CRITICAL ACCLAIM FOR BARBARA MICHAELS

"A writer so popular that the public library has to keep her books under lock and key."

—*The Washington Post*

"Miss Michaels has a fine sense of atmosphere and story-telling."

—*The New York Times*

"This author never fails to entertain."

—*Cleveland Plain Dealer*

"Michaels has a fine downright way with the supernatural."

—*San Francisco Chronicle*

"Michaels has a human touch that adds charm to the well-controlled twists and turns."

—*Virginian Pilot/Ledger Star*

"Simply the best living writer of ghost stories and thrillers."

—Marion Zimmer Bradley

MORE PRAISE FOR BARBARA MICHAELS AND *VANISH WITH THE ROSE*

"I leapt on *Vanish with the Rose* as if it were chocolate. . . . This book and this writer are addictive."

—Alexandra Ripley,
New York Times bestselling author of *Scarlett*

"High-voltage mystery . . . a witty, intricate, and ultimately surprising story, with strong characterizations that keep the sparks flying."

—*Publishers Weekly*

"Involving . . . a cleverly spun mystery."

—*Booklist*

"Barbara Michaels can always be counted on for a darned good mystery with fascinating characters and a chilling tale. . . . Magnificent!"

—*Ocala Star-Banner*

HERE I STAY

"An absolutely first-rate job of summoning up the spooky . . . takes on the added dimension besides that of a very good ghost story."

—*Publishers Weekly*

"Scary, interesting. A winner."

—*Pittsburgh Press*

INTO THE DARKNESS

"The suspense builds into a smashing final chapter that does full credit to Michaels' powers of invention."

—Murder Ad Lib

SHATTERED SILK

"Her most enticing yet . . . will capture any woman's fantasy."

—Cleveland Plain Dealer

"An utterly enchanting book."

—Roberta Gellis

"Superior Michaels. . . . Like the antique gowns the heroine collects, *Shattered Silk* glitters!"

—Kirkus Reviews

SMOKE AND MIRRORS

"The perfect curl-up-at-homer for a frosty . . . eve."

—New Woman

"Barbara Michaels tells her story with grace, wit, and unflagging suspense."

—San Jose Mercury News

Books by Barbara Michaels

The Dancing Floor
Stitches in Time
Houses of Stone
Vanish with the Rose
Into the Darkness
Search the Shadows
Shattered Silk
Smoke and Mirrors
Be Buried in the Rain
The Grey Beginning
Here I Stay
Black Rainbow
Someone in the House
The Wizard's Daughter
The Walker in Shadows
Wait for What Will Come
Wings of the Falcon
Patriot's Dream
The Sea King's Daughter
House of Many Shadows
Witch
Greygallows
The Crying Child
The Dark on the Other Side
Prince of Darkness
Ammie, Come Home
Sons of the Wolf
The Master of Blacktower

be buried in the rain

Barbara Michaels

HarperPaperbacks
A Division of HarperCollins*Publishers*

HarperPaperbacks
A Division of HarperCollins*Publishers*
10 East 53rd Street, New York, NY 10022-5299

ISBN 0-06-104469-5

Cover photograph by Travel Pix/FPG International

A previous edition of this book was published in 1987 by The Berkley Publishing Group.

First HarperPaperbacks printing: March 1997
Special Edition printing: January 1999

Printed in the United States of America

10 9 8 7 6 5 4 3 2

To the Delaplaines,
One and All—
Bettie and George,
Buckie and Ted,
Jim and John

be buried in the rain

one

The old pickup hit a pothole with a bump that shook *a few more flakes of faded blue paint from the rusted body. Joe Danner swore, but not aloud. He hadn't used bad language for six years, not since he found his Lord Jesus in the mesmeric eyes of a traveling evangelist. He hadn't used hard liquor nor tobacco either, nor laid a hand on his wife in anger—only when she talked back or questioned his Scripture-ordained authority as head of the family.*

It would never have occurred to Joe Danner that his wife preferred their old lifestyle. Back then, an occasional beating was part of the natural order of things, and it was a small price to pay for the Saturday nights at the local tavern, both of them getting a little drunk together, talking and joking with friends, going home to couple unimaginatively but pleasurably in the old bed Joe's daddy had made with his own hands.

Since Joe found Jesus, there were no more Saturday nights at the tavern. No more kids, either. Joe Junior had left home the year before; he was up north someplace, wallowing in the sins he'd been brought up to hate . . . Only somehow the teaching hadn't taken hold. Not with Lynne Anne, either. Married at sixteen, just in time to spare her baby the label of bastard—but not soon enough to wipe out the sin of fornication. She lived in Pikesburg, only forty miles away, but she never came home any more. Joe had thrown her out of the house the night she told them she was pregnant, and Lynne Anne had spat in his face before she set out on a four-mile walk in the traditional snowstorm, to collapse on the doorstep of her future in-laws. They had raised a real ruckus about it, too. Methodists. What else could a person expect from Methodists?

Another pothole lifted Joe off the seat, bringing his head in painful contact with the roof of the cab and ending his sullen musings about his thankless children. Darned county gov'mint, he thought. New roads, not even a year old, and already gone to . . . heck. Why they'd built it in the first place he'd never understand. Nothing wrong with the old one. This route was shorter, maybe, but . . . Well, he just didn't like it. Especially the steep downhill slope into the hollow. Deadman's Hollow, the kids called it. Said it was haunted. Fool kids . . . He wasn't afraid of haunts or dead men, not with the power of the Lord Jesus in his heart. All the same, there was something funny about that low place in the road . . .

Joe stamped on the brake as the truck approached the downhill curve. The road was slimy-wet after the night's rain; tangled brush and twisted trees, thick with foliage, reduced the sunlight to a golden haze. The fields would be a solid sea of mud; couldn't use a cultivator till they dried. Gol-durned rain, gol-durned gov'mint . . .

Jesus Christ! *The words came bursting out of the deep recesses of his mind, exploding in a high-pitched shout. His heavy boot slammed the brake pedal to the floor. The tires squawled and slid, and he fought the skid with the skill of long years of driving on bad roads in bad weather. The vehicle finally shuddered to a stop, skewed sideways across both narrow lanes; and Joe sat staring down at the thing in the road.*

Had he hit it? He hadn't felt anything. He knew how it would feel. Coons and possums and groundhogs, he'd run over plenty of the varmints. A body—a human body—would make even more of a bump.

Sweat slicked his lean cheeks and trickled into his beard as he climbed down from the truck. He was already composing the excuses he would give the police. It was on the road when he saw it—still and recumbent, dead or dead-drunk—not his fault—sharp curve, wet road . . .

Not his fault. If he could back and turn, go the other way, the old way—leave it for someone else to find . . . Still, better check it out. He'd had enough trouble with the police. That fuss last year, about whipping the kids at church school—all according to the Scriptures, spare the rod and spoil the child—but some busybody had raised cain, and he was an elder.

Slowly Joe went around the front of the truck, dreading what he would see. But everything was all right. He hadn't touched it. The wheels were a good foot away. Must be dead—or dead-drunk. It hadn't stirred. It? She. Woman's dress, but a durned funny one—long, covering even the feet, a faded calico print that had once been blue. She lay facedown, the back of her head covered by a scarf or shawl. Her arms were crooked, one over her head, the other at her side. The voluminous folds of fabric were strangely flat, and as he edged closer, Joe's fears faded, to be replaced by rising anger. It was just an empty dress. Couldn't be a body under that. Some fool kids—could've caused an accident, playing a trick like that.

He lifted the scarf.

It grinned up at him, baring twin rows of earth-browned teeth. The ivory curve of the skull was pale against the black macadam of the road. A drop of water, caught on the rim of the empty eyesocket, winked in the sunlight.

Somehow he got the truck backed and turned. The last wild twist of the wheel produced the faintest crunching sound, and an echoing quiver ran through Joe's own bones. For some reason all he could think of was Lynne Anne, struggling through the winter storm. He could see her face drawn into ugliness by her hate, superimposed on that fleshless horror in the road.

He had not seen the other, smaller bundle of cloth that lay half-concealed by the full sleeve and crooked armbones, as if it had fallen from a failing grasp. A very small bundle, not of calico, but of finer stuff, stained with rust and mold in a strangely beautiful pattern of greens and browns. Once it had been white—delicate, fragile lawn, lace-trimmed, hand-tucked and embroidered, just the right size to fit a child's doll-baby. A life-sized doll-baby.

The story was macabre enough to make the national newswires. I suppose I was one of the few people in the eastern United States who didn't read it. I wasn't watching TV or reading newspapers that week. Final exams were looming, and that first year in med school is the one that separates the sheep from the goats. When I wasn't crouched over my desk rereading pages I had read a dozen times, I was pacing the floor mumbling to myself. The twelve cranial nerves, the facial nerves—optic, trigeminal, glossopharyngeal . . . Now and then I heard myself break into song. "The hip bone's connected to the thigh bone, the thigh bone's connected to the leg bone . . ." Then I would do aerobics for a few minutes or dash out to the store for another jar of instant coffee.

Actually, I have a vague recollection of seeing a headline on one of the trashy journals near the check-out stand in the grocery store. Waiting in line, one couldn't help glancing at the headlines. Princess Di's private life vied with lurid lies about Hollywood and rock stars, promises of wonder diets, cancer cures, and proof of life after death. That was the sort of headline I noticed: "Returned from the Grave! To Seek Revenge????" Just more gruesome sensationalism, and it made no lasting impression on a mind stuffed to overflowing with anatomical terms.

If I had read the story, would I have gone to Virginia? Yes, of course—all the more readily, no doubt, because of the coincidence and the intriguing aspects of the case. On the other hand, I was awfully sick of bones.

The summons came. I use that old-fashioned phrase deliberately; it was one *she* would have used. The call didn't come from her, however. It came from my mother, who informed me irascibly that she had been trying to reach me for three days.

"I told you I was in the middle of exams."

It was five o'clock on a rainy spring afternoon and I was in bed with a beer and a mystery story and a bowl of pretzels. I had not yet received the exam results, but at that moment it was enough just to be done with them. Mother's grumbles washed over me without making any impression. I had heard it all before: I had no business cutting myself off from the world; what if someone became ill? What if . . . She had a superstitious reluctance to say the words, so I said them for her.

"If somebody died I'd find out soon enough. That's not the sort of news I'm anxious to get."

Though she had lived in Pittsburgh for years, Mother had never quite lost her pretty Virginia accent. It softened her voice even when she was angry, and was, I think, partially responsible for her success as an executive secretary. "Mrs. Newcomb is so ladylike!"

She sighed gently. "Julie, I wish you wouldn't joke about such things. It makes you sound so callous."

It was a mercy the dear woman couldn't hear some of the jokes that pass around the dissecting room. She thought I was growing callous, did she? I was beginning to wonder if I would ever become callous enough.

"I was going to call you this evening," I said, sliding away from the subject of my sense of humor. "I really was. So, what's new?"

"What are you going to do this summer, Julie?"

"You know what I'm going to be doing. Same as last summer."

Another sigh trembled along the miles of wire, and I said firmly, "Now, Mother, don't give me a hard time. I know you think being a cocktail waitress is one step away from prostitution, but it's a perfectly respectable occupation, and I can make more money that way than I could at any other job. Lord knows we need it. I feel bad enough using your savings and letting you borrow from your boss . . ."

She let me run down before she spoke. "It isn't that. It's Martha. She needs you, Julie."

The idea that Martha needed anyone, much less me, was so incongruous I laughed aloud. "Don't tell me she's dying at long last."

"I wish you wouldn't talk that way!"

"Sorry. But she's ninety if she's a day."

"Eighty-five."

"Oh well, that's different."

"Julie—"

"All right, all right. But be honest, Mother. Her death can hardly come as a shock. Eighty-five isn't exactly the springtime of life, and to call our relationship tender and loving—"

"You shouldn't speak of her that way, Julie. She *is* your grandmother."

She was my grandmother. She was also my mother's mother. Neither of us used the familial, affectionate words. We called her Martha, when we didn't refer to her simply as "she."

Mother went on, "She wants you to spend the summer at Maidenwood."

I spilled the pretzels all over my lap. Out of respect for my poor mother, of whom I am really very fond, I did not yell. All I said was, "Why?" and I spoke in a quiet, controlled voice.

She was relieved at my calm. "It's logical, Julie, when you think about it. She was recovering rather well from the stroke until a few days ago. Then she had another. The doctor thought it would be the end, but it seems she has rallied in the most amazing way . . . What did you say?"

"Nothing."

Mother decided to let it go. "She is paralyzed. She can barely speak."

"Then how did she manage to ask for me?"

She hadn't asked for me. Mother finally admitted as much, but not until I had pressed her; she insisted Martha would have asked for me if she hadn't been—er—well— "You know, Julie, how a stroke affects a person's brain . . ."

Accustomed as I am to my mother's conversational style, it took me a while to sort through the clutter of conventional clichés that obscured the facts.

"Wait a minute, Mother, let me get this straight. Martha had another stroke? And she's at home—in that tumble-down wreck of a house—not in a hospital?"

Another shower of conventionalities rained down on me. The wishes of the dying, the last days in the old home, et cetera, et cetera. What it all came down to was that Martha wanted it that way. And what Martha wanted, Martha got.

"Yes, I understand," I said resignedly. "What I don't understand is why I've been chosen as the sacrificial lamb. It's Matt's problem. He's on the spot, he's Martha's heir, he has no family or financial responsibilities—let him deal with it."

"But, honey, he's a man."

"I figured he must be. Last time I saw him he was a boy, so—"

"Julie, your cousin is doing all he can. He has his career to think of. This is an election year and he is very busy."

From the awe in her voice you'd have thought Matt were in the running for the presidency, instead of being only a lowly state senator. The key sentence had been the first. Matt was a male and hence automatically exempt from the family tasks that are a woman's responsibility. The dirty, unpaid, boring tasks—like bedpans and cooking, scrubbing floors and carrying trays.

It would have been a waste of time and energy to try to convince my mother of the injustice of this attitude. She had grown up with it; it was engraved on her brain. So I didn't yell, "What about my career? What about my needs?" I listened in mounting depression as Mother outlined the arguments in favor of my going to Maidenwood. I felt sure she had got them from Matt; they had the glib, specious appeal of a political speech.

"You wouldn't have to do any actual nursing, Julie. No—er—no nasty things. Shirley Johnson is there—maybe you remember her? Such a fine woman, very conscientious, and Matt says she has her certificate as a practical nurse."

Mother probably did not realize that her argument affected me in a way she had not planned. I didn't remember Shirley Johnson, but I pitied her with all my heart.

Another convincing argument was that Matt had agreed to compensate me for the wages I would lose. I cheered up a little, because I was pretty sure Matt didn't know how much a good cocktail waitress can earn in three months. Of course he counted on getting the money out of Martha. I wished him luck. Maybe she'd die before the summer was over. . . .

But the argument that turned the trick was the one Mother didn't make. If I did not go, she'd have to. I knew how she felt about Martha, even if *she* didn't. She would never admit to herself or anyone else she hated and feared her own mother; she would risk her job and her health for some outmoded notion of duty. I was her surrogate, and like the paid substitutes during the Civil War, I would have to shoulder arms and march out to be killed.

I had to go. And I would have gone even if I had known that the fanciful analogy about the sacrificial lamb was more accurate than I imagined.

two

Matt met me at the bus station in Richmond. Cost was certainly a factor in my decision to take the bus—so far I hadn't got any money out of Matt, only promises, promises—but I must admit another reason was my suspicion that Cousin Matt would rather be caught dead than mixing with the hoi polloi who traveled by Greyhound. I had expected he would send one of his lackeys to pick me up, so when I saw him standing there at the door, I almost fell over.

He was wearing slacks and a blue denim shirt, the sleeves rolled up and the collar open. He waved and called out, in a voice loud enough to make heads turn, "Cousin Julie! Good to see you, honey!"

Well, of course I should have figured it out sooner. This was an election year. It wouldn't hurt Matt's image to be seen mingling with the underprivileged, dressed like one of the boys. I fully expected a flash to explode, but there didn't seem to be a photographer in sight.

Matt gave me a big brotherly hug and held me out at

arm's length, his hands on my shoulders. "You're a sight for sore eyes, honey. Prettier than ever."

"So are you," I said. It wasn't much of a compliment. The last time I had seen Matt he had been sixteen years old, with all the normal tribulations of that age—acne, long, gangly legs and arms, and a voice that turned from soprano to bass at odd moments. He was thirty now, seven years older than I, and in spite of my sarcastic semicompliment I had to admit that he had turned into a good-looking guy. His casual clothes showed off his tan and his muscles and his flat stomach. I felt sure that all three were the products of an expensive health club, but the working-man image wasn't bad. He had the family features, the jutting nose and high, prominent cheekbones and heavy jaw. Unfortunately I had them too. One of the reasons I let my hair grow long was the hope of softening those pronounced and prominent protrusions. My best friends wouldn't call me pretty. The women of my family are seldom pretty. By the time we reach middle age we all look like tribal matriarchs. But on a man the "Carr face" is attractive; it gives a (deceptive) impression of strength and reliability—the Abe Lincoln look, only handsomer. We looked enough alike to be brother and sister, Matt and I, even to the dark chestnut-brown of our hair.

Matt noticed the resemblance too. His smile faded and he gave me another, longer inspection before he said, "No mistaking you for anybody but a Carr, Julie, even if you don't have the name."

The driver had unloaded the belly of the bus and I indicated my three suitcases. I picked up the lightest of the three, ignoring Matt's polite protest. When he had hoisted the other two he stopped protesting. An expression of mild distress crossed his face, but he carried them easily enough; the health club must be doing its job.

"What the hell have you got in here?" he asked.

"Clothes, books, the usual. If I'm going to be here all summer I can't get by with one pair of jeans."

He nodded, saving his breath. I was soon to discover what he was saving it for; as we neared the exit a man stepped into our path, hand outstretched. "Senator Ellis! Hello, Senator."

Matt dropped the right-hand suitcase—on my foot—and took the extended hand. He didn't raise his voice, but all of a sudden you could hear him all over the station. It's called projection, I believe.

"Well—Mr. Busby, isn't it? Good to see you, sir. How's the wife?"

"Much better, Senator, since she had that operation. Had to thank you, sir; hadn't been for you, we couldn't have afforded it. Just no way to tell you, Senator, how much we all think of you and the great job you're doing for us—"

"Please." Matt dropped his admirer's hand and gave him a friendly slap on the shoulder. "You good people deserve everything you get and a lot more. I'm delighted to hear that Mrs. Busby is doing well."

They played it to the hilt as a small crowd gathered. Matt introduced me—"My li'l Cousin Julie, come to nurse our granny—the dear old soul is sinking fast . . ." Finally Mr. Busby—if that was his name, which I rather doubted—backed away, bowing and scraping. Matt spread a friendly, self-deprecating smile around the watching crowd, picked up my bags and shepherded me toward the door, followed by an admiring murmur.

We were out on the street before I spoke. "Can I throw up now, or would you rather I waited until the chauffeur can clean it up?"

The fourteen-year-old Matt would have turned purple

with rage and tried to slug me. Senator Ellis smiled. "That's the way it's done, honey. And I do it well. I'll be governor in five years."

He wasn't smiling now. His voice was dead serious. I believed him.

"And then?" I asked.

"Every little boy in America envisions being President."

"And every little girl."

"I agree, darling. You can't fault me on women's rights. Look at my record."

"How do you get away with that in your district? The word 'redneck' comes to mind . . ."

"The word is one we use pridefully," said Matt, with a twist of his lip. "I get away with it because I am also great at huntin' and fishin' and man-talk. It's all image, honey."

He stopped by a nondescript vehicle—a five-year-old tan Chevy with rust stains. I took one look at it and burst out laughing.

Matt joined me. "Image, Julie. I told you—I'm good at it."

He helped me in with a burlesqued gallantry and got behind the wheel. We kept up a desultory spatter of conversation as he drove skillfully through the noonday traffic—the usual polite catching up on each other's lives. Not until we had left the city and were heading south did I break a long silence. "How is she, Matt?"

He didn't need to ask who "she" was. "Same as ever. She could be deaf, dumb, blind, and paralyzed and still rule the roost." He waited for me to comment. When I didn't he said, without looking at me, "Are you still afraid of her, Julie?"

"No. Yes. How the hell should I know? I haven't seen her for five years."

"I am," Matt said. "Afraid of her."

"You were always her favorite."

"Isn't there something in the Bible about chastening those you love?"

"Oh."

"She did favor me," Matt admitted. "I was the boy. The only boy born into the family for God knows how many generations. It's funny, how we run to girl-babies . . . Your standard male chauvinist has nothing on these tough old ladies when it comes to putting down other women. And I'm sure that when she talked about me to you, she praised me to the skies. That was a favorite trick of hers—invidious comparisons. But she never allowed me to have a very good opinion of myself."

"Matt, she's a sick old woman and you're a successful young man with your life ahead of you. Don't tell me you are suffering from some neurotic obsession—"

"No." Matt's tight grasp of the wheel relaxed. When he went on, the strained bitterness had left his voice. "No, I think I've come to grips with my neuroses. Whatever she did, she is paying for it now. There could be no worse punishment for her than lying helpless. If you could see her—"

"I will."

He took one hand off the wheel and patted my knee. "Don't think I'm not grateful, Julie. I'll try to make it up to you. If there's anything in the house you want—furniture, china, that sort of thing . . ."

The sympathy and affection I had begun to feel for him abruptly vanished. I don't know why the offer repelled me so. Heaven knows I had no reason to feel sentimental about my grim old grandmother.

He felt me stiffen and removed his hand. "That wasn't expressed too well," he said.

"No. I don't intend to prowl the house like a ghoul looking for loot. She's not dead yet."

"She can't last the summer," Matt said flatly.

We went on for another mile in silence. For all its battered appearance, the old car was in excellent condition. The engine ran smoothly and the air conditioning kept the interior comfortably cool. Under a bright hot sun the level fields of the riverbanks were green with new crops.

Finally I said, "She's a tough old lady, Matt. She might recover. I'm going to do everything I can to ensure that she does."

"Naturally."

His expression was so glum I had to laugh, though without much humor. "We're a fine pair of loving grandchildren, aren't we? You'd better start briefing me—things to do and not do, subjects to mention and to avoid, topics that might raise her blood pressure or improve her disposition—if there are any of the latter . . ."

"There aren't," Matt grunted. "But don't mention the skeleton on the road. She doesn't know about that."

"The skeleton on the . . . What on earth are you talking about?"

Matt glanced at me. "Didn't you hear about it?"

"No."

Matt touched the brake and signaled for a turn. "It's time we stopped for lunch anyway. I'd better fill you in on the local sensation before you see Martha."

The restaurant was one of those roadside types that have names like Joe's Place or Flo's Place or Harry's Place. This "place"—fake Tudor stucco and beam construction, two whiskey barrels filled with petunias flanking the entrance—belonged to Sam, whoever he was. It was obviously one of Matt's hangouts; the waitress greeted him by name and asked if he wanted the usual, which turned out to be bourbon on the rocks—a lot of bourbon on a few rocks. We were only half an hour from Maidenwood and I figured that Matt was in the habit of stopping at Sam's for a shot of Dutch courage before confronting his grandmother.

"Now," I said, sipping my gin and tonic, "about that skeleton."

There had, in fact, been two skeletons; one was that of a newborn infant. I listened with my mouth open, too astonished to question or interrupt. When the waitress came along to ask if we wanted refills on our drinks, Matt laughed at my aghast face and nodded at the girl.

"Drink up, Julie, you look as if you need another one."

"I never heard such a crazy story in my life! Come clean, Matt. You made it up. You used to tell me things—"

"I never made up one like this. It's crazy, all right, but if you read the newspapers as conscientiously as you ought, you would know that cases just as weird turn up from time to time. Unfortunately this one happened in our backyard, so to speak. The new road cuts through our land."

I finished my drink and shook my head, marveling. "I can see why you warned me not to tell Martha. She'd view it as a personal insult. Was that the motive, do you think? And where did the bones come from? I'm not as ignorant as you suppose; I've read about cemeteries being desecrated—"

"That was the first place the police looked, naturally. There are three cemeteries in and around Carrsville—the Methodist, the Episcopal, and the old Catholic cemetery. There were no signs of disturbance."

"Medical-school specimens, then."

"Use your head, Julie—and give your colleagues and the police some credit. Sheriff Jarboe called in an anthropologist from William and Mary to examine the bones."

"Oh, of course. That would be the thing to do." I pondered the matter while Matt watched me quizzically. The waitress brought our second round of drinks. Without looking at the tattered menu, Matt ordered for both of us. "Well?" he said.

"Well what?"

"You med students are supposed to know something about bones. How much can an expert tell from a skeleton?"

"I'm no expert. But I took a course in forensic medicine, and I've done some reading on my own. A pathologist can determine the age of the individual, within a few years. The sex of an adult or adolescent—sexual characteristics don't mark the bones until after the onset of puberty. Medical history, general health, sometimes cause of death . . ."

"Sometimes?"

"Only if the cause of death left a mark on the bone. A fractured hyoid bone may indicate the individual was smothered or strangled. A fractured skull suggests a fatal fall or a blunt instrument. But breaks in the bones can be post-mortem injuries, and it's hard to tell for sure whether they occurred just before or after death."

The waitress put two chef's salads in front of us. The lettuce was brown around the edges but I was too hungry to care. "You can tell a lot more from the soft tissues, if any fragments remain. I remember reading about an examination of Egyptian mummies, where the pathologists were able to perform histological sections, after rehydrating the hardened tissues with sodium carbonate. They found parasitic worms in the intestinal mass . . . Aren't you hungry?"

Matt pushed his salad away. "I'm sorry I asked. Let's change the subject."

I took a roll and buttered it. "Okay. I assume your tame anthropologist was not able to determine the cause of death. Not surprising. What did he find out?"

"Just the age, and in the case of the woman's remains, the sex. She was between sixteen and twenty years old." Matt continued to contemplate his food with faint disgust.

"Mmmm. He wouldn't have been able to determine the sex of the infant. Maybe the woman died in childbirth. When?"

"That's the question." Matt picked up his fork and looked at me dubiously. "Are you finished talking about—er—histological sections?"

"For the moment. If they could determine when the woman died, it might give some clue as to where the bones came from."

"That's what I was about to ask you. How they deduce something like that."

"It wouldn't be easy. A lot of factors affect the rate of deterioration of animal bone and tissue. The type of soil, the weather, the absence or presence of a coffin, whether the body was embalmed—"

Matt had taken a bite of salad. He stopped chewing and looked at me reproachfully. I laughed. "Okay, we'll skip the details. The truth is, archaeologists usually depend on other factors to date skeletal remains, such as the objects buried with the bodies, like scraps of clothing, buttons, coins, and so on. Without such clues, or the use of a process like carbon fourteen—"

"I've read about that. Why couldn't it be used in this case?"

"First, because it only works with specimens that are hundreds of years old. The margin of error is too great. Second, because you have to destroy the specimen in order to get results. Matt, why are you worrying about this? Surely it's obvious where the poor girl and her baby came from. There are old forgotten cemeteries all over the state. Indian, colonial, Civil War . . . We're walking on the dust of our ancestors every time we take a step."

"Very poetic," Matt said distastefully.

"Very true. It is also true that illegal digging has been going on around Maidenwood for a long time. That old lie about Blackbeard's treasure—"

"It's not so farfetched," Matt protested. "Teach, aka Blackbeard, did operate in the Tidewater area; after he was killed in a sea fight, some of his crew were hanged at Williamsburg, and he—"

"Matt, my boy, I detect a greedy gleam in your eyes. Don't tell me you dug for treasure in the pastures of Maidenwood?"

"Sure I did. What red-blooded American boy could resist a story like that?"

"You never let me help."

"You," Matt said solemnly, "were just a girl."

I couldn't help smiling. Matt grinned back at me, and I found myself liking him again. "I did most of my treasure hunting in the years after you left," he said, half-apologetically. "I didn't spend that much time at Maidenwood when you were in residence."

"I suppose I was something of a nuisance," I admitted. "Seven years is quite a gap in age when people are children. I mean, when children are—I mean—"

"I know what you mean. But Blackbeard's treasure isn't a myth, and every now and then public interest revives. Martha caught some idiot in the woods with a bulldozer a few years back—she ran him off with her shotgun. He had bought a treasure map from a con man for fifty bucks."

"There you are then. A gang of kids, looking for pieces of eight, came upon an old grave and decided to be cute. Isn't that the conclusion the police arrived at?"

"Yes . . ."

"So that's it. Are you going to eat the rest of your salad?"

He shoved it toward me and I began picking out the good parts—strips of country ham and fragments of cheese. I should have known from the way he kept glancing at me that we weren't finished with the subject.

"That's why I decided to give the archaeologists permission to excavate," he said. "Their presence will deter trespassers, and if they find the cemetery the bones came from, the police can close the case."

I speared an olive and popped it into my mouth. "Martha will have a fit," I mumbled. "She's always refused to allow . . ." Then I caught on. The pit flew out of my mouth and bounced uncouthly on the table. "Archaeologists? You wouldn't be referring to one archaeologist in particular? Not—not . . ."

"His name is Petranek," Matt said. "He claimed to be an old friend of yours."

I picked up the olive pit and put it on my plate.

I could tell by the smug set of Matt's handsome mouth that he suspected the truth. It was the same smirk the fourteen-year-old had worn when he put snakes in my bed and told me I was going to get rabies from a rooster that had pecked my legs. I was determined not to let him see the news had disturbed me. Actually, I told myself, I wasn't disturbed. It had been a long time—five years.

I was a wide-eyed innocent freshman at William and Mary, and Alan was a grad student in anthropology, earn-ing his stipend by teaching an introductory anthro course. He looked like a young Indiana Jones—lean and bronzed, his brown hair sun-bleached after a summer in the field. I practically swooned with rapturous disbelief when he picked me out of the gaggle of adoring girls who surrounded him. There was some vague talk of an engagement—mostly from my mother—before I caught on to Alan's real reason for courting my favors.

Even then he had his future career mapped out. Historic archaeology was a relatively new discipline, applying the standard techniques of excavation to recent historical sites. You might think we know all we need to know about the early settlements in America; not only were those people literate, they seemed to have spent most of their spare time writing letters, declarations, diaries, and documents. But there are gaps, especially in our knowledge of the living conditions of ordinary people, that can only be filled in by archaeology. Digs around Williamsburg, Plymouth, and other sites have proved that.

I could go on. I knew a lot more about historic archaeology than I wanted to know. I heard a lot about it that year, in coffee shops and college bars, in my room and in his apartment, in and out of bed. He even talked about it in bed. That should have told me something.

I didn't catch on, though, not even when Alan complained about the difficulty of advancement in a field so poorly funded and so competitive. He had no doubt he'd make it to the top eventually. Humility was not one of his virtues—or failings—and he had reason for vanity. He was good—intelligent, innovative, hard-working. But he didn't want to wait until he was fifty before he fought his way to a full professorship or to one of the big curatorships. He wanted instant success, and the only way he could get it was to make a really sensational, significant discovery.

He didn't lust after my maidenhood; he lusted after Maidenwood. (It shows you how young I was, that I could get a grim relish out of that poor pun.) I never really understood why he was convinced that the discovery that would make his career lay hidden under the tangled brush and weedy clay of my family's land. Like all old houses, Maidenwood had its share of legends; the buried pirate treasure was only one of them. And, as Matt had pointed out, not as farfetched as one might think.

Then there was the story of beautiful Lady Jocelyn, who had fled the dissolute court of James I to find freedom in the wilderness of the New World. This was not only farfetched, but downright ridiculous, in my opinion. Women of seventeenth-century England were not their own mistresses, they couldn't hop a boat and take off on a cruise without the permission of husband or father or guardian—especially if they were wards of the King, as Lady Jocelyn was supposed to have been. However, Alan always insisted the tale contained a germ of truth.

And there was Maydon's Hundred. Or, if you were credulous enough to believe in Lady Jocelyn, Maiden's Hundred. Duller (i.e., more sensible) scholars scoffed at the claim put forth by some of my romantic ancestors that the Carrs were descended, in a roundabout and questionable manner, from the Lady. They attributed the name to an otherwise anonymous settler named Maydon.

Maydon's or Maiden's, it had been one of the "hundreds" granted to Virginia Company emigrants in the early 1600s. There had been a settlement at Maidenwood in 1622, when the first Indian uprising almost destroyed the young colony of Virginia. Three hundred settlers massacred out of a total of twelve hundred, two of the four towns burned to the ground, many of the "hundreds" reduced to smoking rubble strewn with the corpses of the inhabitants. I didn't know why Alan believed he could make his reputation by digging up burned timbers and rotted bones, even if he could find them in Maidenwood's five hundred acres. But that is what he believed, and that is what he was after. Permission to excavate.

He met his match in Martha. She saw through him, damn her. Damn her, not because she read his mind but because she was careful to explain his motives to me.

I had taken Alan to Maidenwood that afternoon, at his request. I remember the sunlight slanting through the windows and gleaming on the silver tea service that had been in the family for two hundred years. I remember the smile on Martha's face . . .

Alan buttered her up with great skill. Not too much, only the best butter. It didn't work. She turned him down flat. She had never allowed outsiders to profane the soil of Maidenwood, and she never would allow it—not developers, nor archaeologists nor treasure hunters. She left him with no illusions of eventual success, but he took it with seeming grace. Not until after he had gone for a walk, so I could have a little time alone with dear Grandma, did Martha really get to work. With pitiless accuracy she described my failings, physical and emotional. How could I possibly imagine that a man like Alan—handsome, sophisticated, worldly—could be interested in a callow, homely girl like me? Flat-chested, with lusterless stick-straight brown hair, and the Carr features—"so unfortunate on a woman"—and, of course, no charm whatsoever.

I retreated, not in good order, before she had quite finished. The next year I transferred to the University of Pennsylvania, even though I lost the family-connected scholarship that had been my principal reason for returning to Virginia for college. Alan made a few attempts to see me, but he wasn't a man to persevere in the face of such sullen resentment, such unreasoning demands for reassurance. Oh, yes, I had been unreasonable, I could admit that now—now that it was too late. The past can't be changed. Alan probably wouldn't want to change it. He had been, and still was, all the things Martha had called him—handsome, sophisticated, worldly. There must have been countless other women in his life . . .

"You don't mind?" Matt asked, as we left the restaurant.

"Mind what? Oh—the excavations." I laughed lightly, and then caught my breath as the warm air closed over me like a sauna. "I feel sorry for the archaeologists, that's all. I had forgotten what Virginia summers are like. They'll be up to here in sweat when they aren't drowned by rainstorms."

"I felt it was the proper thing to do," Matt said. He started the engine and the air conditioning blasted out.

"How did you convince Martha?"

"Are you kidding? She doesn't know about it. If she finds out she'll probably have another stroke."

"You have her power of attorney?"

"No." Matt scowled, and swung out to pass a tractor that was chugging down the road at ten miles an hour. "I'm expecting to get it—my legal advisers are working on it. At the moment, Martha's lawyer is acting for her. You remember him?"

"No."

"He's seventy-eight. It's ridiculous, allowing a man that age to handle Martha's affairs. I'm sure the court will allow my application, but until then I have to sue for favors from Ronald Fraser McLendon, and I do mean sue—hat in hand. He had to agree with me about the excavations, though."

We were back to the excavations again. Did Matt know he was probing an old wound? I hadn't realized the spot was still so tender till he brought the subject up. Over the years the memory of Alan's features had faded into a blur. Now, suddenly, I could see him in my mind as clearly as if he stood before me—his eyes alight with enthusiasm, his brown hair tousled, his hands moving in quick, emphatic gestures as he spoke. I had heard the arguments so often . . .

"Martha should have given them permission to excavate a long time ago," I said. "The heritage of the past belongs to everyone. Treasure hunters and casual diggers can destroy a site; the light it might throw upon our history is gone, forever. The best way of preventing vandalism like that is to let the archaeologists go in first."

Matt smiled. "Is that a quote?"

"I'm sure it's been said before," I murmured. "Wasn't that Mr. McLendon's argument?"

"Well, not exactly. He was more concerned with the legal ramifications. We want to do everything we can to cooperate with the police. Until they identify those bones . . ."

I didn't want to hear any more about bones, or excavations, or archaeologists. "Where are you going?" I asked. "Wasn't that the turnoff we just passed?"

"There's a new road," Matt explained. "That's it, ahead."

He swung on to the narrow road, its entrance half-concealed by the branches of the trees that crowded close on either hand. The road surface shone with wet, and Matt slowed to a cautious twenty-five.

"Looks just like the old road," I said.

"You remember."

"It hasn't been that long."

Long enough, though, to make the contrast between

the well-traveled state highway and this unnumbered county road even more striking than before. There were new developments all along the highway, clumps of crackerbox houses, shopping centers, factories. The county road might have been in another country or another time; there was no sign of the present century except for the power lines and poles flanking the rutted macadam. Not even fences. Yet I knew it was all Maidenwood land. Cut by ravines and gulches, carved by the streams that emptied into the James River and the Bay, its tangled woodland had not changed for three hundred years. It must have looked much the same when the first settlers came to Maydon's Hundred—Jacobean cavaliers in high boots and half-armor, women in long gowns carrying their babies in their arms. Had the girl-mother and her infant been among them? It was not likely. The heavy Virginia clay would have reduced their delicate bones to dust long ago.

The car rounded a steep curve and glided down into a shadowy hollow. "Is this where she was found?" I asked.

Matt's eyebrows lifted. "How did you know?"

"It is what you might call a suitable ambience," I said.

Even as the words left my lips I realized that the casual, half-joking comment was literally, grimly accurate. Through the lichen-smeared trunks of the trees whose branches shadowed the narrow road, I could see masses of tangled green vegetation on either side, fecund and overgrown like a tropical rain forest. I could almost feel the dampness, even through the closed car windows.

"What a horrible place," I said involuntarily. "Has it got a name?"

"You don't remember it?"

"No. Should I?"

The road leveled out and straightened. We crossed a

one-lane wooden bridge, and sunlight dispelled the shadows. "Should I?" I said again.

Matt shrugged. "Probably one of the places forbidden to you, as a mere female. The local kids have some weird name for it—Deadman's Hollow, something like that."

I didn't pursue the subject. Neither of us spoke again until we reached the entrance to Maidenwood.

Five years before there had been traces of the gateposts—tumbled piles of stones intertwined with weeds. The stones had vanished now under heaps of rank greenery. Pink trumpets of bindweed raised triumphant heads over the ruin. The narrow track between them had been freshly graveled but, from the way the car bounced along it, not graded. The trees edged closer as if resenting our presence—scrub pine and dogwood seedlings and sycamore, strangled by the hangman's noose of honeysuckle. Matt's hands were tight on the wheel and I realized he was as reluctant to reach Maidenwood as I was. When we came out of the trees and saw the house ahead I felt like a stranger, viewing with detached and critical appraisal a monstrosity that had long since outlived usefulness or beauty.

The decay of the house was something they couldn't blame on the damn Yankees. It had survived the "War Between the States," as they called it in these parts, intact, thanks, family legend claimed, to a daughter of the house who had charmed the Union captain into sparing the mansion and its contents. In the 1880s the lord of the manor had had less compunction than the Yankees. An inveterate gambler, he had sold the family treasures and gutted the house, stripping off the hand-carved walnut paneling and even selling the lead off the roof. Another family legend claimed that his long-suffering wife had finally poisoned him before he could hock her jewelry and her best bed. The jewels had carried the family through the next lean half century. In 1917 fire had destroyed the east wing, and since there was no money for repairs, that part of the house had been abandoned to the ravages of wind and weather and weeds.

I saw it as a stranger, and yet I had visited often, when my parents lived in Richmond, and I had lived in the house for four endless, aching years, from the age of eight until I was twelve. Mother had had no choice but to hand me over to Martha. Left alone, untrained and unskilled, she had a long uphill struggle before she could send for me. In the intervening years I had returned only once—on that single disastrous visit with Alan—and only because he made me go. I couldn't admit to him that I would rather have paid a visit to the Fifth Circle of Hell, and I had assumed that his presence beside me would make it easier . . .

Five years ago. It was only a moment in the life of the old oak trees shading the front lawn. They looked the same. The lawn was unchanged too—not soft green grass but acres of cropped weeds.

I remembered the trees. I remembered the slope behind the house that led through pastures thick with clover to the riverbank. I remembered, only too clearly, the formal drawing room where Martha had torn my pathetic little love affair to ribbons. And that was all I remembered. It was as if a black wall shut off the rest of the house and the years I had spent there—a wall more than ten years thick.

Matt stopped the car and reached for a cigarette.

"I didn't know you smoked," I said curiously.

"I never want to smoke except at Maidenwood," Matt said wryly.

I laughed—but not loudly, and not long. We sat in

silence while Matt blew furious clouds of smoke between pursed lips and I stared at the house in a queer confusion of emotion.

The house was of bricks shaped from clay dug on the site. A flight of steps led up to the entrance door in the center of the western face. The wrought iron railings that had flanked the steps were long gone. One of the chimneys was only a stub, and the famous leaded roof had been replaced by rotting wooden shingles.

"What a mess," I said.

There was no chagrin in my voice, only a satisfaction so strong it couldn't be missed, even by Matt, who had never been sensitive to innuendo. However, he answered as if my comment had been a criticism instead of a crow of triumph. "I can't keep the place up. Martha doesn't have a bean, and I'm up to my eyeballs in debt. Politics is an expensive profession."

I didn't ask why he could not get help from his mother. I am named after my Aunt Julia, but the names are all we have in common. A pretty, frivolous creature, who had been spared the tragedy of "the Carr features in a woman," she had married a struggling young lawyer of good family—that is, poor—and had given birth to Matt before she got bored with genteel poverty. She was on her fourth husband now, and he was no more inclined than Aunt Julia herself to waste money on a decaying house in the wilds of Virginia. None of that Tara sentiment for them! It would never have occurred to anyone, least of all her son, to suggest that Julia give up her summer in Europe to care for her dying mother. That was the kind of person she was. I only wished I knew how she got away with it.

"I don't know why you care," I said. "Houses like this are anachronisms. Let it collapse."

Matt didn't reply. He sat smoking and staring at the

house with a mixture of loathing and longing, and I read his thoughts as clearly as if they had been printed on his face—which in a sense they were. He was seeing Maidenwood as it had once looked and as it might look again if he had half a million bucks to spend on it—gracious and beautiful, a perfect background for the aristocratic governor of the Old Dominion.

"So sell the land," I suggested. "I don't suppose it's worth much, but there are hundreds of acres, aren't there?"

"You know Martha would never allow that. And," he added, with a sidelong glance at me, "I wouldn't go against her wishes."

I smiled to myself. Matt was so transparent. He wouldn't make any damaging admissions for fear I would betray his nefarious plans to Martha and try to supplant him as her heir. Even supposing I were low enough to attempt such a trick, it wouldn't work. If Maidenwood were mine I would sell off every damned acre, assuming I could find a buyer stupid enough to invest in a tumble-down house and five hundred acres of weeds—and Martha must know I would. Matt would at least try to keep the house, poor romantic snob that he was; but unless Martha could tie the estate up in some sort of trust it would be broken into quarter-acre lots before she was dead a year. I felt confident it was sheer spite that had made her refuse to let Matt sell before this, but maybe she had been smart to hang on to the land. Property values had gone up, if the new subdivisions along the highway were any indication.

Matt opened the car door. "Let's go," he said, and ground the cigarette butt to scraps under his heel.

* * *

My first thought was: My God, she looks terrible. My second was: She's just the same.

She had been eighty the last time I saw her. That's old by any standards. By the standards of eighteen it's antique, ancient, older than the Pyramids. But there was an ironic truth in the seeming contradictions of my impressions. Martha had always had one of the most expressionless, rigidly controlled faces I had ever seen. Frozen by the partial paralysis of the stroke, it was no colder now than it had been.

She lay propped up by pillows in the big bed—Mary Carr's bed, the one she had saved by poisoning her husband. My third impression was that Martha looked a lot better than I had expected. Her white hair, still thick and healthy, had been cut short, and it cupped her head in a surprisingly modern, stylish look. It was a well-shaped head, sleekly rounded, elegantly curved. Though her hands lay limp on the counterpane, they were beautifully tended. She had always been proud of her hands—a Carr feature I had not inherited. The room was stiflingly warm, but she wore a pink flannel bedjacket that cast a flattering glow on her sallow, lined features.

She had been looking to one side when I entered—deliberately slighting me, I thought. Now she turned her head on the pillow, very slowly, and I understood her real motive. The stroke, one or both, had chiefly affected the left side of her body. The drooping eyelid and sagging mouth would have appeared pitiable on any other old woman. But her right eye was wide open and it blazed with intelligence and pride that defied pity. Either my mother had been mistaken about the extent of the paralysis or Martha had regained some muscular control in the past few days. She could move her head, though with difficulty, and she could speak, in a fashion. The croak that issued from her tight lips was obviously, "Come here," and it was accompanied by a flexing of the fingers of her right hand.

I had made up my mind I would call her "Grandmother," but I couldn't do it. I said, "Hello, Martha," and bent to kiss her cheek. She turned her head. A trickle of hair brushed my lips and I straightened, feeling the familiar surge of frustrated anger.

She looked me over from head to foot. One black eyeball rolled like a jet marble in its socket. She didn't speak again. Her voice had always been one of her best weapons, its soft southern cadences lending a special sting to the cutting words she used with such deadly effect. She gestured again, a gesture all the more imperious for its slowness, and I obeyed, turning to greet the woman who sat in a chair by the head of the bed.

Behind me, Matt said, "You remember Shirley Johnson. I don't know what we'd do without her."

"Mrs. Johnson." I held out my hand.

"You'd best call me Shirley." She shook my hand and released it. Her palm was slick with perspiration and the hair that had escaped her cap curled into wiry coils around her forehead. "You don't remember me, Miz Julie?"

I couldn't fit her placid, coffee-brown face into any niche of memory. She was a comfortable-looking woman, plump and sweet-lipped, with warm brown eyes. I shook my head, smiling apologetically, and she said, "It was a long time ago. You were only eight or nine. I was thinner then."

"Shirley's husband was one of Martha's tenants," Matt prompted. "They moved to Atlanta where, luckily for us, Shirley got her training as a nurse."

"Practical nurse," Shirley corrected. Her eyes shifted to

the bed. "She wants to rest now. She wants me to show you your room and tell you what you're supposed to do."

"Good idea," Matt said heartily. "You get your rest, Martha, and I'll see you this weekend—"

Martha's fingers writhed. Shirley said in the same, soft, calm voice, "She wants you should stay, Matthew. Come along, Miz Julie."

She closed the book she was holding—Tennyson's *Poems,* of all things—and rose. I followed her to the door. I should have been relieved that the interview was over, but I had an odd feeling of incompleteness. Not that I'd expected a loving welcome, but all the same . . . I said, "I'll see you soon, Martha. Have a good rest."

I got the response I might have expected—none. Matt winked at me before turning to Martha.

It wasn't until Shirley had closed the door and started down the hall ahead of me that I realized how tense the atmosphere in that steamy room had been. Was it only the heat? The temperature in the hall was almost as hot. Shirley was wearing nurses' whites and as she preceded me I saw the wet patches on the back of her dress.

"Can't you get Matt to install a window air conditioner or at least a fan?" I asked, catching up with her. "That room is like an oven."

"Old people feel the cold," Shirley said. "The blood runs thin at her age, Miz Julie."

"Skip the 'miss,' Shirley. You and I are about to become sisters in misfortune."

She didn't acknowledge the poor joke except to say sedately, "I'll be glad of someone to spell me, and that's a fact. Miz Martha takes a heap of care."

"You don't mean you've been alone with her all this time?"

"Miz Danner comes most days to clean and cook. She sits with Miz Martha afternoons."

"When do you sleep, Shirley? Or do you?"

"I'm used to sleeping with one ear open, like you might say. It's no different than in a hospital; if you're at the far end of the corridor from the nurses' station, you could fall out of the bed before anybody'd notice, and—"

"I wasn't criticizing, Shirley, I was commiserating. We'll split the shifts from now on. You tell me what you want me to do."

Shirley indicated a closed door, and I stopped short, almost in pain. The lost memories of my childhood at Maidenwood were returning, not sliding smoothly into place as I saw again the rooms and corridors I had known, but thudding into the vacant spaces in my mind with jarring force. I remembered this door and the room behind it. I had spent many hours shut in that room, as penance for my various misdeeds.

The room had changed less than Martha had. Dark and gloomy, its single pair of windows overlooking the kitchen yard, it contained a small iron bedstead, a pair of faded rag rugs, and a cheap chest of drawers. A calico curtain across one corner of the room concealed the rope on which I had once hung my clothes.

Shirley stood silent beside me, but I think she sensed my outrage. Martha had assigned me my former room, at an inconvenient distance from her own, as part of a deliberate campaign. Well, I wasn't a cowering eight-year-old now. I glanced at Shirley, but I didn't have the heart to ask her to move furniture; she had more than enough to do already. I would do it myself—strip the other bedrooms of anything that would make this one more comfortable.

"My room is next to Miz Martha's," Shirley said. "We

share the bathroom. You'll have to use the one down the hall, I guess."

"Okay. I'll be in to relieve you as soon as I change."

"No, that's all right; Miz Danner will sit with Miz Martha for a while. *She* wants you to sit with her mornings. Mostly she wants you to read to her."

"Tennyson's *Poems*?"

Shirley permitted a small smile to curve her lips. "It's better than Dickens. We tried him, but Miz Martha says I don't read good."

"I doubt that my efforts will please her any better, Shirley."

"Then she wants you should sit with her again after supper. She wants you—"

"She wants? What about you? I'm not squeamish, Shirley. I'll empty bedpans and bathe her and change sheets. I didn't come here to read Tennyson and Dickens."

"She don't want you should do those things." Shirley added, "She's the patient, Julie. It's my job. I've done worse."

I could believe that. And I thought I understood why Martha wanted my services restricted to those of a genteel lady's companion. She'd fight to keep the shreds of dignity remaining to her while there was breath in her body. Well, I could sympathize with that feeling. At least I wouldn't have to brush her poodle. Martha hated animals. She had never allowed pets at Maidenwood.

Matt came in just then, ending the discussion. Shirley gave him a smile, much warmer than any I had received, before slipping out. Matt had my suitcases. He dumped them willy-nilly onto the floor and mopped his brow.

"God, what an awful room. Why did you pick this one?"

"I didn't. It was Martha's selection."

"Take another one—the Green Room, or the Jefferson Room. She'll never know the difference."

"No, I rather like being this far away from the throne room. But I'm going to borrow some furniture."

"Go ahead. Uh—want me to help you?"

He looked so hot and rumpled and distraught I took pity on him. "That's okay. I'm sure you're busy. If I yearn for something I can't move myself I'll enlist your services next time you come."

I walked him to the front door, trying to think of things I had forgotten to ask him about. He had given me a list of phone numbers, some money for expenses, and promised me the loan of a car as soon as he could find someone to deliver it. "I'll have it here by the weekend," he promised. "That's only a couple of days. If you need to go out before that, I'm sure Shirley will let you borrow her car. Doc Green said he'd stop by tomorrow . . . Let's see—is there anything else?"

"Probably. I'll think of it after you've gone. Where is the archaeological team working?"

"The southeast pasture. I told them not to come near the house. If Martha hears sounds of activity and asks about them, the story is that I'm setting out young pines as a windbreak."

"Okay."

"You won't see anything of them unless you want to, Julie."

"I don't care one way or the other."

"Right. Well . . ."

He opened the car door and got in. The air was as clammy as a wet sheet. To the west the piled cumulus clouds had changed from white to dirty gray. We were going to have a thunderstorm—probably one of the humdingers common to the area. The basement would flood, the power would go out. A horrific picture flashed into my mind, a preview of the evening ahead: reading Dickens by candlelight, with the sweat running down the back of my neck and Martha's single eye fixed on me in silent mockery.

It was all I could do not to wrench open the car door and jump in.

three

The evening wasn't quite that bad. The lights flickered and dimmed periodically but the power did not go off. Thunder rattled the windowpanes and rolled among the trees. I cringed when a particularly violent crash shook the house like a cannonball dropped onto the roof, and I could have sworn Martha's watching eye brightened.

By the weekend I felt as if I had been there forever. I didn't mind the morning duty so much, but I really dreaded the evening round. The days were stretching out, but darkness had usually come by the time I settled myself for another session of Dickens. Shirley had not been kidding about Dickens. The book Martha had me reading was *Bleak House*. The plot was rather interesting, but the heroine, Esther Summerson, was so pious and goody-goody she turned my stomach.

Martha only permitted one lamp, the one by my chair, and the big, high-ceilinged room felt like a dark cave occupied by a half-visible, shapeless thing that might have been animal or human. Occasionally, when I paused for breath, I heard a faint rustle of linen—fingernails, scratching at the sheet. It sounded like dead leaves crackling as the creature crouched in its lair, shifting before it sprang.

Martha never asked me for any personal service, not even a sip of water. One evening, when the air was especially hot and sticky, I asked if she would like me to wipe her face with a damp cloth. Her response was instantaneous, and unmistakably negative.

Shirley relieved me at ten o'clock, so I really had quite a bit of free time—the rest of the evening and every afternoon from noon till about seven. At first I had no trouble filling the hours. It gave me a mean satisfaction to loot the unoccupied rooms for furniture that would give my own shabby bedroom some comfort. Not that there was much to choose from. I hadn't realized just how little was left from what had presumably been a wealthy and well-equipped home. There were no Chippendale highboys or Sheraton chairs. Great-Great-Grandpa had really screwed his descendants; the objects he had disposed of, probably for pennies, were fetching five- and six-figure prices at antique auctions these days. I suspected the late Victorian replacements had some value, since antique freaks are into Victorian these days, but they weren't of much use to me since most were too heavy to be moved. I swiped the mattress from the only bedroom, aside from Martha's, that was decently furnished. Shirley confirmed my assumption that it was the guest room, occupied by Matt when he condescended to spend the night. She seemed faintly amused by my activities, but did not ask why I just didn't move into the guest room. Maybe she knew the answer. It was directly across the hall from Martha's room. Besides, I got a childish pleasure from taking the things, late at night when Martha was deep in the drugged slumber the doctor had prescribed.

Aside from Shirley and Martha, and "Miz Danner"—of whom more later—the only human being I saw for four dreary days was Dr. Green, who came the afternoon following my arrival.

The doctor was in his late fifties. He had watchful, hooded blue eyes and a thatch of snow-white hair, and an accent that made him sound as if he were talking through a mouthful of syrup. I cracked a joke about doctors who made house calls, to which he replied with deadly seriousness. "I've practiced in this region for thirty years, Miss Julie. Anyhow, Miss Martha is a special case."

"In what way?"

We were sitting in the drawing room partaking, if you will excuse the expression, of sherry. At least the doctor partook, and with gusto; I sipped politely at the glass I had taken to keep him company. I had learned from Shirley that Maidenwood sherry was supposed to be something special, and that it was one of the doctor's perks for making house calls. I wasn't impressed, but then I've never claimed to be a connoisseur of fine wine.

He stared at me as if he thought I wasn't quite bright. "She can hardly come to my office, can she?"

"Why isn't she in hospital, or a nursing home?"

"Well, now, Miss Julie—"

"I know hospitals don't like to give space to terminally ill patients, and I also know that it is good medical practice, as well as common decency, to allow the dying to pass their last days at home, if it is at all practicable. But Martha is a long way from dying, in my humble opinion. Considering her age, she is making a remarkable recovery."

He looked surprised, as if a dog had addressed him in understandable English. "Now, Miss Julie, it may seem that way. The patient's attitude is important, and Miss

Martha hasn't made up her mind to give up. But if you could see her records—"

"I'd like to see them."

"You wouldn't . . ." He broke off. He could hardly tell me I wouldn't understand the technical terminology, but he obviously resented being questioned by a lowly student. "I can't show them to you, my dear. Medical ethics—"

"I know I've no right to see Martha's records. But I am responsible for her care and I ought to know what I should be doing for her."

His frown smoothed out. "There's nothing to worry about, child. Shirley Johnson is one of the most capable nurses in the county. She knows what to do. It's only a matter of time, Miss Julie. You must resign yourself. You are giving her what no one else can—the tender love of a woman of her own blood."

He left soon after that remarkable and exasperating statement. Still, the fact that he had burbled nonsense instead of giving me a straight diagnosis wasn't necessarily a sign of professional incompetence. A southern male of his generation would find it hard to take a woman seriously.

Competent or not, he was no specialist, only a country G.P., and I couldn't help wondering why he had not insisted that Martha be moved to a city medical facility for treatment. The problems of aging had received greater attention in recent years; a good doctor didn't shrug his shoulders and write a patient off just because she was eighty-five. Modern therapy might preserve Martha's life for several more years.

The question was—did I want it preserved?

The fact that I could even think the question horrified me so much I took another sip of sherry, reminding myself to lay in a stock of something stronger when I went shopping. The point was not what I wanted, but what decency and the ethics of the profession I hoped to enter demanded.

I replaced the decanter on the sideboard and collected the used wineglasses. Before I could pick up the tray there was a timid tap at the door, and "Miz Danner" sidled in.

"I heard the doc leave," she said. "Shall I take the tray, Miz Julie?"

I had told her to call me Julie, but she couldn't or wouldn't do it. I had met her the day before; I was in the kitchen making myself a glass of iced tea, after Matt left, when she shuffled in, her shoulders hunched as if she expected a blow or a reprimand, and I had the odd feeling of looking at a double exposure. Her scrawny body and nondescript features left so fleeting an impression on the senses that she might have been transparent. Yet, behind the woman that she was, I seemed to get a picture of the woman she once had been—heavyset and plump-cheeked, with cosmetics inexpertly but cheerfully smeared across her face.

She greeted me by name, before I could introduce myself, and her implicit assumption of previous acquaintance jogged my recalcitrant memory. Of course—that was the reason for the double image. I had known Mrs. Danner way back when; her husband was one of Martha's tenants. They lived in a ramshackle frame house a few miles away, and farmed a few acres, ran a few cows, raised a few chickens and pigs—not poor white trash, but not exactly upwardly mobile. Visiting them had been a rare treat for me. They had a daughter about my age with whom I was sometimes allowed to play; Mr. Danner used to take me for rides on the tractor, and Mrs. Danner gave me cookies.

She had been a pretty woman—pounds overweight, but rosy and smiling.

Consternation filled me as I saw what the years had done to her. Gray hair strained back into an ugly knot, gray sunken cheeks, a gray-and-black dress that covered her arms to the wrists and closed tight around her neck.

I tried to think of something to say. Even "How are you?" carried ironic overtones. I could see how she was—terrible. In my attempt to avoid a minor faux pas I committed a worse blunder. Something Matt had told me slipped into place, and I said, "How is Mr. Danner? It must have been a terrible shock, finding the—er—remains. He was the one who found them, wasn't he?"

Mrs. Danner's face froze like an ice sculpture. Without replying she turned to the cupboard and began banging pans around.

Mercifully Shirley had appeared then and I escaped, berating myself for my tactlessness. I hadn't seen Mrs. Danner since. Now she appeared to have forgiven me. She repeated the question, "Shall I take the tray?" with something approaching animation.

"No, thank you, Mrs. Danner. I'll get it. Can I do anything to help in the kitchen?"

She shook her head. "Dinner's fixed. I got to go. Mr. Danner'll be fetching me any time."

"Go on, then. I'll take care of the tray."

She looked as if she wanted to insist, but then came the insistent blast of a horn. Mrs. Danner started, her hand going to her breast. "He's here. I'm late."

"He's early," I corrected, glancing at my watch.

Mrs. Danner didn't debate the issue, but moved at a rapid shuffle toward the door. I followed, curious to see what sort of man could inspire such frenzied obedience. She hadn't called him "Mr. Danner" when I knew them. It was "Joe," then, or sometimes "Stud." I liked that name; once I called him "Mr. Stud," and he laughed so hard he almost fell off the tractor. Then he warned me not to repeat the word in front of Martha . . .

I was too late to see whether an equivalent transformation had affected Joe Danner. The pickup pulled away as I reached the front door. It rattled down the drive, emitting black fumes from its tailpipe.

Deprived of even that uninspired hope of social intercourse, I went back to the drawing room. It was an oasis of cleanliness in the general decay, and the few remaining antiques of which Maidenwood could boast were gathered there. Mrs. Danner earned her pay in the cleaning line; I wished I could give the same praise to her cooking. If the meal I had eaten the previous night was any indication of her culinary talents, I might be driven to take drastic actions—such as doing the cooking myself. The stew had been a disaster—chunks of meat and mushy vegetables swimming in a bland, tan, watery gravy. To accompany it we had been offered store-bought bread and frozen coconut pie.

I took the wineglasses to the kitchen. It was the most pleasant room in the house, which admittedly isn't saying much. The appliances were old, the linoleum was worn down to the nub, and the woodwork needed painting. An antique refrigerator chuckled and grumbled in the corner; like Martha, it couldn't last long. But there were windows on two sides and a screened-in porch beyond; the plank-bottom chairs were surprisingly comfortable, and the big table had a lovely patina from years of scrubbing. There were none of the country-chic touches one might expect in a house that age—no fireplace, or exposed beams. The kitchen wing had been added during a relatively affluent period in the late nineteenth century, when the lord of the manor got tired of food served ice-cold after it had been carried clear across the yard from the separate kitchen house. It was still a considerable distance from the dining room, at the end of a long windowless corridor with rooms on either side—pantries and storerooms and small cubicles that had housed some of the servants.

I opened the oven door and found my most dire suspicions confirmed. The casserole within consisted of noodles mixed with the remains of the stew and covered with a leathery layer of cheese.

I was contemplating this catastrophe with my hands on my hips and a sneer on my lips when Shirley came in. "Is Martha supposed to eat this?" I demanded. "I don't think I can force it down myself."

Shirley reached for a saucepan that stood on the back of the stove. It contained soup, which she ladled into a bowl. The aroma of the soup did nothing to tickle my taste buds; it was a canned variety. She added a few slices of bread to the tray.

"There's cans of soup and tuna in the pantry if you don't fancy the casserole," she said.

"How about lending me your car? I'll run into town and pick up a few things. Even fast food would be better than this."

The request caught her off guard; for the first time I saw her serenity ruffled. "I can't. I mean—didn't Matthew say he'd fetch a car for you to use?"

"Saturday. I can't wait till Saturday."

She frowned, and I burst out laughing. "Sorry. I sound like a whiny kid. I'm a good driver, Shirley, honestly. Or if you would rather, I'll give you the money and you can go shopping later."

"It's not that. Truth is, I don't have the car. I lent it to—to someone."

I almost asked to whom, but caught myself in time. It was her car, after all. She muttered, "I'm sorry." Picking up the tray she went out, moving rather more quickly than usual.

Have I mentioned that it rained every day? Not all the time, just during my hours off, so I couldn't even indulge in the dubious pleasure of a walk. By Friday I was ready to climb the walls and I'd have killed for a bacon cheeseburger. I kept myself sane by making a shopping list, to which I added daily. Not only food and drink, but basic necessities such as light bulbs; the only one-hundred-watt bulb in the house was in the reading lamp in Martha's room. In the other rooms they were forty or sixty watt, or missing altogether. Even in daylight the grey gloom was so depressing I felt as if I were walking through a tropical rain forest. My list got longer and longer. Electric fans, flashlights, paperback books, magazines, newspapers . . . Martha wouldn't have a TV in the house, she didn't take a daily paper, only the twelve-page local weekly, and I had finished the mystery I had brought with me. Stamps. I hadn't even written my mother.

On Friday after lunch I left Mrs. Danner to her criminal activities in the kitchen and went on a tour of exploration. She was making spaghetti sauce, I assumed—canned tomatoes bubbling furiously on the stove, with a chopped onion for seasoning.

There was one flashlight in the house. I took it with me when I started toward the part of the house I had not yet visited. It was pouring outside, the afternoon skies were as dark as a winter evening, and I knew the lights would be cut off or the bulbs burned out in the regions where I was headed. That wing of the house was closed. But there was, or had been, a library, and that was my destination.

Why hadn't I gone there before? It's a good question. I know the answer now; at the time I was only aware of a vague disinclination to open the door into the west wing.

The long gloomy corridor led past closed and cob-webbed doors—drawing room, dining room, music room, billiard room . . . I was glad I had brought the flash-light. I was sorry I had come. Dark and depressing, smell-ing of mold and mildew—even the boards of the floor felt soggy under my feet.

The library was at the end of the wing, with long win-dows like French doors opening onto a flagstoned terrace. I reached for the knob and then it happened again—an-other of those thuds of returning memory. There had been a number of them the first day I arrived, but this was the first in some time. I literally flinched, as if something had struck me, before I opened the door.

I had spent a lot of time in this room during the years I lived at Maidenwood. Reading was almost my only plea-sure. I had no one to play with. Martha wouldn't permit me to invite schoolmates to the house, and I was seldom allowed to go to the Danners' place. The Danners weren't "our kind." Neither were the other families whose chil-dren attended my school.

The heavy draperies were open. Sun had rotted their linings; they hung in tatters from the gilded rods. The furniture and chandeliers were swathed in cobwebs like soft gray dustcloths.

The flashlight beam moved erratically around the room, spotlighting familiar objects. The sagging leather chair near the window, my favorite seat. The row of chil-dren's books on the bottom shelf of the bookcase to the left of the fireplace—books that dated, all of them, from my mother's youth, or from times even farther back. *Ruth Fielding at College, Kim,* and a lugubrious little masterpiece called *Beulah,* about a homely orphan girl who grew up to be one of the most appalling prigs in the history of literature. Remembering Beulah, I felt a positive affection for soupy Esther Summerson.

Martha did not forbid me to use the library, but she effectively censored my reading by putting the verboten volumes on shelves that were too high for me to reach. Another memory made me cringe—the night I was caught in flagrante, climbing up the steplike shelves to get a book called *The Golden Bough.* I thought it sounded like a fairy tale. When I asked about it, Martha said, no, it was not a fairy tale (she was right about that, at any rate!) and I was not under any circumstances to read it. There must have been a few smoldering embers of rebellion still burning in me, because the prohibition made me all the more determined to see for myself. I waited until late one night, when I was sure Martha must be asleep. A spring night, it must have been—the smell of blossoming, burgeoning new greenness came back to me, when I remembered . . . I had almost reached the top shelves when the French doors flew open and there she stood. She didn't speak, she just reached out, as if to grasp me, and the moonlight fell full on her outstretched hands. They were stained and streaked with black clear to the wrists, as if she had plunged them into a bucket of oil or liquid mud.

I lost my hold and fell, a good ten feet. I must have knocked myself out, because I woke up in my bed, with a bandaged head, and without the slightest notion of what had happened to put me there.

No wonder I had fought to suppress so many of those childhood memories. I couldn't have handled them then.

I wasn't sure I could handle them now. My hands shook so violently that the yellow beam of the flashlight darted up and down, and side to side, like a hysterical firefly. It would have been completely in character for Martha to lie in wait for me, let me make that painful, dangerous climb before revealing herself—suddenly, silently, shockingly, like some monster from a child's worst nightmare. But she had not followed me through the house. She had come through the French doors, out of the night. What had she been doing out there, to stain her hands with darkness? Or had I only imagined that?

I grabbed a couple of the children's books, without looking at the titles, and ran.

The clouds lightened as the day wore on, and a daring idea occurred to me, born of desperation. I had to get out of that house. Shirley had said nothing more about her car and I didn't like to ask. Either she didn't want to lend it, or the unknown borrower had not returned it. But there might be another way.

I was waiting, purse and list in hand, when Mr. Danner sounded his asthmatic horn. Mrs. Danner gave me a startled look when I followed her out, but she got in the truck without comment, and I circled around to look in the driver's window.

"Hello, Mr. Danner. Remember me? It's been a long time. You're looking—you look—uh—"

I would never have known him. He had been a tall, burly man with a red flush of health under his tan and a ready grin. The face that looked back at me was that of a well-preserved mummy, the cheeks cadaverous, the wrinkles etched as if by acid, sour-shaped and ugly. His lips parted just enough to let a few words squeeze out. "Evening, Julie. How's your mama?"

"Fine, thank you. How is . . ." I couldn't recall the girl's name, much less that of her brother, whom I hadn't known as well. "How are the children?"

"I have no children. Good-bye, Julie."

I was so taken aback I didn't respond immediately. He had shifted gears and taken his foot off the brake before I woke up. I made a desperate grab at the car door and yelled, "Wait. Wait a minute. Can you give me a ride to town? I need to get a few groceries. It won't take long . . ." He continued to regard me with stony disapproval and I added, "I'll be glad to pay for the gas, and your time."

His scowl deepened. "It ain't that. A Christian don't take money for doing a deed of charity."

"Well, then—"

"I don't have the time. Services tonight. I could take you in, but there's no way you could get back."

"I'll hitch a ride. Or—is there a taxi?"

He shook his head. Mrs. Danner squeaked, "There's Will Smith, Mr. Danner. He obliges for some of the ladies—"

"Be quiet, woman. Will's a drunk and a fornicator. No decent female would get in that car of his."

I had my head in the window, intent on winning the absurd argument. He came across the rain-softened grass, silent as a snake. I didn't know he was there until he spoke.

"Looking for a lift, Julie?"

I straightened up so fast I hit my head on the window frame. Danner promptly gunned the engine and took off. I jumped back, slipped on the wet grass, and would have fallen if Alan had not caught my arm.

"Typical Joe Danner courtesy," he remarked. "Are you okay, Julie?"

The rap on the head had brought tears to my eyes. I blinked them away, hoping Alan hadn't noticed them, or mistaken their cause. I'd known I would have to face him sooner or later. I had worked it all out in my mind—the casual smile, the cool, composed words of greeting. So much for that scenario. I did what I could to retrieve my dignity, trying to ignore the treacherous warmth that was spreading from his hand, up my arm and shoulder, into my body.

"Yes, thanks, I'm fine. I'd better get back to the house. Martha—"

"I thought you wanted a ride."

He hadn't changed. He was the only person I had seen who had not changed. Bareheaded, his hair darkened and sleeked by wet, he towered over me by almost eight inches. He was wearing jeans and a long-sleeved shirt, buttoned up to the neck—you don't wander Virginia's woods with your muscles bared, not if you have any concern about poison ivy, mosquitoes, ticks, chiggers, and brambles. But I didn't have to see the muscles to know they were there. I could still feel the pressure of the fingers that had gripped my arm. Long slender fingers, capable of an infinitely delicate touch in excavation—and elsewhere.

I reminded myself that I was a grown-up person, not a silly adolescent. That my feelings for Alan Petranek were those of polite indifference. And, most important, that he had the only set of wheels available.

"Thank you," I said. "If it's not too much trouble."

"No trouble at all."

The Jeep was parked behind the house, near the old stables that served as a garage. Instead of heading back to the front of the house, Alan turned onto a track I hadn't known existed. It had never been paved, and if there had been gravel laid, it had sunk into the mud. Two tracks filled with water led east toward the woods, curved sharply, and debouched on to the road just below the bridge.

As we rattled over the bridge I looked down. The stream was up; water the color of dried blood rushed between banks that showed the raw, new scars of flooding.

"It'll be higher before morning," Alan said, reading my thoughts with the uncanny accuracy I remembered—and resented. "Maybe over the bridge. Nothing to worry about, though. The house is on high ground."

"I'm not worried. Why are you going this way? Carrsville is back—"

"I know, to my sorrow, where Carrsville is located. The dullest town in Virginia. I thought you might prefer something more exhilarating than Millie's General Store."

"I didn't know there was anything more exhilarating."

"There's a shopping center a few miles down the highway. Compared to Carrsville, it offers a wealth of amenities."

"Oh. I—uh—I appreciate this, Alan. You needn't worry that it will take a lot of time. I have to be back by seven."

"How is Miss Martha?"

"Stable."

He nodded. "And your mother? I hope she's well."

"Fine, thank you."

The stiff, formal sentences might have been uttered by strangers who didn't like each other very much. He sounded even more ill at ease than I felt. I couldn't believe that he was; a glib tongue and charming manner were part of Alan's stock in trade; he could carry on a conversation with a mortician and sound as if he were genuinely interested in the composition of embalming fluid.

I said, matching his polite, disinterested tone, "How is your work progressing?"

"Do you really give a damn?"

"No, not really."

Ahead, through a break in the trees, a bar of crimson showed where the clouds were breaking, but under the trees twilight deepened. Alan switched on the headlights. He seemed more relaxed; perhaps my blunt and not entirely honest reply had relieved some of the strain.

"I'll tell you anyway," he said amiably. "At the moment my work isn't progressing. Every time we dig a hole the rain fills it."

"Too bad."

"Your sympathy warms the cockles of my heart."

"Whatever they are."

"Are we going to go on sniping at each other all summer?"

"I don't intend . . ." I stopped, before I dug myself into a hole of my own, a hole I might not be able to climb out of with dignity. Unless Martha obliged me by dying, I had a long hot summer ahead of me, with massive boredom the least of the difficulties that might ensue. Matt obviously had no intention of spending any more time at Maidenwood than he could possibly help, the Danners were, to say the least, uncooperative, and Shirley . . . Shirley had problems of her own. It was distinctly possible that I might find myself facing an emergency, the result of bad weather, Martha's condition, or any number of other contingencies. If I did, the proximity of a few husky archaeologists might come in handy.

Besides, hadn't I told myself that the past was over and done with?

"No more sniping," I said. "I am interested, naturally. What is it you're looking for? Maydon's Hundred?"

It was surprisingly difficult for me to pronounce the name. The last time I had used it to him I had hurled it like a missile, accusing him of using me to get the site he wanted. But once the words were out I felt as if I had jumped a hurdle. The barricade was behind me now.

If he remembered that occasion, he gave no sign of doing so. "That's what I'm hoping to find, yes. But there are other things."

"Such as?"

"The remains of the first manor house. Property and tax records show that there was a house here in the late seventeenth century. The present building wasn't begun until 1735, so presumably it replaced an earlier structure which was destroyed. I don't expect to find traces of that, though. It probably lay close to the present house and we're supposed to keep our distance."

"What about cemeteries?"

We had reached the highway. Alan gave the "Stop" sign a jerk of acknowledgment and turned on to the pavement. "You heard about our local scandal?"

"Not till I arrived. Matt said it was because of that that he decided to give you permission to dig."

"He didn't magnanimously yield, he was forced to give in. There was some public pressure."

"Public, hell," I said, forgetting my resolution. "The pressure came from you, I'll bet."

"I orchestrated a certain amount of it," Alan said smugly. "To refuse wouldn't have been good for the senator's image. The proud aristocrat, letting vandals flout the law . . ."

"Much you care for the law."

"I care about vandalism. There has been too much looting of archaeological sites. Especially at Maidenwood, with all that crap about pirate treasure. Here we are . . ."

I forgot about his problems as the full glory of the shopping center burst upon me. Bright lights, people, cars . . . I felt like a backwoods hick seeing the big city for the first time.

Alan pulled into a parking space. "I'll wait for you at the coffee shop. Take your time."

He strode off without a backward glance, his briefcase in hand. I hesitated, torn between the exotic offerings of Safeway and Drug Fair. There were a liquor store, a gift shop, a McDonald's . . . I would not have believed the golden arches could be so enticing. I hadn't even seen a newspaper for four days.

I bought groceries and booze and stowed them in the Jeep before heading for the drugstore. The coffee shop was part of it, and when I went in I saw Alan in one of the booths, his head bent over the papers spread on the table. He used to complain about the amount of paperwork necessary in a dig . . .

I acquired an armful of magazines and paperbacks and newspapers. When he saw me, Alan gathered his work up and shoved it into his briefcase. "Ready?"

A glance at my watch told me it was later than I had thought. I asked him to stop at the drive-in window at McDonald's and got something to eat along the way, for I knew I would not have time to prepare a meal if I was to be on duty by seven, and Mrs. Danner's spaghetti was a horror I preferred not to face.

I offered Alan a french fry. He shook his head. "That stuff is poison to your system. I'd rather starve."

"There speaks a man who has not eaten Mrs. Danner's cooking."

He chuckled. "I haven't had the privilege, but if her cuisine resembles her personality—"

"It's so bad I may be driven to take over the cooking."

I half-expected some crack about my culinary talents, or lack thereof; it had once been a standing joke between us. But Alan seemed as anxious as I to avoid unfortunate references to the past. He went on, "Do you ever get an evening off? We can do better than Mrs. Danner, or even Ronald McDonald."

It sounded like a dinner invitation—a surprisingly tentative invitation. Perhaps he had learned some humility in the past five years. His invitations always used to sound like orders.

I said I didn't know. "Shirley is the only other person there full-time, and I hate to ask her to do more than she is already doing. I sit with Martha mornings and in the evening from seven to ten."

I hadn't meant it to sound like a hint. Anyhow, he didn't take me up on it. "If you get bored in the afternoon, come out and join us. I can always use another pair of hands."

That sounded like the old Alan. Since I did expect I would be bored, I said I would think about it.

He dropped me at the front door. He didn't offer to help me carry in the groceries, but took off in a spatter of mud and gravel as soon as I had removed the bags from the Jeep. No doubt he was late for his Friday-night date, I thought.

I carried the groceries to the kitchen. Shirley had been in the room during my absence. The lights were on and the tray with the remains of Martha's dinner was on the table. The back door was open.

A trickle of uneasiness touched me. I had not been surprised to find the front door unlocked, for Shirley knew I was out. But Mrs. Danner had closed and locked the kitchen door when she left, and the only reason why it should be open now was because Shirley had gone outside—and had not returned. What could she be doing in the dusk-shrouded, empty kitchen yard?

The clouds had closed in again. It was dark outside—how dark, only those who have lived in an area without street lights and nearby houses can possibly realize. I put the groceries on the table and tiptoed to the door.

Shirley was there. Or someone was there . . . I could see a crouched darkness beyond the porch steps; it was still, but not silent. She was talking, apparently to herself, in a low crooning voice. I could not make out the words.

I crossed the porch and opened the screen door. Shirley got to her feet. I heard the rustle of leaves as something fled into the bushes. Shirley's body had concealed the object on the path—a bowl, filled with an all-too-familiar mess, the remains of last night's casserole.

"What are you doing?" I asked.

It was a stupid question. Yet I half-expected her to tell me she was feeding the local brownie—the atmosphere was that uncanny.

"I was going to throw it out anyway," she said defensively. "I knew you wouldn't want it—"

"For God's sake, Shirley, you can have all the food you want and you can do anything you want with it. Is it your pet? Dog or cat?"

"It's not mine. Just a stray—a dog, that is. It's been hanging around. I guess I shouldn't feed it, but—"

"Not that stew. It's only fit for the buzzards. I bought a couple of pounds of ground beef; let's try that."

I took the meat out of the bag and put some of it onto a plate. The plate was cracked and its design was faded, but there were traces of gold remaining around the rim, and I smiled as I put it down next to the bowl of stew. Feeding stray dogs with hamburger in a Sèvres plate—typical of Maidenwood.

"Here, doggy," I said.

The bushes rustled, but the animal didn't show itself. Shirley said, "It won't come out while you're here. Took me all week to get it to come near me."

I followed her into the house. "What about some milk?" I asked. "Or water? It must want something to drink."

"There's plenty of water around," Shirley said, straight-faced.

"True, too true." I folded the plastic wrap around the remains of the ground beef. "It can have the rest tomorrow. I'll buy dog food next time I go to the store."

"That's nice of you, Julie."

"Nice, shmice. I'm not going to let some animal starve right under my nose."

"I don't suppose it would starve. There's plenty of game around. But it's used to somebody feeding it, you can see that, even though it hasn't been treated right. Guess the owner got tired of it and dumped it here."

I muttered something, not quite under my breath, and Shirley looked at me severely. "Doesn't do no good to swear, Julie. People are . . . people."

"People are no damn good. Shirley, would you mind putting the groceries away so I can get up to Martha? Fix yourself something decent to eat—I got cheese and ham and fresh fruit—"

"That's all right, you run along. I'll take care of it."

I grabbed a banana and ate it as I ran upstairs. I left the peel on the table outside Martha's door. What the heck, she wouldn't know the difference.

I was late and Martha let me know it. If looks could

have killed, that glaring eye of hers would have turned me into a block of stone. Her hand moved with almost normal vigor as she gestured toward the chair and the book.

I wish I could say I learned to love the Victorian novelists that summer. I wish I could say it, but I can't. The sight of a volume of Dickens on the library shelf brings on an almost physical revulsion, as if the events of that incredible summer had permeated the pages, and opening the volume would set them free, like a bad-smelling fog. But, as Dickens might have said, all that was in the future. In the early days I despised Dickens for his own sake—his egregious sentimentality, his soupy, soppy heroines. God, but they revolted me—especially sweet Esther Summerson. Already I had learned to mouth the words like a tape recorder while my thoughts strayed.

Had Shirley really believed I was such a monster that I would scold her for feeding a hungry animal? Anyhow, she had warmed to me; her parting smile had been broad and friendly. I was glad. I needed friends. Even a dog. It would be nice to have a pet. I had never had one. Mother was allergic to animals . . . For the first time I wondered whether her supposed allergies might be based on other factors—her own mother's violent dislike of animals, for instance.

As I read on, page after close-printed page, the night breeze turned pleasantly cool and stars began to bloom in the night sky. I should have been in a good mood. I had a collection of munchies to eat before I went to bed, and a new mystery story to read; Shirley felt more kindly toward me; God willing, I would have wheels of my own next day. I don't know why I was depressed. Maybe it was the muffled cry I heard, just before I stopped reading to Martha. It sounded like an animal in pain or distress.

It could have been any animal. The cycle of life is a

cycle of death as well, and natural selection seems to consist mostly of things eating other things. But long after I had turned out my light I lay awake thinking of all the homeless, hungry creatures that cower in the dark; and I dreamed that something young and troubled came to my window and pressed a white drained face against the screen. Its eyes were empty holes in a framework of polished bone, and the fingers that scratched at the window, pleading for entry, had no flesh to strengthen their appeal.

four

At any rate, it was not the stray dog that had met an untimely end in the night woods. I caught a glimpse of it next morning when I replenished its empty food bowl—only a pair of worried eyes and a long muzzle poking through the bushes. When I went toward it, it vanished altogether, so I left it to its breakfast. The bowls had been licked to gleaming cleanness, as if they had been washed.

I was usually the first one down in the morning, for Shirley stayed with Martha until I relieved her and Mrs. Danner didn't come until noon. She worked for someone else in the morning. On Saturday she didn't come at all; according to Shirley, the church to which she and her husband belonged celebrated the Sabbath in the old style. No, Shirley said, she wasn't Jewish, or Adventist; it was one of those small sects—she couldn't remember the name.

Mrs. Danner's religious needs had left Shirley to carry the burden unassisted on Saturdays. Shirley said she didn't mind; it gave her a chance to run over home for a few hours on Sunday, when Mrs. Danner condescended to stay late.

I had not given much thought to Shirley's domestic arrangements. I guess I had assumed the family had imported her from Atlanta when the need arose, and that her husband and children were still in that city. When I said as much, her friendly smile froze. "I moved back here ten years ago," she said, and changed the subject.

But she wasn't reluctant to gossip about the Danners. I had been brooding about my faux pas when I asked about the children, wondering what nerve I had inadvertently struck. If the boy and girl I remembered had died, I didn't want to be guilty of arousing unhappy memories.

No, Shirley said, they weren't dead. They were alive and well and, last she'd heard, doing just fine. Lynne Anne had three kids and Joe Junior was somewhere up north, working in construction.

I listened greedily. You can laugh if you want to, but small-town gossip is the stuff of which great novels are made. Look at Jane Austen. Look, for that matter, at Dickens and Tolstoi. As I was to learn, there are few quirks of human behavior that don't exist in small towns. In fact, they show up all the more strongly for being isolated.

The bizarre transformation of the Danners from nice, amiable slobs to stern Puritans was the first such case I had encountered, and it left me aghast. "I can't believe it," I said. "I remember them—he laughed a lot and smelled of beer, and she made terrible cookies—she never was a good cook—but she handed them out lavishly, and teased the children . . . He really, literally, threw that girl out into a snowstorm?"

"It wasn't like sending her out to die," Shirley said practically. "There was some traffic on the road, and a neighbor half a mile away. It was plain spite that made her walk so far. That's how they are at that age."

"Even so . . ."

"He's got some virtues," Shirley conceded. "He don't get drunk, or fight; and he used to be a real heller with women."

"Well, I'm glad you told me, Shirley. I won't mention the children to them again."

We were standing outside Martha's room talking in whispers. She had settled down for her afternoon nap; I was on my way out, freed for a whole afternoon of mad, frivolous pleasure. I thought I might clean out the refrigerator or maybe do something really exciting, like take a walk.

I had a ham-and-cheese sandwich and a cup of coffee and washed my dishes. There was no need to clean out the refrigerator; there was nothing in the refrigerator to clean out, except one lonely chicken and some fruit and cheese. As I contemplated the bare shelves I felt like giving Matt a swift kick where it would hurt the most. I wasn't feeling as kindly toward Shirley as I had, either. How the hell was I supposed to run this house without food or the means to acquire it? The mystery of Shirley's missing car was still unsolved; obviously it had not been returned, since it wasn't there. I wished I had asked Matt precisely when he meant to arrive. Was he expecting to stay for dinner? The chicken wouldn't stretch far, especially if I gave half of it to the dog. The hamburger was gone—long gone.

I decided there was no sense in hanging around the house waiting for Matt. He might not come until evening. If he arrived at 6 P.M. with a big hungry smile on his face, expecting a meal, he was out of luck. And if he arrived without a car for me, I *would* kick him.

Having settled that point in my own mind, I went out. The food I had left for the dog was gone, but there was no sign of him, or her. I had placed a pan of water under the steps, but I couldn't tell whether it had been touched.

I suppose that first stroll around the family estate should have depressed me. The place was certainly a sad ruin, overgrown and unkempt; but I could not remember it as ever having been otherwise, and since I tend to be something of a radical in my social thinking, I wasn't cast down by what some people might describe as the decay of a once-proud old family. There was nothing left of the terraced gardens and wide lawns that had once surrounded the house, or of the outbuildings, extensive as a small village, that had served its needs. The dairies, tobacco barns, craftsmen's shops, and slave cabins had crumbled into ruin long ago. When I lived at Maidenwood I was forbidden to go near that part of the grounds, for there were abandoned wells and sunken cellars under the weeds. A few small structures had been kept up—the old smokehouse, solidly if crudely constructed of field stone, and two tiny brick buildings where garden tools and junk were stored.

The ridge of higher land on which the house stood ran roughly north and south, paralleling the river half a mile to the east. To the south, separated from the house by a belt of trees, was pastureland, uncultivated and overgrown. Another stretch of open ground sloped down from the ridge to the riverbank. In the distant past it had been the river approach to the house, from the landing on the James. Visitors sometimes came by water instead of risking the rough, muddy roads, and the tobacco from which the wealth of the plantation flowed was loaded there for shipment. Most of the area between the house and the river was thickly wooded; small streams had cut the ground into ravines and gullies.

The ground was still damp in shady places but the sun shone bright in a cloudless sky, and everything that could bloom at that season was blooming its head off. White blossoms starred the vigorous green of tangled blackberry and raspberry thickets, wild roses raised crumpled pink clusters out of the weeds.

I followed the track toward the woods. It was early in the year for mosquitoes, but the poison ivy looked very healthy, and there would be ticks in the tall grass. Snakes too. I stuck to the track so I could see where I was putting my feet. I had added "boots" to my shopping list, but all I owned at the moment were sneakers, and they don't offer much protection against snakebite.

Later in the season the woods would be almost impenetrable except in the deep secret places where heavy shade and fallen leaves restricted plant growth. Even now the edge of the forest was fenced by head-high tangles of bramble and honeysuckle, wild grape and poison ivy, like a barbed-wire barricade. The vines had been hacked away at one point, where a footpath left the track and plunged into the dusky shade.

I wandered on, keeping a watchful eye out for creatures. Wild animals are shy and wary; I knew that if I met one, even a harmless variety like a possum or a rabbit, and it just stood there glowering at me instead of running away, there was a good chance it had rabies. I armed myself with a stout branch and marched bravely onward. If I was going to get nervous about things like that, I wouldn't dare leave the house all summer.

I had another motive for exploring, other than boredom and the need for some exercise. I was curious about what Alan and his crew were doing. This seemed like a good chance to have a look around. I didn't expect to understand what I saw, assuming I saw anything; in the old days, Alan had dragged me out to a couple of digs, and without a program or his comments I couldn't have distinguished an archaeological site from a hole in the ground—which some sites decidedly resemble.

I didn't meet any snakes or rabid possums, but I found an archaeologist. The first thing I saw was his rear end. The rest of him was head down in a hole between two pine trees. A broad patch of brown mud stretched across the seat of his jeans, but I had no difficulty in recognizing him.

The opportunity was too good to pass up. No, I was not tempted to employ my stick. That would have been childish and uncouth.

At least I wasn't much tempted.

"Hi, there," I said loudly.

The results were even better than I had hoped. His foot slipped on the mud at the edge of the hole and he fell flat. When he wiggled to a sitting position, there was mud on his face to match the mud on the other end.

"Did I startle you?" I inquired.

Alan spat out a chunk of dirt. "My God, but you're a petty woman. Feel better now?"

"Much." I squatted. "Are you finding anything interesting?"

"Four beer cans, five Big Mac wrappers, and a random sampling of contraceptives. Plus some bones."

"Human?"

He handed me a sample. It was a long bone, stained by the red clay and ominously splintered.

"What is this, a test?" I asked. "No, it's not human, as you know perfectly well. Equine?"

"What would you say to a deer?"

"Very little." I tossed the specimen aside. "Looks to me as if you've come upon a local trysting place. Not my idea of an ideal location for lovemaking."

"Oh, I don't know." He leaned back, supporting himself on his elbows, and lifted his face to the sky. "It's private and peaceful; and at night, you can see the stars."

I decided not to pursue the matter; he had spoken with the air of a man who knows firsthand what he's talking about.

"Well, it was nice seeing you," I said.

"Wait a minute." He scrambled to his feet.

"Well?"

He hesitated. Then he said bluntly, "Five years ago we parted on bad terms. I never knew why—"

"Didn't you?"

Alan's eyes narrowed. "Maybe I was to blame. Maybe you had a few hang-ups of your own. I don't really give a damn who was responsible. I've never believed in the popular modern fallacy that people can solve all their problems by talking them out. The procedure usually results in a new exchange of old accusations. So far as I'm concerned, the past is dead and buried. I had hoped you felt the same."

"It's okay with me," I said. "I stopped caring a long time ago."

"Good," he said coolly. "Because I meant it last night when I said I could use some help. I'm damned shorthanded."

"What do you want me to do, dig?"

"No. I've got a couple of muscular jocks to do the heavy work. But I need practically everything else—record-keeping, surveying, photography. I'm running this dig on a shoestring."

"What, no grants from the university or the *National Enquirer*?"

He didn't smile. Where his work was concerned he had very little sense of humor. "The national rag has already been here. I had to run one persistent reporter off with a club. But that is an area in which you can be most useful—getting rid of unwelcome visitors. As a member of the family, you can threaten trespassers with the full force of the law."

"I'd do that in any case. You talk as if you were expecting an invasion."

"It could happen, now that the weather has cleared. The sheriff tells me these woods are popular with local hunters and trappers and lovers." A sweep of his hand reminded me of the evidence littering the ground. "It's the only large undeveloped tract of land in the area. The publicity stirred up the old pirate-treasure rumor, and I don't want a gang of louts wrecking a potentially valuable site."

"You still haven't found out where the skeletons came from?"

"For God's sake, there are over five hundred acres to search, most of them overgrown. I can't even be certain the bones came from Maidenwood, though it certainly is the likeliest possibility."

I grimaced. Alan looked at me curiously. "Don't tell me you're superstitious. If the bare idea of a skeleton gives you the shivers, maybe you've chosen the wrong profession."

"Don't be insulting. It isn't the skeleton, it's the sickies who put it on the road that bother me. How could anyone do a thing like that?"

"I've no answer except the one you suggested. There are a lot of sick people in the world. But looting graves isn't necessarily a sign of sociopathic behavior; there are good practical reasons for the exercise, including my own. Even our culture inters valuables with the dead."

"Like wedding rings," I said. "Was she wearing one?"

"Not when she was found. Which doesn't mean she never had one."

"Why haven't the police been able to track down the people who did it?"

"They don't have much to work on, Julie. No fingerprints, no footprints, no tire tracks. And the clothes it—she—they were wearing—"

"Clothes! What clothes?"

"I thought you knew."

"All I heard from Matt was the word skeleton. I never read the story. Can't you date the remains from the clothing?"

"The dress and the baby's gown couldn't have been the clothes they were buried in, Julie. The cloth was too well preserved. It was cumpled and musty, as if it had been packed away in a trunk, but not rotted."

"You mean someone dressed those pathetic bones in clothes he found in his granny's attic? That really is sick, Alan."

"Weird, but not necessarily sick," Alan said, sounding so pompous I wanted to shake him. "Kids have a peculiar sense of humor; some of the fraternity hazing procedures are just as bizarre, believe me. The clothes obviously came out of someone's attic, as you suggested. So we haven't a clue as to the origin of the bones. That's why I get so incensed at this kind of vandalism. If we had found the skeletons in situ, there would have been evidence with them—buttons, scraps of fabric—"

"How old?"

"Huh?"

"How old were the dresses? Were they made by hand

or by machine? What kind of fabric? You could get a rough idea of their age by the style."

Alan looked blank. "I don't know."

"Neither would any other man." I sniffed. "I don't suppose it occurred to any of you experts to have a woman examine them?"

"What difference does it make?" Alan demanded irritably. "I told you, they weren't the original grave clothes."

"It might give a clue as to whose attic had been raided. If the police could locate the jokers, they could persuade them to tell where they found the skeletons. Then you wouldn't have to dig up five hundred acres of dirt."

The suggestion was so eminently reasonable it infuriated Alan—because he hadn't suggested it first. His face reddened. "Why don't you talk to the sheriff? I'm sure he'd love to have your advice."

"I may do that."

It was clear that he was not interested in the subject; with a preoccupied frown he was squeezing the damp lumps of clay between his fingers, as if he expected to find gems hidden in them.

"Look here, Alan," I said. "I'm not superstitious or anything . . ." No, not me—but I dream of fleshless faces wailing at my window.

"Bones are bones," I went on firmly. "Objects. Things. I'm not concerned about the dead; it's the live bastards that worry me, as somebody once said. The ones that may be prowling around the house."

"I see your point," Alan said agreeably.

"Damn it, Alan, where did they come from?"

"The skeletons?" Alan wiped his muddy hands on his pants. "I've no idea. Possibly from your family cemetery."

He saw how the suggestion jolted me, but he didn't understand why. Relenting, he said in a more friendly voice, "I feel sure the police have looked there, Julie. Though these local clods wouldn't notice an open grave unless they fell into it."

"Why don't you look?"

"My dear, we low archaeological types aren't allowed near the house. Your stupid cousin insisted on that; every goddamn crook in Virginia strolls in and out, but we can't. Look at this." He indicated the hole at his feet. "It's recent—within the past week. I do try to patrol the area from time to time and this wasn't here last weekend."

"You don't think this was—"

"Her grave? Couldn't have been. The skeletons turned up two weeks ago. No, I think the treasure hunters are with us again."

"Why doesn't somebody do something?" I demanded angrily.

"Who? It would be impossible to guard this area twenty-four hours a day." He was silent for a moment. Then he said awkwardly, "I didn't mean to yell at you, Julie. It's just that this kind of destruction makes me so damn mad—"

"I know."

"Still interested in helping me out?"

"Sure. When do you want me to report for work? Tomorrow?"

"I don't work on Sunday. Not," he added, scowling, "because I have any qualms about the Sabbath, but because I've already had trouble with some of the local religious nuts about profaning the Lord's day. They can't seem to make up their minds whether he favors Saturday or Sunday, so they ban both. How about Monday?"

"Okay. Where?"

"I'll show you."

"I had better get back. Matt said he'd come today and I don't want to miss him."

"This won't take long. It's on the way."

He picked up a shovel that was propped against a tree and started forward. Before long we came out of the trees into a meadow high with grass and wild flowers. Several hundred yards away the river sparkled in the sunlight. To the left were the roofs and chimneys of the house. The air was thick with insects. A couple of bees floated inquisitively around my face, and I began flailing at them.

"Ignore them and they won't bother you," said Alan, striding manfully forward.

They didn't bother him, but something about me was irresistible—my shampoo, maybe; I wasn't wearing perfume. When we left the meadow my admirers turned back, presumably because they had decided that although I smelled delicious, I was disappointingly devoid of nectar.

The neighboring field had been mowed but not plowed. The surface underfoot was soggy; we were on low ground, not far from the river. Big sheets of black plastic were spread here and there. Pools of water shimmered in their folds. Alan's Jeep stood next to another vehicle, a small van whose back doors were open. He tossed the shovel in, where it clattered onto an assortment of other tools, and then closed the doors.

"How did you get the van in here?" I asked, looking in vain for any sign of a road.

"With great difficulty," Alan said sourly. "And I won't be getting it out until the ground dries. This is not exactly the most convenient dig I've ever run."

The memories that stirred as I surveyed the field were devoid of emotional overtones or jarring shocks—just your ordinary conventional memories of past experience.

The plastic sheets covered test holes and trenches; they were not as random as they appeared, but formed a pattern, part of a grid overlaying the mowed area. I reached for a loose corner of the nearest piece of plastic, which was weighted down with stones. Alan struck my hand away, hard enough to sting the skin.

"Never put your bare hand near anything you can't see," he said. "I found a six-foot copperhead sheltering under a flap of plastic once."

"Oh."

"There's nothing to see anyway," Alan went on. "This area appears never to have been occupied; it's sterile. We'll dig a few more holes just to make sure and then move to another spot."

"It sounds absolutely thrilling. I can hardly wait."

"Don't blame me if it's dull, blame your cousin. If I could dig nearer the house, I'd find foundations and rubbish pits and . . ." A speculative gleam warmed his eyes. "Did you say he was coming this afternoon? What time?"

"He didn't say. If you're thinking of hanging around in the hope of seeing him, forget it. Martha would have another stroke if she knew you were on the premises."

"She wouldn't know."

"Forget it, I said. I don't know when, if ever, Matt will turn up."

He didn't say yes, no, or maybe, just stood smiling at me with his lids half-veiling his eyes. I had seen that look before. "Till Monday," I said, and turned away.

He yelled at me when I had gone a short distance, to point out I was heading in the wrong direction. I waved—it was a "Mind your own business, get lost" flap of the hand rather than a friendly gesture—and went on.

Something about the excavation bothered me, and it was not the prospect of being bored out of my skull. I could see why Matt didn't want an archaeological team working near the house. Martha's hearing had always been abnormally acute—at times I thought she wasn't hearing, but reading people's minds at a distance. But that restriction left Alan with a lot of territory at his disposal, and if he was supposed to be looking for an abandoned cemetery, from which the girl's skeleton had been taken, he wasn't going about it in the right way. Nobody would dig a grave in a low-lying spot near a river that flooded frequently, and if he had, there would be nothing left of the contents of the grave by now. I remembered one flood when that whole stretch of pasture had been under water.

I was walking uphill as I headed away from the river. The slope was gradual, but it meant that the house stood well above the flood plain, and so did the old family cemetery, half a mile north of Maidenwood. The higher ground was the only sensible site for a house, or a cemetery—unless you didn't care whether your relatives' remains got washed away every few years.

I climbed a rotting wooden fence and cut across the corner of another field, chest-high with weeds. Alan had, not surprisingly, misinterpreted my reaction when he mentioned the cemetery. Another memory had thudded into place. Without hesitation I turned away from the house along a brick walkway enclosed by appropriately funereal cypresses.

The cemetery was surrounded by a brick wall and by more of the cypresses, so dark their foliage looked black, so tall they cast a perennial shadow over the graves. Family tradition claimed the trees had been brought from England, seedlings of venerable giants carried home from the Holy Land by a crusading ancestor. (When it comes to inventing romantic legends, nobody beats the Carrs.) In the center of the plot was a red brick mausoleum. Its roof was a startling, brilliant green, the slate shingles completely coated with moss.

The wrought iron gates were closed with a brand-new shiny padlock. A case of locking the barn door after the horse has been stolen? It was impossible for me to tell from outside the gate, but the padlock was evidence that someone had checked the place out recently. There was no sign of regular upkeep or renovation; the weeds were knee-high and some of the stones leaned drunkenly, their inscriptions blurred by smears of lichen.

Ah, the nostalgic memories of childhood! The last time I had stood peering through the bars with the pitted metal biting into my palms I had been eight years old—and I had stood *inside* the gate, with night drawing in and a wind rustling the long grass over the graves. Matt had locked me in and run away. I was hoarse with crying by the time the grown-ups finally found me. I still had a scar on the ball of my thumb, where rust had ground into a bleeding cut.

Dear Cousin Matt. If he didn't show up pretty soon with that car, I would kill him.

He had not arrived when I got back to the house, nor was Alan anywhere in evidence. I hoped Alan had taken my warning to heart. Martha might not realize he was there, but I didn't want him around. One male menace from the past was enough.

Without stopping to change or wash my hands, I went to Martha's room. Shirley was changing the bed. I didn't offer to help; I had tried that once before and had been refused in no uncertain terms, by both parties. I suppose it was easier for Shirley to do it herself, without my unskilled assistance. It was a job for an expert or a weightlifter; Martha was a tall, big-boned woman, and she had not lost any weight to speak of.

"I'm about to start supper," I said. "It's chicken—is there any special way you'd like it prepared, Martha?"

Martha had got over her self-consciousness about talking to me, but I couldn't understand her very well. Shirley translated the harsh gabble. "She wants to know where you've been."

I suspected that wasn't all she had said. The inimical eye fixed on my untidy person spoke volumes, and she had never been reticent about criticizing my personal appearance. I said, "I went for a walk. Don't worry, Martha, I'll shower and change before I handle the food. I'm not much of a cook, but I can't do worse than Mrs. Danner."

"Better stew the chicken," Shirley said. "She shouldn't have fried food or anything with a lot of seasoning."

Martha's eyes rolled in Shirley's direction and the movable half of her mouth drooped. I felt an unwilling tug of sympathy for her; she had always had a hearty appetite, and when you're lying in bed, helpless and bored, food means a great deal.

"I'll think of something," I said. "Will Matt be here for dinner? When will he be here?"

I didn't need Shirley to translate the reply; the gist of it was that Matt was a law unto himself; he came, and went, when he felt like it. I caught another word. "Doctor? He is coming today?"

"He called up when you were out," Shirley said. "Miz Martha wants to know if there's enough wine."

"Wine? I don't know."

Martha mumbled at Shirley, who nodded reassuringly. "I'd best go and show her. I'll only be a minute."

As we descended the stairs, Shirley explained. "Miz Martha's daddy was noted for his wine cellar. There's still a few bottles left, and she likes to offer it when the gentlemen come. I'll show you where, then you can make sure the decanters are kept filled. But you aren't to give the doctor more than two glasses of the amontillado."

"If amontillado is what I think it is, he got three last time," I said.

"Miz Martha figured he'd take advantage. He likes his wine, does the doctor."

No jarring shock of memory struck me when Shirley opened the cellar door. Evidently Matt had never shut me in the cellar. I wondered why he hadn't thought of that one, and then remembered that the cellar door always used to be locked. We weren't supposed to play there; the stairs were unsafe, there might be rats or snakes, and the lower regions had never been electrified.

Conditions underground had not improved in the last ten years. Creatures scuttled away from the beam of the flashlight as we cautiously descended stairs that sagged ominously under our feet. Shirley made quick work of extracting the bottles from their cobwebby bin, and we beat a hasty but equally cautious retreat.

I really needed a shower after hugging those filthy bottles. Clean and refreshed, I went to the kitchen. Matt still hadn't appeared, and it was after four o'clock.

There wasn't much sherry left in the decanter. I splashed it recklessly onto the chicken. I needed sour cream and fresh mushrooms and wild rice, and a lot of other things without which the dish would not amount to much, but it was the best I could do. I put the back and neck on to simmer for soup. Then I sat down at the kitchen table with the bottle of vodka. I seldom drink alone, but I was mad at Matt. If he didn't show up pretty soon, I would not have time to go to the grocery store, and there was nothing in the house, not even eggs for breakfast.

A clinking sound sent me to the kitchen door just in time to see the dog head for the bushes. He had been licking his empty bowl; the noise I made had sent him flying. He made pretty good time, considering he only used three legs. There was something wrong with one of his paws, the back left.

I stood by the screen door, biting my lip. There went my dinner. I didn't mind that so much—there aren't many women who think they are thin enough. What bothered me was the injury. It would nag at the back of my mind until I did something about it. Don't get me wrong. I am not noble—you must have realized that, after reading some of the admissions in these pages. I just can't stand seeing misery without wanting—no, needing—to do something about it.

I didn't find out until after that you aren't supposed to feed dogs chicken bones. I kept the breasts for Shirley and Martha, and gave the rest to the dog, including the quondam soup. He was hiding in the bushes when I went out. He didn't emerge, but he didn't retreat, either; I decided we were making progress. He didn't belong to any breed I recognized. He was brown and white and medium-sized—that was all I could tell. A mutt.

I sat down on the step. The dog stayed where he was, but I could hear him sniffing hungrily. I wasn't trying to tease him; I thought maybe if I stayed still and didn't move or speak, hunger might overcome his fear of people. Once he knew me, he was sure to love me.

I didn't hear the car until it came to a crunching halt out in front. I abandoned the dog to his—my—dinner and went flying to the door. But it wasn't Matt; it was the doctor, already inside the house. Since he didn't apologize for intruding, I deduced that in this neck of the woods it was correct social conduct to walk in without knocking.

He said he'd go right upstairs. I was about to accompany him, uninvited, when I saw another car approaching. This time it *was* Matt. Strain my eyes as I might, I saw no sign of another vehicle, and I went out with my sleeves rolled up, metaphorically speaking.

"Where's my car?" I demanded.

Matt's broad smile faded. "Is that any way to greet your favorite cousin?"

"Unless you have brought me a car you are not my favorite cousin."

Matt extracted himself and stretched. He was dressed formally on this occasion, in a lightweight summer suit and a tie. "I brought you a present," he said winningly.

"I don't want flowers or candy. I want a car."

"It's coming, it's coming. Not quite as fast as a speeding bullet, but it is coming. I had to ask one of my aides to drive it down. He left half an hour after I did."

"Oh. Well, that's all right, then."

"Hi, Julie."

"Hi, Matt. What did you bring me?"

Matt started to laugh. I gave him points for that; lots of people wouldn't have considered my rude behavior amusing. I didn't consider it amusing myself. So I apologized. "Sorry, Matt. I'm out of my head with loneliness and a sense of abandonment. If I had to face another week without some means of escape from this place, I'd run amuck."

"Don't whine to me. I spent vacations with Martha for years before I got a driver's license. Here's your present for being a good girl."

He handed me a brown paper bag. I sat right down on the steps and investigated it. Pâté, French bread, smoked baby clams, anchovies . . . He must have visited one of the gourmet delis in Richmond. I flung my arms around him and gave him a resounding smack on the cheek.

"You *are* my favorite cousin. I even forgive you for locking me in the graveyard."

"What on earth are you talking about?"

He helped me return the goodies to the bag, while I told him what I was talking about. "You're kidding," he said incredulously. "I never did a thing like that."

"I said I forgive you."

"I can't believe it! I was a rotten kid, but that was . . . Well, if you say so, I must have done it. You're sure it wasn't an accident?"

"Don't worry, I won't tell the press. Smoked clams compensate for a lot of sins. The doctor's here."

"I know."

"Are you going up?"

"I am going to get a head start on the sherry," Matt said. "And the clams."

He carried the food to the kitchen and made himself useful with openers and glasses. I glanced out the back door. The dog was gone and so was the chicken. I decided not to mention the animal to Matt. It was my problem. Anyhow, it wasn't important.

Dr. Green couldn't have been upstairs more than five minutes. He greeted Matt deferentially, addressing him as "Senator," and accepted a glass of wine.

"How is she?" Matt asked gravely.

Green shook his head. "You know it is only a matter of time, Senator."

"How much time?" I asked.

Green's solemn expression changed. He shot me a disapproving look. "You are a student of medicine, I believe. Would you care to hazard a guess? That's all it can be—a guess."

"Since she is eighty-five, I wouldn't be guessing too wildly if I said her chances of making ninety weren't high," I said. "But her condition has improved markedly even in the few days I've been here. Her muscular coordination is visibly better, her vital signs are good—"

"You carried out an examination?" Green demanded.

He sounded as if he were about to have me arrested for practicing medicine without a license. "She asked me to," I snapped. "Obviously I'm not going to prescribe for her, or carry out any procedures for which I'm not qualified. I'm not stupid! But there's no law against taking someone's blood pressure or using a stethoscope—people do it for themselves all the time, you can buy the instruments at any medical supply house. If you are accusing me—"

"No one is accusing you of anything, Julie," Matt said smoothly. "We're all grateful to you for giving up your vacation to watch over Martha, all the more so because your training makes you better qualified to act quickly in an emergency, should one arise. Isn't that right, Doctor?"

"Yes, yes," Green muttered. "But I know Miss Martha; she is a very—er—determined woman. It is hard to resist her when she demands something she should not have."

"She won't overrule me," I said. "I'm pretty determined too, Doctor. And she is completely helpless right now."

It was an idle boast, born of resentment, but as the words left my lips I realized it was the literal truth. Martha had dominated me and frightened me all my life. Now I had the upper hand.

The doctor did not linger after his second glass of sherry. As he rose to go, I heard the sound for which I had been listening. Matt caught my eye and grinned. "That must be Joel. He made better time than I expected."

The man at the door was not the unknown Joel, however. It was Alan.

"What the hell are you doing here?" I demanded in a furious whisper.

He didn't answer me. Instead he spoke to Matt, who was behind me. "I saw your car, Senator. I've been trying to reach you all week. There are one or two things we have to talk about."

"Come in." Matt opened the door, adding, dismissively, "I'll see you next week, Doctor. Thank you."

Green went out, Alan came in. He paid no more attention to me than if I had been a sofa or a potted plant. Matt gestured him into the drawing room. They left me to close the door, which I did.

"I thought I would give you a progress report," Alan said.

"*I* thought you weren't supposed to come to the house," I said.

"Relax, Julie," Matt said. "Even if Martha hears voices, which is unlikely, there's no way she could tell who the visitor is. How are things going, Dr. Petranek?"

"No luck so far. I'm planning two more days on the site. If nothing turns up, we'll try somewhere else."

"Where?" I inquired.

"I haven't decided yet."

"So long as it isn't near the house," Matt reminded him.

"I am well aware of the restrictions," Alan said coldly. "Have you any objection to my making a few trial digs around the smokehouse?"

"Well . . ."

"Look, Senator . . ." When Alan used the title it sounded like an insult. "I can't do a proper survey of the site if you are going to keep me away from the one area where habitation was most likely. I'm not proposing to bring in my crew, I just want to do some solitary prospecting. You can tell the old lady I'm fixing the cesspool."

"All right. But if she asks too many questions you'll have to quit." Matt's voice was slick as oil, but it was obvious he didn't care much for Alan. I didn't blame him. That hectoring manner would annoy anyone. "Is that all you want to talk about?" he added.

"No. You're still having trouble with trespassers. I found signs of recent digging this morning. I want you to post some new signs, and insert a notice in the local paper warning people off."

"Good God, man, that's the wrong approach entirely," Matt exclaimed. "Why draw attention to the problem?"

"Is that the way a politician solves a problem?" asked Alan, with his usual tact. "Ignore it, and hope it will go away? I've received a dozen crank letters in the past week." He took a manila envelope from his pocket and dumped the contents onto the table. "Look at these."

Matt eyed the untidy pile distastefully, but made no move to follow Alan's suggestion. "I've had my share of such things. These people are all crazy."

I picked up the letter atop the pile. It was written on cheap lined paper torn from a dime-store tablet. The letters were round and unformed, the writing of someone who did not often indulge in the art of correspondence. "Dear Mr. Arkeologist," it read. "You are sinning against God's Holy Word when you dig up dead bodies. If you dont stop you will be struck by His Rath."

"Crazy? Of course they're crazy," Alan said. "Who do you think commits crimes, sane people? There ought to be a guard here at night—"

"The sheriff doesn't have enough manpower for that," Matt interrupted. "How many men would it take to patrol all this territory?"

Alan brushed this minor tactical problem aside with a wave of his hand. "You may not care about your property rights but you ought to give some thought to the three women who are here alone—one of them bedridden. If anything happened—"

Fortunately, at that moment I heard the long-awaited sound. I ran out, without saying good-bye. If I had spoken a word, it would not have been printable.

I can't tell you what Joel looked like. He was a man with a set of car keys, that was all I cared about, and if he had not been Joel, but an insurance salesman or a cop, I would have done exactly what I did—snatch the keys, mumble, "Go on in, the room to your right," and leap into the driver's seat like a romance hero vaulting into the saddle of his mighty stallion. I was off, in a cloud of dust and a roar of the exhaust . . . No wonder I had heard Joel approaching; that engine hadn't been tuned in years and there was something funny about the muffler. I did not care. The thing moved.

If I had not left the house I would have said something rude to Alan. Curse the man! It had never occurred to me to be nervous. Now I'd lie awake starting at every creak of a branch or squeak of a mouse. I knew I was safer here than I would be in a city apartment. I did not doubt that drug abuse, vandalism, and burglary had invaded Carrsville's rural innocence; but the random, sick violence that occurs in cities was not likely to happen here.

Yet in a way, Alan had done me a favor. I now had an excuse to acquire a dog.

When I got back, there were no cars in the driveway. Matt had decamped, without even waiting to say good-bye to me. He had also not waited to give me any money.

By the time I had carried in the groceries and put away the perishables and filled the Sèvres saucer with a heaping pile of dog food, I was starved. Shirley had served herself and Martha; she had taken exactly half the chicken, dividing it as punctiliously as if she had used a ruler. I made myself a sandwich and headed upstairs, munching. One of these days I would get a decent meal, but this wasn't the day. It was after seven, and Shirley had been on duty all afternoon.

Martha's door was open. Shirley was reading—Milton, this time. I don't think Martha was listening. Her eye was fixed on the doorway, and the moment I appeared she began gabbling.

"I know, I know," I said thickly, through my sandwich. "I'm sorry I'm late. This has been a wildly exciting afternoon. I'm not sure I can stand such a whirlwind of social activities. How was the chicken?"

Martha said, "Grmph." Shirley said, "She enjoyed it very much, Julie."

I offered to go on with Milton, but Martha said no. I never did figure out why she kept poor Shirley reading poetry—and the dullest, most pompous poetry in the language at that. Maybe she enjoyed hearing Shirley struggle with the long words and the sedate, difficult meter, just as she enjoyed my loathing of sweet Esther Summerson. Esther was recovering from smallpox, which she had caught through nursing an abandoned waif. Her face scarred, her lover lost to her forever, she was so revoltingly noble any sane woman would want to murder her. She talked to herself all the time too. "Once more duty, duty, Esther! And if you are not overjoyed to do it, more than cheerfully and contentedly . . . you ought to be. That's all I have to say to you, my dear!"

I exchanged a few words with Shirley when she came up to take over for the night. She said Matt had paid his usual fifteen-minute duty call on Martha. He had left no message for me.

When I went downstairs I found Shirley had cleaned the kitchen and put away the rest of the groceries. The dog had come and gone. Whatever else was wrong with him, his appetite was excellent.

five

It was after midnight when I turned out my light and settled down. The night was cool and dry. The night was also very dark. What the hell had happened to the moon, I wondered? As I lay there listening for bumps in the night I cursed Alan again.

I finally fell asleep, to be awakened minutes later—at least it felt like only a few minutes—by an outrageous noise. A human voice raised in pain and anger mingled with the howls of a dog.

I was out the door, my shins aching from a couple of encounters with the furniture, before I realized I had moved. At least my professional instincts were working; my first thought had been for Martha, shocked out of sleep by the racket.

The door of her room opened as I ran into the hall, shedding some welcome light on the scene. One look inside reassured me as to Martha's condition; she was wide awake, alert and staring, and the expression on her face was not of fear but of indignant interest. She raised a wobbly hand and jabbered to me. I said, "Right, I'm going."

"Wait—Julie—" Shirley made a grab at me.

"Call the police," I told her and took off again.

She knew how to reach the cops; I would waste time looking up numbers and arguing with the operator. Besides, I was twenty years younger and twice that number of pounds lighter. I went down the stairs, flicking on the lights as I ran, and snatching up a bronze statuette from the hall table as I passed.

The noise had subsided to a duet of growls, one animal, the other a monotonous undercurrent of profanity. Shirley's notion of locking up was perfunctory, to say the least. There wasn't a bolt or a chain on the door, and the key protruded from the lock, a flimsy old-fashioned affair I could have picked with a bobby pin. I turned the key and opened the door.

At least Shirley had turned on the outside lights. The sixty-watt bulbs shone on a recumbent form sprawled at the foot of the steps. If he was a burglar he was either stupid or very confident; he had parked his car, a vintage sixties' Olds, smack in front of the house. He was a young black man wearing a sleeveless T-shirt that displayed muscular arms and shoulders, and blue jeans so tight it was a wonder he could move at all. He wasn't moving, but he was swearing, with admirable inventiveness. The least obscene term he used was "son of a bitch," and I had to admit it was appropriate. Attached firmly to his left leg was the dog—my dog—the mutt.

I went down the steps. A suspicion of the truth had dawned; I let the bronze swing carelessly from my hand. The man turned his head to glower at me. "I didn't know you had a damn dog!"

I sat down on the bottom step. "I don't. Who are you?"

"Ron Johnson. Tell him to let me go."

"I don't know how. You're Shirley's son?" He nodded, grimacing. "What the devil are you doing here at this hour?"

"Bringing her car back."

"At four in the morning?"

"She wants it to go to church," Ron said sullenly.

I started to laugh, but turned the sound into a cough. His dignity had already taken a beating. It appeared to be the only part of him that had really suffered.

I said, "I'm Julie."

"I know." After a moment he added, "I'm sorry I woke you up."

"That's okay, I wasn't doing anything except sleeping. How are you planning to get home—assuming, that is, that I can persuade the dog to let go?"

"Buddy of mine's waiting for me." A movement of his head indicated the end of the driveway.

"Fine buddy. Why didn't he come to your rescue?"

Ron's expression strongly indicated that he thought we were wandering off the subject. He was younger than I had thought at first—eighteen or nineteen, at a guess. The drooping pirate's mustache made him look older—no doubt that was why he had grown it—but his cheeks and forehead were as smooth as a baby's. The night air was strongly scented with the smell of beer, though he didn't appear to be incapacitated. His remarks had been more to the point than mine.

I turned my attention to the dog. It had stopped growling as soon as I spoke. Now, sensing my eye upon it, it raised its tail and flopped it up and down in a tentative wag. I said experimentally, "Good dog. Three cheers for the dog. You can let go now."

The tail wagged more confidently but the dog did not let go.

"I told you it wasn't my dog," I said. "What do we do now?"

"Don't ask him, tell him," Ron said in an exasperated voice.

"Oh. Let go, dog! Drop it!"

It worked. I felt as amazed and pleased as Aladdin must have been when he said, "Open Sesame," and the magic door responded.

It took a while to get Martha settled down. I told enough lies to get me a couple of hundred years in Purgatory—a stray dog, a lost, drunken coon hunter. . . . Shirley was no help. She remained silent, avoiding my eyes. I figured it was safe to assume she had not called the police.

I checked Martha's pulse and blood pressure. She was in fine shape. That was probably just what she needed, a little rumpus now and then to maintain her interest in life.

I was in the kitchen watching the dog polish off a bowl of food when Shirley came in. "He's not hurt," I said. "Ron. The dog didn't lay a tooth on him, just tore his pants."

"His new Calvins!" Shirley's anguished tone echoed the outrage that had colored Ron's voice when he examined the damage. I had not laughed then, and I didn't laugh now. I'd have howled myself if I had ruined a new pair of designer jeans.

Shirley dropped heavily into a chair. "I'm sorry, Julie. I don't know what I'm going to do with that boy. But he's a good boy—he's never been in any real trouble. . . ."

"He has very nice manners." The amusement I had been repressing for the past half hour would not be restrained any longer. I added, through my laughter, "Under the circumstances, very nice manners indeed. Honestly, Shirley, it was funny. You'd have laughed too."

"No, I wouldn't," Shirley said grimly.

"He brought your car back."

"He should've had it back last night. Told me he needed it to look for a job. Don't suppose he found one, or he wouldn't have snuck in here in the dead of night."

"I don't imagine it's easy for him to find work," I said, sobering.

"Not here."

"Teen-age black unemployment is high everywhere. But he might have a better chance in a big city."

The dog had finished his food. I got down on the floor beside him and lifted his foot.

"I know I'm selfish to keep him here," Shirley said with a sigh. "There's three others at home and he's a real help to me. But it's not just that. I'm scared of what he'll get into if he's away from home. There's so many temptations."

"I don't blame you. Steady there, boy," I added, as the dog winced and turned his head. "I'm just taking a look."

"What's the matter with him?"

"I can't tell for sure. There's a great deal of swelling and some infection, maybe a couple of bones broken. He could have been struck a glancing blow by a car, or been caught in a trap."

"Can you fix him up?"

"I'm no surgeon." I got up and filled a bowl with warm water. "I'll try soaking it, but I suspect he needs a vet. I'll take him in tomorrow—no, I guess it will have to be Monday."

"You're going to keep him?"

"I wouldn't turn a dog . . . I mean, I wouldn't turn

any injured creature away. To be honest, I'd feel better with a dog on the premises. Weren't you nervous here alone with Martha?"

Shirley shook her head. Her eyes were fixed on the dog but it was obvious she wasn't thinking about him, or about my argument for keeping him. I suspected it was not physical fatigue—though heaven knows she had good cause—but worry that made her mouth droop and her eyelids sag.

"He'll be all right," I said awkwardly. "All kids go through periods like this."

"I know. But it's hard, raising a boy without a man in the house."

"It's hard raising any child with only one parent to do the work of two," I said. "You're divorced?"

"No. I never—I guess he never, either . . . He walked out, Ron's daddy—there was some woman . . . Haven't heard from him in ten years."

"So did mine."

"What?" She raised her drooping head.

"So did my daddy. Walk out. It's been almost fifteen years."

"But I thought . . ."

"Sure. So did everybody else in Carrsville and vicinity. Martha told people my mother was widowed." The water in the bowl was an ugly reddish-brown. I rose, rinsed and refilled the bowl, and found a cloth before resuming my place. "I don't understand," I said, half to myself. "Why did it matter so much to her? Why did she care?"

"Miz Martha? No, you wouldn't understand. Small town, old family, pride . . . She was born in 1900, Julie. Appearances were everything when she was growing up. Some people adjust to change, but she's not that kind. To her, divorce is still a shame just next to murder. Maybe worse."

"And for my mother. Can you believe I didn't find out until two years ago that my father was still alive?"

"I can believe it. I guess—I guess I feel that way too."

"You've got better sense," I said curtly. "You feel betrayed and angry and humiliated. Those feelings are bad enough without adding a gratuitous load of guilt."

Shirley's smile was wry. "Thanks for the advice, Julie. I'll bet your mama really took it to heart, didn't she?"

"She told me to mind my own business." I grinned at Shirley. She laughed softly. I said, "Look, I know you can't change your feelings by pushing a button. I'm telling you how I feel, that's all. And you can tell me to mind my own business whenever you want."

"I will." She laughed again. "That looks better."

"Huh?" I realized she was referring to the injured paw. The other subject was closed. That was okay by me. I didn't particularly relish discussing it; can't imagine why I had done so. People say funny things when they are awake in the dead dark hours before dawn.

"Actually," I said, inspecting the paw, "it looks worse than I thought. Do you think one of the local vets would see him on Sunday? He needs antibiotics, the sooner the better."

"I'll call my doctor in the morning," Shirley said. "She's a nice lady. I think she'd make a special case."

"Do you have a dog, Shirley?"

"Cats." Shirley rose heavily to her feet.

"How many?"

Shirley hesitated. "Five. No, six. There was another stray dropped off last week. They do that, you know—city people—bring them out and dump them in the country, think they'll make out all right. Most of them get killed by cars or wild animals, or starve, or get sick . . ." Her voice trailed off.

I said, "I think I love you, Shirley. Go to bed."

"You too."

She left the room. I wondered whether she had meant that I should go to bed too, or . . . The dog licked my hands.

Later, I lay awake watching the curtains blow in the pre-dawn breeze. I wasn't nervous any longer. The thought of the dog, sleeping on the back porch on the old carpet I had found for him, was that little extra touch of reassurance I needed. I only hoped he would not feel duty-bound to bark at every moth that blundered into the screen.

Shirley was some woman. I didn't know what Matt was paying her, but knowing Matt, I felt sure it was no more than he could get away with. She had held that family together for ten years—four kids, she had said. Three younger than Ron, who was about nineteen. And she still managed to squeeze out enough money to take in abandoned animals and pay a vet to care for them.

I got out of bed and set my alarm. I didn't want Shirley to be late for church. If she didn't have clout Up There, nobody did, and you never know when you may need a friend in high places.

Shirley came downstairs next morning with a spring in her step and a light in her eyes and a handsome flower-bedecked hat on her grizzled head. She looked marvelous.

After some bullying on my part, she had agreed to take the whole day off, providing I let her make it up to me during the week. Maybe it was the prospect of spending the whole afternoon with her kids that brought that light to her eyes. Mothers are peculiar.

"Get going," I said, propelling her toward the door. "And stop worrying. A whole day with Martha isn't going to kill me. It may reduce me to babbling idiocy, but it won't kill me . . . Just kidding, Shirley. Go, leave, vamoose."

She lingered, pulling on her gloves. White gloves! "Miz Danner will sit with Miz Martha while she naps . . ."

"I know. Run along. Depart. Take your leave."

"And the Judge will be here this evening. It's his day."

"Who's the Judge?"

"I knew I forgot to tell you something. That's Miz Martha's lawyer. He's a very old friend of hers and always spends Sunday evening with her. They like to be private, so you can sneak off and have a little time to yourself."

I meditated a ribald remark, but decided it would be tasteless. "I suppose I bring out the sherry."

"She'll tell you what to do."

"I'm sure she will."

"You can't go wrong with the Judge," Shirley assured me. "He's a real gentleman. You'll like him. Everybody likes Mr. McLendon."

She finally left. I squared my shoulders and gritted my teeth and went up to Martha.

She seemed brighter that morning. There was no doubt in my mind that she was getting better. Old fussbudget Green was right, sooner or later she would have another stroke; nothing can prevent the inevitable when the patient is eighty-five. But I was beginning to think that it would be later rather than sooner. Or was Green giving Matt, not a medical diagnosis, but what he thought Matt wanted to hear? If Matt shed tears at Martha's funeral, they would be crocodile tears. He could hardly wait to get his hands on the property.

With Martha, feeling livelier was synonymous with feeling meaner. She kept nodding off, but every time I stopped reading her eyes would snap open and a growl would remind me to continue.

The fourth time she woke from a pleasant doze to demand that I go on reading, I rebelled. I had been at it for two solid hours and Esther was more revolting than ever. She had just welcomed her former lover back to England and was rejoicing over the fact that he seemed to be very sorry for her.

When Martha croaked, "Go on," I shut the book. "You've been struggling to keep awake for half an hour," I said. "I'm going to see about lunch."

Martha snarled at me, and I went on, firmly, "If I don't do something before Mrs. Danner gets here, she'll dish up some revolting mess. How would you like a nice juicy hamburger with cheese, and a tossed salad?"

A gleam of greed replaced the gleam of outraged malice in Martha's eyes. (It's a subtle difference, but I could tell.)

"Good," I said. "I'll be back in fifteen minutes."

I had the salad made by the time Mrs. Danner arrived. I was very tactful; I told her I was taking over the cooking because I thought she had too much to do, even though she was a better cook than I . . . It was wasted effort. She didn't care. She didn't appear to care about much.

I took Martha's lunch up and fed it to her. She grumbled at my awkwardness. She had cause—I wasn't very good at it; but she would have grumbled anyway, so I didn't take her criticism to heart. Her appetite was excellent; she ate every scrap. I hoped the food had mellowed her, but when I started to assist with the more intimate needs her helplessness demanded, she began thrashing around and sputtering.

"I told Shirley to take the afternoon off," I said, interpreting the gist of her complaints without difficulty.

Martha never used profanity, not even a teeny damn or hell. She didn't have to. I got the idea: I was an officious, interfering brat, and I had no right to decide what Shirley's duties should be.

I interrupted the tirade, principally because I was afraid she was hurting herself. "Might is right, Martha. I'm in charge now. When you get back on your feet, you can kick me down the stairs and out the door. My advice to you is to conserve your strength so that that happy day is quick to arrive. Now. I'll just lift you up and slip this in . . . Oh, sorry. I'll improve with practice."

It was not a pleasant time for either of us, but I finally got her washed up and tucked in and settled down. She looked exhausted. I felt guilty about my clumsiness, and about bullying the poor old witch, so I offered to read her to sleep.

"How about some Milton?" I offered. "God in him for her, and that sort of thing."

She shook her head. "Talk," she mumbled. "Mother?"

It was the first time she had indicated any interest in my maternal parent—her daughter. I sat down on the side of the bed and started talking. Told her about Mother's job and her recent promotion, about her apartment, about her friends and her arthritis and so on. Martha seemed to enjoy it—at least she didn't stop me—so I went on, and told her about me. Med school was rough but I thought I was keeping up; my grades were good, and I had had a half-hearted compliment from one of the professors.

After a while she interrupted. "Bows?"

I couldn't figure out what she meant at first. My failure

to comprehend brought a faint flush of rage to her cheeks. It wasn't until she fumbled for my hand and jabbed at the third finger that the light dawned. "Beaux?" I repeated. "Boyfriends? One or two. I'm not engaged, no. Nothing serious. I don't intend to tie myself down until I finish school."

Martha stared at me without blinking. The drooping eyelid and the slight twist of her mouth turned her expression into a cynical leer.

She said, quite clearly, "Judge coming."

"I know, Shirley told me. I'll break out the sherry. And shall I make some hors d'oeuvres?"

"Bring here."

"Okay."

"Change . . . dress. Look decent."

I glanced at my faded shirt and jeans. "All right."

"Some respect . . . Manners . . ."

"I said, all right."

"Sleep now." She closed her eyes.

She had outscored me again. She wasn't interested in Mother's life, or in mine; it had all been designed to lead up to the humiliating admission that I was still unsought and undesired—not a beau to my string. Then the curt orders, the kind she'd have given a servant . . . It was such a petty way of getting back at me, not so much for my clumsiness in helping her as for the fact that she needed help. I should have pitied her. I didn't. But I did not feel humiliated. She had lost the power to hurt me.

I had left part of the salad for Mrs. Danner, but she hadn't touched it. When I went to the kitchen she was finishing a thick sandwich made of cheese and bread—no lettuce, no tomato, no nothing. She started guiltily to her feet when I entered.

"Take your time," I said.

"I was goin' to clean the parlor."

"I'll clean the parlor. If you've finished, go up and sit with Miss Martha."

She began gathering up the luncheon dishes. "I'll do that," I said impatiently. "Go on upstairs. I have to go out for half an hour or so, but I won't be long."

She turned, alarm written plainly across her drab features. "I don' like to be alone with her. What if somethin' happens?"

"Then you pick up the phone and call the doctor. Nothing is going to happen, Mrs. Danner. I'll be back in half an hour—an hour at the most."

"But I don' like—"

"Don't be silly. The doctor's phone number is on the pad by the telephone. So is Shirley's. She's home today. Run along."

I could hardly blame her for her reluctance. I too would rather have scrubbed floors or cleaned privies than sit with Martha. Did she insist that Mrs. Danner read aloud to her—T. S. Eliot, perhaps, or Dostoevski?

After I had rinsed the dishes, I went to the back door. The dog was nowhere in sight. I realized I should have had sense enough to tie him up or confine him when he came for his breakfast. Shirley's veterinarian had agreed to meet me at her office at one. There was no point in my going unless I had the dog with me. I couldn't even call him. I didn't know what to call him.

Finally I got one of my brighter ideas. I put some of his dry food in a dish and went out on the back step and rattled it, calling softly. It was, perforce, an anonymous call. "Here, dog—come on, dog."

It was probably the sound and smell of the food, rather than my voice, that attracted him. In daylight he had lost the confidence he had demonstrated the night before. He came skulking, tail low, eyes wary.

I didn't know much about dogs. I couldn't tell one breed from another. He had long drooping ears and a low-slung body that ought to have been heavier than it was. He was brown and white. He was either very nearsighted or very absentminded, because after a few feet of slow forward progress he finally recognized me; then his tail started flapping and he advanced more quickly. While he gulped the food I tied a scarf around his neck. He came with me readily and climbed into the front seat of the car as if he knew what was going on.

It was my first visit to Carrsville in years. The town had not changed much. A sign on the outskirts reminded me that the population was 1350. The houses on the main street—the only street—looked as if they hadn't been painted since I left. There was one block of commercial establishments—two gas stations, a grocery store, a drugstore, a five-and-ten. The visit convinced me of one thing—except for the vet, there was absolutely no reason for me to return to Carrsville.

I had wondered how a woman veterinarian could establish a practice in an area like this, where macho traditions prevailed and most of a vet's practice involved farm animals. When I saw May Rubin I understood. She was about six feet tall and must have weighed a hundred and ninety pounds, most of it muscle. Those brawny arms could easily hobble a cow or throw a sheep—if that's what you're supposed to do with cows and sheep. Her graying hair was cropped short, and she had not bothered with makeup. Her eyes were gray too; they appraised me, without prejudice, from behind her horn-rimmed glasses.

I started to tell her how much I appreciated her coming in to work on Sunday. She shrugged the speech away with the air of a person who has no time and little sympathy for meaningless courtesies. "Let's see what you've got here," she said.

I drove back to Maidenwood half an hour later and sixty dollars poorer. Rabies shot, distemper shot, parvo shot, penicillin shot, bottles of pills, ointment, flea shampoo . . . I had the feeling that I was in much deeper than I had expected. The dog thought so too. He sat bolt upright on the seat beside me, with a distinctly proprietorial air.

I also had a little book called "How to Care for Your Dog."

When May realized I was as ignorant about the canine species as I claimed, her contempt turned to pity. She even presented me with an old collar one of her clients had left behind.

My brain was reeling with new information. The dog was a mixed breed—part hound, part shepherd, part God-knew-what. He would always limp; several of the small bones in his paw had been broken and they had already started to knit, badly. It would require a painful and expensive operation to put them right, and May saw no point in doing so. She supposed I didn't care whether he ever won any prizes catching rabbits? I assured her that was not one of my aspirations. So, she said, all we had to worry about was the infection. Make sure he had his pills twice a day, use the ointment four times a day, keep him from licking it off, bathe him, de-flea him, worm him . . .

I groaned aloud. The dog glanced at me and flapped his tail sympathetically, but he didn't appear at all embarrassed at putting me to so much trouble. I don't know how he knew, but he did; anybody who has spent sixty hard-earned bucks on a dog *owns* that dog.

I drove around to the back and left the car in the yard. The dog curled up on his rug and prepared for a well-deserved nap. He had yelped once or twice while May was cleaning and disinfecting his foot, but he had not snapped at her. I told him he was a good dog. I'd have to think of a name for him. Couldn't keep calling him "dog."

The trip had taken longer than I anticipated, but I figured I had another half hour before Martha woke up. I browned the roast, poured a generous dollop of wine over it, and set the burner to simmer. Martha still had all her own teeth, but I thought pot roast would be easier to chew than oven roast. That only took ten minutes. I was about to sit down for a rest when I remembered I had promised Mrs. Danner I would tidy the parlor. It shouldn't take long; no one had been in the room since Friday, and I had carried the used wineglasses to the kitchen that evening.

As I approached the room I saw the door was open. Mrs. Danner must have been a little deaf. I stood in the doorway for several seconds before she realized I was there. She started and turned. Her hands were empty, but there was a can of furniture polish and a dustcloth on the table.

"I thought I told you to stay with Miss Martha," I said.

"She's asleep. I was gonna—"

"Please go back upstairs."

"I was—"

"I said I'd clean this room. Go on, please. Tell me when she wakes."

She obeyed without further argument, ducking her head as she passed me like someone expecting a blow. She was so damned humble and Uriah-Heepish she made me feel guilty; but what the devil was she there for, if not to relieve Shirley and me in watching over Martha? Not that the house couldn't have used a full-time housemaid; in its heyday, it must have had a large staff. But there had been no attempt to maintain the old standards, just keep a few rooms habitable.

And why, if the idea of being in the same room with Martha terrified her so, had she accepted the job?

I knew the answer, of course. She had accepted it because she needed the money. I ought to know; I had done a lot of things I detested for the same reason.

The table on which she had been about to operate was mahogany, with the soft reddish patina of age. I picked up the can of polish. It was one of those spray jobs, and even I knew you aren't supposed to use it on fine old wood. Mother used a special polish on hers, together with a lot of elbow grease. Actually, the furniture didn't need polishing, only dusting.

I rather doubted that Mrs. Danner had intended to polish anything. She had been looking at some object, and it wasn't hard to figure out what that object was. It lay on the table, where she had dropped it when she heard me at the door—one of the letters Alan had brought to show Matt, in order to make his point about the need for protection from trespassers. The rest of the letters were there too. I could see Matt stubbornly refusing to look at them, and Alan stubbornly refusing to take them back. I hadn't noticed them when I cleared away the wineglasses.

I was a little surprised that Mrs. Danner would be curious enough to examine the peculiar documents. I gathered the papers and took them to a chair by the window.

The one she had been inspecting was the letter I had read—the difficult, childish handwriting, threatening Mr. Arkeologist with the Rath of God. There were half a dozen others. They had nothing in common except the craziness of their contents. One, on scented pink notepaper with fancy gold initials, offered the services of the writer to "Professor Alan" in terms that left the extent of those services wide open. She had seen his picture in the newspaper and she just knew they would have an awful lot in common. Another, neatly typed on business stationery with a printed letterhead, was from an organization named The Research Center for Psychic Archaeology. It requested—perhaps demanded would be more accurate—permission to excavate at Maidenwood, at a location that had been revealed to the writer during a séance. A third offered to sell Alan a map showing the exact spot where Blackbeard had buried his treasure. The price was a mere ten thousand dollars—no personal checks, please, only cash or certified check.

The others were even more exotic. If these were a sample of Alan's mail, I wondered what kind of trash Matt had received. I also wondered whether any of the letter writers and their ilk were given to prowling the fields and forests of Maidenwood by night. Someone had done so—someone with a very unpleasant sense of humor. I lavished a few silent but passionate adjectives upon my cousin Matt. He might have had the decency to warn me about this feature of the job. However, to give him his due, he probably never thought of it as constituting a potential danger. He had very little imagination. I, on the other hand, probably had too much.

I picked up the letters and went in search of Mrs. Danner. She was in the kitchen, motionless as a monolith, staring at the door. The dog stared back at her, eyes pleading, nose pressed against the screen.

I poked her. "Mrs. Danner—"

She pointed. "It's a dog."

"I know."

"I'll run him off."

"You'll do nothing of the kind. It's my dog."

"It's the Beekins' dog. Beekins run him off a while back."

"Beekins must be a real charmer," I said. Mrs. Danner transferred her glazed stare to me. "Anyhow, he's my dog now," I said firmly. "You needn't have anything to do with him. Just leave him alone."

"Miz Martha won't have no animals around the place."

"Miss Martha won't know unless you tell her. And," I added, "if you do, it will be your fault if she has another stroke. Clear?"

Mrs. Danner stared.

"Okay," I said. "If you get bored you can—you can dust the parlor. Don't use that polish, just a dustcloth. Got it?"

Mrs. Danner stared.

Martha was too dignified to yell for me; had that not been the case, I'd have heard her at the bottom of the stairs. She had plenty to say once I had made my appearance. She started by complaining about being left alone.

"I've been thinking about that," I said. "You're so much better, I don't believe you need constant attendance. You must be sick of people around all the time. Oh, I don't mean you would be left alone in the house; but if I could get Matt to install a bell, like they have in a hospital . . . Wouldn't you like that?"

She indicated she would think about it. I smothered a smile as I went about my nursing duties, because I knew she was considering pros and cons I had not mentioned. The idea of pressing a buzzer to bring her slaves running, panting and puffing, from far corners of the house, had its appeal.

I flattered myself that I was rather deft in tidying her up that time, but she wasn't satisfied. She wanted her hair brushed and arranged, she wanted her new bedjacket—not that one, the other one—no, not that one . . . she wanted her nose powdered and her nails buffed, and a touch of cologne. Her vanity was a little pathetic and more than a little grotesque. It is hard to believe when you are still firm-fleshed and unwrinkled that you will ever be old; yet I think the pathos would have outweighed the grotesque with anyone except Martha.

When I had finished the job she glowered at me. I knew what she was going to say. My only defense was to beat her to the punch. "I'll run and change now," I said. "I didn't have time before."

She nodded grudgingly.

The Judge was early. I was on my way upstairs with the plate of "hors d'oeuvres"—crackers and cheese—when I heard his car; but it wasn't that sound that made me drop the plate onto the nearest piece of furniture, and bolt for the door. It was the sound of a dog barking.

However, the dog was easily seduced. When I went out, he was sprawled on the ground, squirming with pleasure because his belly was being scratched by the tip of a gold-headed cane.

The Judge was a handsome old man. He had probably not been handsome when he was young; sagging muscles and loosened skin had blurred and softened features that might have appeared too bold, even coarse, thirty years earlier. He had a beautiful mop of snow-white hair, brushed back from a high forehead, and he looked as if he had dressed for a wedding—dark grey three-piece suit, white shirt, silk tie.

When he saw me, his eyes widened. "Julie?"

There was a questioning note in his voice. I said, smiling, "I suppose I've changed."

"Yes. Yes, I thought for a moment . . . The family resemblance is very strong."

I decided not to pursue that subject. I definitely did not want to be told that I reminded him of Martha.

He had to make a wide circle around the dog, who was staring admiringly at him. "A fine animal," he said politely.

The dog wound itself into a pretzel and began biting furiously at its flank. By now I knew what that meant. "I'm afraid he has fleas," I said.

"A fine hound," the Judge repeated. "What is his name?"

It must have been the word "hound" that put the idea into my head. Normally I am more inventive.

"Elvis," I said.

"Elvis?"

"Elvis."

The stupid dog stared off into space, paying no attention. "Elvis," I repeated loudly. "Good dog, Elvis. You can go and—er—do whatever dogs do . . ."

Elvis continued to gaze raptly into the infinite, so I gave up. "Do come in," I said, opening the door. "Martha is looking forward to seeing you."

"And I her. But first, may I have a word with you?"

I led the way into the parlor. He waited for me to take a chair before seating himself.

"How is your mother?" he began.

I should have known he would have to go through the formalities first. If the house had been ablaze he would have asked after Mother before he yelled "Fire." We established that Mother was fine and I was fine before he got down to business.

"I fear you found Martha sadly changed."

"Actually, I think she's doing remarkably well."

"Do you?" A glow of pleasure warmed his sallow cheeks. "I am delighted to hear it. Dr. Green has not been encouraging."

"He's the doctor," I said quickly. "I mean, don't take my word for anything. I wouldn't want to raise false hopes, since I don't know what I'm talking about. I was just giving you an inexpert opinion."

"You are being modest." He smiled approvingly; modesty was a proper attribute for nice young women. "I did not want an expert opinion, I wanted encouragement. Green is a good man, but . . ."

"I'm sure he is. However, I can't help wondering why Martha is not in a hospital—a city or university medical center, with up-to-date facilities. I'm in a difficult position. Dr. Green hasn't volunteered any information, and I can hardly ask questions without sounding like some smart . . . like some smart-aleck med student."

"You have the right to ask any questions you like. But it isn't Dr. Green's fault that Martha is here. He recommended the University of Virginia Hospital. Martha refused."

"I can understand her feelings," I began.

"You can't really understand," the Judge said gently. "You are too young. Old age is, above all else, ignominious. One by one our strengths are stripped away. Arthritis and rheumatism cripple our limbs, hearing and vision diminish, beauty fades . . . Martha is clinging to the only shred of dignity remaining to her—the right to die in her own home. Here she is an individual, not one of many bodies in many sterile rooms—addressed as 'mother' by impertinent interns who can't be bothered to remember her name, and as 'dear' by nurses young enough to be her grandchildren . . ."

"I do understand. I'm sure I'll feel the same way when my turn comes. But you must admit the situation places a considerable responsibility on my shoulders. Shirley is first-rate, one couldn't ask for a better nurse; but she is not a young woman, and we are so far away from help if an emergency should arise—"

"Yes, I see. You must be nervous here alone, especially at night."

"I am not nervous. I am understandably concerned. We are isolated, and some peculiar things have happened."

"Is that why you got the dog?"

"I didn't get the dog, he got me. But I do feel better with him here. I know Martha hates animals—"

"You are quite mistaken."

"She never let me have a pet," I said. I had not meant to say it. It made me sound sullen and childish.

"Martha doesn't hate dogs. She had a dog, long ago—a beautiful hound named Jason. Her father gave him to her on her twelfth birthday, and she had him for over ten years. She found him dead—shot—one morning, and it almost broke her heart. She vowed then that she would never own another pet."

Moisture sparkled in the corners of his eyes. Poor dear old man, he found the story touching. But I couldn't agree with the idea of cutting oneself off from love because of the fear of losing it.

"I didn't know that," I said gently, but noncommittally. "Martha doesn't know about the dog—Elvis—and I don't intend to tell her unless I have to. But if she refuses to go to a hospital she must accept the consequences. Don't you agree that it would be irresponsible of me not to take security measures?"

The Judge began, "A gun—"

I laughed. "I'd probably shoot myself in the foot, Judge. Besides, I don't want to kill some harmless screwball, just scare him away."

It was the second reference I had made to the neighborhood sensation. Again Judge McLendon tiptoed delicately away from the subject.

"You are a very persuasive young woman, Julie. And a very sensible one. I am much more at ease about Martha's safety now that I have talked with you, and I am in complete agreement with your arguments. I had better go upstairs now, if you will excuse me." He pushed himself to his feet, with the help of the cane. Then he winked. "I won't mention—er—Elvis," he whispered.

I got to the kitchen in time to prevent Mrs. Danner from dumping a quart of water onto the roast. I splashed in more wine; as I turned to reach for a fork I caught her staring, not at me, but at the bottle, with an expression I could not mistake.

The only thing that surprised me was my own obtuseness. I should have known, the day she had been so eager to take the wineglasses, one of which was more than half full.

Well, I didn't begrudge her an occasional nip. If I were married to born-again Joe Danner, I'd have taken to the bottle myself.

"You can run along if you like," I said.

"Mr. Danner's not here yet."

"Suit yourself. But I can't think of anything else for you to do. Unless you'd like to read the rest of those letters."

In detective stories a sudden, unexpected accusation

produces a guilty start, or a guilty blush, or a guilty something. Mrs. Danner just stared blankly.

I elaborated. "The crank letters. The letters on the table in the parlor."

"I wasn't reading nothing. I was dusting the table."

"I'm not blaming you. I suppose a phrase in one of them caught your eye. They were peculiar letters."

"I wasn't reading nothing."

I shrugged. "Go on, then. Sit on the step and wait for Mr. Danner, if you can't think of anything else to do."

She couldn't.

Elvis was at the back door, ears up and tail flapping. I had not had time to read my manual on dog care, but I had a feeling I wasn't supposed to feed him four times a day. I decided the hell with it. He was too thin anyway.

I slipped a pill in his food and rubbed ointment on his foot while he gobbled his dinner. The fleas hopped merrily up and down on his back. I thought I'd bathe him in the morning, after I had studied the manual. No need to be precipitate about such things.

Mr. Danner duly arrived, just as the grandfather clock in the hall struck five. I watched the truck drive off; the Danners sat side by side staring straight ahead, not speaking. American Gothic on wheels.

I wondered if they ever spoke to one another, beyond the basic remarks dictated by common needs; and if they did, what they talked about. Not their children. Perhaps they read aloud to one another from the Bible, with particular attention to doomsday prophecies.

How much of a fanatic was Joe Danner? He was fanatical enough to disown his daughter and alienate his son. A man like that might feel duty-bound to write threatening letters to blasphemers and heretics. It wouldn't have surprised me to learn that Joe had penned the letter his wife had been examining; but was he crazy enough to fall upon the heretics with fire and the sword? I certainly hoped not. But I found myself unwillingly remembering a movie I had been fool enough to see with a friend who was an aficionado of horror films, the bloodier the better. This film had featured an insane handyman who did in a dozen people with various tools—hammer, saw, chisel. Moviemakers do amazing things with special effects these days. Blood spouted, heads fell off, arms and legs littered the terrain. I could see Joe Danner, in his faded dungarees, coming up the stairs at Maidenwood, brandishing an ax . . .

Nonsense. If Joe decided to exterminate anyone, it would be Alan, who was planning to desecrate graves. Comforted by this reasoning, I went back to the kitchen and had a drink.

I was waiting in the parlor when I heard Martha's door open and Judge McLendon descend.

"I hope I haven't tired her," he said, as soon as he saw me. "She'd like you to come up now."

"I'm sure it did her good to see you."

"I'll run along now. Please telephone me at any time, day or night, if there is anything at all I can do."

The visit had certainly not pepped him up. He looked ten years older than he had when he arrived—and that is very old. To me, Martha might appear to have improved, but her condition must seem pitiable to an old friend who remembered her in her vigorous youth—especially a friend who knows that only good luck or the Grace of God has preserved him from a similar fate.

Martha hadn't much to say that evening, but she never took her eyes off me. She didn't scare me—not any longer—but that bright, unwinking glare would have affected anyone's nerves. I handed her over to Shirley with enormous relief.

Another neglected duty was nagging at me, and I decided to get it over with. I had forgotten to buy stamps, and I owed Mother a call. She had written once, a conventional note hoping I was not finding my duties too onerous, but I knew she wouldn't use the phone unless she was desperate. Long distance, to her, was not a convenience but a last resort.

She said she had been hoping I would call. "Such a long time, Julie. I always worry—"

"You could have called me, you know."

"Oh, honey, I've just been so busy. Work is frantic, you've no idea."

I laughed at the complacent enjoyment in her voice. She loved the frantic schedule and the compliments that followed her achievements. "I don't know how you keep so calm, Mrs. Newcomb. I don't know what we'd do without you."

"I wish I could say the same, Mother. I had anticipated being driven crazy by Martha, but I didn't realize it would be so damn boring."

"How is she getting on?"

"I am sorry to report that the patient is recovering nicely," I said.

Mother had a way of responding to particularly outrageous remarks with pained silence. It was much more effective than a scolding, and usually ended with me scolding myself.

"That was a terrible thing to say," I offered.

"Yes, honey, it was."

"So I apologize. But she is so . . . Why does she hate me so much, Mother?"

Mother's ladylike laugh was a little strained. "Now, Julie, you know she doesn't like anyone, not even her own daughters. You mustn't take it personally."

"It's more than dislike. It's active, malevolent . . . When she looks at me I feel as if she isn't seeing me, but someone else—the child I used to be, perhaps. Was I that bad? Lord knows I hated every second I spent in this house—"

"Julie, I took you away the instant I could. It was impossible for me to have you with me at first."

The child I had been didn't believe that. As an adult, I could understand her reasons. She had had a desperate struggle at first, working at minimum wages during the day and going to secretarial school at night. Not impossible with a young child, but close to impossible, and there were other major disadvantages—inner-city schools, a cheap room in a bad neighborhood, drugs, child molesters . . . I understood, yes, but I also wondered, with my grown-up wisdom, whether there had not been another factor, a kind of social snobbery, sometimes called pride, that made Mother refuse to have anyone, even me, see her until she had attained the goals she considered minimal—a nice garden apartment in a pleasant suburb, a car, a good school for her daughter.

I had never voiced any of my doubts to her, and God willing I never would. She went on protesting, excusing, anxiously demanding my acknowledgment that she had acted for the best.

I cut her short. "Sure, Mother, I know. How's the weather up there?"

Hot. The weather was hot. I said it had been raining here. Finally she said, "So Martha is better. Still bedridden, though? Well, we can't expect miracles, can we?"

"No," I said. "At least I hope not."

I made my farewells and hung up before she had that comment figured out, and before I had to admit it was a terrible thing to say.

six

I reported for work the following afternoon, to be received with something less than enthusiasm. I didn't take it personally; the weather was hot and muggy, and the open field swarmed with insects of all varieties. I couldn't blame Alan for being in a glum mood, particularly since it was apparent that his new trial trenches had yielded nothing. (I deduced this because a big young man was filling them in.)

"I came to tell you I can't come today," I told Alan.

Through the cloud of gnats that hovered around his nose he said, "Why not?"

"I have to wash my dog."

"Your dog," Alan repeated. His lips barely parted; whether he was controlling passionate emotion or trying to keep a bug from flying into his mouth I was not certain.

"And see the sheriff."

"The sheriff?" This time, voice and expression indicated rising interest. "Has something else happened?"

"Sorry to disappoint you. It's about that other matter."

"Ah. Any new information?"

"I don't know why it's any of your business, but since there is no new information, I have no hesitation in informing you that such is the case." After a moment, during which I decided there really was no reason for keeping the facts from him, I added, "He wants to know what to do with them. The bones."

"That is my business."

"Since when have you been the residuary legatee of all the miscellaneous bones found in this county?"

"Let me rephrase my remark. I have an interest in those bones." He tossed his clipboard and pen onto a card table that had been set up to serve as an extremely temporary and portable office. "I'll come with you."

I lied. "Sheriff Jarboe specifically requested that you not attend."

"But—"

"I don't want you either."

"But—"

"I can't stand around here arguing with you. I'm late. See you tomorrow."

I didn't look back. The big young man with the shovel stopped shoveling and gave me a hopeful "Hello" as I passed him. I smiled and went on.

I had a drive of almost forty miles ahead of me, so I wasn't lying when I said I was short on time. On back roads encumbered by slow-moving farm machinery, it took an hour—ample time to think over what the sheriff had told me.

I had been in the kitchen when the telephone rang. It was eight-thirty, and breakfast cooled on the stove as the sheriff rambled on. He had called me by my first name. That didn't mean anything; everybody in these parts called everybody by first names, unless prefixed by "Mr."

or "Miz" if the person addressed possessed the dignity of age or social position. Yet there had been an underlying assumption, in the way he talked to me, that he knew me and expected me to remember him. I didn't. It was beginning to worry me, how little I did remember from those years with Martha. It had not worried me before this visit because there was no reason for me to remember—no reason to think about that time. I had blotted out four years of my life with a thoroughness that was rather unnerving.

At any rate, he knew me, if I didn't know him, and he granted me a status I had not realized I possessed—that of resident relative-in-charge.

"I been tryin' to reach Matt," he said aggrievedly. "That boy is never in his office."

"It's an election year."

"Yeah, well, it's damn early to start campaignin'. When I vote for a man I want him there workin', not ridin' the roads lookin' for more votes."

I didn't care whether the sheriff voted for Matt or not, so I had no reason to placate him. "I haven't seen Matt since Saturday evening, and he didn't tell me what his plans were. Is there anything I can do?"

"Well, yeah, sure—that's why I called. I got to do somethin' with those damn bones, Julie. They can't lie around here forever."

"Oh. Those bones."

"You know the ones I mean. The ones that was found—"

"I know the ones you mean. What do you want me to do about them?"

"It's rightly Miz Martha's responsibility. But I don't want to bother her when she's so poorly. I can't find Matt.

So I figured you'd be the one to speak for the family, or at least get them to make up their damn minds."

I could have told him it was not my responsibility, or my right, to decide anything. I don't know why I didn't simply refer him back to Matt. Yes, I do. I was flattered at being asked to participate in a decision, instead of obeying orders, like hired help.

With one eye on my congealed eggs, I said, "I'll come to your office and talk to you about it. Would this afternoon suit you?"

He allowed as how it would, always providing he was not called away by a murder or an accident. I said I'd take my chances; we agreed on two o'clock.

Apparently it was a quiet day for crime in the county. The sheriff was in his office, feet on the desk and cigar in his mouth, in approved county-sheriff style. He swung his feet off the desk when I appeared and rose, stubbing out the cigar.

He was a little man. From the rumbling, grumbling voice that had vibrated over the telephone I had expected someone taller and heavier, with a beer belly hanging over his belt, like the caricature sheriffs in the television programs. If I had met him on the street I'd have taken him for a barber or bank clerk. Thinning hair that had once been blond and was now an indeterminate shade halfway to gray framed a narrow, almost ascetic face, with lined cheeks and wide ingenuous blue eyes.

"Well, now, it sure is good to see you again, Julie," he said. "You sure have growed up to be a pretty girl."

He *had* known me back then. I hadn't the faintest recollection of ever having seen him. I didn't say so; I shook his hand and took the chair he indicated. He asked after my mother and I asked after his family—a photograph on the desk, of a little woman and three hulking children, gave me the clue.

"I really don't know what I can tell you," I began. "I tried to reach Matt this morning; his secretary said he was in Washington and wouldn't be back till the end of the week. Surely he has talked to you about this business?"

"Not for a couple of weeks. See . . ." He paused, studying me, and I realized that the baby-blue eyes were not as naive as they appeared. "How much do you know about this? Did Matt talk to you? Was it in the northern papers?"

"I don't know much," I admitted. "Only the bare facts and the reasonable assumptions one might draw from them."

"Reasonable assumptions." Sheriff Jarboe looked as if he wanted to spit. "I'm gonna tell you what the law says, not what some professor *assumes*. Human remains turn up, then the law's gotta be notified. They turn up oftener than you might think—sewer lines, new roads, building sites—not to mention the damn archaeologists. Now if they turn up in the course of digging, whether it's construction or something else, the professors can tell us how long they've been in the ground. If they're what you might call real antiques, then we don't worry about how they died; but we do have to worry about what's done with them. There are laws about disturbing Christian burials, and lately the Indian groups have stirred up a fuss about their people. So that's one problem. Everybody raisin' hell about what to do with the remains."

He reached for his cigar, then glanced at me. "Go ahead," I said.

"I think better with the damn thing in my mouth," he said apologetically.

"You haven't done badly without it, Sheriff. I see what

you're getting at. There is a problem of jurisdiction even with skeletons found in situ. But in this case you can't even be sure whether they are—antiques, as you put it—or remains that might demand a criminal investigation. Right?"

Jarboe's blue eyes narrowed. "There was a crime committed, no question about that. Those bones didn't walk out onto the road and lay down. I want to find the kids who played that little joke. But near as I can tell, that was the only crime committed. There was no evidence of violence. I've gone through the missing-persons files for thirty years back, and nobody fits the description. I don't understand why the damn-fool professors can't tell me how old those bones are, but they say they can't."

"That's the way it is, though. Soil conditions, type of burial—"

"Yeah, well, I've heard all that stuff. Point is, she must have been dead a long time or we'd have some record in our missing-persons file. Without evidence of identity or criminal violence, I've got no reason to keep the case open. I want to get her out of the morgue and back into the ground. The question is, where?"

"Why ask me?"

"Because—" He stabbed the air with his cigar. "Because that reasonable assumption you talked about suggests that she came from Maidenwood. The road cuts through your land; I can't think of any reason why the jokers would carry those bones very far. If they'd been left on somebody's porch I'd figure the comedians had a grudge against that person, but they couldn't predict who would be the first one to drive that road. The doc says she was white—not Indian or nigra—so it's possible she was an ancestor of yours."

"Are you suggesting the family cemetery at Maidenwood?"

"Any objections?"

"It's okay with me. I can't imagine why Matt would object, but I'll ask him. What do you need—some kind of legal document?"

"I'm not sure what I need," Jarboe mumbled, scratching his head. "But I can't move without the family's permission."

"You have mine, for what it's worth. I can't understand what all the fuss is about, to be honest."

"Yeah, well, most of the fuss came from that big-mouthed young prof who's digging at Maidenwood."

"Alan?" I leaned back in my chair. "What does he want you to do?"

"Wants me to give him the skeletons so he can study them. He acts like they were—you know—pieces of wood."

"Sounds like him. He hasn't actually seen the remains?"

"No. He barreled in here and pounded on the desk and . . . I maybe would have let him if he hadn't been so damned high-handed," Jarboe added, with a sheepish grin.

"I know what you mean."

"Hell, he's not even an anthropologist," Jarboe said rather defensively. "We had a prof out here from UVA; I did all the right things. You can see 'em if you want."

"Who, me?" I said, startled. "I'm not an anthropologist either. I couldn't tell you anything you don't already know."

"You are a member of the family," Jarboe said. "Seems as if somebody ought to go through the formalities. Course if it would upset you—"

"It would not upset me. I just don't know . . . Oh, well, why not?"

You have to be fairly hardened in the handling and viewing of cadavers to find yourself at ease in a morgue. More hardened than I was, at any rate. There's a smell about such places, and a cold, hard, white look. I certainly was not upset, however. In fact, I had been annoyed by Jarboe's assumption that I would come all over queer with faint feminine flutterings at the sight of a harmless old skeleton. I was not prepared for the emotion that seized me when Jarboe yanked out the drawer in which the bones had been placed.

Never before had I been quite so conscious of the frailty of the inner structure that holds us upright. She had been a small woman. The soft ivory bones had a sculptural delicacy.

I hadn't been completely honest with the sheriff when I disclaimed any knowledge of bones. I was no expert, but I had attended a couple of seminars given by Kaufman, the "bone man" at Pennsylvania. He was a popular lecturer because he had served as consultant to the state police, and he had a repertoire of gruesome case histories. So I knew enough to observe some technical details. Such as the teeth. They were in excellent condition—no sign of caries or abscesses. No fillings, either. The absence of dental work would have made positive identification difficult, even if the missing-person files had come up with a possible candidate.

The baby's skeleton lay next to that of its presumed mother. Whether by design, or because the space was limited, it huddled close to her latticed rib cage. The bones were not so undamaged as hers; the frail shell of the skull had not withstood the weight of earth. I assumed the pathologist had determined that the injuries were postmortem. I assumed it because I had no intention of handling those softly curved scraps.

I don't think I exhibited any sign of distress, but Jarboe was determined I should react like a lady. He put a fatherly arm around me. "I shouldn't have let you look."

I shrugged off his support. "I'm all right," I said curtly.

Jarboe closed the drawer. "I shouldn't have let you. Let's go back to the office. I just might be able to scare up a little bourbon, strictly for medicinal purposes."

"The clothes," I said, remembering my comments to Alan. "Could I see the clothes they were—er—wearing?"

"Yeah, sure."

The clothes had been wrapped in brown paper. Jarboe cleared his desk, pushing the accumulated debris to one side, and opened the package.

Psychologists say the sense of smell is more evocative than any other sense. I don't know why, or even whether it is true. But the faint aura surrounding those faded garments evoked images, and vivid ones at that—attics of old houses, sunbeams stretching across worn floorboards, hot closed-in air, dust tickling my nose, and a strong, distinctive odor . . .

"Mothballs," I said faintly.

Jarboe nodded. "Yep. Stored away someplace, these were. I showed them around, nobody recognized them. Thought maybe they came from Maidenwood."

"I wouldn't know. There's a lot of junk in our attic; I used to poke around up there . . ." Another shuddering jolt of recollection—but this one didn't drop neatly into place, it streaked through my mind and vanished. I didn't realize I was swaying gently to-and-fro, like a windblown weed, until Jarboe's arm guided me to a chair.

"There, now," he said, not without satisfaction. "I knew

I shouldn't have let you. Here, this'll make you feel better."

I took the glass he pressed into my hand. The momentary faintness was gone, but I couldn't deny him his amiable revenge. Served me right for being so smug.

I assured him the liquor had indeed restored me, and brushed away his apologies. "I'm only sorry I can't help you, Sheriff. I don't remember . . ."

"Pity I can't ask Miz Martha."

"It's not likely that they came from our attic, is it? We've had trouble with trespassers, but I can't believe thieves could get into the house without leaving signs of forced entry. Shirley Johnson has been on duty ever since Martha became ill, and if anyone had broken in before that, Martha would have raised Cain. She was always a light sleeper, and she had ears like a hawk."

Jarboe nodded agreement. "Not to mention a double-barreled shotgun. I guess you're right, Julie. If Martha had caught a burglar on the premises, she'd have peppered him good."

"Martha has a gun?"

"Well, sure; she always did, didn't she?"

"Oh, yes. I—uh—I'd forgotten. I haven't seen it since I arrived."

"Better find it and keep it handy." I stared at him in consternation and he added hastily, "In case of trespassers, and there's rabid animals around . . . You don't need to worry about anyone getting into the house, you were one hundred percent right about that. Carrsville is a nice quiet little place, not like Pittsburgh."

A nice quiet little place inhabited by people who got a kick out of playing with human bones. The expression on my face convinced Jarboe he had better drop that argument.

"Nothing familiar about the clothes, then?" he asked.

I picked up the dress. The calico was a drab print, small white figures on dark grey-blue ground. It looked as if it had been made at home, and by an unskilled seamstress; the sleeves were unshaped tubes, the neck was high, unadorned by collar or frill, and the body of the dress fell straight and full from a narrow yoke.

"I'll tell you one thing," I said. "This was never made for *her*. It's miles too big."

"That fits our reasonable assumption," Jarboe said. "Somebody took this out of his mama's attic."

"It's maddening," I muttered, examining the dress more closely. "I mean, there is absolutely nothing distinctive about this dress. It was made on a sewing machine, but women have been using them for—at least a hundred years, I suppose. The fabric doesn't look like a synthetic and the print is old-fashioned, but these old prints are popular for quilts and country clothes. The style doesn't tell me anything because the dress hasn't any style to speak of."

"Some old ladies in the country still wear dresses like this," Jarboe agreed. "We thought of all that, Julie."

"It's a hideous dress," I said vehemently. "No girl that age would be caught dead in it . . . Sorry. That wasn't intentional."

Jarboe grunted.

"Now this," I went on, touching the folded white garment with my fingertip, "is altogether different. Handmade and probably old."

"Pick it up if you want," Jarboe said, watching me. "Can't hurt it."

I didn't want to pick it up. The stains were probably rust but they looked like dried blood. I told myself I was acting like a fool and lifted the garment from the table.

"Hand embroidery," I said. "Every inch of it, all along the ruffles and frills. I think it's what they call *broderie anglaise*. The fabric is lawn or batiste—I'm not up on such things. All handmade." I dropped the stained small dress onto the table. "No clue there either. Both boys and girls wore dresses like this years ago. If that matters . . ."

"Well, no, it doesn't. Except people save things like this, handmade, family heirlooms like. The woman's dress is no heirloom."

"You can say that again." I realized I was unconsciously wiping my fingers on my skirt. I put my hands in my pockets. "Sorry I can't be more help."

"You sure you won't have another nip?"

I had another nip. I needed it. I had not been able to conceal from Jarboe that I was "upset," as he tactfully put it, but he didn't know how upset I had been—or why. It wasn't good old-fashioned female squeamishness at the sight of a few bones. The skeletons hadn't frightened or repelled me. They had only made me feel sad. But the clothes . . . Why couldn't I pin down that flash of memory, as I had so many others once lost and unwanted? My arguments as to why the clothes could not have come from Maidenwood were convincing, so far as they went. And I certainly didn't relish the idea that unknown persons were prowling freely around the house . . .

I said good-bye to Jarboe and left the building, but I still couldn't get those pitiful garments out of my head. That baby's dress, so lovingly and exquisitely made—and such a contrast to the woman's dress. Well, but that didn't mean anything. Both garments must have been picked at random from a trunk of old clothes; the mother who had fashioned that dainty gown would never have worn such a homely dress.

As I drove out of the parking lot, I thought of something I should have realized earlier. The dress would not have been too big for a woman in the last months of pregnancy.

After a quick stop at a supermarket to lay in more dog food (my estimate of Elvis's appetite had been wildly wide of the mark), I started back to Maidenwood. I was annoyed with myself for a number of reasons, and it did not improve my disposition to find that Mrs. Danner had made soup out of the stew-meat I had intended for supper. It had obviously been boiling for a long time. The package of frozen vegetables she had added to the pale gray broth had been reduced to mush, and the kitchen felt like a steam bath.

I would have dashed upstairs to yell at her, but the sight of a flea-infested muzzle and two hopeful brown eyes peering in at the door reminded me of another duty. Why do dogs have such soulful eyes? According to approved theology they have no souls. I took a dim view of approved theology—or I had always believed I did. So why was I so perturbed at the thought of the pitiful bones lying in a cold metal drawer? Why were images of chanting priests and neat gravestones with "Here lies . . ." pressing at my mind?

I turned off the burner under the soup and filled a bowl with dog food. Elvis started whining at the sight of it, but before I took it out onto the porch I surreptitiously gathered my equipment, whisking around the kitchen with my back turned to the door so he wouldn't see what I was doing. I waited until he was deeply immersed in his food before I carried the big washbasin and the brush and the flea shampoo and the towel and the kettle of hot water outside. Elvis didn't look up. Maybe he had never had a bath. He certainly looked as if he'd never had a bath. I sat down on the step and rechecked the pertinent pages of

"How to Care for Your Dog." It didn't sound formidable: Put the water in the basin and the dog in the water.

Five minutes later I was drenched from hair to sneakers. The only damp parts of Elvis were his paws. He stood a few feet away, grinning and wagging. Obviously he considered this a new and fascinating game—you pick me up and put me in the basin, then I jump out. The wetter you get, the more points for me.

I was about to try again when Elvis turned and dashed off, rounding the corner of the house at a good clip. He was back before I had time to swear, escorting Alan and acting as if they had known one another all their lives. He hadn't even barked.

I said bitterly, "How sharper than a serpent's tooth to have a faithless dog."

Alan acknowledged the witticism with a polite smile. "We met earlier."

"Oh?"

"Your cousin *said* I could investigate the smokehouse area."

"Oh."

"I think I've located a rubbish dump."

"Gee, that's wonderful."

"If your cousin would let us work there—"

"Oh, come off it, Alan, you aren't really interested in the first manor house. You're only interested in harassing Matt. I suppose," I added, as Elvis squirmed unbecomingly at Alan's feet, "you found some eighteenth-century steak bones in the trash. Or did you bring the wherewithal with which to bribe my dog?"

"He didn't need bribing. He's a smart dog; he recognized my charm and sterling character immediately."

I sighed. "What do you want, Alan?"

"I came to help you give the dog a bath," Alan said.

"Oh, to coin a phrase, yeah?"

"I figured you might have a little trouble." Alan surveyed me from dripping hair to soggy sneakers, and grinned offensively. "You used to be terrified of dogs."

"I was not terrified of dogs. My mother was terrified of dogs."

"Anything you say. Come here, dog."

"His name is Elvis," I said, in a more amiable tone. I am not too proud to accept help, and besides, I hoped Elvis would saturate Alan too.

"Elvis? Good God." Alan grabbed the dog and popped him into the tub. The damned animal stood like a rock, with his tongue hanging idiotically out of his mouth.

Alan got pretty wet, which soothed my ego somewhat. I decided it is not possible to bathe a dog without getting wet. "The tricky part is to keep him from rolling in the dirt the instant he gets out of the tub," Alan explained, taking a firm grip on Elvis's collar. "Give me that towel . . . Damn!"

I backed away out of the shower Elvis produced by vigorously shaking himself. "Oh, sorry, Alan. I'm new to this."

"To coin a phrase," Alan began.

He showed me how to brush out the dead hair and dead fleas. Elvis loved that part of the process and I was able to return to a more pertinent topic of conversation.

"You really came to find out what the sheriff said," I remarked, watching with mild revulsion as Alan disposed of a few fleas whose stronger constitutions had resisted the shampoo.

"What did he say?"

"He wants to get rid of the bones. Not," I added, "give them to you. He pointed out that there are laws governing the disposal of human remains."

"Don't I know. I suppose he wants you to plant them in the family plot."

"I can't think of any reason why not."

"Neither can I," Alan said agreeably.

Elvis, lying on his side in blissful abandon, stiffened and started to squirm. "Hold on, I'm not finished," Alan said. "What's the matter with him?"

"Now and then he remembers he's supposed to be a watchdog. That sounds like Mr. Danner's pickup. Damn it; I thought Mrs. Danner would come to the kitchen before she left. I wanted to read her the riot act for making mush out of my dinner."

I realized after I had said it that it sounded suspiciously like a hint. Alan didn't take it up. He went on brushing, and I said, "Why aren't you looking for burial sites?"

"What makes you think I'm not?"

"In the middle of a pasture that's under water a good part of the year?"

Alan cocked a quizzical eyebrow in my direction. "Have you been taking archaeology courses, or can it be that the pearls of wisdom I dropped all those years ago—"

"It's just common sense. You're looking for evidence of occupation, not for vandalized graves."

"The two are not incompatible."

"In this case they are. The settlement at Maydon's Hundred dates from the first quarter of the seventeenth century. I saw the skeletons. They are too clean and well preserved to be that old."

"I know."

"How do you know? You haven't seen the skeletons."

"Perkins, the pathologist, is a friend of mine. Anyway, I knew as soon as I read the story in the newspaper that the bones couldn't be three hundred and fifty years old. Unless . . ."

"Unless what?"

Alan might not have heard me. He released the dog, who promptly flung himself into the nearest patch of dirt, and rolled. Sitting cross-legged, hands resting lightly on his knees, Alan stared dreamily into space as if he were visualizing the scenes he described.

"It's hard to imagine what it was like for them. Tangled wilderness as far as the eye could see, none of the comforts, even the necessities, they had always taken for granted. Elizabeth the First had been dead only a few years. James was king—that sour-faced Scot who amused himself with handsome young men and solemn researches into witchcraft. The men who landed at Jamestown wore ruffs and swords; they boasted of being 'gentlemen,' too good to dirty their hands clearing land or building houses. The settlement almost died because of their gentility . . .

"But it survived. Towns grew up; the Hundreds sent representatives to the Assembly at Jamestown. There were seventy-eight people at Maydon's Hundred in 1622. They had built homes, and a church, all clustered around the fort they believed would intimidate the 'savages.' The Indians weren't intimidated. The uprising of 1622 wiped out one third of the Virginia colonists. Maydon's was the hardest hit. The slaughter was so terrible, the destruction so complete, that no attempt at resettlement was ever made. For years afterward, hunters camping near the site swore that the spirits of the dead crowded around them in the darkness, baring their bloody wounds and wailing for vengeance in thin, high voices. The spot was shunned, its very location forgotten. Maydon's became 'the lost Hundred.' "

I had heard it before, but the spell of his voice was as strong as ever. Even the dog lay still, his head on his paws, his liquid brown eyes fixed on the speaker.

"But they say she still lingers in the green shadows of the forest," Alan went on softly. "Not as a mutilated victim but in all her youthful beauty. Raven-haired and blue-eyed, gems at her throat and in her hair, long velvet skirts rustling the dead leaves—"

The spell was broken. I sat up as if I had been stung. "You're wasting your talents in archaeology," I said rudely. "You ought to write romantic novels. That story *is* a romantic novel. I read it, *To Have and to Hold*, by Mary Johnston. One of those fatuous, sentimental, old-fashioned—"

"Sure it is," Alan said. "Pure fiction. The high-born Lady, fleeing a hated marriage with the king's favorite, disguising herself as one of the servant girls the Virginia Company had recruited as wives for the settlers. But there's a germ of fact behind that story; there was a Lady Jocelyn Cartwright among the residents of Maydon's Hundred—"

"You told me that five years ago. Alan, I understand why Maydon's is important. So little has survived from those first settlements—only a few have been located, much less excavated. But your fantasy about the Lady was what ruined your article. Every scholar in the field ridiculed it; it almost wrecked your career. She never existed."

"She wrote to the king. There was a letter."

"Then where is it? The only person who claimed to have seen it, in a collection of family papers, was one of those dilettante nineteenth-century historians. He probably made it up."

Alan refused to be provoked. He gave me a sweet, lazy smile and said cheerfully, "You've seen the portrait."

I had not seen the original. It was in the National Portrait Gallery in London—an exquisite miniature on ivory, attributed to one of Holbein's students, and done with almost the master's genius. I had seen copies. They were all over the place, including Maidenwood. One of my crazier ancestors had claimed we were descended in a roundabout way from Lady Jocelyn. Very roundabout, considering that if she wasn't a figment of someone's imagination, she had died in 1622 without issue.

"The attribution is questionable," I said, in my nastiest pseudo-scholar voice.

"But just suppose," Alan persisted. "Suppose it did happen, in the way the lost letter described it. When King James realized she was in earnest, he relented. He granted her a vast estate here in Virginia—so long as she never married. If the husband he chose for her wasn't good enough, she could damn well live and die a virgin. Doesn't that fit his peculiar personality, the blend of cruelty and sentiment that distinguished his actions?"

This time the magic of his voice failed to entrance me. I suppose, in an odd way, I had always been jealous of the Lady. Jealous, not even of a ghost—the ghost of a fantasy! But the miniature was so beautiful. The raven hair, the wide blue eyes . . .

"And then the massacre," Alan went on. "One version of the story claims she was captured and carried away by the Indians; that she fell in love with her stalwart brave and bore him children. Another version suggests that she killed herself rather than be taken alive. When the rescue expedition arrived, too late, they found the dead lying where they had fallen, decomposed and torn by wild animals. The bodies were tumbled into hastily dug, unmarked graves. But just suppose . . . suppose they thought her worthy of more respectful treatment. A well-made coffin, a leaden shroud—some method that would preserve her bones through three and a half centuries."

"Alan," I said, half convinced, "you are just—just romanticizing—aren't you? You don't really believe—"

"Hell, no." He looked directly at me. His eyes were no longer dreamy; they sparkled with devilish amusement. "But doesn't it make a great publicity story? You haven't heard the rest of it—the infant, born in defiance of the king's command—"

"You son of a gun," I exclaimed. "Are you really going to print that yarn? Your colleagues will crucify you."

"Oh, I'll hedge it around with all the proper scholarly reservations. But if all else fails—sure, I'll publish it. I have to do something to get funding, Julie. I've waited too long to let a little thing like money stop me."

"I have never heard anything so immoral, dishonest, unprincipled, shameful—"

"I said it was just a story." Alan grinned. "But Maydon's Hundred isn't. It's here, damn it, and I'm going to find it."

"So that's where you got to," said Shirley, at the porch door. "Is this mess on the stove supposed to be supper?"

We ate soup for supper, because that's all there was. I promised Shirley something exotic next day—crab, lobster, whatever she wanted.

Martha grumbled over the meal, which I took as a compliment to my cooking. After supper we settled down to *Bleak House,* and for once I found Esther's hideous optimism almost soothing. Every time I thought of Alan's underhanded scheme for raising the money to carry out his heart's desire, I couldn't decide whether to laugh or swear.

After Martha dismissed me I was too restless to sleep. What I needed was exercise—a long brisk walk, attended by my faithful dog. But the darkness intimidated me, not only because there was a chance I'd fall over something and sprain an ankle, but because the night teemed with dangers—ancient phantoms and crazy live people. I made sure everything was locked and bolted, and then I went to the library.

It was a grisly promenade at night, with only the sallow light of a single flashlight to push the dark away. I didn't prolong my visit, but went straight to the shelves containing volumes on history. I had not been much interested in those books in the past, but I vaguely remembered having seen a book about Maidenwood. The shelf was shrouded in cobwebs, but the book was there; my memory was working admirably now that it had been jogged so often. I took the Maidenwood book and a few others on Virginia history, and left the room, almost running. There were ghosts haunting Maidenwood all right, and the most terrifying of them was the shade of the angry, unhappy child that I had been.

I woke next morning with a bad taste in my mind, like a mental hangover. The window was opaque with soft white mist. The air felt close and hot; it was going to be a warm day once the fog burned off, which it inevitably would. A super day for digging in an open field full of bugs.

I heard Martha's voice raised in protest as I stumped grumpily past her door. I was not moved to stop and inquire what she was complaining about. I put the kettle on; then a scratching at the back door reminded me of my new responsibilities. The sight of Elvis, clean and eager-eyed, and unashamedly delighted to see me, wiped away some of my evil humor. I was beginning to understand why people own dogs. It's nice to have someone adore you uncritically, even if your position as a source of food is a large part of that adoration.

He didn't want to eat out on the step all by himself. He wanted to come in. My mind was so muzzy I had to concentrate before I figured out the solution: close the kitchen door. Elvis had polished off his breakfast by the time the kettle boiled. He settled down at my feet while I drank my coffee, his tail making a soft rhythmic sound.

I knew why I was in a bad mood, and it was not lack of sleep, though I had sat up late reading. It was the content of what I had read that bugged me.

The little book about Maidenwood, written at the turn of the century by one of my dippier distant relatives, was an uncritical hodgepodge of fact and fancy, legend and history, served up with a generous dollop of self-esteem. Anything that augmented the pride and glory of the Carrs was fact, to him. Not only did he believe in the Lady, he referred to her as "my ancestress."

The other books reduced Lady Jocelyn to her proper position—"a pretty legend," as one historian condescendingly put it. Maydon's Hundred had a more solid foundation. There had been such a settlement, the authorities agreed on that. They did not agree on its location. Nobody had ever mounted an expedition to look for the remains of Maydon's Hundred, and for very good reasons. The biggest reason was lack of money. Archaeology is an expensive activity, and there were dozens of other sites that attracted greater interest. The author of the book on Maidenwood, who (erroneously) fancied himself a scholar, had done some casual digging. He was convinced that the lost Hundred had been located at Maidenwood, and he offered, as proof, a rusty piece of metal he claimed was part of a suit of armor dating to the reign of James the First. There was a photograph of this artifact in the book; it looked like a fragment of a fender from a Model-T. I could see why it had not impressed the historians. Some of them agreed that Maidenwood was one possible site, but only one of several, and nobody really cared enough to find out.

I guess I had hoped to discover that Alan was as far off-base with regard to Maydon's Hundred as he was about the Lady—for I still was not convinced he had wholly abandoned his "pretty legend." No such luck.

The kitchen door opened. "How come you closed—" Shirley began. "Oh, I see. Now, Elvis, don't do that—you get me distracted . . . Julie, there's a woman at the front door and she—"

The woman wasn't at the front door, she was at the kitchen door, right behind Shirley. Elvis, who had greeted Shirley with lickings and waggings, began to growl. I caught his collar in time to keep him from launching himself at the newcomer.

"Who—" I began.

"Restrain your dog, please," the woman said in clipped tones. "If he attacks I shall be forced to take legal action. My card."

Keeping a safe distance from the dog, she flipped the card at me. I let it fall on the floor. With some effort I got my wits together—Elvis out, Shirley back to Martha, a cup of coffee in her deserving hand, the kitchen door closed. Then I turned my attention to the intruder, who had stood her ground, immovable as a granite statue.

She looked like someone's secretary, stocky and shrewd-eyed, wearing a grey pinstripe suit and sensible shoes. Horn-rimmed glasses dominated her face; her features were otherwise unremarkable except for those knowing eyes. She had retrieved her card. When she thrust it at me a second time, I took it.

"Pauline A. Hornbeak, P.A., B.A., M.B.A. . . ." I looked up. "P.A.?"

"Psychic Archaeologist."

"Oh, damn," I exclaimed.

Pauline A. Hornbeak raised her eyebrows. "I beg your pardon?"

"You should. What's the idea of barging into a private home without an invitation—and at this ungodly hour?"

"I apologize for the earliness of my arrival," said Pauline, sounding as insincere as a politician explaining what he was doing with that fan dancer. "I have written Senator Matthew Ellis without having received the courtesy of a reply. My letters to Professor Alan Petranek have also gone unanswered. Their unaccountable rudeness left me with no alternative but to come to you."

My adrenaline had begun to flow, tardily but strongly. I shouted at her. "No alternative? You had the obvious, reasonable alternative of staying away. What the hell is the matter with you people?"

From outside the door Elvis let out a sharp, agitated bark, and I moderated my voice. "I can't believe you, lady. Go away before I call a cop."

Pauline gave me a pitying smile. "Your lack of courtesy does not touch me, Miss Newcomb. I am in tune with my Masters. I am insulated by a blanket of karmic invulnerability. Are you going to ask me to sit down?"

"No."

"A cup of coffee, perhaps. Normally I do not indulge in stimulants, they are rank poison to the system and cloud the psychic senses. But as a symbol of good feeling—"

"I am not going to offer you a cup of coffee. A cup of rank poison, if I had it . . . See here, Miss—Mrs.—"

"Call me Pauline."

"Thank you, no." I straightened the card, which I had squashed between my clenched fingers. "The Research

Center for Psychic Archaeology. I read one of your letters."

"Then you understand my purpose in coming. Let me explain further. I know where—"

"If you run, you can probably get into your car before the dog catches up with you. He's a little lame."

I had to lead her to the door and shove her into her car. She kept talking every step of the way. Only the advent of Elvis, limping but full of zeal, prevented her from continuing her lecture. I held him, stroking and praising him, to keep him from chasing the car down the driveway, and from barking. Either he was sensitive to atmosphere or he had been trained not to bark unnecessarily. He certainly paid no attention to most of my other orders.

I went back in the house. Shirley was waiting at the top of the stairs. "Miz Martha—" she began.

"Right. I'm coming."

Shirley always left the lying to me. I told Martha the visitor was a Jehovah's Witness, hoping that group was as prevalent and as pushy here as it was in my neighborhood. Apparently it was, for Martha didn't question my story.

It was an inauspicious beginning to a day that held little promise of anything better. I asked Shirley's indulgence while I made a quick trip to the grocery store. When Mrs. Danner arrived, I dashed downstairs to threaten her with a painful death if she laid a hand on the pots and pans. I had changed to jeans and a long-sleeved shirt; they clung like molten lead, it was so hot, and when I went out the back door and saw Elvis sprawled lazily in the shade, I had a strong inclination to join him.

He was bored, though. When I started along the path

to the pasture, he went with me. We found Alan folding his tents. A few patches of raw earth were the only remnants of his unsuccessful excavations, and he was loading his card table into the van.

"Where are you off to today?" he inquired.

"Whither thou goest," I replied.

He gave me a dirty look. "Come and meet the others."

There were only four of them—a skeleton staff, to use a not-too-nice pun. The hulking young man was a football player—third-string tackle, he proudly informed me. His name was Willkie. He would have told me more, but Alan whisked me away and introduced me to the girls. They really were girls, not more than eighteen, and obviously infected with the same virus that had blinded me to Alan's character defects when I was the same age. One was blond and one was brunet; both looked at him with wet-lipped adoration and at me with identical expressions of hostility.

The fourth member of the team was Alan's protégé, a graduate archaeology student from the University of Virginia. He was even bigger than Willkie—very handsome, very black, very muscular. He could have been a football player, but, as he informed me, he had never really enjoyed being mauled by other big muscular males. He was obviously intelligent as well as handsome. Alan treated him with a courtesy he did not accord the others; he ordered them around like galley slaves, but he occasionally said "please" and "thanks" to Jono.

Alan left Jono to supervise the packing up, and offered me a seat in his Jeep. We went bouncing off across the pasture toward a belt of trees on a ridge to the northwest. I expected Alan would stop when we got to the trees; instead he drove over a mound of rubble that had once been part of a fence and headed straight for a pine tree two feet in diameter.

He didn't hit it, or the tree behind it, but he didn't miss either by much. After I had opened my eyes I saw that a rough trail had been hacked through the woods. It ended in a clearing—not a natural glade, but a man-made opening. The uprooted trees and brush had been pushed to one side, where they stood like a wall.

"You had a bulldozer in here," I said, as Alan stopped the Jeep next to the brush pile. "Did Matt give you permission?"

"I didn't ask him. Watch out, that's poison ivy."

It was, and there were equally unpleasant plants among the debris that loomed at my shoulder. Instead of getting out, Alan rummaged under the seat, emerging with a paper bag, from which he took a sandwich and a bottle of beer.

"Want some?"

"No, thanks."

He applied himself to his lunch with the same single-minded concentration he applied to his work. After a while I said, "Aren't bulldozers frowned on in your profession?"

"I'm not crazy about using them myself. In this case I had no choice."

"I assume you had a reason for picking this particular spot? It doesn't look promising to me."

"That's because you don't know anything about it," Alan said. "This is probably where your Great-Great-Uncle Albert found the piece of armor. You do remember my talking to you about Albert?"

I didn't tell him my memory was as leaky as a sieve. There was some excuse for its inadequacy in this case, since at the time he had lectured me about his pet theories I had been intent on the cadences of his voice and the way his lips shaped the words, instead of paying attention to what he was saying. I saw no reason to go into this, in view of the fact that I was freshly informed about Great-Great Uncle.

"Where did you find that book?" I asked suspiciously.

Alan crumpled the bag and tossed it and the bottle into the back of the Jeep. "Not in your library, my dear. I was never admitted to that holy of holies, if you recall."

"I thought we agreed not to call up the past."

"We did. Sorry. Your ancestor presented copies of that inane book to every library in the state. I don't suppose he actually sold more than ten. They were received with proper gratitude and promptly filed away in the farthest possible storeroom. A few are still in existence, forgotten but not beyond reach."

"And this is where he found the—whatever it was?"

"I can't be certain. He was no surveyor, and his measurements are vague in the extreme. The pasture was one possible site. I started there, partly because it was more accessible, and partly because many of the early settlements were close to the river. This is farther away, but in a healthier situation, not so susceptible to the malarial mosquitoes that wiped out so many of the settlers at Jamestown. This was an open field ninety years ago. If you look at the vegetation you can see it has grown up in the last half century."

The fallen trees looked older than that to me, but what did I know? Before I could comment Alan said, "Here they come," and got out of the Jeep.

In spite of my grounding in archaeological technique I still harbored a few fantasies—plunging my spade into the earth and turning up a golden necklace glittering with gems, or a chest of pieces of eight. Nobody plunged a spade or anything else into the earth that afternoon. The entire time was spent in what Alan called plotting the site.

I would have called it plain ordinary manual labor. The bulldozer had left the ground littered with broken branches and twigs, tangled vines and roots. So our first job was to finish clearing the ground. We used rakes—plain ordinary garden rakes—and Alan yelled at us every time we disturbed a clod of dirt.

He had already surveyed the site. He and Jono brooded over the papers for a while, muttering about things like base lines and datum points, and then we all got to help lay out the grid. The area was divided into equal squares approximately eight feet on a side, and stakes were driven into the corners at the intersections of the grid squares and the balks.

I asked what a balk was, and everybody looked at me with varying degrees of contempt and pity. Everybody except Willkie—he didn't know what a balk was either, and I suspected he didn't care. (It is an earth partition left between squares, so the digger doesn't have to walk on the area he has dug. By keeping the edge of the balk perfectly straight, he can also check the stratification and chart the precise depth of any objects that are found.)

I was prepared to pound in a stake or two, but that wasn't good enough. They had to be set in concrete and then surveyed so that their precise elevations could be scratched into the concrete before it hardened.

It struck me as an awfully complicated procedure, in view of the minuscule staff and the limited time at Alan's disposal, but I didn't want to ask any more idiotic questions. Everyone was visibly wilted by the end of the day, and I was relieved to throw down my tools and announce my imminent departure. Willkie and the girls looked as if they would have been glad to join me.

Alan looked up from some abstruse calculations he was

scribbling on a yellow pad. "Are you leaving already?" he demanded.

"It's after five. I have to get supper. Are you going to drive me to the house?"

"I can't quit yet."

Glowering, I started toward the track by which we had come. Jono intercepted me. "My scooter is over there. Want a ride? It's the long way around, but easier than walking."

I accepted with alacrity. "How come you get off early?" I asked. "Clout or blackmail?"

Jono grinned. "I work nights. Short-order chef. It drives Alan up the wall to have me leave at five, but he can't afford to pay me and I can't afford not to work, so he has to put up with it."

"You work all night and dig all day?"

"So I'm crazy. It's an occupational hazard for archaeologists."

"Is Alan that hard up? I thought the university funded operations like this."

"Some. Not this one. It's strictly a one-man show."

The scooter was leaning up against a tree. I got on. "That's why he's so uptight," I said thoughtfully. "So meticulous about the procedure."

"You got it. If he can find something—anything—that is incontrovertibly early seventeenth century, he can apply for funding to several places and stand a good chance of getting it."

"If I were in his place, I'd be tempted to salt the site."

Jono had mounted. Foot poised over the pedal, he glanced at me. "He wouldn't do that!"

"Just kidding."

"Oh. Right."

I wrapped my arms around his narrow waist and we

were off. As we bounded over ruts and boulders I shook with silent laughter, imagining what Martha would say if she could see me.

Mrs. Danner had left when I got back. There was a note on the table, a short list of cleaning items she needed. The writing was nothing like the penmanship of the crank letter; though just as laborious, it was stiff and spiky rather than rounded.

After I had dinner started, I went to the library to return the books I had taken. I put them back and looked to see if I could find anything fit to read. The place had lost its terror for me now; it was just a dusty, abandoned room.

When I examined the set of shelves devoted to classics and belles-lettres, I remembered something else I had forgotten. It was almost the only happy memory connected with those years—the summer I had discovered poetry. Martha had censored the poetry section too, but she couldn't find much to complain of in Keats and Tennyson. (I didn't find out about Lord Byron until later; he led, you know, a most dissolute life.) And there was one book Martha had overlooked. Squeezed in behind *The Collected English Poets,* leather-bound and gilt-edged, was a slim volume of verse by Edna St. Vincent Millay. After Milton and the rest, her poems hit me like a fresh wind blowing off the sea.

The book was still there. I picked it up and blew the dust off the spine.

> Love has gone and left me and the days are all alike;
> Eat I must, and sleep I will,—and would that night
> were here!

But ah!—to lie awake and hear the slow hours strike!
Would that it were day again!—with twilight near!

I smiled as I read the lines, but I felt my eyes filling. It is so awful to be almost thirteen years old. All those burgeoning hormones and romantic dreams, all those pimples and long, bony legs . . . There was no acceptable vent for such emotions, certainly not for me, with Martha hovering over me like a Puritan witch-hunter searching for sin. What was that boy's name? Ragged and sunburned, the child of one of the nearby farmers. He liked me too. He brought me daffodils from his mother's garden, and dusty field flowers that withered in a day. When Martha found out, she hit the ceiling. There had been nothing but innocence in those shy encounters until she started calling me names, calling me . . .

I groped toward the nearest chair and sat down, my head on my knees, until the spots stopped dancing in the air. When I left the room, I took Edna St. Vincent with me.

seven

As the days passed, the neat excavated squares in the clearing sank lower and lower. We found some fascinating items. A Coca-Cola bottle, circa 1956. (Willkie collected bottles; he became inarticulate with pleasure when Alan grimly presented him with this specimen.) A rusted sickle blade, circa nobody knew when. A few scraps of coarse white pottery, Sears Roebuck, circa 1946. Alan's face got longer and longer. The only one unaffected by the general atmosphere of gloom and despair was Willkie. His oars weren't always in the water, but I found his good cheer very soothing. Even the "girls" got gloomier as Alan's temper wound tighter and tighter. The temperature rose another couple of degrees every day. I got into the habit of accepting a ride home from Jono every afternoon. He understood why he couldn't drop me at the house; once, when he had a few minutes to spare we sat on the crumbled gateposts and had a cigarette and talked. I liked him, even if he did view Alan as a cross between Heinrich Schliemann and Saint Peter.

I kept trying to reach Matt, without success. His secretary coyly refused to tell me where he was. She admitted he telephoned twice a day to get his messages; yes, she had told him I wanted to speak to him. Of course, if it was an emergency . . .

"His grandmother isn't dying, if that's what you mean," I said crudely. "Where the devil is he—making a deal with organized crime?"

Shocked noises came from the other end of the line. The woman had no sense of humor. (Or maybe she was shocked because the accusation was true.) In fact, I figured Matt was probably taking a few days off with a girlfriend.

It was not until Thursday that he condescended to get in touch with me. After I had explained what I wanted, he let out a loud, exasperated sigh. "Is that all! You said it was important. I thought Martha was worse."

"You did not. You thought I was going to quit and leave you stranded. And I may yet."

"Now, Julie, honey—"

"We have to talk, Matt."

"Sure, honey."

"And don't call me honey. These fifteen-minute visits of yours are a pain in the butt. I need at least two hours to tell you what is bugging me."

"Okay. When?"

His capitulation left me speechless. I had been braced for an argument. Finally I said, "I want to get this other business settled first. Have you any objection to my telling the sheriff he can go ahead with the burial?"

"I guess not. Though I don't see why he has to foist this on to us."

"Because we're the lords of the manor," I said. "The Big Cheeses. A little moldy, and full of holes, but still the best they've got. Hell's bells, Matt, I'd give grave space to a dog! It's only a hole in the ground; what's the problem?"

"None." The uncertainty had left his voice. "You're right, Julie. I'll call Jarboe right now and tell him to make the arrangements. Call you back."

He did call back, an hour later. "I'll take you to dinner Friday evening," he announced. "Seven o'clock. I'll be spending the night. Shall I bring my own sheets?"

He sounded pleased with himself. I assured him that sleeping accommodations were available, and waited for the next announcement. "The services are set for eleven Saturday morning," he said. "I have to leave immediately afterward, since I have a political dinner in Richmond. Can you—"

"Services?" I bleated. "What services? I assumed they would just dig a grave and—"

"If we're going to do this, we're going to do it right," Matt interrupted. "Now don't you worry about a thing. I have it all arranged."

He rang off before I could ask any more questions. I almost called him back, but decided there was no need; I had a premonition of what Matt intended, and since there was no way of stopping him, there was no sense in worrying about it.

I'm not sure why I decided to take Elvis with me to the dig that day. Mrs. Pauline Hornbeak, P.A., et cetera, would undoubtedly have claimed I had received a message from the Infinite Whatever. The message came, I think, from my nasty suspicious subconscious, which found something a trifle peculiar in Mrs. Danner's behavior. The first thing I noticed was that she was carrying a purse—a "pockabook" as she called it. I had never seen her carry one; not surprising, since she didn't use cosmetics, or smoke, and it was a good bet that Joe Danner didn't trust her with cash or credit cards. She handled this one as if it contained the family savings; when I picked it up to move it out of my way she bleated like a nervous sheep.

It also seemed odd to me that she made a timid attempt to ingratiate herself with Elvis. She had never paid the least attention to him before; he had learned to tolerate her but he showed her none of the affection he showered on me and Shirley. Now, when she stooped to give him a gingerly pat on the head, he didn't respond at all, not with a growl nor with a wag. I can't honestly say I was suspicious, though, not even when she offered to feed him before she left that afternoon. I told her not to bother; but when Elvis proposed to escort me I let him come along.

Willkie was delighted to see him. Willkie was bored. Alan wasn't so enthusiastic, especially after Elvis started to help dig. Elvis ended up tied to a tree, at a safe distance. He didn't seem to mind; sometimes he watched what was going on, sometimes he slept, and sometimes he carried out his own excavation. He was hurt when I wouldn't let him ride home on the scooter with me and Jono, but he enjoyed running after us.

He had fallen behind when Jono and I reached the gate in time to observe the Danners' pickup turn on to the highway. They were going in the opposite direction, but they saw us; Danner stared so fixedly he almost ran into a tree.

I waited for Elvis to catch up and then, since he was with me, I went around to the back door. The first thing I saw was his food dish, filled to the brim with a noxious blend of dry dog food and what appeared to be Mrs. Danner's famous stew. Fearing the worst, I left Elvis to it and dashed into the kitchen, but she had not been cooking; my supplies were undiminished, and there was no ghastly mess on the stove.

I was chopping onions and tomatoes and peppers for the western omelet I planned for supper when a series of horrible sounds from Elvis sent me flying to the door. He had eaten about half the mess in the bowl. It hadn't stayed with him long.

In retrospect I can't believe I was so stupid. But at the time I had no grounds for doubt. Mrs. Danner's cooking was enough to make anyone throw up. I assumed she had brought something from home in an attempt to win over the dog—something that had been around a little too long. I abominated her cooking, but I had no reason to question her motives.

Elvis, looking as green around the gills as a brown-and-white dog can look, had gone to his water dish and was lapping furiously. Cursing Mrs. Danner, I dumped out the rest of the stew, and rinsed and refilled the bowl. Then I decided I had better do something with the remains; I didn't want a pile of garbage right outside the porch. It would attract flies, if nothing else. Cursing Mrs. Danner some more, I looked for a shovel. There must be tools in one of the sheds.

I had not explored the outbuildings. The second one I looked into had the tools, rusted spades and rakes. But it was the contents of the first shed that puzzled me; I kept wondering about them as I dug a shallow hole and scooped the detritus into it.

The things in the first shed had not been rusty discards. Wooden packing crates were neatly lined up along one wall. The floor had been swept and the place smelled faintly of bug spray. Rolled up in a corner was a down sleeping bag.

The explanation was not long in coming. Alan had admitted he had done some test digging near the smokehouse. He had probably stored some of his supplies in the shed; he had nerve enough to do something like that, without bothering to ask permission.

I gave the incident no more thought. I had lost time, and Martha would be yelling for her supper. I went back to my innocent omelet without the slightest suspicion of what was to come.

Yet deep in the distant recesses of my mind some taint of trouble ahead must have persisted. I found Martha more than usually infuriating that night; it seemed to me that her half-smile was more pronounced, as if something amused her, and from time to time she let out a hoarse little sound that might have been a cough—or a chuckle. When I asked if she was catching cold, the smile turned to a glare. Lord knows there was no excuse for her to catch cold; the weather was stifling, and I was sticky with perspiration by the time I left the room.

Heat lightning flickered in the sky when I looked out the back door before locking up. If only it would rain! Elvis looked as if the heat was getting him down too. Sprawled on his rug, he wagged his tail but did not rise to greet me.

He was so limp and depressed I knelt to feel his nose. It was warm. According to the book, that didn't mean anything. My nose was warm too. His lethargic air made me a little uneasy, though. Perhaps the food had been tainted. It would seem logical to Mrs. Danner to feed something that was not fit for human consumption to an animal. His tongue rasped the skin of my hand as I examined him. He had got rid of the stuff almost immediately; and surely, if he had been afflicted with food poisoning he'd be worse by now . . .

"Come on, old boy," I said. "You can sleep inside tonight. I wish I could take you to my room, but the kitchen will be more comfortable than the porch, especially if we have a storm, which I hope we will."

He followed me in. I offered him a dog biscuit; the relish with which he crunched it reassured me as to the state of his stomach. Then I said good night and closed the kitchen door.

It may have been the heat that kept me awake, or it may have been my worry about Elvis. I dozed and woke and dozed again, before falling into a sticky, heavy slumber.

A sound woke me. Struggling back to awareness after a nightmare of Elvis writhing in fatal convulsions, I thought at first I had heard him bark. Then I realized I couldn't have heard him, not from the kitchen. The horrible vividness of the dream got me out of bed, however. I knew I wouldn't rest until I made certain he was all right.

I had bought half a dozen flashlights and distributed them around the house. I took mine from the bedside table and went out, moving quietly to avoid waking Martha or Shirley. We left a light burning in the hall, near her door; I didn't need the flashlight.

I had almost reached the head of the stairs before I heard something. Not the same sound that had wakened me, but softer and less distinct; not a distant crash or thud, that might have had any number of innocent explanations—but nearer at hand and familiar, and all the more frightening because I knew exactly what it was: the creak of the sagging boards of the floor in the downstairs hall.

Someone was there. Old houses moan and mumble in response to changes in humidity and temperature, but this was not such a sound. I had heard it too often to be mistaken—whenever my feet crossed that spot.

I wanted to believe it was a paw, and not a human foot, on that creaking board, that Elvis had escaped from the kitchen and come in search of me. I wanted to believe it, but I couldn't. There was no way Elvis could push the door open. I had tested it to make sure.

Another, softer crack as the unseen foot shifted position. It wasn't courage that forced me to fumble for the switch of the flashlight, it was fear—fear of the dark and of the unknown. Surely no visible horror could be as bad as the monsters created by my own imagination.

The light caught him and froze him like a germ on a slide. Joe Danner, in his faded dungarees and work shirt, a long glittering knife in his hand.

I don't know why I didn't drop dead on the spot. I suppose I was in a state of shock, but sheer incredulity was a factor too. I do remember thinking, My God, you're so brave! when I heard a voice that didn't even *sound* like mine say sharply, "What are you doing there?"

His face turned livid. The knife fell from his hand. "Who is it?" he gasped. "Oh, Lord—who is it?"

"Julie." I started down the stairs, keeping the light in his eyes.

The nightmare had faded. Instead of the maniacal handyman from that horror movie, it was just disgusting old Joe Danner, caught in the act, and more afraid of me than I was of him. At least I hoped he was. At any rate, it was too late to retreat, and on the assumption that a good offense is the best defense, I continued in the same aggressive voice, "Stay right where you are, don't move. How did you get in the house and what do you want? You're not leaving until I get an explanation."

He backed slowly away as I descended, as if I were the homicidal maniac. That was reassuring, as was the fact that he had not tried to retrieve his weapon. However, I stopped a safe distance from him.

"All right, Mr. Danner, what's your excuse?"

He was not a quick thinker. He licked his lips and looked away. "I—uh—I came in the front door. I got a key. We's always had a key. In case somethin' happened to Miz Martha."

"Nothing has happened to her. What were you after? You were going to steal something."

"No, ma'am." The firm denial sounded sincere. But I had a feeling Joe Danner's definition of theft might not be the same as mine. He went on, "I was—uh—I seen somebody prowling around the house. I thought he come in."

Though I had tried to keep my voice down, our conversation had been heard. A door opened upstairs and Shirley called out. "Julie? Is that you? Miz Martha heard voices—"

"It's all right," I called back. "At least I think so. . . . Now see what you've done, Mr. Danner. You scared the liver and lights out of an old woman who is in poor health—"

"No, ma'am!" Disconcertingly, the mention of Martha put him more at ease. "You ask her. She'll tell you it's all right for me to be here. Keeping watch over Miz Martha, that's my job."

"I will ask her. Stay where you are."

Martha was sitting upright in bed. She started yammering at me. I cut her short. "It's Joe Danner. He says he's here with your knowledge and permission, but I don't believe him. I'm calling the sheriff."

"No!" The word came clear and strong. The rest of her speech was not so articulate, but the meaning was clear.

"You told him it was all right?" I demanded. "You knew he had a key?"

Martha nodded.

I reached for her wrist. She flung my hand away. The only word I caught in the next tirade was "faithful."

"You might have told me," I said angrily. "I'm supposed to be responsible for you."

Martha's wide-open eye shone with unholy amusement. "Now you know," she mumbled. "Go to bed. Sleepy." And with that, the old witch closed her eyes and lay back.

I left her to Shirley—I was afraid if I stayed any longer I'd throttle her. Danner was waiting for me, his expression little short of insolent. "You want I should look around the house?" he asked.

"No. What I want is your key." I held out my hand.

"But Miz Martha—"

"Give it to me."

He had a key, all right. I took it, knowing my gesture was no more than a meaningless assertion of authority. If the Danners had one key, they might have a dozen. But it reinforced the lecture I delivered, in my most belligerent voice.

"Don't ever do this again, Mr. Danner. I'm in charge here now, not Miss Martha, and if I find you inside the house, or prowling around outside without permission from me, I'll charge you with trespass. Is that clear?"

He didn't argue, but he didn't apologize, either, and the look he gave me just before I slammed the door on him told me that I had not made a friend.

Before I went back to bed I checked on Elvis. He was his old self; I had to grab his collar to keep him from bolting out of the room to see what had happened. His look was one of reproach: If you hadn't locked me in here, I'd have warned you.

Right, Elvis, I thought. But if you hadn't thrown up the

food Mrs. Danner put out for you, you might not have been in any condition to warn me.

I couldn't complain to the police about Danner without Martha to back me up. But I could, and would, complain to Matt. It was a good thing he planned to stay the night on Friday. I had lots to say.

I was almost asleep before I figured out something else that had been nagging at my mind—the weapon Danner had been holding. He had picked it up and put it in his pocket while I was upstairs talking to Martha, but I had got a good look at it before that—and it wasn't a knife. It was a pair of scissors.

What on earth was Joe Danner planning to do with a pair of ordinary household scissors? I mean, if you have a chain saw, why use scissors?

My indignation had not lessened the following morning. I held forth at some length on the subject of the Danners to Shirley when she came to fetch Martha's breakfast. Her only reaction was a resigned shrug and a comment to the effect that Miz Martha was a law unto herself. But when I told her about Elvis getting sick her expression turned to one of shock and surprise.

"I been wondering . . ." she began.

"What?" She didn't answer. "Do you think it could have been deliberate?" I persisted.

"I wouldn't want to say that. But why don't you just run Elvis in to the vet's and make sure he's all right? It's Dr. Rubin's day in Carrsville."

Actually, I had planned to do just that. I had even scooped up a sample of the revolting meal to take with me.

Elvis didn't look like a dog who required medical attention. He loved riding in the car; it was not until we actually got into the office that he remembered what had happened to him the last time, and it took both Dr. Rubin and me to drag him out from under my chair.

She gave him a checkup and pronounced me a qualified dog owner. The foot had healed well, and the flea population had decreased. When I told her he had thrown up his dinner she smiled. "That happens sometimes. They aren't fussy about what they eat. Dead birds or rodents—"

"I know that," I said indignantly. "It says so in the book. It also says in the book that if there is any question, take the dog to the vet."

"Is there any question?" She gestured at Elvis, who was struggling to get off the table. "He's fine. Did he eat this morning?"

"Yes. But I wondered . . . Is there any chance he could have been poisoned?"

Her smile faded. "You mean deliberately?"

"I'm not sure. Someone gave him some scraps. They could have been contaminated . . ."

"There's no way I can tell now," she said slowly. "Whatever it was, it's out of his system."

"I know. That's why I brought this."

I produced my sample. Her heavy brows lifted. "You're taking this seriously, aren't you?"

"Yes."

"Okay. I'll let you know when I get the results. It may take a few days."

I thanked her. She nodded brusquely, but as Elvis and I started for the door she said, "Talk to you soon, Julie," and, for the first time since I had met her she patted me on the back. It felt like an accolade.

* * *

I hadn't intended to tell Alan about the latest developments; if I had wished to unburden myself I'd have been disappointed, because he was in no mood to sympathize with other people's troubles. His temper had been visibly worsening all week. Later that afternoon he finally cracked. Willkie presented his glorious leader with a new find—two rusty arrowheads and the jawbone of a deer. Alan placed them in the box devoted to finds from that square—otherwise empty—and gravely recorded the information in his work book. Then, as we all stared in fascinated horror, he ripped half a dozen pages from the book, tore them into confetti-sized scraps, and flung them into the air.

"Go home," he said in an ominously quiet voice. "That's it. No more."

"That's it?" Willkie was being paid—minimum wage, but he *was* being paid. He looked horrified. "You mean you don't want me to come no more?"

"What are you talking about?" Alan demanded. "Be here Monday as usual."

"Oh, right. Sure."

"Before you go, put the tarps over the squares."

"It's not gonna rain," Willkie said innocently. "Weather man said more of the same till—"

Alan cleared his throat. The crew scattered, quaking.

After the tarpaulins had been spread, Willkie and the girls piled into the Jeep. I was about to follow Jono when a roar from Alan stopped me. "I want to talk to you, Julie."

I gestured. "I was going—"

Alan moderated his voice—not in deference to me, but out of respect for Jono, who was watching him interestedly. "I'll take Julie home, Jono. You go ahead."

"Right, boss." Jono's expression was so preternaturally

solemn I knew he was struggling to keep from smiling. I could not imagine what he thought was so funny.

Alan waited till the others had left. "Are we going to walk, or what?" I asked.

He yanked open the door of the van. "Get in."

"You can't drive that out of here. Not unless you squash your precious excavations. There isn't room to turn."

"I said, *please* get in."

He backed the van out—all the way out, through the trees. I was not capable of watching. When I felt the vehicle reverse in a wild swing, I opened my eyes.

"I'm sorry the site is turning out to be a bust," I said.

"That's life." The insane ride had rid Alan of some of his bad humor. "I'll check my calculations over the weekend. Looks as if we are in the wrong place again."

"Looks as if," I agreed. "Alan, don't you have any leads except the ones you got from that crazy book of my crazy ancestor's?"

"I wish I did. The terrain is a factor, of course; some areas are more suitable to occupation than others. Local legends can be useful—even place names. That's something I had hoped you might help me with. Any old tales of Maidenwood you never told me?"

"A couple of hundred, I should think. The one about the gal who poisoned her husband to keep him from gambling away the estate—"

Alan grinned. "I've heard that one. I'm not interested in modern scandal, but in stories you would probably dismiss as myths or fairy tales. Buried treasure, ghost stories—"

"Ghost stories?" I repeated incredulously.

"Most of them are standard fiction, of course. But you'd be surprised how long the memory of a startling or tragic event can survive, passed down from father to son. Distorted and misinterpreted in the transmission, of course, but often retaining a grain of truth among the chaff. A massacre like the one at Maydon's would be such an event. As I think I mentioned, stories about wailing ghosts sprang up soon afterward, and the ghost stories might survive after the initial cause was forgotten. A certain room or a certain spot, reputed to be haunted—shunned by those whose fathers had warned them about it, and who warned their children in turn . . . Names that linger on centuries afterward, like Gallows Hill or Deadman's Dyke or—What is it?"

"That's the name!" I exclaimed. "Deadman's Hollow. It was one of the places on Maidenwood land that was strictly off limits for me when I was young. Martha said the ground was boggy, crawling with poisonous snakes and insects . . . The boys went there sometimes, though; they would dare one another to spend the night, especially at Halloween. A boy I—a boy I knew, back in sixth or seventh grade, told me about it. You don't suppose . . ."

Alan shook his head, smiling. "Sorry. I've heard that one too. I even checked the place out. Next to the new road, at the bottom of that steep curving hill?"

I nodded. "That's where she was found."

"She?" It took him a few seconds to figure out what I was talking about. "Oh, the skeleton. That doesn't mean anything, Julie. The comedians who found it could have carried it some distance in order to put the fear of God into good old Joe Danner. Or were you thinking she crawled up on to the road by herself?"

His smile vanished abruptly when he saw the look on my face. "Julie! I didn't mean—I'm sorry! It was a stupid thing to say."

I pressed my hands to my cheeks. Hands and cheeks were icy cold, as if all the blood had drained out of them. Gradually feeling and warmth returned, and I summoned a sheepish smile. "It's all right. I don't know what came over me. It was such a gruesome idea . . ."

"Gruesome, sick, black humor," Alan agreed quickly. "And not very humorous."

I really couldn't imagine what had come over me. I felt like a fool. "So," I said, to prove that I wasn't a fool, "Deadman's Hollow is a washout."

"In every sense of the word." Alan acknowledged the horrible pun with a polite smile. "Even the reputation of the place seems to be fairly modern. I haven't come across any reference to it in the older records."

"Oh. Well, I'll give it some thought. Maybe I can come up with something."

"How about dinner tonight?"

I was so surprised I lost my grip on the window frame and hit my head on the roof as the van bounced over a ridge.

"I can't," I said.

"Aren't you entitled to an evening out occasionally? You've been on duty for almost two weeks."

Two weeks . . . The phrase triggered a flood of memory. Our "two week anniversary . . ." I had been so anxious to impress him with my culinary skills; but I forgot to turn the heat down after the veal had browned, and then we got a little distracted . . . I had paid eight dollars a pound for that veal. The stench of charring meat finally tore me from his arms, screaming like a Victorian virgin as I rushed to the kitchen. Too late . . . Alan had laughed so hard I thought he'd choke—and insisted on eating every blackened, leathery scrap of that wretched meat.

I glanced at him out of the corner of my eye. He was

staring straight ahead, his profile impassive, but a muscle at the corner of his mouth twitched, as if he were remembering that arduous exercise in mastication. I almost said something—but I got cold feet.

"I can't," I repeated. "Matt is coming to take me to dinner, and there are some things I want to discuss with him."

"Oh, yeah? Why the change in routine? I thought Saturday was his usual day."

His cool, calm tone hit me like a slap in the face. The memories that had softened me hadn't touched him at all. I hated myself for succumbing to sentimentality, and I hated him for making me succumb.

"How did you find out?" I demanded.

"Find out what?"

"Don't be clever. You knew Matt was coming this evening and you knew why. Who told you the burial service was tomorrow morning?"

"You did." A slow satisfied smile curved the corner of his mouth. "I knew it was on the agenda, but I didn't know when."

"You really are a bastard."

"For asking you to dinner? When are you going to overcome that stupid . . ." He stopped. Then he said quietly, "I didn't know Matt was coming out this evening. The invitation was made in good faith. It still stands."

"Thanks, but I'd hate you to waste precious cash that could be spent digging holes."

Alan shrugged. "Do you mind if I attend the obsequies?"

"Yes, I do mind. But short of an injunction, which I couldn't get in time, and a shotgun, which I disapprove of on principle, I can't think of any way of preventing you from coming."

Alan stopped in front of the gates. "See you tomorrow, then. Er—what time did you say?"

"I didn't say. Eleven o'clock."

As I started down the long road to the house I saw Elvis coming—a brown-and-white blur enclosed in a cloud of dust. He always seemed to know when I was due back. I hastily sat down. Once he had knocked me off my feet with the exuberance of his greeting. Now he flung himself into my lap and we exchanged pleasantries—licks, hugs, compliments, excited whines. He was too big to be a lap dog, but he didn't know that.

I had had a few words with Mrs. Danner about Elvis before I left the house. Quite a few words. I would have said even more if she had not taken the wind out of my sails by starting to cry.

It was awful. I wouldn't have felt quite so bad if she had burst into loud lamentations, but she didn't utter a sound. It was not until the first tear oozed down along one of the deep lines in her cheek and twinkled in the sunlight that I realized what was happening.

So what could I do but tell her I was sorry? I *was* sorry for her. Poor woman, she was caught between a rock and a hard place, with me on one hand and her husband on the other. If there had been an attempt to poison Elvis, Joe Danner was behind it; his wife wouldn't have had the gumption to take such a step on her own, nor would she dare resist his orders. All the same, I repeated my warning before I left. Shirley had promised to keep an eye on Elvis, but the most reassuring fact, to me, was that Mrs. Danner didn't have her "pockabook."

I was in no hurry to get to the house, so I continued to sit, with Elvis sprawled across my legs drooling onto my jeans. Martha's supper was prepared—tuna salad, for the second time that week. I was running out of ideas. No wonder women hated cooking. Three meals a day, year after year after deadly year . . . Chicken and beef and pork and fish, chicken and beef and pork and fish . . . If Matt tried to take me to that local hangout of his, I'd have hysterics. I wanted tripe or brains or sweetbread—anything but chicken or beef or pork or fish.

I decided I would not tell Matt that Alan planned to attend the funeral. He'd find out soon enough—and probably blame me. I condemned both Alan and Matt to an even hotter climate than the one that prevails in Tidewater Virginia in the summer.

I had planned to dress in my best, in the hope that my gorgeousness would inspire Matt to take me someplace fancy for dinner. The heat defeated me. I settled for bare legs and sandals and the coolest sundress I owned. My hair got bushy and unmanageable when the humidity was high; I yanked it back from my face and bundled it into a knot at the back of my neck.

Martha had been in a snit of excitement all afternoon, running Shirley ragged with orders. Matt's room had to be cleaned and garnished with flowers. (Little did she know I had swiped his mattress; the one on the bed now was the musty, hard object that had been allotted to me, and I sincerely hoped he would sleep well on it.) I had been summoned to the presence three times, to get *my* orders. I had also been told to come in before I left, to say good night. After I was dressed I decided I might as well get it over with, so I knocked on her door.

Her movable eye surveyed me from top to bottom and stayed fixed on my bare calves.

"It's too hot to wear stockings," I said, anticipating the

criticism. "We're not going to the Ritz-Swank-Carlton, Martha; I'll be lucky if I get a Big Mac and fries."

The next complaint was about my hair. She waxed so vehement on the subject that I couldn't understand what she wanted me to do about it, but she obviously disapproved of the style. "It's too late now," I said ambiguously.

Matt was on time, I'll say that for him. I suppose punctuality is a political necessity; he had never exhibited that trait as a child.

I was ready for him. "Get me out of here," I hissed, as he came in.

Matt laughed with professional heartiness. "Can you hang on for ten more minutes? I ought to spend a little time with Martha."

I knew it would take longer than ten minutes. Martha was lying in wait, bedecked in pink and smelling of cologne. As I had hoped she would, Shirley took advantage of Matt's presence to slip downstairs for her supper. I had it ready—tuna salad and sliced tomatoes, rolls, and iced tea.

"That's nice, Julie," she said appreciatively. "Looks pretty, too."

"I feel guilty enough walking out on you. Are you sure you don't mind?"

"Goodness, honey, I did it for two weeks before you came. Anyhow, I owe you an evening out."

"You look awfully tired."

"It's the heat. Gets to you when you're my size."

"Gets to you, period." I sat down across the table from her and sipped my tea. "I'd forgotten how awful summers can be down here."

"You get used to it."

"I don't plan on getting used to it."

She smiled but said nothing, and for a while we sat in

silence. She was a comfortable person to be with; I felt my frazzled nerve endings smooth out and wondered why the hell I was letting myself get uptight about petty things. Compared to Shirley, I had little to complain about.

"How is Ron?" I asked.

"He's got a job." Shirley beamed.

"Really? That's great! Why didn't you tell me?"

"Just got it today. Night shift at the chicken-and-chips place on the highway. It's only six hours a day, but it's a help."

"What about the other kids?"

"The neighbors will keep an eye on them. Frannie is sixteen, big enough to watch the little ones."

A suggestive whine at the back door interrupted the conversation. "I'm sorry," I told him. "You can't come in. Believe me, Elvis, it is just as hot inside as it is out."

Elvis looked as if he had more to say on the subject, but the arrival of Matt prevented further discussion. Matt's eyes widened at the sight of the furry face pressed pensively against the screen, but another aggravation was uppermost in his mind. "Let's get out of here, Julie," he grumbled, mopping his brow. "This house feels like an oven."

"That's one of the subjects I wanted to discuss."

"I offered Martha a window air conditioner. She said no."

"Try forcing one on me and you won't hear any objections. Shirley too."

"Of course she can have an air conditioner if she wants one," Matt exclaimed. "Why didn't you say something, Shirley?"

"Now, Matthew, it's been quite comfortable until the past few days. Julie's not used to it, she feels it more."

Matt put his hands on her shoulders. "You don't complain enough," he said affectionately. "You know, Shirley, that all you have to do is ask. How am I supposed to know what you want if you don't tell me?"

It seemed to me that only a minimal degree of intelligence was required to note that the temperature was sizzling; but Shirley, like so many women, was easily seduced by a sweet smile and a pat on the shoulder. She told Matt not to worry, everything was fine. "Run along now and have a nice time."

Matt helped me into the car and closed the door. "Where do you want to go for dinner?" he asked, starting the engine and flicking on the air conditioning.

"I don't care." The rush of cool air dispelled a great deal of the aimless animosity I had felt. In our controlled environment many of us have forgotten how excessive heat affects the emotions; there's a definite correlation between temperature and violent crime, and I can understand why.

"I don't suppose," I added wistfully, "that there is such a thing as a taco or a piece of moussaka anywhere around? I'm so sick of chicken and hamburgers."

"Spoiled, effete city girl," Matt said. "But you have it coming. I'll find you a taco if we have to drive to Washington. What else do you want?"

There were so many things, I hardly knew where to begin. I started with the worry uppermost in my mind. "More help—or better help. Surely there's someone better than Mrs. Danner."

"I can't fire her," Matt said indignantly. "The Danners have been with the family for thirty years."

"What is this, the Old South? I don't care if the Danners have been around since Sherman ravaged the old plantation. She's incompetent, and her husband is crazy. He broke into the house last night."

I expected a cry of outrage or an exclamation of disbelief—something. Matt didn't even look at me. "Why would he break in? He has a key."

I was the one who emitted the cry of outrage. "Is that all you can say? I tell you the man was wandering around the house at three A.M., and you calmly inform me he has a key. He scared the hell out of me!"

"I suppose it was a shock," Matt said broad-mindedly. "I'll have a word with him."

"I already had a word with him. But I suppose he'd pay more attention to you. I'm just a weak-minded female who gets all het-up about finding strange men in her house."

"You don't understand the local customs—"

"If you give me that crap about faithful family retainers I'll scream. Danner scares me. He isn't right in the head."

"He's perfectly harmless, Julie. Martha wasn't upset about it, was she?"

"Well—no. But she isn't right in the head either."

Matt laughed tolerantly. "She knows and trusts Joe. He has a rather feudal attitude toward Martha—unusual in this day and age, I admit, but no less admirable for all that. I admit he's a little peculiar, and he hasn't fully recovered from the shock of his discovery that morning a few weeks ago. That's probably why he was wandering around last night—he's hoping to lay hands on the pranksters who played that gruesome trick on him."

The explanation was so glibly reasonable it cut the ground out from under my protest. I knew there was no hope of persuading Matt to get rid of the Danners; secretly he adored the idea of having a faithful serf to protect the manor. I gave it one more try.

"At least let me fire Mrs. Danner. There has to be someone better—if something happened to Martha while she was on duty she'd just stand there wringing her hands. It's not fair to Shirley. She has the brunt of it, even with me there."

"Shirley's quite a gal, isn't she," Matt said fondly.

I'm sure Matt honestly believed he was paying Shirley the highest tribute in his power. I saw through the evasion, but instead of telling him that Shirley didn't need compliments, she needed help, I heard myself ask him a question that had nagged me for some time.

"How long have you known her, Matt?"

"Years—I hate to think how many. She helped raise me, you know."

"I didn't know."

Matt glanced at me in surprise. I said, "I don't remember. I've forgotten her. I have almost no memories of the years I lived at Maidenwood."

"You remember my sins," Matt said lightly.

"I had forgotten about you shutting me in the graveyard until I went there the other day. Oh, I don't mean those four years are an absolute blank, but I should remember more than I do."

"Have you talked to anyone about it?"

"A shrink, you mean?"

"Anyone. A friend, your mother . . . Why not a shrink? I didn't expect ignorant prejudice about psychiatry from you."

"I didn't talk to anyone because I didn't know I had a problem," I said, my voice rising. "How often would you reminisce about the good old days when you were ten, if you were miles away from where you had lived and nothing happened to remind you? Mother hardly ever talked about Martha—"

"That's a clue for you," Matt said dryly. "Face it, Julie. Martha is a mean old devil. She used to be a mean younger devil. She isn't the person I'd pick to look after a child."

"You mean she beat me?"

Matt burst out laughing, and I blushed for my brief descent into melodrama. "Martha handed out a few spankings and slaps," he said. "But she didn't have to resort to physical violence. She could cut you to pieces with a look and a few words. I don't know much about psychiatry, but I suspect we both have reason to blot out many of our childhood memories."

We didn't have to go as far as Washington to find tacos. Matt knew a good Mexican restaurant in Petersburg. Though he advised me not to take my missing memories seriously, he told a lot of "Do you remember?" stories that evening, without ever asking a direct question. As he talked, the incidents and people and places he mentioned began to come back to me. It was a gentle, sensitive probing into the past, without pressure and without risk.

We were on our way home when I told him I knew what he had been doing and thanked him for it. "You've reassured me, Matt. I remember a lot more than I thought I did. Maybe I am playing with a full deck after all."

"You're no crazier than any of us—if that's any consolation. To tell you the truth, Julie, I enjoyed talking about it. The memories weren't all bad, were they? It's nice having kin who share a common heritage. The tie of the blood, and all that stuff."

"The old blood is running thin, Matt. There aren't many of us left."

"Only two of us, in the direct line of descent. It's a pattern that has repeated itself for a long time—your mother and mine in the generation before ours, Martha and her sister before that."

"Didn't Martha's sister have children?"

Matt chuckled. "She may have. Didn't your mother tell you about her? She ran away from home with a totally unsuitable man, as Martha put it. That's another pattern that seems to run in the family—unsuitable marriages. Martha hasn't spoken to my mother since she divorced Dad, and she has never referred to her sister. The poor woman wrote several times after she fled the nest, but Martha never answered. Finally Melissa gave up, and no one has heard from her in years."

"If Martha never talks about her, how did you hear all that?"

"From the Judge. He warned me not to mention Melissa to Martha."

"You mean Martha has never forgiven her, after all those years? We aren't a very nice family, Matt."

"We're okay; it's Martha who isn't. In my opinion, her marriage was a worse sin than any divorce. You know she married a cousin in order to keep the family name. Did you ever see a picture of our grandfather?"

"I think Mother has one somewhere. Didn't he have a mustache?"

"Not just a mustache—big, black, sweeping mustachios, like a pirate's. And under them, the softest pursed lips . . . The poor devil died young. Martha kept him around just long enough to breed two children off him."

Chilled by the contempt in his voice, I said, "And I thought I had a grudge against her! What did she do to *you,* Matt?"

I expected him to reply with an equivocation, but the form it took surprised me.

"Here lieth one who would resign
Gladly his lot, to shoulder thine.
Give me thy coat; get into mine."

"Matt! Poetry?"

"I'm not a barbarian, Julie. But don't tell my constituents."

"What's wrong with quoting poetry?"

"Nothing, if it comes from Lincoln or the Bible. If it were known that I read lyric poems, it could lose me the election." His voice was back to normal—light, amused, concealing emotion.

Shirley had left the outside lights burning. When we got out of the car I lifted my face to the breeze. "It's cooler," I said. "Maybe we can sleep tonight after all."

"Rain by morning," Matt said.

"It is not going to rain."

"Sure it is. Look at those clouds." As if in affirmation a red light flared in the belly of the clouds, followed by a mutter of thunder.

"Heat lightning," I said firmly.

I heard the first drops patter on the roof after I had got into bed. Alan had been right—he was always right, even about the weather.

It was a lovely morning for a funeral. Fog clung to the trees like bolls of dirty gray cotton; water dripped from the leaves. As we walked down the path toward the cemetery I was still in a state of shock. When Matt had mentioned services I had expected some inappropriate demonstration, but I had not imagined he would go this far.

His suit wasn't black, but the charcoal gray cast a suitably somber note. The umbrella he held over my uncovered head was black. Ahead of us, another of the same hue shielded the minister. Ahead of *him,* six stalwart men, recruited by the undertaker, carried the coffin—a pine box so ostentatiously simple it almost ranked as a valuable antique.

Matt had my hand firmly imprisoned in the crook of his arm. My canvas sandals and yellow cotton dress were the only incongruous details in the decorous scene. Dire suspicions began to take shape in my mind. They were soon confirmed by a bright light that blinded me and left spots dancing in front of my eyes. Behind the spots I saw the photographer, camera at the ready.

Matt stopped. "Please," he said reproachfully.

Another photographer advanced from the left flank. Matt repeated his plea for privacy, but he was careful to give the second man a good profile. I put my tongue out and grimaced. Matt didn't notice what I was doing until the photographer started to giggle; then he jabbed me in the ribs.

"Don't make a farce of this, Julie."

"I can't do any worse than you. Damn it, Matt—"

"Not now," the future governor muttered, sotto voce. "Let's get on with it."

Accompanied by reporters, we wended our damp way onward. At the gate of the cemetery Matt stopped and faced the press. "Keep a straight face, or no air conditioner," he told me, out of the corner of his mouth. Aloud, he said, "Ladies and gentlemen, I understand that this is your job and I respect the public's right to know. But I beg you won't follow us into this sacred enclosure. I'll answer any questions you may have afterward. Fair enough?"

He closed the gates, leaving the pack outside. I noticed that the grave had been dug in a spot not far from the gates, and that the open grille did not impede the photographers.

I was furious with Matt, but I knew that making a scene would only prolong the discomfort. At first I didn't see Alan, and hoped he had had the sense to stay away. Then I found him, kneeling by one of the stones near the east corner. He rose to his feet when the procession entered, but kept at a distance. He was wearing tan slacks and a white shirt instead of his working garb of jeans and blue shirt—respectable but not theatrical.

He was not the only spectator. Also at a respectful distance from Alan, and from the grave, was Sheriff Jarboe. Catching my eye, he nodded, without smiling or speaking. I had expected he might be there; I had not expected the Danners. They stood apart from the others, and neither of them looked at me. Mrs. Danner's head was bowed. Her husband never took his eyes off the open grave.

The pallbearers went about their business, supervised by the undertaker, a plump man in black. He had full cheeks and a couple of chins, but years of looking solemn had trained his face in lines that made it look longer and thinner than it really was. The minister took his place at the head of the grave and opened the book.

"I am the Resurrection and the Life . . ."

Traditionally the Carrs were Episcopalians, when they went to church at all. I assumed Matt had chosen an Episcopal minister for that reason; but the formal service had its advantages, leaving the pastor no awkward problems of how to eulogize an unknown. I hoped she didn't mind, whoever she was. Joe Danner would have minded. He had transferred his inimical stare to the minister, and I had the distinct impression that if someone had read the wrong service over his bones, those bones would have risen in protest.

The service was quickly concluded. The minister looked up from the book. "Would you care to say a few words?"

Though I felt sure Matt had planned that last, outrageous gesture, he seemed for once at a loss for words. I was as surprised as anyone when I heard my own voice break the stillness; and although, like another well-known person, I can quote Scripture for my own evil purposes, the phrases I repeated did not come from the Bible.

> "Down down, down into the darkness of the grave
> Gently they go, the beautiful, the tender, the kind;
> Quietly they go, the intelligent, the witty, the brave.
> I know. But I do not approve. And I am not resigned."

A frown furrowed the pastoral brow at this pagan sentiment, but I didn't care; that was how I felt. And the quotation seemed to strike a responsive cord in Matt. Like an antiphony his words echoed:

> "The sun that warmed our stooping backs and withered the weed uprooted—
> We shall not feel it again.
> We shall die in darkness, and be buried in the rain."

"Where did you get that?" I whispered, surprised but impressed.

"Your fault." He was as good as a ventriloquist; his lips

scarcely moved. "I had a Biblical quote ready, but you got me off the track . . ." He took my arm to lead me away, but I shook off his grasp. Alan was coming toward us and I didn't want him to think I had been an active participant in the proceedings.

The cameras flashed as Matt and Alan confronted one another.

"I don't recall inviting you to be present, Professor," Matt said. "This was supposed to be a private family service—"

"I suppose they're all cousins," Alan said, indicating the reporters. "I wouldn't have missed this for the world, Senator. Particularly the last act."

"Last act? What—what—" Matt's voice failed him, a phenomenon I had never expected to see once, let alone twice, in a day.

Alan pointed. "She's been there behind the mausoleum the whole time."

She emerged, trying to look as if she had been planning to make her appearance at that point. She wore the same pinstriped suit, but she had tied a transparent rain bonnet over her head. Ignoring the rest of us, she minced through the rain-soaked grass till she stood by the grave.

"Hail to you, sister. Hail, Lady Jocelyn! Not to your mortal remains, which lie here, but to your immortal spirit, with which I spoke last night. Your wishes have been followed, Jocelyn; you lie in holy ground at last."

This speech wiped the grin off Alan's face. He started for Mrs. Hornbeak, who skipped nimbly aside without interrupting her cozy chat with the ghost of Lady Jocelyn. "Fear not, sister, I will impart to these skeptics the tidings you gave me. Rejoice in the sunshine and love of the hereafter with your wee babe—awk!"

She slipped but recovered herself, and I went in pursuit of Alan, who really looked as if he wanted to strangle the woman. The photographers were having a field day. Flashes exploded like fireworks.

It was Sheriff Jarboe who halted the farcical pursuit. Darting forward, he took Mrs. Hornbeak by the arm and stood between her and Alan. "Shame on the both of you," he said sternly. "Don't you know better than to act up at a time like this?"

"I came on an errand of love and mercy," Mrs. Hornbeak cried. "My messages have been unanswered, my offers of help ignored—"

"I don't care what you came for, lady; the fact is, you're guilty of trespass. Want I should arrest her, Senator?"

"No, no, of course not. I'm sure Mrs. Er-um's motives were of the best. If she will leave quietly I'll forget the whole thing."

"But I know where she once rested," Mrs. Hornbeak insisted. "I can show you the place—she wants you to know, you who are her descendants."

"If you don't shut that woman up, I will," Alan said, trying to get at Mrs. Hornbeak.

"You shut your own face, Professor, or I'll arrest you for creating a disturbance. Everybody out of here."

The undertaker wrung his hands. "But, Sheriff—"

"I don't mean you, Sam. Get on with it."

Alan shrugged. Thrusting his hands into his pockets he strode angrily toward the gate. One of the reporters hesitated, and then took off after him.

The others converged on Matt. "Please follow me to the house," he instructed. "I'll talk to you there. Julie . . ."

"Go on," I said. "I'll be there in a minute."

Mrs. Hornbeak was led away by Jarboe. The minister had made his escape somehow; I didn't blame him for wanting to distance himself from the proceedings. The

Danners had gone too. Mopping his brow, the undertaker followed the others. His assistants began to fill in the grave.

I stood watching them. The mist had thickened; drifting clouds of soft white veiled the ugly scene. The hollow thud of damp earth on the coffin was the only sound that broke the silence.

I wondered if she had been laid to rest in that ugly, ill-fitting dress. I hadn't thought about it before. Perhaps if I had, I would have done something, found a more becoming gown . . . Becoming to bleached bones and grinning skull? Cheap modern polyester trimmed with machine-made lace at so much a yard? But I might have searched the old trunks in the attic . . . Why hadn't I done that?

Because—the answer came swift and clear—because I didn't want to go there. Because I was afraid to climb the narrow, dusty stairs, afraid of awakening hurting memories—afraid of what I might, or might not, find.

"Whoever you were," I whispered, "I'm sorry . . . But none of this really matters, does it?"

I was beginning to sound just like Mrs. Hornbeak. I groped for a more formal epitaph, but nothing came to me. Rest in peace? I had no reason to suppose she did not. Matt's strange quotation came back to me. "Be buried in the rain . . ." At least it was appropriate. Rain is kinder than sunlight on the bowed heads of the mourners.

I went to the back of the house and sat on the porch communing with Elvis. He had better manners and better sense than most of the people I had seen that morning. I had heard voices, even laughter, from out in front, where Matt was entertaining the press and getting his picture taken on the steps of the family mansion. He'd make sure the photos didn't show the broken windowpanes and overgrown boxwood. It would be so easy to despise Matt, if it weren't for those occasional moments of communication. I liked him so much, when I didn't want to murder him.

Eventually the tumult and the shouting died. I continued to sit on the steps. I ought to do something about lunch. This was Mrs. Danner's day off and I owed Shirley some Martha-sitting time. I felt as shapeless and forlorn as the fog that hung over the trees. No wonder Matt had given in to the sheriff's request. He had seen a chance to get his name in the papers; for the ending to the bizarre story was bound to attract media attention. Alan was just as bad. He had sneered at Matt, but he had not avoided the photographers.

Shirley found me still sitting, with Elvis's head on my lap. "Here's where you're hiding. Miz Martha's having a fit. She wants to know what all the racket was about."

"Tell her to ask Matt."

"He left already."

"Damn him." I scrambled to my feet, pushing poor Elvis out of the way. "As usual, he's left me holding the bag. What are we going to tell Martha?"

"I don't know," Shirley said helpfully.

I went to the kitchen and started taking things out of the refrigerator. "I'm tempted to tell Martha the whole story. All this tender concern for her sensibilities—she doesn't have any, she's tough as steel."

"You want to take the responsibility, you go right ahead," Shirley said. "It's not my place to do it."

"Nor mine, I guess. Oh hell. Go home for a few hours, why don't you? I'll give Martha her lunch, such as it is, and tuck her in. I've nothing better to do anyway."

* * *

I told Martha part of the truth—that the people she had heard had been reporters and photographers, interviewing Matt about something to do with his campaign. She was more restless and agitated than usual, and when I started to tuck her in for her nap she shook her head in vigorous refusal.

"Do you want me to read?" I asked resignedly.

Another shake of the head. She wanted something from the shelves next to the fireplace.

I guess I've forgotten to mention that Martha's bedroom was as crowded as a pack rat's nest. It was spotlessly clean—Shirley and Mrs. Danner saw to that—but every drawer and shelf was crammed with odds and ends. Photograph albums, scrapbooks, boxes filled with clippings, other boxes filled with God-knows-what. Several of the scrapbooks were devoted to Matt's career. Until she had had her first stroke, Martha had kept them up to date.

She didn't want the scrapbooks. She didn't want this box or that one. I finally found the one she had in mind, an antique cookie tin, and handed it to her. Her nails scratched ineffectually at the lid.

I said, "Here, let me—" and reached for the box. Martha's claws closed over it. "No!"

"Okay, okay."

"Read."

When I looked up from the book a little later she was asleep, hands resting protectively on the tin box.

I dozed off too, lulled by the dripping rain and gloomy skies. Waking from a dream of fire—one of my recurrent worries in that old barn of a house—I realized that the siren ringing was that of the telephone. By the time I reached it, Martha was awake and cursing—or maybe not, her mumbles usually sounded as if she were swearing.

It was Matt. "Hi, Julie."

"You son of a—" I began, and broke off, seeing Martha's beady eye fixed on me.

"What's the matter?"

"What's the . . . We were sorry not to see you before you left. You and your buddies made a lot of noise. Martha was disturbed."

"What did you tell her?"

"The truth."

A gurgling noise at the other end of the wire made me feel better. I waited a few seconds before relieving his anxiety. "I couldn't tell her what it was all about. Your political machinations leave me baffled."

"Oh." He let out a sigh of relief. "I knew I could count on you, Julie."

Martha was waving her hands and mumbling. I said, "Martha wants to talk to you."

"Holy God, Julie!"

"Here." I handed Martha the phone and settled back to enjoy the proceedings.

Matt did most of the talking. I don't know what he said—I'm sure ninety percent of it was cover-up and the rest was a lie. When I retrieved the phone, Matt's first remark was, "I owe you one for that, Julie."

"I haven't begun to even the score, Matt."

"Why don't you buy a couple of air conditioners to-morrow? Tell them to send me the bill."

"Tell who? I think you're trying to bribe me, Matt."

"Me? Now, Julie, you know—"

"Forget it. What's on your mind?"

"Has that woman shown up?"

"You mean Mrs.—"

"Ssss!" The sound blasted my ear. He went on, "You're with Martha still, aren't you?"

"Yes."

"We don't want her to find out about Hornbeak."

I said, "Let me call you back. Where are you?"

"You can't call me back. I'm—er—at a friend's."

"You little devil," I said.

Matt ignored the comment. "She was very persistent. If she bothers you, call the sheriff. I wouldn't put it past her to break into the house—"

"Thanks. That makes me feel great."

"She's not dangerous, she's just a bloody nuisance. I don't want her bugging Martha, that's all."

"Well, I don't want her bugging me either. What do you suggest I do with her while I'm waiting for the sheriff to arrive?"

"Damn it, Julie, if you can't watch what you're saying in front of Martha, I can't talk to you. Just keep your eyes open, that's all."

He hung up before I could think of an appropriately withering response.

I turned to find Martha staring at me with a face like stone. She might have died between one breath and the next. Cursing my temper and my big mouth, I reached for her limp wrist.

Her fingers writhed like worms, clamping over my hand. "Who?" she mouthed. "Woman—who?"

The unexpected, painful strength of her grasp was another shock. I can lie with reasonable facility when I have time to concoct a story, but I'm not good at spontaneous invention.

"Uh," I said brilliantly. "Uh—er—nobody important. She calls herself a psychic or something like—"

Martha cackled. Her grasp relaxed and she pushed my hand away. "Hornbeak. Institute."

"Yes, right."

I should have expected Mrs. Hornbeak would have been in touch with Martha. Maidenwood had been the object of interest to a lot of people and institutions, from land developers to treasure hunters. Martha enjoyed running them off, threatening them with lawsuits. Since she knew so much, I couldn't see any harm in telling her the rest.

Her reaction was typical of her. "Gun," she said emphatically. "Shoot."

"Gun," I repeated. "That reminds me. What became of that shotgun you had?"

Martha's open eye narrowed suspiciously, so that it matched the other eye. I said guilefully, "I can't shoot her if I don't have a gun, can I?"

She hesitated, almost believing me. Then she muttered, "Gone. Not here. Get one."

I was half tempted to tell her about the dog, but decided to follow the path of least resistance. Elvis's presence might reassure her, or it might make her furious.

She kept muttering about shooting, and guns, and buckshot. Vindictive old witch . . . Didn't she realize that if I peppered a trespasser I could be sued—and I'd probably lose the case?

Suddenly she said something that brought my train of thought up short, like crashing into a boulder on the track.

"Bones. What did you do . . . bones?"

eight

I stopped breathing. Martha's fingers crooked and twitched. She looked as if she wanted to slap me, but lacked the strength. Her other hand fumbled at the box that now lay open on the bed beside her. It was filled with an untidy tangle of objects, mostly sewing materials—spools of thread, scraps of cloth. And newspaper clippings.

The clipping she indicated had not been neatly cut out. It was ripped and crumpled. She must have done it herself, struggling to overcome the handicap that had paralyzed one arm.

"You've known all along," I gasped. "Matt was so worried about your finding out . . . Why didn't you say something before this?"

Martha's lip curled. She never explained her actions or her failure to act. "Bones," she repeated insistently. "Where?"

I didn't know what to say so I sought refuge in the

truth. "We buried them in our cemetery," I said. "Nobody knew who they were or where they came from, so . . ."

The sounds coming from her parted lips froze my voice and sent chills coursing through my body. They resembled the screeching of rusty hinges, but after a while I realized she was laughing.

For once I was glad to return to Bleak House. It had been, to say the least, an unnerving ten minutes. Martha had been, for her, absolutely garrulous; she had asked questions and even answered a few. What had happened to shake her out of her customary close-mouthed habits? Could it have been something I said? She had only heard my side of the conversation with Matt, and I couldn't recall having made any startling pronouncements. Something about a woman coming to the house, causing trouble . . . When Martha found out it was Hornbeak I was talking about, she had appeared relieved. Was there some other woman she feared, as she did not fear the psychic? Then the sudden change of subject, from shotguns to skeletons, and her horrible, eerie laughter . . .

I didn't ask any more questions. I wasn't sure I wanted to know the answers.

That night I did not dream of skeletons. I dreamed I was six years old and Mother had taken me to a revival of *Snow White*. When the Wicked Queen turned into the Wicked Witch and cackled over the poisoned apple, her laughter sounded just like Martha's.

Sunday dawned dreary and wet. Shirley eschewed her flowery hat in favor of a raincoat with a pointed hood, in which she looked like a benevolent gnome.

"I hate to leave you alone all day," she said anxiously. "Are you sure—"

"I'm sure. Mrs. Danner will be here, and I haven't anything to do anyway. Run along. And, Shirley—"

"Yes?"

"Say a prayer for me. That I won't lose my cool and smother my grandmother."

Under the shadow of the hood her eyes shone like sunken stars. "I will."

She must have prayed. Mrs. Danner never showed up, and by late afternoon I was sorely tempted, not to smother Martha, but to run howling out into the fog. Only Shirley's arrival, late in the afternoon, saved me from self-destruction.

"You're back early," I said, restraining myself with difficulty from embracing her.

"Figured I should get here before dark. It's a miserable day—foggy and dark."

"I'll start dinner." I rose. Martha flapped her fingers.

"Sherry," she said, quite clearly. "Late. Coming soon . . ."

"She means the Judge," Shirley said. "It's his day."

I had forgotten. I hurried downstairs. Everything in the house was soggy with damp, except for a single box of crackers I'd had the foresight to put in the refrigerator. I smeared cheese on a few of them and arranged them on a plate. Four o'clock struck, but there was no sign of Judge McLendon. I began to think he wouldn't come. The weather was miserable. The fog had thickened as the day wore on; it pressed against the windows like white sheets hung out to dry. Even Elvis was depressed. He sat by the door moaning until I opened it, and then he slithered into the kitchen, crawled under the table, and lay down, his head on his paws. I didn't blame him for wanting company.

I had almost given the lawyer up when I heard the

sound of a car, and I went quickly to the door. The fog came in with him like a cloud of ectoplasm; the pallor of his face, his snow-white hair and white suit completed the ghostly image. I took his hand, not so much as a gesture of courtesy as to reassure myself that he was actually there, in the flesh. His hand was as cold and damp as that of the specter he resembled.

"You shouldn't have come," I said.

"Come now." He smiled. "Surely I don't look that bad."

"Oh no. I meant—the fog is so thick—driving must be hazardous."

"My eyes are as good as ever," he said firmly. A sudden fit of coughing spoiled the picture of good health; his shoulders shook, and he reached for a handkerchief. "I beg your pardon, Julie. A touch of bronchitis. Damp weather always brings it on, but it's nothing to worry about."

"I'll get the sherry."

"Thank you, my dear. Just what I need to clear my chest."

When I returned from the kitchen with the tray he was only halfway up the stairs, leaning heavily on the balustrade and pulling himself from step to step. I backed up and stayed out of sight until he had reached the landing, knowing he would be humiliated if I followed his difficult progress and bitterly offended if I offered an arm.

After I had arranged the wine and crackers on a table, Shirley accompanied me back downstairs. "He looks terrible," I said.

"Well, he's not a young man," Shirley said reasonably. She glanced at the shrouded window and shivered. "It sure isn't a fit night for man nor beast. Fit for . . . for other things . . ."

"For God's sake, Shirley, give me a break! I'm ready to

howl like a banshee already." Shirley smiled faintly, but did not reply. After a moment I said, "Do you believe in . . . other things, Shirley?"

"I don't believe in them," Shirley said. "I don't *not* believe in them, either. Especially on a night like this."

"Let's have a drink."

"You go ahead. Coffee's what I need; I'm so sleepy with this weather, I can't hardly keep my eyes open."

I put together a rather slapdash meal while she sat yawning over her coffee. Neither of us spoke; I couldn't think of a cheerful topic of conversation, and I certainly didn't want to discuss "other things" or the Judge's fragility. I had forgotten about Elvis, who was keeping very quiet under the table. Like all canny canines, he knew he could stay where he was, in the nice lighted, friendly kitchen, if he didn't remind anyone of his presence. Shirley had not seen him. When he rose to his feet, growling softly, she let out a shriek and I dropped the plate I was about to give her. The hamburger slid off onto the table and a shower of french fries flew into the air.

Close upon the dog's signal came a sound that echoed down the hall and through the kitchen door, which neither of us had remembered to close. A series of muffled thuds, followed by a final, louder thud . . . Shirley struggled to get out of her chair and I bolted for the door.

I knew what had happened before I reached the scene—that slow, painful ascent of the stairs should have warned me. I fully expected to see the old man sprawled lifeless on the floor, but when I got to him he was struggling to sit up.

"Lie still," I begged. "Don't move, let me—"

"I assure you—no damage done . . ." His smile was like the bared teeth of a death's head. "Clumsy of me. Lost my footing . . ."

Shirley knelt beside him. Her firm brown hands moved capably up his legs and over his chest. "Don't seem like anything's broken . . ."

"No, no. Just bruised." In a sudden, frightening burst of strength he escaped our hands and staggered to his feet. "You see? Fully recovered. So sorry to have worried you."

His color was so ghastly I would not have been surprised to see him drop at my feet. "You can't drive home after a shock like that," I exclaimed. "I had intended to ask you to stay anyway. Matt's bed is all made up—"

"No. No, thank you, child—I must go. I can't stay. I must . . . There are matters I must attend to tonight—at once."

Short of physically restraining him there was nothing I could do except continue to plead, which I did as I followed him to the door. He walked steadily, but I had a feeling—professional instinct or feminine intuition—that he was making an enormous effort to keep from collapsing. When he reached the door he turned and put his hand on my shoulder.

"You're a good girl, Julie," he said gently. "I hope—I am certain—that all will be well with you. Go upstairs now. Reassure Martha. Tell her . . . Tell her not to worry."

The door closed right in my face. By the time I opened it the car was already in motion.

I turned to Shirley. "I'm tempted to call the sheriff."

"He's driving all right."

The taillights were red blurs in the fog, but they held a steady course. They flared brighter as the car reached the road, and then disappeared.

"We shouldn't have let him go."

"Child, there wasn't nothing you could do to stop him. Now stop fretting. You're in a state of nerves tonight, and no wonder. I'd better get up to Miz Martha. She'll be thinking he broke his neck or something. You get on out to the kitchen and eat that hamburger—unless Elvis already ate it."

Elvis was under the table, looking angelically innocent. The hamburger was gone. I preferred to assume he had eaten it rather than blame its absence on . . . other things.

Come to think of it, his performance had been a bit on the uncanny side. He had moved and growled a moment before the Judge fell.

I told myself not to be absurd. The dog's keener ears had caught a sound mine had missed, a scuffle or a stifled cry of alarm.

I didn't feel like eating. I put another hamburger on to broil for Shirley and sat down at the table to finish my wine. Elvis put his head on my feet. The warm prickly weight felt good. I wished I could take him to my room. If I were awakened during the night, to hear howling in the woods and see fog shifting at the window like hollow-eyed, white faces looking in, it would be comforting to know he was there.

Out of the question, of course. But it gave me an idea. I got up and went into the hallway.

I had never had reason to investigate any of the closed rooms along the kitchen corridor. The first one turned out to be a pantry, the shelves empty of everything except spiders. The second and third were low-ceilinged and small; rain had beat through the broken windowpanes and rotted the floor boards.

I worked my way along the opposite side of the hall, back toward the kitchen. Another miserable little cubby hole—a servant's room, perhaps. The last room on that side was a small bathroom, antiquated but functional.

There was only one other door I had not opened, and for a while I thought I wasn't going to be able to open it. The door was not locked, though; it was only stuck. When I threw my weight against it, it suddenly gave way and I staggered a few steps forward before I could get my balance.

At first glance it was no different from the other rooms except that it was a little larger. In the foggy twilight, I could make out few details; there seemed to be something obscuring the window, like shutters or draperies, that cut off even the misty evening light.

I went back to the kitchen and got a flashlight. With its assistance I found the light switch. When I pressed it, nothing happened. I hoped the only problem was a dead or missing bulb, for if the wiring was faulty I wouldn't be able to use the room.

I don't know why I wanted to use it. If someone had asked me, I could have produced glib, rational reasons. I could keep Elvis with me at night. This room adjoined the bathroom. It was in no worse shape than the others . . . Perhaps this reasoning influenced my decision, but I don't think so. I simply knew, without hesitation or reservation, that this was where I had to be.

I'd have moved in that very night if the room had been habitable, but it really wasn't, not even by my relaxed standards of housekeeping. I decided I'd favor Mrs. Danner with the job of cleaning it. If I couldn't get rid of her, she might as well earn her keep.

I carried Martha's tray upstairs and sent Shirley down to have her supper. I was definitely out of sorts with Martha, and she did everything she could to push my temper to the breaking point. I had to cut her food for her, but she insisted on feeding herself, and a sloppy mess she made of it. After I had cleaned up, she ordered me to read.

The tin box she had been inspecting earlier was back on the shelf. That news clipping had been taken from the local paper, the weekly that came to us in the mail. The skeleton episode had occurred after Martha's first stroke, so someone must have brought the paper to her. It had been naive of me, and of Matt, to believe she would submit to being cosseted and coddled and kept in ignorance of what was going on in the world—especially in her own immediate world, where she ruled like a despot. And it was just like her to let us go on thinking we were getting away with our plan to protect her. No wonder she had howled with laughter—mocking my stupidity, proving that, though physically helpless, she was still in command. She had known all along. What else did she know? Had Matt's decision to allow excavation at Maidenwood been reported in the local paper?

I read on and on. Mr. Bucket, the great detective, drove the erring Lady Dedlock toward her doom. Esther wrung her hands and bleated platitudes. Martha drowsed and woke and drowsed again. " 'Miss Summerson,' said Mr. Woodcourt, 'if without intruding myself on your confidence I may remain near you, pray let me do so.' " Men didn't talk that way nowadays. And a damn good thing too, I thought. Or was it a good thing? A little kindness, a little courtesy . . . " 'Twas brillig, and the slithy toves/ Did gyre and gimble in the wabe . . .' "

Martha lay still. I finished the first couple of verses of "Jabberwocky" without arousing a protest. She was asleep. I tiptoed to the bed and bent over her.

Sound asleep and snoring—the harsh, difficult breathing of old age. Her eyes weren't quite closed. Between her folded lids shone narrow slivers of shining white eyeball.

The slits were not quite symmetrical; one was wider than the other. I thought, irrelevantly and cruelly, that she looked like a vampire—one of the undead, in her coffin, waiting for sunset before she rose to suck the blood of the living. She had derived pleasure from the pain of others. She was still doing it. Perhaps that was why the stroke that would have killed a weaker woman had left her with strength enough to fight back.

Shirley wasn't in her room. I went downstairs, stumbling with fatigue but too wakeful to sleep. For two cents I'd have dragged a mattress into the kitchen and sacked out there, with Elvis's wet muzzle in my face.

I expected Shirley would be in the kitchen, and she was; but she was not alone. Elvis was under the table and across the table from Shirley, slurping coffee like an old friend of the family, was Alan.

Shirley started guiltily when she saw me. "Oh Lord, Julie, I'm sorry. I didn't realize it was so late."

"You're not late, I'm early. Martha must have been tired. She conked out a few minutes ago."

"I'll go right up."

"Take your time. She's dead to the world. If you'll pardon the expression." I got a cup out of the cupboard.

Shirley murmured something unintelligible and made her escape. Smart woman, Shirley. Never explain, just walk out. She must have picked that up from Martha.

The kettle was still hot. I made a cup of coffee and pulled out a chair. Alan didn't move. Elvis twitched and whimpered in his sleep.

"Aren't you going to demand to know what I'm doing here?" Alan asked.

"No." I drank my coffee.

"Shirley and I are buddies."

"That doesn't surprise me."

"It doesn't?"

"You're good at making friends with people who can be useful to you." A gigantic yawn interrupted me before I could develop the insult. It hardly seemed worth the effort.

"My so-called charm didn't win Shirley," Alan said. "What won her heart was my offer of a commodity nobody else has bothered to provide—protection. I usually spend the night out there." He waved vaguely in the direction of the great outdoors, but I knew he had a more specific location in mind.

"The gardener's shed?"

"Oh, you found my lair, did you?"

"Mmmm."

"Unlike some people, I take my responsibilities seriously."

"So where were you the other night when I was confronting a maniacal handyman?"

The dramatic question fell flat. Apparently Shirley had spilled the beans.

"Sorry about that," Alan said calmly. "It was one of my nights off."

"Mmmm."

"I'll do better from now on."

"I wondered if it was you Danner saw. Assuming he was telling the truth about following a prowler."

"It wasn't me. Did you check the house to see if there were any signs of unlawful entry?"

I might have resented his hectoring tone if I hadn't been so tired—and if I hadn't been so grateful for his efforts. He must care a little, or he wouldn't spend his nights in that comfortless shed . . . Then, wearily, I told myself I was jumping to conclusions. He did take his responsibilities seriously. His actions meant no more than that.

"Alan, this house is such a wreck I couldn't tell if someone had broken in. Actually, I had the impression Danner was lying about seeing a prowler. Another funny thing—he was carrying a pair of scissors."

"Nasty weapon."

"Your sense of humor is as sick as Martha's." I didn't feel like explaining that slip of the tongue; before he could ask what I meant, I hurried on. "What would he want with scissors?"

"The logical conclusion is that he wanted to cut something."

"Oh, clever."

"Were they heavy scissors, like tin shears or metal clippers?"

"I don't think so. Just ordinary household scissors."

"Hmph," Alan said.

"Never mind about the scissors. Danner's mind works in ways incomprehensible to the normal world. Did you have any luck with your research? Any ideas as to where to excavate next?"

"A few," Alan said coyly.

"So don't tell me. I don't care. I think I'll go to bed."

"Not yet. I've had a few ideas about another subject that is of more immediate concern to you."

I sighed ostentatiously and propped my chin on my hand. "Proceed. There's no way of stopping you when you decide to deliver a lecture."

A lecture was just what I got.

"Maydon's Hundred was founded in 1619," Alan said. "And totally destroyed in 1622. The other towns and hundreds were resettled after the massacre. Not Maydon's.

The site was abandoned until your ancestor began the first manor house, a century later. In spite of your entertaining family legends, there was no connection between the inhabitants of Maydon's Hundred and the first Carr—except for the name Maidenwood, indicating a lingering tradition. Hey—wake up, I'm talking to you."

He jogged my elbow. Lulled by the familiar academic tone, I had fallen into a semidoze.

"I'm listening."

"The first manor house was destroyed in 1735. The present house was built on or near the foundations of the first one. I'm not much interested in either of the houses. What does concern me—and it should concern you and your dim-witted cousin—is where the original Carr burial ground was located. The earliest graves in the present cemetery date from the middle of the eighteenth century—contemporary with the second manor house. There must have been an earlier graveyard with burials dating from the building of the first house."

I was wide awake now. "You think that's where the skeletons came from?"

"The connection is unproved, but logically seductive. A lost cemetery and bones from a lost grave. What I don't understand is why the earlier cemetery was abandoned."

"It's a good question . . . Oh my God!" I started upright, kicking Elvis, who woke with a yelp. "Under the house! It's the only explanation, Alan; they couldn't go on using the old graveyard because they put the house—"

Alan burst out laughing. "You've been seeing too many horror films. Get it out of your head, Julie. There was no break in occupation between the destruction of the first house and the building of the second. The location of the cemetery would not be forgotten, and people weren't that callous about the remains of their kin. Besides, how could the jokers who found the skeletons get to them if they were under the house? Your grandmother is old, but she would have noticed if people were digging in the basement night after night."

"Oh." I wiped perspiration off my forehead. "It's getting hot in here."

"It's cooler, if anything. You're the one who is uptight. Shirley is spooked tonight too. What's the matter?"

"Nothing's the matter. I've had a tedious day. And there are . . . things out there."

"You're drunk," Alan said.

"Not yet. But I'm considering it. This weather isn't exactly soothing. Was that an owl I just heard or a vampire?"

"Owl. Good hunting weather."

"There *are* things out there," I said. "Cute characters who think it's funny to dress up dry bones and leave them littering the road. Crazy people like Mrs. Hornbeak. I wouldn't put it past her to want to dig in the basement."

"I ran her and her crew off the property not long ago."

"You what?"

Alan grinned reluctantly. "The stupidity of the woman is only equaled by her effrontery. They drove right in along the track we've been using. Flashlights and lanterns all over the place, pickaxes and shovels . . ."

"I didn't hear anything." I leaned down and stared at Elvis, who yawned. "What were you doing while all this was going on, noble dog?"

"It happened before you adopted him," Alan said. "Acquiring that dog is the smartest move you've made. Why don't you put the old lady in a nursing home and get the hell out of here?"

"You know how she is."

"Yes, I have good cause to know how she is. What I have never understood is why the rest of you let her bully you. For Christ's sake, Julie, she's eighty-five years old and she has never been quite sane. Matt has considerable influence; why can't he have her declared incompetent and get her into a hospital?"

"I don't think that's any of your business."

"I guess not," Alan said.

"You just want her out of the way so you can have a free hand. You and your Lady Jocelyn—"

"I don't know why you want to drag her into this."

"Neither do I." I put my head between my hands. Elvis, sensing my mood, began to lick my ankles. "I'm sick and tired of virginity," I mumbled.

Alan's smothered gasp of laughter made me realize what I had said. I felt my cheeks burn. When I looked at him he had his face under control, except for his eyes, which shone with amusement.

"I didn't mean that the way it sounded," I explained haughtily.

"What did you mean?"

"The motif—the—the theme. Isn't that one definition of the very word 'maiden'—a woman who hasn't lost that oh-so-precious commodity men make such a fuss about?"

"Well, I wouldn't say—"

"They *used* to make a fuss about it, anyway. Brand the Scarlet Woman, drive the erring daughter out into the snowstorm . . . Look at your Lady Jocelyn. One of the main fascinations of that story is the virginity angle. If she had been a widow with five children, nobody would give a damn about her. Including Mrs. Hornbeak."

"I don't know what you're so excited about," Alan said mildly. "I agree with you on every point, from the absurdity of the virginity fetish to the stupidity of Polly H. The skeletons can't possibly be those of Jocelyn Cartwright and her baby; they aren't that old. They may have come from the original cemetery of Maidenwood. Though I am only peripherally interested in the remains of that period, I am willing to turn my complete attention to the location of the cemetery, if only to prevent other people from looting it and possibly threatening you and Shirley."

"And Martha."

"She doesn't need me," Alan snapped. "She's got you and Shirley ready to die in her defense. I can't do the job, though. Matt has thrown too many barriers in my way."

"I'll talk to Matt."

"Good luck. I tried that."

"I said I'd talk to him." Far off in the dark night a faint cry rose and fell. I shivered. "Damn owls."

"That wasn't an owl."

Alan got to his feet. The dog was already at the door, whining and scratching. Alan said, "Quiet, Elvis." He took a piece of rope from his pocket and attached it to the dog's collar.

I followed the pair, man and dog, on to the porch. Elvis tugged at the leash but obeyed Alan's low-voiced command to refrain from barking.

The weather was clearing. Fog lay along the river meadows like a pale carpet, but in the black reaches of the sky, stars shone incandescently. Lower down, there were other lights—half blurred by the mist that lingered among the trees on the ridge north of the house, fluttering like will-o'-the-wisps—the dead man's lanterns.

"Son of a bitch," Alan muttered, and trotted off, towed by Elvis.

I stopped to close the porch door before I followed. I had to run like crazy to catch up with Alan, which I did at the start of the path leading to the cemetery. The lights were east of the path, between the ridge and the river.

Alan didn't order me back to the house; he only muttered, "Don't make any more noise than you can help." After that he ignored me, letting me climb over a rotten section of fence and snag my pants on rusty barbed wire without offering a helping hand.

The owls were hooting and the mist swirled along the ground, but I felt a hundred percent better than I had all day. In spite of the eerie appearance of the drifting lights, I knew they were human in origin. The only thing that puzzled me was the boldness of the invaders; they didn't seem to be concerned about their lights being seen, and as we came closer I heard voices. Surely trespassers wouldn't be so open. Could it be a search party, looking for a missing child?

I should have known. Alan knew; restraining the eager dog, he marched into the clearing where the group was assembled, and though his voice was not raised above its normal speaking level, it stopped conversation. "I warned you once, Mrs. Hornbeak. This time I'm calling the police."

Mrs. Hornbeak had changed from her pinstripe suit into riding breeches and knee boots. She must have copied the outfit from an old lithograph showing turn-of-the-century archaeologists; she even wore a pith helmet. Her glasses flashed as she greeted Alan, brandishing a shovel with an enthusiasm that made him retreat a few steps.

"Just in time to share the great moment," she exclaimed. "I bear no malice, Professor; those of us on the path are above petty revenge, and I invite you to join me—"

"You're trespassing," Alan said.

Mrs. Hornbeak leaned picturesquely on her spade. "You have no authority to evict me, Professor."

"She does." Alan pushed me forward.

"Ah, Miss Newcomb." Mrs. Hornbeak nodded familiarly. "I intended to call on you in the morning. How much more fitting that you should be present when we disinter the remains of your ancestors!"

She indicated the muddy hole beside her. Two of her cohorts stood nearby; one held a trowel, the other a shovel. A flash went off in my face as I stepped forward.

I knelt by the hole. One of the cohorts obligingly turned his flashlight into the depths. Odd shapes made lumps and bulges under a thin layer of dirt. Other shapes protruded, pale against the surrounding soil.

I couldn't bring myself to look at Alan. "It's a grave, all right," I said. "Those are human ribs."

Another flash blinded me. Mrs. Hornbeak had brought several assistants to do the actual digging, but at least some of the people in the clearing were newspapermen. The fat was in the fire and sizzling merrily.

nine

Mrs. Hornbeak wasn't intimidated by Alan or by me, but she was afraid of dogs. Alan used Elvis, who was more pleased to oblige, to run the woman and her crew off the property. The reporters were not so easy to disperse, but after a rain of "No comments" from Alan, they decided to follow the more cooperative interviewee. They didn't even get "No comment" out of me, only muffled, inarticulate grunts. I didn't dare open my mouth for fear I'd laugh. The situation was so horribly, comically grotesque I almost felt sorry for Alan. All his scientific study and intelligent research had come up empty, while Mrs. Hornbeak's dippy excursions into the infinite had led her straight to the gold. Even a nonexpert like me could tell that the grave she had found was old. The bones were fragile and discolored, and there was no trace of a coffin. So maybe Mrs. Hornbeak wasn't that dippy after all.

Alan sent me back to the house with Elvis. He stayed, brooding over the grave like a vulture. Before I went to bed I called the number he had given me and asked for

Jono. I explained what had happened; Jono said incredulously, "You're kidding."

"I'm not kidding. She found something, Jono. Alan is out there now, and he wants—"

"I'll be there in half an hour."

I passed on the rest of Alan's instructions. Jono could hardly wait to get off the phone and get going. The last thing I heard from him was a rapturous "Hot damn! This could be it!"

Alan had also suggested—by which I mean ordered—that I telephone the police. I decided that call could wait until morning. I was in no mood to explain the situation to a sleepy cop, and I doubted Mrs. Hornbeak would return that same night. She'd be too busy talking to reporters.

I should have done what Alan told me. I was awakened by Shirley shaking my shoulder. "There's some people down there, Julie. Reporters."

I sat upright. Sunlight blinded me. "What time is it?"

"Eight o'clock. One of 'em's been there since six. I tried to let you sleep, but—"

"I'll get up. Give me a minute."

"I brought you some coffee."

I grabbed the cup. "You're a saint, Shirley. Call the sheriff and tell him we're under siege. I'll go down as soon as I put on some clothes."

"Did something happen last night? Don't tell me there was more—"

"No, nothing like that. I'll explain later—just make that call, will you please?"

I scrambled into pants and shirt and sneakers, and trotted downstairs. The front door was closed. I opened it. "I just called the police," I said.

The invasion consisted of one balding middle-aged

man. Apparently the others had given up or gone after Alan.

"How did you feel—" he began.

"Is that the only question you people can ask? Look, there's an old lady upstairs recuperating from a stroke. She needs peace and quiet. Why don't you give her a break?"

The reporter looked thoughtful. I made sure he understood the implications. "What paper did you say you were from? I mean, I want to know whom to sue if she has another stroke."

I closed the door before he could think of a counterargument. Looking through the window, I was pleased to see him retreat to the end of the drive. There was nothing I could do about that; the road was public property.

I was dying to get out to the site and see what Mrs. Hornbeak's discovery looked like in daylight. Maybe I had been misled by the general air of rapture; maybe she had only uncovered the carcass of a horse or a deer. I doubted it, though.

Shirley didn't respond to my suggestion that she go and see what was happening. She had no interest in archaeology. "I don't care about bones so long as they stay where they're supposed to be," was her summary of the situation, and I had to admit she had a point.

The law didn't appear until almost midday. I was in the kitchen making Martha a sandwich when I heard the knock at the front door. I greeted Jarboe with reproaches.

"What kind of service is this? I called almost four hours ago."

"They been bothering you?"

"Well, no, not lately. But no thanks to you and your men."

"That's not what I come about."

"What did you come about, then?"

"Judge McLendon. He's dead."

"No," I said. "He can't be. I saw him last night."

"Well, he is." The sheriff scratched his head. "Can I come in the house?"

I said dazedly, "Sure. I'm sorry. I can't believe it. Damn, damn, damn! I should have made him stay here. He wasn't fit to drive in the fog, after that fall—"

"Fall?" The sheriff followed me to the kitchen and sat down at the table.

"He tumbled down the stairs in the front hall. I tried to persuade him to stay all night—"

"That accounts for the bruises, then. Got a cup of coffee, Julie?"

"Sure." Then I realized what he had said. "Bruises . . . Wasn't it a car accident?"

"No, he got home all right. Don't blame yourself on that account. It was a heart attack. He lives alone; it was his first client that found him this morning, slumped over his desk."

"That doesn't make me feel any better." I filled two cups and joined him at the table.

"Maybe this will." Jarboe took a folded sheet of paper from his jacket pocket. "He was writing you a letter."

The handwriting was quite firm, with none of the tremulousness one associates with old age. "My dear Julie," it began. "I must apologize for startling you as I did this evening by my clumsiness. As I assured you, there was no damage done except to my pride. Please tell Martha I will see that her wishes are carried out to the best of my . . ."

The final "y" trailed off and ended in a ragged gouge. It was surrounded by ink spatters, like flecks of blood around a wound.

"He was always writing people notes," the sheriff said, averting his eyes from my stricken face. "Old-fashioned habit of his."

"I see."

"His heart was bad. He knew it; told me once the doc was after him to retire, but he wanted to die in harness, not rotting away in a nursing home. He got his wish. You could say he was lucky."

"You could say that." I folded the letter. "I'm sorry, Sheriff, I didn't mean to get teary, but—well, I liked him. He was a good man, and a kind man. I don't know how I'm going to break it to Martha. She'll be devastated."

"I wouldn't be too sure of that. Old people are peculiar about friends dying. Oh, they're grieved, sure, but there's a kind of funny satisfaction too—like they won another round by surviving."

If that was true of old people in general, it would be particularly true of Martha. She'd be annoyed, though. McLendon had handled all her legal affairs.

"Have you notified Matt?" I asked. "I suppose he'll have to find another lawyer."

"Called him a couple of hours ago. He said to tell you not to worry about the business end, he'd deal with that. He'll call you this evening to find out how Miz Martha took the news."

I thought of several replies to this cool announcement but decided I would save them for Matt. "Is there anything I can do?" I asked.

"No, thanks. Just thought you ought to know, seeing as I was coming out this way anyhow. Don't worry about reporters, this story will die in a day or two. It's pretty small potatoes."

"What you're telling me is that you can't spare a man to patrol the place."

" 'Fraid not. What I can do is put up a barricade at the entrance."

"How am I supposed to get out?"

"Oh, it'll be something you can move—a sawhorse, like, with a 'No Trespassing' sign. There's no way you can wall this place off, Julie; all you can do is create a moral effect. Your pal the archaeologist has things under control in his work area—ropes, signs, and a couple of husky kids with spades standing around looking aggressive."

I had hoped for more but I knew I wasn't going to get it. He was probably right about the news being a purely overnight sensation. So I thanked him and showed him out, and then went up to tell Martha her old friend was dead.

I held her hand when I told her. The pulse under my fingers didn't skip a beat or change tempo. There was a cry of surprise and distress, but it didn't come from Martha. Turning, I saw Shirley in the doorway of the bathroom that connected her room with Martha's. I said, "I'm sorry," and it was to her I spoke.

She shook her head dumbly. Tears filled her eyes.

Martha twitched her hand from my grasp. "Note," she said. "Note?"

"It was a heart attack, not suicide," I said. "People don't leave . . . Oh." She of all people would know of the old man's note-writing habit. Perhaps he had told her he would write her that evening.

"He was writing to me," I said, taking the paper from my shirt pocket. "But there is a message for you."

She read it without the slightest sign of emotion. Perhaps the corner of her mouth lifted a fraction of an inch, but that was all. The sheriff was right. Under her grief was a kind of satisfaction.

"Matt," she said. "Get him here."

"He said he'd call this evening. It's hopeless trying to reach him during the day, Martha. I know; I've tried."

"Hmph," said Martha, quite emphatically, and for once I agreed with her.

When I went downstairs to retrieve a somewhat wilted sandwich, Mrs. Danner was there. "What happened to you yesterday?" I demanded.

"Truck broke down."

No apology, no expression of regret. I said, "If you had called, I'd have picked you up."

"Weather was bad."

"Not that bad."

Mrs. Danner stared.

I abandoned the inquisition, wishing I could decide whether Mrs. Danner was abysmally stupid, or smart enough to know how to defend herself against such assaults. "I've got a job for you," I said. "I want the room next to the kitchen cleaned. Here, I'll show you."

The room was hardly brighter by daylight than it had been the night before. The windowpanes were opaque with dirt. Mrs. Danner stood watching as I struggled to raise the window. Finally it shuddered up; I propped it with the stick lying in the sill, and then I saw something the dirty glass had obscured. There were bars on the window—thick iron bars, set in a grilled frame that had been nailed or screwed onto the outside of the frame.

The sight of them made me feel easier about sleeping downstairs. Nobody would get in that window, at any rate. Perhaps the other rooms on the remote ground floor corridor also had barred windows. I hadn't looked.

I turned to Mrs. Danner. "You had better start by sweeping the floor. I want it and the walls scrubbed—get off as much of the old wallpaper as you can, half of it's hanging in strips anyway. The windows and woodwork need washing too."

Mrs. Danner put one foot forward, and then pulled it back, as if she had stepped on something slimy. She shook her head.

"What's the matter?" I asked impatiently. "You don't do windows?"

Her head kept moving mechanically from side to side. "I do windows real good. But I don't like . . ."

I didn't interrupt; her voice just trailed off into echoing silence.

I was in no mood to be patient with Mrs. Danner's vagaries. "I know it's a filthy mess, but the longer you stand there gaping, the longer it will take to get the job done. Where's the broom?"

I practically had to push her into the room. She kept glancing from side to side like a nervous animal who scents a hunter hidden in ambush. Once inside, she seemed to resign herself to the inevitable. She began sweeping while I carried in a ladder from the shed and replaced the light bulb in the ceiling fixture. It worked. That was a relief, though I had been prepared to make do with flashlights and electric lanterns if necessary.

I left Mrs. Danner to get on with it, hoping she wouldn't turn tail the minute I walked out of the house. She was obviously not a happy woman, but I couldn't figure out what was bugging her. Nor, to be honest, did I really care.

I changed into work clothes and reminded myself again to buy some boots. When I went out the back door, Elvis rose from his rug and ran to greet me.

The sound of voices led Elvis and me to the site. There was no path from the direction of the house, and it took a long time for me to get through the underbrush, since I had to untangle the dog's leash every few steps. When I emerged into the clearing I was immediately accosted by a large young man, Willkie-type, who politely but firmly asked me to go away.

"It's okay," Jono called. "She's one of us. Over here, Julie."

The opened grave had been refilled. Only a square of blank dirt indicated its presence. "I thought you'd have the bones out by now," I said.

"Good Lord, no. There's a week's work here before we can start digging. Actually, Julie, there's nothing for you to do unless you want to help clear the brush. Alan didn't say anything about you . . ."

"Where is he?"

"In Richmond, getting some more equipment and starting the paperwork. The Commonwealth has laws about disturbing human remains; it'll take several days to get a court order. We've got to clear the site and survey it, lay out a grid, sink some test holes . . ."

"It seems to me you're going to a lot of trouble without being certain you have something to take trouble for. Wouldn't it be smarter to sink your test holes first?"

Jono shook his head. His eyes were shining. "I saw it, Julie—last night, before we filled it in. We've found it. It's the right period."

"You're sure?"

"I can't show it to you; Alan took it with him. A tinned brass hook, the kind used on clothing around 1600–1650."

"Then this is it. Maydon's Hundred."

A veil dulled Jono's sparkling eyes as professional caution moved in to cool his excitement. "Well, we can't be sure, not until we find some evidence of occupation. But the grave is definitely of the right period, and he wouldn't have been stuck out in the woods, miles from the settlement."

"He?"

"The hook was used to hold men's pants to their doublets."

"I see. Well, if manual labor is all you have to offer, I can find plenty of that elsewhere. I'll drop in again tomorrow."

"One of us will be here all the time from now on," Jono said. "So don't worry about trespassers."

"What about your job?"

"I haven't quit yet. But I hope to soon."

"I see," I repeated.

Alan's big problem, aside from Martha's intransigence, had been money. It was a classic dilemma for archaeologists; without results there was no funding, without funding the chance of getting results was lessened. Alan was the world's fastest talker, but even he couldn't build a convincing case out of nothing. With a grave and a seventeenth-century gizmo, he could probably con some foundation or university into backing the dig. Once he got the money, he could afford to pay his staff and hire others.

I wished him well. If he got a big grant, I would demand wages too.

So I spent the afternoon scrubbing dirt off walls and floors instead of digging it out of a grave. Prodded and assited by me, Mrs. Danner accomplished wonders.

The end result was still not very attractive. The woodwork was blistered and cracked, and the dingy old wallpaper had peeled off in long strips, except where it refused to come off at all. At least the room was habitable.

I left Mrs. Danner washing the window and went upstairs to reconnoiter for a bed. When I reached the head of the stairs Martha's door opened and Shirley came out.

"Goodness, what have you been up to?" she asked. "You never got that kind of dirt on you out in the woods."

I explained what I had been up to. Shirley looked dubious. "I don't know what Miz Martha will say."

"I don't intend to tell her. We can rig up some kind of signal system—a cowbell, if I can't find anything better—so you can summon me in case of an emergency. Never mind that now; what the hell am I going to make for supper, Shirley? I'm completely out of ideas."

"That's what I was going to tell you. *He* called a while back. Said to tell you he was coming about six, and he'd bring some fried chicken."

"Matt?" The suggestion didn't sound like him, so I was not surprised when Shirley shook her head.

"Alan. He's a devil, that boy. Didn't give me a chance to say yes, no, or maybe, just told me."

Beware of archaeologists bearing gifts. But when the gift is edible and you are extremely sick of domesticity . . . "Sounds great," I said. "I had better clean myself up. Is she all right?"

"Kind of restless. Been looking at old pictures and papers this afternoon. She keeps nagging at me to call Matthew again. Well, I tried, and left a message, and they told me the same thing. He'll telephone tonight."

"I suppose he has a lot to do," I admitted. "The Judge was handling all Martha's affairs. But I still think Matt ought to come out here."

Shirley wisely refused to comment.

After I had cleaned up, I scouted the bedrooms. All I really needed was a bed and a table and chair, and maybe a lamp. I found a small table and took it down. Mrs. Danner was still washing the window. I pried her away from it and set her to scrubbing the table. The outside of the window was still dirty. There was no way of getting at it through the bars, but enough light came in to convince me that I couldn't stand those scabby walls after all. There was just enough time to run to the shopping center and buy a couple of gallons of paint. Yellow, I thought. The room was dark, with only one narrow window.

When I looked in my purse I found I only had about twenty dollars. I'd have to tap Matt for more money for expenses. And had there not been some vague talk of a salary? I added another damn to the pile I was heaping on my cousin, and informed Mrs. Danner I was going out.

Elvis decided to come along. I wasn't keen on leaving him with Mrs. Danner, though I believed my lecture had had the desired effect—and, perhaps more significantly, the "pockabook" had not reappeared. As we drove along, with Elvis's ears flapping in the breeze, I wondered how I had existed so long without a dog.

The man in the hardware store was willing to take my credit card, so that still left me with twenty dollars. I ducked into the grocery store. Elvis ate dog munchies and I ate cookies all the way home, crunching in chorus.

My nice big cans of paint made me itch to start on the walls, but I controlled myself; it was almost six, and I knew from past experience that painting is fun for the first hour. After that, it isn't. Anyhow, the best time would be in the morning, so that the paint smell would have a chance to dissipate before I went to bed.

The table I had brought downstairs was standing in the middle of the kitchen, where Mrs. Danner had left it. A cheap rickety affair of painted green pine, it was still damp from her scrubbing. I carried it into my new room. The place looked even emptier with that single piece of furniture in it.

I was scraping wallpaper when Alan arrived. Scraping wallpaper has a bizarre, hypnotic fascination; once you get started it's hard to stop. Alan walked right in the back door without knocking; only Elvis's rapturous whines warned me of his arrival.

There were two brown paper bags on the table, and Alan was taking out cartons of food. "Put this in the oven to keep warm," he ordered.

"Don't you ever say please?"

"Please put this in the oven."

I put it in the oven. "Want a drink?"

"You talked me into it. What are you doing with that?"

The scraper was covered with flakes of white plaster and scraps of wallpaper. I decided not to put it on the kitchen table.

"Scraping wallpaper, obviously. I'm going to move into that room next to the kitchen."

"Any particular reason?"

"To make it more convenient for burglars and rapists to get at me, of course."

"Mmmm," Alan said absently. "Not a bad idea."

"What, making it easier for burglars and—"

"Moving downstairs. You'll hear the dog if he barks, and you'll be closer to me if you need help. I won't be sleeping in the shed tonight, though."

"What are you going to do, camp by the grave?"

"Right."

"Nice cheerful place."

"It's no worse than any other place. I didn't expect you of all people to be so spooky about a few bones."

"Me, spooky? Listen, buster, I just finished anatomy. There isn't a bone in the human body I don't know by its first name."

"That's what I meant. Where do you keep the liquor?"

"Under there. No, there."

Alan took out my two bottles. "What, no fine vintage wines? Never mind, they'd be wasted on me. But you'll have to hide the liquor if you want to keep Mrs. Danner from tippling."

"She does drink on the sly, then. I wondered."

"If you were married to Joe, you'd drink on the sly too. I hear she used to be the toast of the town, the belle of the bars. Big, cheerful, laughing woman, with a vocabulary like a truck driver."

"I remember her. She sure has changed." I took the glass he handed me.

"She didn't change, he changed her. And himself. Finding Jesus can have a revolting effect on some people."

"That's an awful thing to say."

"I'm not blaming it on Jesus," said Alan, compounding the blasphemy. "Danner scares me. He's one of the reasons why I've been sleeping in the shed."

"Thanks for cheering me up, Alan."

"Oh, I don't think he'll bother you." I didn't care for the faint emphasis on "think"; before I could protest, Alan went on, "Danner is a bigot and a sadist, and religious mania takes peculiar forms."

"Like writing crank letters?"

"Yes, like that. After he kicked his daughter out of the house he apparently made a bonfire of everything she owned—which wasn't much, poor kid—and almost set the barn on fire. He's stupid as well as sadistic, and that combination can be dangerous."

"How do you know all this?"

"I frequent the local taverns," Alan said with a grin. "You think women are the only ones who gossip? To revert to the original topic—"

"I don't remember what it was."

"Bones," Alan said. "Anatomy. Why didn't you tell me you had studied with Kaufman?"

"Because the subject never came up. Because it's none of your business. And," I said, warming to my theme, "because I might have known you'd find out anyway. What the hell is the idea of checking my credentials?"

Alan ignored the question. "You're not qualified, of course. But at the moment I can't afford an anthropologist. I have a job for you."

"Paid or volunteer?"

Alan blinked. "I might be able to scrape up a few bucks."

Honesty forced me to admit the truth. "Alan, if you're talking about the skeleton you found last night, you were right the first time; I am definitely not qualified to tackle something like that. Those bones are so fragile they'll crumble if you try to lift them. I don't know how—"

"Oh, I can deal with that," Alan said confidently. "That's a simple matter of preservation. I had something else in mind for you."

"What?"

Instead of answering he reached into one of the paper bags. He used both hands; his long, blunt fingers and broad palms half covered the object he drew out, and since I was thinking in terms of food, for one wild moment I thought he was holding a cauliflower. A distorted, peculiarly shaped cauliflower . . .

Fortunately for me—not so fortunately for her—Shirley chose that moment to walk into the room. Her shriek drowned my gasp of surprise. Alan started. "Damn it," he exploded, juggling the skull.

Finally he got a firm grip on the thing. With a reproachful look at Shirley he said, "You shouldn't have startled me. It's fragile; would have shattered if I had dropped it."

"Don't put it on the table," I said squeamishly.

"Why not? It's nice clean plaster."

He propped the skull against one of the grocery bags. It grinned whitely at Shirley, who retreated a step. "Perfect copy," Alan said, regarding the grisly object affectionately. "I've still got the mold, but making another one would be a devil of a job. It's not really plaster, but one of those new synthetics."

"I don't care what it's made out of," Shirley said. "Just you take it with you when you go. I come down to get Miz Martha's supper and see you waving that thing around . . . Good thing I come, too. What's wrong with you, child, putting that paper in the oven? I could smell burned cardboard all the way upstairs."

She whisked the charred container out of the oven.

"I hadn't forgotten about it," Alan said in injured tones. "That's the way I always heat it. The chicken isn't burned."

"Hmph. I think I'll take my supper with Miz Martha tonight. No, you stay sitting, Julie—I'll just get a couple of plates and then you two can enjoy your meal. You got company already, so you don't need mine."

"Ouch," Alan said. "Here, Shirley, I got biscuits and cole slaw and potato salad."

Shirley watched him warily when he reached into the bag, but all he took out were a few plastic containers. She filled the plates and left.

Alan pushed the container of potato salad toward me and picked up a chicken leg. "That's the job," he said, waving the leg at the skull. "Reconstruction. You know the technique, don't you?"

"I watched Kaufman do it. Would you mind putting that out of sight while I eat?"

"I thought you might like to study it while you chewed."

I informed him he was mistaken. With a shrug he returned the cast to its bag. "Can you do it?" he asked.

"I'd need the reference tables."

"I can get them for you."

"Materials—"

"Those too. What have you got to lose, Julie? It's just an experiment. Good experience for you."

He knew I was tempted. Reconstruction is one of the most evocative techniques of anthropology—the restoration of musculature and flesh to dry bones, the re-creation of a face from its underlying structure. Two German scholars were the first to approach the problem scientifically, back in 1898; their paper included a series of tables that gave the average thickness of soft tissue at various points on the human face. The results could only be approximations; the measurements varied according to age and sex and a number of other factors. But some of the results had been astonishing; in one case Kaufman had mentioned, reconstruction had enabled a murder victim to be recognized and identified.

I remembered how Kaufman had gone about it. He had worked on molds too. Measuring out from the established points, setting his markers—he had used pencil erasers—then building up layers of clay, following the curves of the bones to the limits designated by his markers. He had completed the process by painting the plaster, adding false eyelashes and glass eyes, a wig. Building a person. I had always thought it must make you feel like Dr. Frankenstein.

"I could try," I said.

"Good." Alan took another piece of chicken.

"Why?"

"What do you mean, why?"

I touched the paper bag. "This is from the skeleton Joe Danner found, isn't it?"

"Right."

"You and your pathologist friend talked Jarboe into having a cast made before the bones were buried. No reason why he shouldn't agree to a request like that. But why reconstruction? That's your idea, not Jarboe's. And don't give me that bull about knowledge for its own sake. What you're proposing is time-consuming and complex. Why are you so curious about what she looked like?"

For a moment Alan concentrated on his chicken. Then he said, "I don't suppose you have seen today's paper."

"No. We only get the local weekly."

Alan reached into one of the bags and produced another item—the *Pikesville Bulletin,* dated that morning. It took me a few minutes to find the story. The headlines concerned the latest disasters in Africa and South America, and the latest presidential lies about the deficit. In a box at the bottom of the page was a smaller headline. "Grave of Virginia legend found by psychic investigator. Lady Jocelyn was real! See page C-1."

I turned the pages. The story was featured in the Style section, first page, and the first thing I saw was a photo of myself, glaring at the camera. My hair stood out in a frizzly bush and my eyeballs reflected the flash. The caption under the picture read, "Julia Newcomb, Lady Jocelyn's descendant, at her ancestress's grave."

"Oh, hell," I said.

"Read on," Alan said.

There were photographs of Alan, and of Mrs. Hornbeak, shovel in hand. Elvis was in one of them. He photographed better than any of us. Mrs. Hornbeak had had her revenge. The discovery was (correctly, I must admit) attributed to her. She claimed to have been in touch with Lady Jocelyn, "the aristocratic beauty who fled the lust of a royal favorite to find love and freedom in the New World." But the grave Mrs. H. had uncovered was not that of the Lady. Jocelyn's violated sepulcher was nearby; from it she had been wrenched by impious hands, and although she had found rest among her descendants, she wanted the world to know the truth and save her friends who rested near her from a like fate . . .

The real kicker was in the final paragraph. Even Mrs. Hornbeak's purple prose paled by comparison to the revelation contained therein. The newspaper fell from my hand. "She's offering to finance the dig?" I exclaimed.

"You got it."

"But she—you—where does she get her money?"

Alan wiped his greasy fingers carefully on a napkin. His neatness was an ominous sign, but he had his temper well in hand. "The organization she heads is loaded. There are a lot of rich nuts in the world."

"But she—you . . . You aren't going to accept the offer, surely."

"I'm trying to get funding. So far this is the only offer."

"You can't. It would ruin you."

"Not if I found Maydon's Hundred."

The depth of his obsession was greater than I had realized. But for once I was right and he was wrong. If he found the remains of Lost Atlantis or the Fountain of Youth, it would still be the end of his career. In the eyes of the academic world, the results would be hopelessly flawed by the nature of the expedition's funding.

"You can't do it," I said.

"Do you want to help me avoid it?"

"Well—yes."

"Then do that reconstruction for me."

I thought I understood what he had in mind. The basis of Mrs. Hornbeak's claim was Lady Jocelyn. Anyone with an ounce of sense knew the forlorn skeleton could not be hers, but bare bones have no identity. Put the reconstructed face on view, next to the famous miniature of the Lady, and Mrs. Hornbeak's error would be demonstrated by a display worth more than a thousand words. And if the reconstruction was clever enough, it might attract the attention and the funding Alan wanted. Most people, even learned foundations, are more attracted to pretty copies than ruined originals.

"You're on," I said. "The works—false eyelashes and all."

Alan nodded. He had known all along he had me hooked. "Are you going to eat any more?" he asked, reaching for the last piece of chicken.

"I haven't had any of it yet," I said, grabbing the piece from him. My appetite and my good humor were restored. He thought he was using me, but I had a few axes to grind as well. If the reconstruction was good, it wouldn't do me any harm to get my name in the papers. Besides, this was a chance to do something requiring skill and intelligence—something I needed, after two weeks of bedpans and *Bleak House*.

And it would put Lady Jocelyn to rest forever.

Alan insisted on leaving the cast with me. He also insisted on knowing where I intended to keep it; he didn't want to risk damage or loss. At first I couldn't think what to do with the damned thing. The kitchen was out of the question; Shirley had already indicated she hoped never to see the cast again, and if Mrs. Danner came upon it in the course of her quest for dirt and liquor, she'd probably have a fit. We finally decided to stow it away in my new sleeping quarters, since that room would be my workshop. Alan pointed out that the light was poor. I pointed out that I'd be working under artificial light in any case, and that it was up to him to supply me with proper lamps. Part of the equipment.

"Equipment? You don't even have a decent table," he complained, rocking the rickety object I had brought downstairs.

"I don't have a bed, either, but all that will come. Let's put it in the closet for the time being."

Mrs. Danner and I had not done much about the closet, since I did not intend to transfer my clothes from upstairs. We had swept up the fallen plaster and removed the cobwebs, but that was about all. The closet had been wallpapered—they had an excess of cheap labor in the old days. I had ripped off the loose, hanging strips and left it at that.

"First thing you need in here is a light," Alan said, squinting into the dark corners. "And a few shelves. You could store your materials in here."

"The first thing I need is bug spray," I said, shying back as a big fat black spider swung toward me, like Tarzan. "But right now I have to get up to Martha. I'm overdue."

"Go ahead." He whipped a folding rule from his pocket and, bravely ignoring the insect life, began measuring the dimensions of the closet.

"If you start hammering and banging things around—"

"With this door and the one into the hall closed, your grandmother couldn't hear me if I set off a charge of dynamite."

I couldn't argue with that, so I left him to it.

The evening had never seemed so long. Now that I had something I wanted to do, I begrudged the boring hours with Martha. She insisted I read, though I doubt that she paid attention. She had an enameled box on her lap, and she kept fumbling through the papers it contained.

Matt finally called at a little after nine. I tried not to watch the clock, but I couldn't help it. The bell roused Martha from a doze and she began grunting demands even as I lifted the phone.

"She wants to talk to you," I said, after I had exchanged greetings with Matt. "And so do I, dear favorite Cousin."

"Put her on," Matt said wearily. "Might as well get it over with. Then I'll talk to you."

I haven't reproduced Martha's speech patterns precisely. To do so I would have to eliminate about half the consonants. She couldn't articulate clearly; understanding her was partly a matter of knowing what the subject was, and partly watching her lips and her expression. She started by asking Matt when he was coming to see her, but this is what the sentence sounded like: "We'e' 'oo cuh?"

Matt figured that one out; he was expecting some such inquiry. But as she rambled on he appeared to comprehend less and less, and every time he asked her to repeat a phrase she got madder and less intelligible. Finally she tried to throw the telephone at me—it fell on the bed—and collapsed against her pillow, glowering.

"It's me again," I told Matt.

"Thank God. How do you cope with that?"

"In my usual inimitable fashion. When are you coming?"

"Saturday, I guess. I have a lot to do."

"Saturday," I repeated.

Martha gibbered at me, her eyes bright with rage. Watching her, I said, "She wants you to come before that."

Martha nodded. " 'A-morrah," she said.

"Tomorrow," I repeated.

"I can't. I had a full schedule before this last disaster happened. You have no idea how much extra work the Judge's death has caused."

"She's quite emphatic," I said, as Martha continued to flap her hands and lecture. "I have a few points to raise with you too. I presume a rising young politico reads the newspapers every day?"

He was quick to catch on. "Son of a bitch," he exclaimed. "There wasn't anything in the *Post* or the *Times* or . . . The *Pikesville Bulletin*?"

"That's it."

"I'll check it out. Is it that important?"

"I think so."

"Oh, all right. Tell her I'll be out tomorrow evening. Maybe we can have a quick dinner somewhere."

I relayed the message to Martha. Another half hour's reading put her to sleep and I decided I had done my duty for the evening.

Alan was gone when I got downstairs. There was a light in the closet and several shelves were in place; it smelled of fresh lumber and bug spray. Inefficiency was not one of Alan's failings.

After Shirley had gone to roost for the night I dragged my mattress downstairs and put it on the floor of the empty room. A few other things followed, all small and portable—a lamp, bedding, a chair. I would need help with the heavier things, and anyway I didn't want to crowd the room with objects that would have to be moved when I painted. I sat in the kitchen reading for a while, and then went to bed. If I had expected raptures from Elvis when I invited him to share my quarters I was disappointed; he settled down on his rug with the air of a dog who has finally established his right and proper place, even if it did take a while to get the idea through to his dull-witted human. We both slept through the night in perfect contentment. I didn't hear the owls wailing in the dark or remember the proximity of the thing in the closet, staring into the blackness with hollow eye sockets.

ten

We slept so soundly that I, at least, didn't wake until Shirley opened the door and Elvis ran to greet her.

"This looks like one of those pads I used to hear about," she said disapprovingly. "I don't know how you can stand being in this room, Julie. It's so dark and gloomy."

"Mrs. Danner doesn't like it either." I sat up, yawning and rubbing my eyes. "The way she acted yesterday you'd have thought I had asked her to clean a medieval torture chamber, complete with mutilated bodies."

Shirley looked around the room. Her expression was not one of fear or disgust, but of increasing puzzlement. "It's not that I feel scared, or anything like that . . . I don't know what it is. Gloomy. Sad . . ."

"It suits me just fine." I followed her to the kitchen. "Sorry I overslept, Shirley. We're out of bacon; how about scrambled eggs for breakfast?"

"Miz Martha has a fancy for hot cakes," Shirley said,

taking milk and eggs from the fridge. "Sit down, Julie, till you wake up."

"I don't know how to make hot cakes. I didn't buy a mix—"

"You kids and your mixes. Don't take offense, child; you're a heap better cook than Miz Danner, but—"

"But that's not saying much. I'm not offended, Shirley, I humbly admit the truth."

"It's not your fault," Shirley said. She mixed the ingredients and began beating them briskly. "Didn't your mama teach you?"

"According to Mother, she never lifted a ladylike finger to manual labor. The servants did everything."

"Servants my foot."

"No servants?"

"Oh, they had girls come in to help out—my own mama worked here for a while. But there hasn't been any money in the family for a long time. And at that, things was better when your mama was growing up than when Miz Martha was a girl."

"I suppose you heard about those days from your grandma," I said, amused.

"You know how it is in a small town. Everybody knows everybody else's business. And the Carrs were always important people, whether they had money or not."

"Why were things better when Mother was growing up?"

"Well, you know Miz Martha married a cousin—same last name. He was an insurance man over at Pikesville, and made a good living. Not enough to keep up this old barn of a house, but they got along all right. Miz Martha's daddy was something else. Never could keep a job. Guess he thought a Carr wasn't supposed to work for a living. An' if you think Miz Martha is hard to get on with, you should have known her mama. A real tartar, she was. Kept those girls close to home. They had to do all the housework, and they had hardly any beaux, 'cause nobody was good enough for one of the Carr girls. It's no wonder the youngest run off the minute she got a chance."

"But Martha stayed." I was fascinated by this glimpse into my family history—a far cry from the hints Mother had dropped of gracious living in the antebellum style. It was easier for me to believe in Shirley's version, and the image of Martha scrubbing and cooking and never going out on dates satisfied my mean streak.

"That kind of treatment takes children different ways," Shirley said philosophically. "Some rebel and break away. Some just fall into the same pattern as their folks, and that's what Miz Martha did. My granny said it was scary to see her turn into the spitting image of her own mama—same way of talking, dressing, doing her hair. Mr. Carr died when the girls were in their teens, so there was just the three of them here. Granny felt real sorry for Miz Melissa—she was the youngest—alone with those two sticks. Now, Julie, you watch what I do. The trick to good hot cakes isn't in the mixing, it's in the cooking."

It looked easy when she did it and the results were divine—I ate three. I had a feeling they wouldn't turn out the same way when I did it. I had never been able to make pancakes, even from a mix. They always stuck to the frying pan.

I offered to give Martha her breakfast so Shirley could eat. "She won't like it if you show up in your nightie," Shirley said dubiously.

"Then she'll have to lump it." Martha scrubbing, on her hands and knees . . . She couldn't intimidate me. I added, "Eat. Even I know there's nothing worse than cold pancakes."

One advantage to Martha's difficult speech was that you had to concentrate in order to understand her and so, if you didn't concentrate, you couldn't understand her. I felt sure her comments had to do with my state of undress and my generally rotten attitude toward life, but I didn't concentrate, and when she saw what was on the menu she stopped bitching and devoted her attention to eating.

"I'll take the tray down," I said, when she had finished. "Back in a minute."

Shirley was washing the dishes. I told her I had a proposition for her.

"You want me to set with Miz Martha this morning? Glad to. If you're going out you can fetch some more eggs."

"I'll get eggs, sure. But what I was going to do was paint."

"That room? Honey, what do you want to do that for?"

"Because I'm going to sleep there. I can keep Elvis with me and—"

"Yes, I know, you told me all that. Well, you suit yourself. How would you like to have Ron paint for you? It's not that I mind setting with Miz Martha, but you shouldn't be doing work like that."

"I'm a damned good painter," I said, wounded. "As for Ron, I'd be glad to have him do it, but—well, to tell you the truth, I don't have the money to pay him. I'm broke."

"Can't you get some from Matthew?"

"That is my intention. But I don't know how much I can wangle out of him."

Shirley snorted. "He's just like all the men—stuff their faces with food and ask for more, then yell when you tell 'em you need money for groceries. Ron don't have to be paid right this minute. You want me to ask him? Might be he could do it this morning."

"Can you call him?"

"He'll be here pretty soon, with my car. I let him have it yesterday. Promised he'd bring it back last night, but . . ."

"After what happened the last time, I don't blame him for not wanting to come around at night," I said, smiling.

"Anyhow, I'll ask him."

"Okay. If he can do it this morning and if he doesn't mind waiting for the money . . . Matt is supposed to come this evening. I'll hit him up for the cash then."

"This evening?" Shirley sounded surprised. "Oh, I suppose it's to do with the Judge's death."

I was ashamed that I had forgotten about the lawyer. So ephemeral is our presence in this world, so soon forgotten . . . When one is old there are few to remember or to care.

However, I reminded myself, it's no better when one is young.

I should have been finished with *Bleak House,* but for the past couple of days I had been cheating. Whenever Martha dozed off, I slid my paperback mystery out from under my shirt and read it until she roused herself and asked why I had stopped. That morning she finally caught me. I was so absorbed in the mystery that when she mumbled, "Read," I did.

"The body lay in a pool of blood on the library rug. Its lovely Bokhara pattern was stained a more deadly crimson. The girl's white bosom . . ." I stopped and looked up to meet Martha's black stare. "Whoops," I said.

She asked, if I understood her correctly, "What is that trash?" I showed her the cover. The victim's white bosom was conspicuous and there was blood all over the place.

"Hmph," said Martha.

"Now, Martha, admit it—you're as sick of *Bleak House* as I am. I'll bet you know it by heart. How about a nice murder for a change?"

I could have sworn she was amused. Such was the distortion of her features that the gleam of humor didn't improve her looks appreciably, but it made me feel more kindly toward her. Maybe I had done her an injustice; maybe there was warmth and kindness buried under the layers of frigid rectitude that were not entirely her fault. At any rate, she allowed as how she wouldn't mind listening to *Murder on the Hearthrug,* so long as I started back at the beginning.

The only disadvantage to the new book was that it kept her awake. I finally excused myself on the grounds that I ought to start lunch. I found that Shirley had been to the store and had put together a ham pie crowned with cheese biscuits.

"I'll pay you back," I said guiltily. "In money and time. It's not fair for you to do the cooking."

"I cook better than you," said Shirley.

"I can't deny that. Well . . ." The smell of the pie overcame my scruples. "We'll take turns. Where is Elvis? I'd have expected to find him drooling at the door."

"Ron took him along to the store. He ran out of paint."

Ron and Elvis returned in time for lunch. The young man greeted me with a sheepish grin, and neither of us marred the occasion by the slightest reference to our first meeting. Nor did I comment on the fact that he and Elvis were now on first-name terms.

Shirley took Martha's lunch up, and Ron and Elvis and I finished the ham pie. Ron also polished off a pint of chocolate ice cream and a box of cookies, assisted by Elvis, and then we went to inspect his painting.

He was my kind of painter—slapdash but fast. I noticed that the closet door was slightly ajar. I had warned Shirley about the cast, and asked her to tell Ron not to touch it for fear of an accident. Evidently his curiosity had gotten the better of him. I couldn't blame him, but I thought I had better reinforce the warning.

"Don't bother painting the closet, Ron. There are shelves up, and some fragile objects inside. If it—if anything got broken, I'd be in trouble."

"Sure, right." He avoided looking at me.

I left the dishes for Mrs. Danner and started for the dig. I left Elvis too; with Ron and Shirley at hand, I figured it was safe. I had warned Ron not to let him eat anything; from the quick, oblique look Ron gave me I knew Shirley must have told him about Mrs. Danner's dog stew, but he didn't say anything except that he would keep an eye on Elvis.

I felt sure I could trust him, and I didn't blame him for sneaking a peek at the skull; but as I picked my way through the tall grass I wondered whether he might not know more about the original of that skull than he cared to admit.

I could understand Jarboe's reasons for believing that local juveniles were responsible for the placement of the skeletons. A gang of kids could have gone into the woods to get drunk or smoke pot or dig for treasure—or all of the above. If they had discovered the skeletons they might have thought it would be funny to scare someone, especially if they knew Joe Danner would probably be the first person along that road. Joe was obviously not the most popular man in the county. Ron could have been one of the gang. At the least, he must know or suspect who was involved.

I wished I dared ask Ron to come clean. It would have

relieved my mind considerably to know there was nothing more sinister involved than the weird sense of humor of some pie-eyed teenagers.

This time there was no guard blocking the entrance to the dig, and I was received with flattering enthusiasm by all concerned. "Just in time," Jono said, smiling. "We're going to sink our first trial trench."

The cleared area was divided into squares, with the now familiar stakes marking the intersections of squares and balks. They must have worked their collective butts off to get so much done. The trial hole was six feet from the grave Mrs. Hornbeak had found. The diggers were not using shovels; squatting, they removed the earth with trowels, inspecting every clod of dirt as if it might contain gold.

Sidling up to Alan I murmured, "I'm ready to start as soon as you get the stuff."

I didn't realize how ambiguous the statement sounded until one of the female acolytes turned from her digging to give me a long, hard stare. Alan said abstractedly, "I've got it. What's that, Willkie?"

The large young man stared stupidly at the clump of dirt he held. From it Alan deftly picked a square of dull metal. Then he shoved Willkie out of the way and took over the digging. The hole was only a foot deep when he stopped. He handed the trowel to Jono, who was beside him; like an operating nurse attending a surgeon, Jono replaced the trowel with a brush. Finally Alan said in tones of deep disgust, "Damn. Another grave."

"What's wrong with that?" I asked.

One of the girls laughed in a sneering way. Alan returned to his careful scraping without comment. It was Jono who explained. "I told you, Julie, we can't disturb burials until we have legal permission. Besides, we know there were burials in this area. What we want now is evidence of occupation. Foundations, rubbish pits—"

"Get started on the second test hole," Alan said, without looking up. "You know where."

Jono left reluctantly. He might pretend to be professionally blasé about graves, but he was as curious as the rest of us. He began digging at the far end of the cleared area, on a direct line with the first hole but fifty feet away.

Alan sat back on his heels and beckoned me. "Have a look."

It was not a pretty sight. The skull lay bedded in the dark soil. The mandible had dropped, so that the mouth was wide open, as if the person had died screaming.

"Well?"

"Well, what?" I pointed. "It's a human skull."

"Male or female?"

"How the hell should I . . ." I leaned over for a closer look. "Sizable brow ridges . . . I'd guess male, but it's impossible to be sure without examining the pelvic and long bones. The incisors aren't shovel-shaped, so it's probably not an Indian. The damage to the skull—"

"Don't touch it," Alan said sharply. "We'll have to undercut the soil and lift it out in a block. It's too fragile to be moved otherwise. Well? What were you going to say about the damage?"

I tried to remember old lectures. "It's broken on the left side. Pressure from earth heaped on the body wouldn't result in lateral damage, but . . . This is ridiculous. I can't tell anything from half a skull."

"Hmmm," Alan said. He began trickling dirt back into the hole. "No point in excavating any further until we're ready to take it out. Jono?"

"Pottery." Jono's voice shook with controlled excitement. "Practically on the surface, Alan. Looks as if there was an old animal burrow here—groundhog, maybe."

"Okay. It may be a rubbish dump. Be careful."

The unskilled help—which, to my chagrin, included me—was put to work enlarging the cleared area. Later in the afternoon I was promoted to sifting dirt. Every square inch that came out of the hole had to be put through a wire sieve so that tiny objects like beads and pins wouldn't be lost.

From the tense silence, broken only by muffled exclamations of pleasure, that reigned over the actual excavation, I could tell that Alan and Jono were delighted with the results, but I found the whole business as boring as I had always expected I would. By the end of the afternoon we had a handful of pottery fragments and a few scraps of rusty metal. The hands of my watch reached five o'clock and moved on. Alan showed no signs of stopping work. Finally I announced I had to go.

"My materials," I said, poking Alan in the back to get his attention.

"In the Jeep."

"And where is the Jeep?"

"There." One arm flapped briefly.

They had not been able to bring the vehicles to the site, since a deep gully intervened. It had been bridged by a couple of planks, over which I crossed with some trepidation. The Jeep was there, and Alan's van. I rummaged in the Jeep and found the charts I had asked for, plus a shopping bag that contained modeling clay and a gross of yellow pencils. I picked up the bag and started for the house.

Elvis was lying by the back steps. He informed me he had not been fed, so I did that first, then took the supplies into my room. Ron had finished. The place looked nice, if you didn't examine the woodwork too closely; neither Ron nor I had thought it worthwhile to scrape off all the old paint. The closet door was closed, as I had left it.

I assumed Mrs. Danner had come and gone, though there were no signs of her presence. The pot of chicken and vegetables simmering on the stove smelled like Shirley's work, thank goodness.

I went upstairs to tell Shirley I was back. She put down the book from which she had been reading; I was amused to note that it was not Milton or Tennyson, but my murder mystery. Martha asked where I had been.

"Walking in the woods," I admitted. There was no point in denying it; I was covered with dirt and leaf mold and bits of vegetation.

I had expected Martha to express disapproval, but her reaction was a good deal more vehement. Her hand moved with something close to normal quickness, the fingers crooked like claws. "Told you," she spat. "Years ago . . . stay away . . . filthy, dirty . . ."

"Take it easy, Martha. I know I'm a bit grubby, but I fully intend to wash."

We had finished eating before Matt showed up. I was reading *Murder on the Hearthrug,* but without pleasure; the section Shirley had read contained several vital clues, so I had no idea what was going on. I had left Martha's door open, and when I heard the car I closed the book.

"I want to talk to Matt for a few minutes," I informed Martha. "About expenses and things like that. I'll send him up shortly."

Martha objected, of course. She wanted Matt right now. I smiled sweetly and closed the door as I left. I must be mellowing, I thought; I almost felt sorry for her, sputtering and helpless and unable to enforce her dictates.

Matt's first remark was not "Hello" but "I can't stay

long. This is damned inconvenient. What does she want me for?"

"She doesn't confide in me, Cousin dear. I suppose it has to do with legal complications following the Judge's death."

"Well, I can't do anything yet," Matt grumbled, following me into the parlor. "He won't even be buried until tomorrow—"

"The funeral is tomorrow? Where?"

"Carrsville, the Episcopal church. Why? You aren't thinking of going, are you?"

"One of us ought to be there. Martha can't go. Besides, he was a lovely man."

"Naturally I ordered a floral tribute," Matt said.

"What time?"

"Ten. Actually, it would be a nice gesture. If you don't mind representing the family—"

"I will even wear a dress instead of jeans."

"Wow. Are you sure that isn't asking too much?"

His smile disappeared when I went on to the next subject. "Money? How much?"

"My God, you sound like a husband," I said disgustedly. "Here, have a glass of sherry."

Matt produced a feebler edition of his original smile. "You don't have to get me drunk, Julie. I know it costs money to run this place, and God knows I owe you. I'm just not sure I can draw on Martha's account right now. The Judge and I were co-guardians, and until the court decides who is to succeed him, or whether to grant my petition to act as sole—"

"For crying out loud, what are people in Martha's position supposed to do while the law sorts these things out? Live on air?"

"The law," Matt said sourly, "doesn't give a damn.

However, I'll see what I can do to expedite matters. In the meantime—will you take a check?"

I was about to say no, when I decided I might get more out of him than if I insisted on cash. After I had the check in my hot little hand I graciously dismissed him and watched him head for the stairs like the schoolboy in Whittier's poem, dragging his reluctant self to school.

I figured I had at least half an hour, maybe more, if Martha was in a garrulous mood. I settled down in the kitchen and looked through the reference material Alan had given me. He had photocopied not only the tables but the entire German monograph. My German isn't too good, but since most of the vocabulary was technical I was able to make it out. The tables were still a basic source, though they were almost ninety years old. Alan had also copied a few articles describing recent reconstructions, including one of a settler from Martin's Hundred, a site excavated by the Colonial Williamsburg people. I wondered if it was this example that had given Alan the idea.

I took the papers to my new room. Ron had piled the odds and ends of furniture on top of the mattress and covered the whole lumpy pile with a drop cloth. It was lavishly spattered with yellow and white paint, like bird droppings. The table was covered with newspapers. I cleared them off and took the cast from its shelf in the closet. Reading the material had fired me up; I was anxious to get started. With a soft pencil I began marking the places where the depth markers would be set. Heel of the mandible . . .

I was so absorbed I didn't hear him coming. His exclamation startled me; I let go of the cast and bumped the table, setting it rocking. I managed to grab the skull as it rolled toward the edge, and turned, cradling it in both hands.

We both spoke at once. I said, "Damn it, Matt, don't do that! If this had been smashed—" And he said, "What the hell is that?"

We stared at one another in mutual indignation. "A present from your boyfriend?" Matt inquired sarcastically.

"In a way." I relaxed; after all, no damage had been done. "I suppose it did look weird, but if this had broken . . . I'm doing a reconstruction of that skeleton—the one Danner found in the road."

The room and the corridor beyond lay deep in shadow, except for the bright circle of light from my lamp. Matt's features were indistinct. I saw a gleam of white as his lips parted, but he didn't speak for a while. Then he repeated, "Reconstruction?"

"It's a process of restoring the person's original appearance. Clay is molded over the bone, following tables of average tissue depths on the human head. Very scientific."

"It can't be accurate," Matt said. "You don't know about skin color or eye color or whether the person was skinny or fat—"

"It's only an approximation. But you'd be surprised what an accurate likeness can be achieved."

"Is that right?" Matt came closer and looked curiously at the cast. "Are you going to do it now?"

"No, I was just fooling around, getting some ideas. It'll take days." I put the cast in its bag and returned it to the closet. "First I have to measure and cut the depth markers, then glue them to the skull, then—"

"Each to his own taste," Matt said, stepping back to let me pass out of the room. "Is this where you'll be working? I'd forgotten this room was here."

"It's convenient," I said, somewhat vaguely. I had no intention of telling Matt I meant to sleep in the room;

Shirley had already given me a hard time about it and I was afraid Matt would lecture me too.

Matt followed me to the kitchen. "Where is your boyfriend?"

"Don't keep calling him that."

"Sorry. I was under the impression that you two had picked up where you left off."

"Well, we haven't. I'm doing some work for him, that's all."

"I'll have to have a talk with him."

"What about?"

"Stopping work. Martha's got wind of what he's doing, Julie. I don't know how she knows, but she does, and she's furious. Your . . . Petranek will have to leave."

"Matt, you can't do that! He's just made a big find—something really important."

"I don't care if he's located Blackbeard's treasure. I'm kicking him out."

I was surprised at the extent of my distress. A few days earlier I'd have said I didn't give a damn whether Alan was allowed to work at Maidenwood or not. In fact, I'd have been happy to have him off the premises. Now I was involved. With the work—and what else? I searched for an argument that would carry weight with Matt.

"It won't look good for your image if you shut down the dig just as they are finding something significant, Matt. Who are you to stand in the way of scientific achievement?"

"Damn." Matt dropped into a chair. For the first time he looked older than his true age. "I'm going crazy with all these unreasonable demands and conflicts. I don't know what to do."

"It's not that difficult, Matt. Just tell Martha—"

"She's crazy," Matt muttered. "Senile. She's talking the

most insane garbage . . . Sometimes I think she does have supernatural powers. How does she know everything that goes on?"

"You really are in a state. Did Martha give you a hard time?"

Matt laughed—a mirthless rattle of sound. "You'll never know, Julie."

"I do know." I patted his hunched shoulder. "Don't let her get to you, Matt. There's a simple explanation for her seeming clairvoyance, and I think I know what it is. Mrs. Danner."

"Rosie?"

What an inappropriate name for that poor frozen wraith of a woman! "Rosie," I repeated. "She hasn't a brain cell she can call her own, Matt. She's scared to death of Martha. I'll bet she's been getting the newspapers for her, and answering all her questions."

The more I thought about it, the more I was convinced I had found the explanation. I only wondered why I hadn't figured it out before.

Matt did not appear cheered by the theory. "That could be," he said listlessly. "It doesn't really make any difference. Look, Julie, I have to go. I'll keep in touch."

I had to sympathize with him. No one knew better than I the power Martha had wielded over her unlucky descendants.

Shirley was disappointed she couldn't go to the Judge's funeral. I hated to take advantage of her, but there was no way we could both go, and Shirley agreed with Matt that someone ought to represent the family. I preferred not to think of it in such formal terms; "representing the family" implied white gloves and a hat, neither of which I owned. Still, I wanted to go.

I was late, since I didn't know where the church was. The service was underway when I slipped breathlessly into a back pew. I was surprised to see the place was almost full. I should not have been surprised; he had been a public figure known to three generations.

I didn't spot Matt until we rose to sing a hymn. He was one of the first on his feet—right up in front, as I might have expected. When the service was concluded I stayed in my seat until he saw me, then joined him.

"Late as usual," he said out of the corner of his mouth, his head decorously bowed.

"I thought you weren't coming."

"Changed my mind."

"Are you going to the cemetery?"

"No. Let's have lunch. I want to talk to you."

That had an ominous sound, but I saw no reason to turn down a meal. One of the reasons why I had been late was that I had stopped to cash Matt's check. I had an argument with the teller, and it was not until one of the bank officials recognized me as Martha's granddaughter that I was able to get the money.

We came out of the dimness of the church into bright sunlight. Matt had taken my arm and I stopped when he did, blinded by the light. When my vision came back I saw the inevitable photographer. Matt always seemed to have one or two following him around; I wondered if he hired them himself.

I refrained from making a face at the camera, out of respect for the Judge, and let Matt lead me to his car. His idea of a restaurant turned out to be a drive-in on the highway, and I grumpily accepted a cheeseburger and shake, which we ate in the car.

"Why can't we go inside?" I complained. "It's hot as hell out here."

"I want to talk privately, that's why," Matt said. "Take a look at this."

He unfolded the newspaper that lay on the seat between us and thrust it at me.

Alan must have gone straight from the dig to his office and called every newspaper in the state. He had even rated a minor front-page headline in the *Washington Post.* "A New Light on Virginia's Dark Ages. Spectacular New Discovery at Maidenwood Plantation."

"Plantation, yet," I said admiringly. "That's pretty fancy."

"The son of a bitch has cut the ground right out from under me," Matt said through his teeth. "Read the last paragraph."

After some fulsome and only mildly inaccurate predictions as to what the new discoveries would mean to historians, the reporter had quoted Alan. " 'Virginia owes a special debt of gratitude to Mrs. Martha Carr and her grandson, the distinguished senator, Matthew Ellis. Without their gracious permission and unfailing support, this magnificent contribution to the cultural and historical traditions of the Old Dominion could never have been made.' "

Through my peals of laughter Matt exclaimed, "You see what he's done? I can't make him leave now."

"No, you can't. His next interview would deplore your strange indifference to tradition, history, and the Old Dominion. He'd probably have the president of the university and the Governor backing him up."

Matt growled and bit savagely into his hamburger.

"So what are you going to do?" I asked.

Matt swallowed. "What can I do?"

"Lie to Martha."

"That, certainly. Listen, Julie, if you're right about Rosie Danner, I'll have to get rid of her. I can't have her blabbing everything she knows to Martha."

"There's a theory in espionage circles that you don't dispose of a spy, you feed him false information."

"Oh, come on, Julie, don't be cute. You can't tell Rosie your buddies have gone when everyone in the neighborhood knows different. Rosie and her husband have always been under Martha's thumb. If she told Joe to shoot a trespasser he'd blast away."

"She's not very bright," I said, reluctant to abandon my idea. "If we told her . . ." Then, belatedly, the implications of his last sentence sank in. "Rosie . . . Joe Danner . . . She's already told Martha. She . . . Start the car, Matt, hurry, I've got to get back."

"Why the rush?"

"Elvis," I said, gulping. "Martha must know about Elvis."

eleven

I forced myself to drive at the speed limit. Though my first impulse had been to make for Maidenwood as fast as the old car would go. I couldn't believe I had been so stupid. Martha had known about the dog for some time—probably from the first. I had suspected the Danners of trying to poison him, but I should have known neither Joe nor Rose would take such a step without being prompted. Martha wouldn't give up after one attempt. She'd tell Joe to try again—another method this time, a rifle or a car. Shirley couldn't protect him from that sort of thing; she assumed, as I had, that the first attempt had been the result of idle malice, and that the Danners wouldn't dare try the same trick twice.

I could have cried with relief when I turned into the drive and saw Elvis lumbering to meet me. He would always limp, although he could cover ground at amazing speed. I brought the car to a stop and opened the door for him. He was surprised but quite pleased when I threw both arms around him and hugged him until he wheezed.

Shirley was in the kitchen, her feet up on a chair, reading *Murder on the Hearthrug*. "I finished it this morning," she explained a little guiltily. "Got me kind of curious; I figured I'd read the beginning and find out how it all happened. Was there a good crowd at the service?"

I sat down and told her all about it—the eulogy, the hymns, the size of the crowd, the number of "floral tributes." She asked if I had seen hers—"Lilies, in a nice pot, with a purple ribbon"—and I improvised. "It was right in front of the casket, Shirley."

"Was Matthew there?"

"Yes, we had lunch afterward. That's why I'm late. I owe you, Shirley."

"Honey, we're not keeping track, we're just trying to get by. It's been a lot easier since you got here, I can tell you."

"That reminds me." I lowered my voice. "Mrs. Danner is upstairs with Martha, isn't she? Then I can tell you . . ."

Shirley wasn't interested in Matt's dilemma with regard to the dig—the archaeological activities had always seemed more than a little absurd to her—but her eyes widened when I explained that Mrs. Danner must be the source of Martha's uncanny knowledgeability.

"That old devil," she exclaimed. "I did wonder, now and then, when she'd let something slip . . . It wasn't me that told her, and it wasn't you, so who else could it have been?"

"Matt and the Judge are the only other possibilities. But I don't believe either of them would play informer. Matt doesn't want her to know he has gone against her wishes, and the Judge didn't want her to be upset."

"Upset?" Shirley sniffed. "It hasn't hurt her one bit. She enjoys having her little secrets."

"You're right about that. As I see it, we've got three choices. We can get rid of Mrs. Danner. At first I was in favor of that, but now I'm not so sure. She's not worth much, but she does give you a break from Martha now and then. The second possibility is to let Mrs. Danner stay and stop playing games with Martha. She knows everything we're doing anyway, so why bother lying?"

"Hmmm," said Shirley, impressed by my logic. "What's the third choice?"

"To go on the way we've been going. Let Martha think she's fooling us. So long as we know Mrs. Danner is blabbing to her, we can take precautions."

"Maybe that's the best way. Miz Martha can fuss all she wants about the archaeologists, but there's nothing she can do to stop them. The only thing is . . ."

Her troubled dark eyes moved to Elvis, whose head was resting on her feet.

"Yes," I said. "For two cents I'd confess to Martha and tell her that if anything happens to Elvis—"

"You'd do what?" Shirley shook her head. "The way I see it, Julie, it doesn't make any difference whether you tell her or not. Only thing we can do is never let that dog out of our sight."

Elvis knew the word "dog." His tail thumped in acknowledgment. Shirley went on, "It's a good thing you decided to stay downstairs at night, I guess. You can keep him with you. I don't like to think Miz Martha would stoop so low as to order somebody to feed him poison, but . . ."

"You're right as always, Shirley. That reminds me—I want to make a phone call."

May Rubin was in her office. "I was going to call you," she said.

I knew from the tone in her voice that it was bad news, and my heart sank. I had hoped I was wrong.

I didn't recognize the name of the chemical. May translated. "It's a weed killer—not the standard commercial variety, but stronger. A lot of farmers use it. Do you have any idea—"

"A lot of ideas. No proof."

"Is there anything I can do?"

"Thanks, May. I'll let you know."

When I told Shirley she didn't look surprised, only grimly determined. "That won't happen again," she said.

Even though I had half expected it, the confirmation of my suspicions made me furious. "I'm going to kick that woman out of here right now!"

"That won't do any good. It isn't Miz Danner so much as her husband."

"A man who would beat children and throw his own daughter out of the house wouldn't think twice about shooting a dog," I agreed. "Well, we'll just have to cope. Which reminds me—I got some money out of Matt. How much did you spend on groceries the other day, and what do you think I should pay Ron for the paint job?"

We agreed on a figure that sounded uncommonly low to my city-accustomed ears, and then I started for the dig. I took Elvis with me.

Apparently Alan had got his court order. He and Jono were at work on the first grave, the one Mrs. Hornbeak had found. The bones had been exposed and they were undercutting the entire mass of soil, preparatory to lifting it out. Watching the work was a newcomer, inappropriately dressed in a tweed jacket and neatly pressed slacks.

Alan hoisted himself to his feet and advanced to meet me, smiling. This demonstration took me so by surprise that I gaped at him. "Here she is," he said. "Our physical anthropologist. Julie, this is Mr. Barton Wilkes—from the National Geographic Society."

Oho, I thought, and also, aha! No wonder I'm getting all the sweetness and charm and professional courtesy. Physical anthropologist yet.

Mr. Wilkes stepped carefully around the open grave, his hand extended. He wore glasses, from which the sunlight twinkled, and there were streaks of gray in his brown hair. "It's a pleasure, Miss Newcomb. Alan is fortunate to have assistance from a lady who is not only qualified, but who is also a member of one of Virginia's old respected families."

"No, not at all," I mumbled, trying to restrain Elvis, who couldn't make up his mind whether to help with the digging or greet my new friend.

"What a handsome dog," said Wilkes.

"Tie him to a tree, will you?" Alan said, trying to keep the irritation out of his voice. "I'd like your advice before we try to lift this."

He knew that I knew that I didn't know a damned thing about the procedure, but I realized this was all part of the plan to impress a potential donor with our dedication and our expertise. If my cooperation could get Alan the grant he wanted, I was willing to do what I could. I handed Elvis's leash to Jono and knelt by the grave.

"Fascinating," I said.

"I know you can't make a proper examination under these conditions," Wilkes said. "But I would be most interested in any preliminary comments you might feel justified in making."

The preliminary comment that leaped to mind was a simple "yuck." This skeleton was even more battered than the other one Alan had found. Many of the bones were disarticulated; the mandible stuck up at right angles. All the remains were darkly stained.

"You understand I would hate to commit myself to anything at this stage," I began.

Wilkes and Alan made encouraging noises. I went on, "The skeletal material appears to be that of a male." That seemed safe enough, judging from the length of the long bones of the legs, and the fact that the hook found in this grave had come from male clothing. The upper teeth were in fairly good condition; all were present, none were worn, and the wisdom teeth had erupted. "He was probably between eighteen and thirty years old," I said. "Laboratory study can narrow it down, but right now . . ."

"Yes, I see." Wilkes sounded impressed. "I don't suppose there is any clue as to how he died?"

Alan didn't nudge me, he just got very, very quiet. I knew what he wanted me to say. Most of the settlers at Maydon's Hundred were killed during the Indian Massacre of 1622. If I said that one of the breaks in the battered skull appeared to have been made by a tomahawk, or that there was evidence the man had been scalped, Alan would be a giant step forward toward the confirmation of his theory and the funding he needed.

I had nothing to lose. I had already qualified my comments to the point of meaninglessness, and as for risking my reputation—how can you risk what you don't have? Something held me back. I would like to think it was integrity.

"No," I said. "I couldn't say, at this point. But you'll notice that the mandible—the jawbone—has been displaced. Pressure from the earth might be responsible for a certain degree of displacement, but this is extreme. It suggests that the mandible had been broken before the body was buried—perhaps that the body was in an advanced stage of decomposition before burial took place."

"Most interesting," Wilkes breathed. "Well. I have a long drive ahead, and I must be on my way. I hadn't planned to spend so much time here, but it has all been most—er—interesting!"

Wilkes and Alan went off together, and I heard Wilkes say, "You will hear from us in a few days, Dr. Petranek. Of course I can't guarantee how the committee will respond, but I can assure you that insofar as I am concerned . . ."

The rest of his words were lost as the two men moved along the track. Jono's lips parted in a wide grin and he gave me a thumbs-up signal.

"You think he's got it?" I whispered.

"Looking good. You were a big help, Julie. Good work."

When Alan returned, his assessment was more cautious. "I've learned not to uncork the champagne until the check is in my hands. But if it does work out, Julie, I owe you a glass or three. Thanks." I was beginning to preen myself when he added critically, "Did you have to bring that damned dog?"

"Yes, I did have to. Can you take a break? I have a couple of things I want to discuss with you."

"I suppose so. Come on, we'll sit in the van."

Thunderheads were piling up on the horizon. Alan gave them a worried look. "Make it snappy, will you? I want to get that skeleton out this afternoon. Rain would ruin it."

"Well, excuse me," I said. Alan stared at me. Then he gave himself a little shake, and I realized he was so tired he barely knew what he was saying. No wonder, if he spent his nights watching out for burglars . . . I was about to apologize when he beat me to it.

"Sorry. I'm a little preoccupied these days. What's on your mind?"

"Well . . . First, congratulations for foiling Matt. Or was that newspaper story a case of coincidental timing?"

"I figured he'd be getting cold feet about letting me excavate," Alan said coolly. "The old lady is bound to know what's going in, with Rose Danner under her spell."

"If you're so clever, why didn't you warn me about Elvis?"

"What do you mean?"

"Well, Mrs. Danner must have told Martha about him too."

"So?"

"So Martha hates animals. Someone gave me a kitten once—from a litter his barn cat had—and she . . ." To my horror I felt my throat close up. I hadn't thought about that incident for fifteen years.

"I didn't know that," Alan said.

I turned away from him, struggling to get myself under control. That's the trouble with amnesia; when memory does return, it is as fresh and painful as if the event had just occurred. For a moment I thought I felt something brush my bowed head; but when I turned, Alan wasn't even looking at me.

He said quietly, "I'll keep the dog with me during the day. He won't like being tied, but he'll have to put up with it. Shut him in your room at night. I'll also have a word with Danner."

Arbitrary, arrogant, bossy man . . . "Thank you. Maybe I had better talk to Mr. Danner. I'm one of the elite to him, and he doesn't think much of you."

"As you like. I have to get back to work. Are you going to stick around?"

"I thought I'd start the reconstruction, unless you need me for anything in particular."

"Oh, that. Sure, go ahead."

His ardor for that project had obviously dimmed. Now that he had a genuine find to show the men with the money, the reconstruction didn't interest him any longer.

"I'll leave Elvis with you, then," I said, getting out of the van.

"Okay. Oh—one more thing—you'd better put that barricade back up at your gate."

"Reporters?"

"Could be. But I was thinking of Mrs. Hornbeak. Her nose may be a trifle out of joint and she may approach you."

"Thanks. That gives me something to look forward to."

I don't think Alan heard me. He was heading away as fast as he could go, back to his rotten bones.

I went the long way around, down the track to where it joined the road, and so to the gates. The sawhorse, with its warning sign, stood where I had left it when I drove out that morning. I dragged it back into place. It was not much of a barrier. And I doubted that the moral effect the sheriff had mentioned would move Mrs. Hornbeak, who appeared to be sadly lacking in rudimentary manners, much less morals. It was the best I could do, however.

I still hadn't made up my mind what to do about Mrs. Danner. We had to have someone. Shirley was working for wages, Matt could impose on her to the extent she allowed—and she obviously had a soft spot for him, heaven knows why. But I was damned if I would let him make a slave out of me. Firing Mrs. Danner wouldn't eliminate the danger to Elvis.

I checked the mailbox to see if the mail had come. It had. Most of it was circulars, but there was a letter from

Mother and a postcard from a friend who was vacationing in Europe, blast her. And one other item addressed to me—a five-by-seven manila envelope thick enough to contain a booklet or brochure. But the address was handwritten, and I recognized the writing.

To receive a letter from the dead gives you an uncanny sensation. I stood turning it over in my hands, noting that the postmark bore Monday's date. Either someone had found it on his desk and put it in the mail, or else the old lawyer had posted it himself, late Sunday evening. The latter seemed the most likely alternative; if he had meant to wait until Monday before mailing it, surely he would have left it unsealed until he had finished the note he had been writing to me at the moment of his death.

I sat down on the grass and opened the envelope. There was another, slightly smaller envelope inside, crisscrossed by heavy tape. A letter had been attached, in such a way that it covered the flap of the inner envelope.

The letter was brief. "My dear Julie. Enclosed is a small memento I think you should have. I know I can trust your honor not to open the envelope until after your grandmother is gone. With most sincere regards, et cetera."

Curiouser and curiouser, I thought. I wasn't tempted to peek, partly because I felt sentimental about honoring the old gentleman's final request, but mostly because I suspected what the "memento" was. He hadn't asked me not to feel the envelope; my fingers traced the outline of what could be a cardboard photo frame, one of the old-fashioned variety with fancy, curved edges. Perhaps it was a picture of me in my misspent youth, or of me and my parents. I could think of a number of reasons why he might not want Martha to know he had given it to me—none of them to her credit.

Mrs. Danner was in the kitchen. She wasn't doing anything, just sitting, staring blankly into space. When I entered she got clumsily to her feet.

"You didn't say what I was to do. I don't know—"

"That's all right, Mrs. Danner." I wished I could dislike the woman wholeheartedly and completely, without any weakening touch of pity. But it wasn't possible to hate someone that miserable. No wonder she was reluctant to sit with Martha. She could no more resist Martha's demands than a gourmand can turn away from a chocolate éclair. She was in trouble whatever she did.

"You want I should start supper?"

My sympathy vanished. She couldn't be that stupid or forgetful. She had her own little ways of hitting back at the people who hassled her. I wondered how she got back at her husband.

I put her to work washing lettuce and vegetables for a salad and went to inspect my room. Though I had told Alan I meant to start working on the cast, there was a lot to do before I could begin the actual reconstruction. I needed a large, sturdy table, and some arrangement to hold the cast steady. And a bed. I was not keen on sleeping on the floor. There were mice in the house and snakes outside the house and I was afraid one of them might decide to go for a stroll across my stomach.

There was a big oak table in the library. I couldn't move it alone, so I enlisted Mrs. Danner. The ease with which she hoisted her end gave me an odd feeling. I had not realized she was so strong.

I also stole a rug from the library—a beautiful old Persian rug, so worn it wasn't worth selling—which is probably why it was still there. Its faded gorgeousness improved the look of the room so much I threw caution to the winds and hauled in all sorts of things, including a brass bed from one of the upstairs rooms.

Any normal person would have asked why I was furnishing the room. Mrs. Danner didn't ask a question or make a comment. She was about as much company as a robot, but she had a machine-like utility, and by the time we finished I had made up my mind what to do about her. I didn't really care what she told Martha. The only thing I was concerned about was Elvis, and Martha already knew about him.

When five o'clock rolled around and Danner's truck rolled up, I was lying in wait. I think he had been expecting a confrontation, and was only surprised it had not come earlier. Not that he appeared embarrassed or apologetic. He didn't even turn off the motor and I had to yell over the untuned rattle-and-chug. I didn't mind yelling.

"You know I've adopted a dog," I began.

I had to wait some time for a reply. Finally his lips parted. "Miz Martha don't want animals around."

"That's between me and Miss Martha. It's not your affair. There are too many unauthorized people wandering around here at night—"

"Miz Martha said I could—"

"Miss Martha isn't in charge here now, I am. She's old and ill and she won't be around much longer. Senator Ellis will own Maidenwood after she dies, and I'm acting by his authority. If I catch you anywhere on the premises after dark, or if anything happens to my dog, I'll swear out a warrant. Is that clear?"

He gave me a long baleful look before lowering his eyes and grunting a reluctant acknowledgment. Mrs. Danner didn't speak or move, but she enjoyed his humiliation. I could almost feel her glee; it puffed her cheeks with laughter she did not dare express. I knew she would pay later—not for her disloyalty, but for my tirade. Joe Danner would vent his rage on an object that could not fight back.

Feeling a little sick, I stepped aside and waved them on.

Before the old blue truck reached the road, another vehicle turned into the drive. Joe Danner had not replaced the sawhorse. I couldn't blame him for that, but I swore under my breath when I saw that the driver of the car was the middle-aged reporter.

I went down the drive at a run and waved him to a stop some distance from the house. "Don't bother to get out," I said. "Just turn around and leave."

I guess journalists have to develop hides like coats of mail. Smiling and unperturbed, he offered me a folded newspaper. "I thought you might not have seen the evening edition, Ms. Newcomb."

I took the paper. "Thanks. Now go away."

"What do you think of the discovery of—"

"I never think. See here, Mr.—"

"Miller. Chris Miller."

"You're wasting your time with me, Mr. Miller. My cousin, Senator Ellis, is Mrs. Carr's representative, and Dr. Petranek is in charge of the dig. Go heckle them. Even if I wanted to admit you to the grounds, which I don't, I couldn't, and I don't know anything except what I read in the paper."

He asked me more questions—all beginning with "What do you think"—but I stood my ground, smiling and shaking my head. Finally he gave up. I followed the car to the end of the drive and dragged the sawhorse back in place.

When Shirley came downstairs I was drinking bourbon and reading the paper. I had had a hard day, and what I read didn't improve my disposition.

The paper was the latest edition, the ink damp enough to stain my hands. Matt must have called a reporter as soon as he left me, and hopped onto the archaeological bandwagon driven by Alan. He had even used some of the phrases I had quoted ironically that morning. "Magnificent contribution—historical tradition—the Old Dominion . . ."

As I read on, amusement replaced my annoyance. Matt had had no choice but to accept a fait accompli with as much grace as possible. He was a smooth talker, all right; platitudes rolled from his tongue like water off a greased pig. The only time he came close to losing his temper was when he was asked about the astonishing psychic discovery of Mrs. Hornbeak. " 'Pure coincidence,' the Senator snapped." Lady Jocelyn was dismissed as a charming legend. " 'She is part of the traditions of Maidenwood, but historians have assured me that there is no factual evidence for her existence, much less her presence at Maidenwood. Mrs. Hornbeak has let her overheated imagination run away with her.' "

I was chortling over this when Shirley came in. I showed her the newspaper, but she refused to read it. "It's all a pack of nonsense. I just hope Matthew can keep those reporters away from here. They get on my nerves."

"One of them was here a little while ago." I folded the newspaper and rose. "I got rid of him. But I'm surprised we haven't heard from Mrs. Hornbeak. She is not going to appreciate Matt's comments."

Perhaps our barricade did deter Mrs. Hornbeak. She called instead of coming in person. At first she was gently reproachful.

"We are accustomed to being ridiculed; but you, Ms. Newcomb, must realize that coincidence cannot explain my success. I would like you to tell the reporters . . ."

She went on in the same vein for some time, despite my denials and interruptions; toward the end of the discussion her voice became shrill and her manner very close to abusive. I had just hung up the phone when something hurled itself against the screen door and I saw Elvis.

We had an enthusiastic reunion on the steps. He obviously shared my feeling that we had been parted too long.

Alan sat down on the steps. "How about offering me a drink, if you can stop slobbering over that mutt?"

I decided to overlook the pejorative comment in view of his contribution to Elvis's continued survival. "Let me feed him first."

I brought Alan's glass of bourbon along with mine outside. The sun hung low over the wooded slope to the west, and a ruffle of rainbow-colored clouds framed its orb. There was the faintest trace of a breeze.

"Have you seen the paper?" I asked, offering it.

Alan smiled sardonically as he scanned the story. "Your cousin is a smart politician. Stupid man, smart politician. Have you had the press here?"

"One. I'm getting pretty good at running them off. Mrs. Hornbeak wasn't as easy to put off."

"She was here too?"

"No, she telephoned. I wish you and Matt would deal with your own enemies and stop foisting them off on me."

Alan smiled wickedly. Leaning back, he braced his elbows and lifted his face to the breeze. His hair clung damply to his forehead.

"She said something, though, that got me to thinking," I went on. "That her discovery was too accurate to be dismissed as coincidence. She's right, Alan. Out of all those acres of wilderness, how could she pinpoint the spot so neatly?"

"No doubt you've thought of an answer too," Alan said peaceably. "Spirit guides?"

"Bah, humbug."

"My sentiments exactly."

"Don't you . . . Do you believe in any kind of . . . well, of survival?"

I was afraid he might laugh at me. Instead he said seriously, "There's no easy answer to that one, Julie. I am willing to accept the possibility that the spirits of the dead might try to communicate with the living, if there was an urgent need, or a strong commitment. What I can't believe is that they would waste their time swapping clichés with a horse's ass like Polly Hornbeak."

"Nicely put."

"Thank you. So what's the explanation for her success?"

"Obviously she has access to information you don't have."

"I wouldn't say obviously. It is one possibility."

"You're a pompous bastard," I said, without malice. "Where could she have found it?"

"Again, there are several possibilities. They have a rather impressive library at the Institute."

"Yes, but it's another possibility that worries me. What if she found her information here?"

"Where here?"

"Huh? Oh. Alan, this house is full of junk that hasn't been sorted for decades. There could be material in the library, in the attic . . . I don't think anyone has broken in since I arrived, but who knows what went on before that?"

"Oddly enough, that possibility had also occurred to me."

"Well, you're damned cool about it, I must say! Weren't you the one who read Matt the lecture about leaving three defenseless women unprotected?"

"I doubt that anyone will bother you now that you

have the dog," Alan said, with maddening calm. "How are you getting on with the reconstruction?"

The change of subject caught me by surprise. "I haven't started it yet," I muttered. "I had to get the room arranged."

"Let's see." He rose.

I displayed my interior decoration, and Alan was kind enough to approve. He was amused by my makeshift stand for the cast: a porcelain cachepot, which cradled the rounded cranium.

"Not bad," he admitted. "That will do for a start, but I'll get you a proper stand."

He seemed disposed to linger, but I showed him to the door, explaining that I had to relieve Shirley. "You're not really nervous about burglars, are you?" he asked.

"I am not nervous! I possess a reasonable degree of logical concern about the subject. Mrs. Hornbeak was really furious. Suppose she decides to come back and have another look for secret documents?"

"I would suggest something if I didn't think you'd bite my head off."

"What?"

"Never mind."

"You mean let you look first?" I hesitated only briefly. "I wouldn't mind, Alan, but the only place I can let you explore is the library. Martha would hear you if you moved around in the attic."

His lip curled, but he said only, "You had better check with the senator first. I don't want to get arrested now that I'm on the verge of something big."

Martha gave me a hard time that evening. She acted like a child who is trying to postpone the moment of bedtime.

She wanted a glass of ice water and a cup of tea and she wanted me to have a cup with her and she wanted toast and the first piece was too dark and the second piece was too cold . . . The final demand was for her sleeping pills, but I balked at that; I had agreed with Shirley that she should be solely responsible for administering Martha's medication.

When Shirley finally relieved me I collected my nightgown and slippers and went downstairs. It was still early, so I decided to work on the cast.

I had already marked the measurement points and begun cutting the markers. The latter was a finicky job, because they had to be accurate to a millimeter. Gluing them in place didn't take long, but it was close to midnight before I finished, and I knew I ought to get to bed. Yet I hated to stop. It would be a good many hours before I could get any sense of what the woman had looked like, but I was beginning to feel quite possessive about her. I took out the modeling clay and started the next stage—connecting the markers with strips of clay, laying a foundation on which the final modeling would be made.

The skull looked really weird by the time I finished. The bands of interconnecting clay resembled the helmet of a Viking warrior or a futuristic Star Wars fighter. It wasn't until I stopped that I realized how tired I was, and I decided to leave the cast in its cradle for the night. If Elvis had been a cat instead of a dog, I wouldn't have risked it, but he was not in the habit of jumping onto tables unless there was food on them.

I let him out for a moment, and as I waited in the doorway I saw a light—not a flickering, distant warning of trespassers, but the square of a lighted window. Alan had not said he planned to sleep in the shed, but I knew the light must be his. It shone steady and unconcealed, and I will candidly admit I was glad to see it.

Elvis finally came back in. I gave him his dog biscuit; he crunched it appreciatively while I locked the door. We were both asleep within five minutes.

I woke with a start, every muscle taut and quivering with the urgency of the dream that had broken my slumber. The dream had been shattered too; nothing remained of it except that sense of desperate need, and a lingering sound—a soft, weak wailing, the lament of something small and helpless, worn out with long weeping.

I knew I was awake, but it seemed to me I could hear it still—the saddest, most heartbreaking sound I had ever heard. Tears filled my eyes and trickled down my cheeks. And then at last—or so I thought—I came fully awake. The sound was not that of a baby crying. It was the dog.

My cheeks were still wet with tears as I fumbled across the tangled bedding in search of Elvis. A dog growling in the night doesn't do a lot for a person's nerves, but it was better—anything would have been better—than that forlorn weeping. Finally I found Elvis's collar. He hushed at my whispered command, but I could feel his entire body quivering.

The night was still. There was no breeze to rustle the branches of the shrubs outside the window, not even a cricket or a tree frog chirping. I had no doubt that Elvis had heard something, and after a moment I heard it too. It didn't come from inside the house. The door of my room was solid oak, an inch thick, and it fit tightly into the frame. The sound came from outside—a metallic scraping at the back door.

Still holding the dog's collar, I slid out of bed. The shrubs outside the window screened off the moonlight and for a moment I was completely disoriented. I couldn't find my flashlight or my shoes. It's funny how defenseless you feel in your bare feet. I couldn't have located the door if the dog had not pulled me in the right direction.

He was practically choking, he wanted so badly to bark. His presence calmed my nerves. He was a combined burglar alarm and defensive weapon, but I didn't want to use him in either capacity. If the burglar entered the house, he or she would have to pass the door of my room on the way to the front hall. I had no intention of going on the offensive, with or without Elvis, but I was determined to find out who the midnight visitor was.

I reached for the doorknob. My fingers had just closed over it when I felt it turn.

It had never occurred to me that the intruder would come into my room, and it scared me so badly that I retreated as far as I could go, and huddled at the foot of the bed, clutching Elvis in my arms. The door opened. A beam of light, slender as a sword blade, invaded the room. It fell full on the skull, with its grotesque tracery of clay. I almost screamed myself at the sight. The person in the doorway let out a soft hiss of breath and started forward.

Elvis had obeyed my orders like a lamb up till then, though it obviously went against all his instincts. This was too much. His barking exploded in my ear and he squirmed free. I sat down ignominiously on my bottom. I don't doubt that the person with the flashlight said something as the dog launched itself at him, but his comment was lost in Elvis's howls. The flashlight wobbled and fell and went out. I heard a sharp cracking sound that I took for a shot, and a yelp from Elvis. That brought me to my feet. I plunged forward, straight into the footboard of the bed.

The top of the post crunched into my diaphragm and my big toe connected with the bottom of the post. It hurt more than I would have believed possible. My yell of pain was drowned in the general uproar—smashes and crashes and the frantic barks of Elvis. He was still alive, at any rate. As I nursed my aching toe I heard footsteps beat a rapid path toward the door. He—she—it—whatever—was getting away. Elvis went after him. The rapidity with which the volume of his barking diminished suggested that pursuer and pursued were setting a good pace. I started to follow. My foot came down on a sharp object that seemed to pierce it to the bone.

Complicated as it sounds, the whole business couldn't have lasted for more than thirty seconds. It seemed to take a lot longer. As I hopped toward the door and the light switch, I couldn't understand why no one had come to my rescue. The racket should have aroused everyone for miles around.

I had just switched on the light when I heard running footsteps returning. If I had been able to lay my hands on a heavy object I'd have brained the newcomer, but luckily I couldn't find a weapon, because the newcomer was Alan.

He was fully dressed, including his heavy work shoes. He held a rusty crowbar. I swayed toward him; he dropped the crowbar and lifted me clean off my feet, holding me so tightly his arms seemed to restrain rather than support me.

"Julie—what . . . Are you—"

"Never mind," I yelled. "I'm all right—go get him!"

The arms that held me relaxed. I couldn't see Alan's face, since his chin was pressing down on my head, but I heard his breath come out in a ragged gasp that might have betokened relief . . . or exasperated laughter, or . . .

"There can't be much wrong with you. Quit kicking, will you? There's blood all over the place. Did he—"

"He didn't touch me. I stepped on something sharp . . . Oh, damn! The cast—it's smashed to smithereens. And Elvis is gone, he chased him out, he'll get shot—"

Alan lowered me onto the bed and knelt, taking my bleeding foot into his hand. My lament over Elvis ended in a bleat of pain as his fingers gently probed and squeezed.

"I want to make sure there are no fragments of glass in the wound, Julie. You must have stepped on the broken glass from the flashlight; the edges of the cast aren't sharp enough to make such clean cuts. His flashlight, I presume?"

"Or hers. Ouch! Alan, stop fussing over me and go look for Elvis."

"The dog is all right, Julie. We'd have heard shots or yells or barks, or something, if Elvis had caught up with the guy. Where do you keep your first aid stuff?"

Fortunately for my blood pressure, Elvis came back before Alan had finished bandaging my foot. At my shriek of joy he leaped onto the bed and allowed me to embrace him. He looked awfully pleased with himself—the Heroic Dog in person. Though he was covered with dirt and dry grass, there was not a mark on him, nor, to my regret, was there a convenient fragment of cloth caught in his teeth.

"Hold him till I get this glass cleaned up," Alan said, and proceeded to sweep the floor while I watched.

"I'm sorry about the cast, Alan," I said. "I should have put it in the closet, but I was so sleepy—"

"I'll have another one made," Alan said curtly. "I've got the mold."

"You may not have caught him, old boy," I told Elvis, "but you sure helped him make one hell of a mess."

As soon as Alan had finished sweeping, I got up. "Where are you going now?" he demanded.

"I'm going to shut Elvis in the kitchen and then check on Martha."

The first thing I saw when I opened Martha's door was the horrid gleam of a white eyeball. She appeared to be sound asleep; but the sound of the door opening, soft as it was, roused Shirley in the next room. She appeared in the open doorway, her wide eyes reflecting the glow of the night light.

"Miz Martha—"

"She's all right. I just looked in to—ah—just looked in. Sorry I woke you."

Shirley padded to the bed and bent over Martha. "Yes, she's sleeping." She straightened and looked at me; though she spoke in a whisper, the hurt dignity in her voice was unmistakable. "You don't need to worry, Julie. I'd wake if I heard her."

"I wasn't checking up on you, Shirley—honest. I just . . . Look, I'll explain in the morning. Go back to sleep now—please."

I retreated, feeling like a worm. I'd apologize and set things straight in the morning; there was no need to ruin what was left of Shirley's repose. I had heard that nurses can train themselves to sleep undisturbed by extraneous noises, and to rouse instantly at the slightest sound from their patients. Mother claimed she had done the same thing when I was little.

When I got downstairs Alan was making coffee. He offered me a cup. I shook my head. Reaction had set in; I felt myself shaking all over and I was afraid I'd drop the cup if I tried to hold it.

Alan gave me a sharp glance and placed the cup on the table. "Drink it. It's half sugar—you need a stimulant."

What I needed was someone to hold me and hug me and tell me there was nothing to be afraid of. But I'd rather have died than say so. I had only imagined that Alan's first spontaneous embrace held anything more than normal concern. Maybe if I had blubbered and clung to him . . . Well, it was too late now. Besides—I assured myself—I wouldn't resort to that kind of emotional entrapment.

Alan was watching me. I sat down and drew the cup toward me, slowly, so it wouldn't spill.

"Are you feeling better?" Alan asked. His voice was cool and disinterested.

"I'm all right."

"He won't be back tonight," Alan said. "It will be light in a few hours. Why don't you go back to bed?"

"I couldn't sleep."

"Do you want me to stay?"

Did I want him to stay! "I'm sure you have other things you'd rather be doing," I said.

Alan got up. "As soon as the sun rises I'll take the dog and try to track your burglar. No sense blundering around in the dark."

"Who do you think it was?"

Alan shrugged. "It could have been one of several people."

After he had gone I sat staring at the closed door. A core of icy cold had settled around me. One of several people . . . including Alan himself. It would be a perfect cover-up for an intruder—to turn on his tracks and return as the heroic rescuer.

twelve

Daylight revived my nerve a little—but not much. What bothered me most was the unavoidable conclusion that the intruder had been after me. There was no other reason why he should have entered that room.

Alan found me huddled over the kitchen table staring at my cold coffee when he returned shortly after six o'clock.

"No luck," he announced. "There are broken branches in the boxwood, where he forced his way through. But the ground is too dry to take footprints and Elvis copped out when we got to the road. He must have left his car there."

"You keep saying 'he.' How do you know it wasn't a woman?"

"I don't. When will the sheriff be here?"

"Huh?" I looked blearily at him.

"Didn't you call him?" Alan snatched at the telephone. "For God's sake, do I have to tell you to do everything?"

"I hated to wake him up," I said yawning.

"Someone would have been awake. You think the cops close down at five and don't reopen until . . . Hello?"

When he hung up he was scowling. "They bawled me out for not reporting the incident earlier. Go get dressed."

"Are they coming?"

"Of course they're coming. Breaking and entering is a crime, hadn't you heard?"

I got the impression that Sheriff Jarboe was getting a little tired of the Carrs and their problems, but he was very nice. He didn't even blame me for not notifying him immediately; he blamed Alan.

Feeling somewhat ashamed of my cowardice, I pulled myself together and started breakfast. When Shirley came down Jarboe and his deputy had joined Alan at the kitchen table and I was serving toast, scrambled eggs, and coffee.

"There was nothing you could have done," I said, cutting short Shirley's broken exclamations of guilt and distress. "It was all over in a few minutes."

"Yes, but I should have woken up. I don't usually sleep that hard."

The sheriff interrupted. "She's right, Shirley. Quit calling yourself names and get back up to Miz Martha. You better not tell her about this."

"No, I sure won't. I just don't know what's going on. We never had things like this happen before. . . ."

She went off with Martha's tray and the rest of us finished the scrambled eggs. "We'll have another look around before we go," Jarboe said, crunching into his third piece of toast. "But I didn't see a damned thing. Must have been the same gang, though."

"Gang?" Alan repeated, raising his eyebrows. "Julie said there was only one person."

"She only saw one. The others were probably outside, waiting for the scout to give them the all clear."

Jarboe was sticking to his theory. Alan didn't reply, but his sardonic smile told me he was as skeptical as I of Jarboe's facile explanation.

Before Jarboe left he examined the debris Alan had swept from the floor of my room. "Smart of you to keep it, Professor," he said grudgingly. "Nothing here, though."

Nothing there *now.* It would be smart to sweep the floor if you weren't sure whether you had left some evidence of your presence. But why would Alan break into the house? He had managed to work his way into my confidence, and Shirley's; he could come and go as he pleased during the day.

Jarboe picked up his hat. "I'll increase the number of rounds the patrol car makes," he promised. "And I'll tell the boys to drive up to the house instead of passing on the road. Don't be worried if you hear a car at night."

"I don't suppose I could talk you into leaving a man here at night," I said.

Jarboe repeated the familiar litany. "Not enough manpower. Uh—Julie—you aren't going to sleep in that room again, I hope."

I said I hadn't thought about it.

"Better not. You're safer upstairs. Not," Jarboe added quickly, "not that I think they were looking for you in particular. But there's no telling what they might do if they found a woman alone . . . I mean, why take chances?"

Having said all the wrong things, he beat a hasty retreat. I turned to Alan. "I feel worse now than I did before he showed up."

"Get a few hours' sleep and you'll be fine." Alan stood up. "Want me to leave the dog?"

"Yes. No . . . I don't know."

"I'll leave him. I have a few errands to run. Stop looking like a wounded doe, nobody is going to bother you in broad daylight. I'll be back about noon."

Shirley also suggested I take a nap, which confirmed my suspicion that I looked as haggard as I felt. I snapped at her and then repented, for she was clearly still blaming herself for my misadventure. "I don't need any more sleep," I assured her. "I get by on a lot less than five hours a night when I'm in school. Why don't you run home for a while?"

"You sure you aren't scared here alone?"

I laughed heartily.

"Maybe I will run over home and do some cleaning," Shirley said. "I need to do something to wake myself up. I must be getting old to sleep so sound."

We were standing outside Martha's door, I on my way in, Shirley on her way down with the tray. "She must have slept good too," Shirley said. "Bright as a new penny this morning. She didn't even ask me what was going on down there, with the police and all. She just lies there and sort of smiles. I hope it's not a sign . . ."

I stifled another laugh—my first genuine laugh of the morning—at the picture of Martha beaming beatifically at the angels who were gliding in to carry her away to the Golden Gates. "It's more likely that she's planning some dirty trick to play on one of us," I said. "Run along, and don't worry about me."

Martha was no more gracious than usual, but I thought I understood the reason for her smiles. When I went in the room I caught her in the act of lowering herself back against the pillow. She had been sitting up—and she must have raised herself, because Shirley wouldn't have left her in that position. The dear old wretch was flexing her muscles on the sly. It was just like her to carry out her own version of exercise, after refusing the help of a trained therapist.

I had not been reading long before the telephone rang. When I heard Matt's voice I realized I should have notified him of the events of the past night. He was concerned, reproachful, and angry in turn.

"How did you find out?" I asked, watching Martha. For once she had the courtesy to pretend she wasn't listening, but her good eye was cocked in my direction.

"Jarboe called me. You ought to have let me know, Julie. It's a hell of a note when I have to find out about my cousin being attacked from the police—"

"I wasn't attacked."

"You're sure you're all right?"

"Yes."

"What the devil were you doing down there anyway?"

The anger in his voice didn't annoy me; I took it as a sign of cousinly concern and was rather more pleased than otherwise. "Do you really want me to explain?"

"Oh—you're with Martha. Never mind, then. I'm going to try to get out there this evening. Let me talk to her for a minute, okay?"

I handed Martha the phone, observing the increased strength with which her hand closed over the instrument. Her speech was the only thing that hadn't improved. She let Matt do most of the talking. Her eyes sparkled as she listened; I assumed he was telling her of his intention of seeing her soon.

The morning wore away in the usual fashion. When twelve o'clock came around, Shirley had not returned, so I closed the book and told Martha I was going to get lunch.

Elvis was under the kitchen table, looking bored and forlorn. I let him out for a run and investigated the food situation. I was stirring an unattractive blend of noodles and peas and cheese when Shirley came in, breathless and apologetic.

"I'm sorry I'm late," she began.

"You'll be even sorrier when you taste this." I waved a spoon over the pan on the stove.

"Ron's lost his job." She dropped heavily into a chair.

"Oh, Shirley, I'm sorry! What happened?"

"He says he got kicked out because a friend of the manager's wanted the job. But I wouldn't be surprised if he smart-mouthed somebody."

"That's a shame, Shirley. Maybe I can find some more work for him around here. Or Alan might need another worker."

"I'd sure appreciate that. Goodness, child, what have you got in that pan?"

She went to work on the noodles. I let the subject drop; I too had heard Mrs. Danner's shuffling approach and I didn't blame Shirley for not wanting to discuss Ron's situation in front of Martha's stooge—especially that aspect of Ron's situation that worried his mother most. She must be well aware of how Jarboe's suspicions were running. That was why she had rushed home, to make sure Ron had an alibi for last night. Obviously he had none, and the loss of his job gave him an even stronger motive for turning, or returning, to burglary.

Shirley took Martha's tray upstairs, and Mrs. Danner and I sat down to finish the noodles, which weren't half bad, thanks to Shirley's intervention. Mrs. Danner ate in silence, her eyes on her plate. I thought I'd try a little detective work of my own, so I said abruptly, "Somebody broke into the house last night."

The even tempo of her chewing and swallowing didn't alter. The element of surprise having failed, I asked point-blank whether her husband had left their house during the night.

"No, ma'am. He didn't. You want I should clean the parlor?"

"What is this strange obsession you have with the parlor?" I asked.

Sarcasm was wasted on Mrs. Danner. She gave me a blank stare. I knew the answer to the question: the wine decanter was in the parlor. I said slowly, "No, Mrs. Danner, I don't want you to clean the parlor. Go and relieve Shirley." I couldn't resist a last shot, mean person that I am; as she trudged toward the door I added, "If Miss Martha asks what went on here last night, go ahead and tell her."

Mrs. Danner's stooped shoulder twitched, the way a cow's does when a fly is biting it, but that was her only response.

I was sitting at the table scribbling a shopping list when Elvis's whines alerted me to Alan's arrival. He was loaded down with parcels, so I opened the door for him.

"I see you're still alive," was his greeting. "No more burglars?"

"Thanks for noticing. What have you got?"

"Presents for you."

"Oh, no. Not another . . . How did you get it done so fast?"

Alan looked smug. "I had an extra on hand."

"In case I screwed up?"

"It's a good thing I did, isn't it?"

I couldn't deny it. "I don't know that I'm in the mood any longer."

"You had better get in the mood." Alan began unloading the bags. "Speed is of the essence. I want this yesterday. I'd like you to start on it right away." After a moment he added, "Please."

"Why? No, don't tell me, let me guess. National Geographic is hesitating."

"I need all the ammunition I can get," Alan said.

"Don't you want me to help you dig?"

"The dig is closed down temporarily until I find out where I stand financially. N.G. isn't my only lead. I should hear from someone by the end of the week, and then I can set up a proper excavation."

It seemed to me that there was some inconsistency in his statement. If he needed the reconstruction to impress potential donors, further evidence from the dig would serve the same purpose. I was distracted, however, by the objects he had removed from the bags. Another cast of the skull—that broad white smile was becoming as familiar as the face of an old friend—a proper stand, modeling clay and erasers, and several new items. I gulped when he took the lid from a box and I saw a pair of eyeballs staring at me.

"Might as well do it right this time," he said. "I got false eyelashes too, and a wig."

"They're brown," I said, staring back at the eyeballs.

"Indubitably."

"But hers were . . ."

Alan pretended he hadn't heard. "Brown is the most common eye color."

"Like mine."

"Yours aren't brown. They're hazel. Anyhow," Alan said, before I could comment, "let's get it set up."

I followed him to my room and watched him lay out the supplies. "What's that?" I asked, as he removed the final object from the bag.

"Lock for the door. I'll install it while you get started."

He had brought the necessary tools. As he set to work drilling I remarked casually, "I am not sleeping here to-night."

"Suit yourself. But I want it kept locked, whether you're in or out of it."

By the time he had installed the lock I was well under way. I had gone through the same process so recently that it was easier the second time. Alan leaned over me, breathing on the back of my neck, until I said irritably, "Will you stop that? I can't concentrate."

"Are you almost finished with the markers?"

"Six more."

"Hurry up, will you?"

I did not reply. When I had set the final, twenty-sixth marker in place, I turned on him. "What do you want?"

"Want? A lot of things." Alan's eyes were veiled, opaque. "But I'll settle for an hour or two in the attic."

"Alan, I told you, I can't—"

"Why not?"

"Martha might hear you. She—"

"She'd do what?" His voice was even, his pose relaxed, but I felt the anger that seethed under the thin surface of his apparent calm. "Call you bad names? Threaten to cut you out of her will? When are you going to get it through your head that she can't hurt you any more? You're not a child, you're a healthy, independent adult—and she's a sick old woman. I swear to God, when I see what she's done to you I could almost believe in witchcraft!"

I stared at him, silent and shaken. It may have been my look of blank helplessness that shattered his self-control; his anger boiled over into quick, hot words. "What the hell is the matter with you and your precious cousin? Don't you care whether uninvited visitors stroll around the house at all hours of the night? I could put locks on every door and window—which is more than the honorable Senator has bothered to do—but that still wouldn't guarantee your safety. Something peculiar is going on here, and I want to know what it is. Are you going to take me upstairs, or do I go alone—stopping on the way to spit in Martha's eye and tell her what I think of her?"

Anger can be a sign of caring. Instead of resenting his outrage, I felt strengthened by it. I even summoned up a shaky smile. "That would be the end of Martha; she'd have a fatal stroke at the mere sight of you. I'll take you. But what do you hope to find?"

Alan relaxed. He could afford to; he had won the argument. "It's more a question of what I hope *not* to find—signs that someone has been up there recently. Polly Hornbeak found a lead somewhere; good old Joe Danner is looking for God knows what—and don't forget the clothes the skeletons were wearing. Nobody in the neighborhood recognized them. They had to come from somewhere." He didn't give me time to reconsider, but reached for my hand and pulled me to my feet. "Come on."

Neither of us spoke again until we stood before the door that concealed the stairs leading to the attic. Martha's door had been closed when we tiptoed past—I tiptoed, at any rate; Alan made no effort to moderate the sound of his footsteps. The attic stairs were at the far end of a wing that had been closed off ever since I could remember. At first the door refused to open, and I felt a cowardly sense of relief, remembering that during my childhood it had always been locked. It wasn't locked now. Alan gave the handle a mighty tug, and the door creaked and yielded.

The smell of stale, musty air triggered the memory flash I had known would come. Sunlight stretching long fingers across dusty floorboards, the shrill buzzing of a fly trapped by the sticky strands of a spiderweb high under the rafters, splinters scraping my bare knees as I knelt to look inside . . .

Inside . . . something. I couldn't see it. It was gone. Alan was gone too—up the stairs, into the attic. I heard the boards groan under his feet.

My hands were sticky with sweat. It would be hot as the hinges of Hades up there; the big circular window under the eaves had probably not been opened in years. Part of me—the coward child—wanted to run away. But another, wiser part knew I had passed the point of no return, that I would never be free of Martha, or of the past, until I saw what was waiting for me at the top of the stairs.

It seemed to take an eternity to climb up there. There was no door at the top, only an opening in the floor. I kept my eyes fixed on the steps until my reluctant feet had reached the last of them.

Dim sunlight, starred by dancing dust motes, lay in remembered pathways across the uncarpeted floor. The center of the big room was bare; discarded furniture, boxes, barrels, crates had been arranged around the perimeter, against the walls. The only footprints that had scuffed the dust were Alan's; he stood with his back to me, head tipped to one side as if he were listening.

I saw it all in a single glance, saw and discarded everything except one object—the humpbacked trunk in the corner farthest from the stairs. I don't remember crying out, but I must have done so, for Alan turned with a lithe, startled quickness. "Julie? What—"

My voice was no more than a whisper. "The trunk. I was looking inside. I forced the lock—I don't know why—it was the only thing that was locked, I thought there must be something special in it . . . She found me. She always found me—she always knew. Alan . . ."

Wordlessly he held out his hands. I caught at them as if they were a lifeline. The next moment I was in his arms, cradled, sheltered; his lips met mine with an urgency no less than my own.

We had made love in some peculiar places before that. Under the table in Alan's office—the only space that wasn't filled with books and desks and filing cabinets; in a muddy pasture outside Williamsburg, with three puzzled cows for an audience. Never could there have been such a wildly inappropriate spot as that filthy, steaming attic—the splintered boards hard under our bodies, the dust tickling our throats and our nostrils.

And never before had our loving been as it was that day—a dizzying, dazzling achievement of oneness that wiped out the last shreds of doubt as a clean flame cuts through clinging cobwebs. I had not known the barrier was there until it went down and I knew I was free of it now forever.

We lay side by side on the floor. Idly, with my finger, I traced a heart in the dust; Alan laughed, and drew an arrow through it.

"She came here regularly—every few weeks. Always alone. She never carried anything up, she never brought anything down. I became curious. Lord knows I didn't have much to occupy my mind in those days. She kept the door locked, but that didn't stop me; I found a key, in one of the other doors, that fit the simple lock. I was scared to death the first time I ventured up those stairs; but in a way, that made the whole thing more exciting. It was an adventure, a small but important act of defiance.

"I must have been up here three or four times before I got nerve enough to attack the trunk. Nothing else was locked; I decided there must be treasures inside, jewels, Blackbeard's gold . . . I didn't really expect I'd be able to open it. The hasp must have been worn with rust; it gave way, with a horrible crack, the first time I tugged at it. I lifted the lid . . . I had been squatting on the floor, you see; I got to my knees and leaned forward to look in . . ."

Alan reached for my hand. "Get it out," he said gently. "What did she do? Hit you, or—"

"No. Oh, no. She . . . I don't know how she crept up on me without my hearing her. One of the boards creaked, but not until she was right beside me. I looked up and there she was, still as a statue . . . She seemed to be ten feet tall. When she stooped down it was like a boulder falling on me. I couldn't move. I heard her say something about satisfying my curiosity . . . She put me in the trunk and closed the lid. I don't remember anything more . . . Alan, you're hurting my hand."

He put his arms around me and held me close. He didn't speak at first; then he said in a stifled voice, "I knew something was wrong, but I never suspected it was that bad. Why didn't you tell me?"

"I had forgotten. I wiped out practically every memory of those years. They're coming back to me now, suddenly and shockingly at times. Now I know why I hate my bedroom upstairs. She'd lock me in there for punishment—usually on stormy days or late in the evening—and take away the lamp. There was one particularly gruesome story connected with that room—it was supposed to be haunted by a girl, a visitor, whose hair had caught fire while she was getting ready to meet her lover. She leaned too close to the candle by the mirror, to admire her pretty face . . . Martha said I'd never suffer from the sin of vanity, at any rate."

"I'd like to kill the old witch," Alan muttered.

"I did—in fantasies—over and over. But my favorite idea of revenge was to have Martha repent. I'd picture myself dressed for a ball, in long skirts and ruffles, with jewels in my hair—and Martha kneeling at my feet, suing humbly for pardon. I've wondered, since, whether Martha made up that story about the girl who was burned to death. She told me a lot of moral tales about 'light women' who were struck down by the righteous wrath of God. I knew words like 'harlot' and 'fornication' before I could spell 'Mississippi.' "

Alan grimaced. "And I wondered why you carried on so vehemently about virginity! Martha made up a lot of garbage, Julie—including your homeliness and lack of sex appeal. I knew you had a low opinion of yourself—though how you could hang on to it, with me falling over my own feet every time I looked at you—"

" 'The Carr features are too strong for a woman's face. I took after my mother's people, but you, poor child . . .' "

"That's a quote, isn't it?"

"Straight from the horse's mouth. Wasn't it a Jesuit who said, 'Give me a child before he is seven and he is mine for the rest of his life'? I was eight when Martha got her hands on me, but she did a thorough job in four years. She had no trouble convincing me that you were using me to get permission to dig at Maidenwood."

"I can't criticize you," Alan said wryly. "She did a number on me too. I don't suppose it ever occurred to you that I had a few insecurities of my own."

"You? I always thought of you as utterly self-confident."

"You don't remember what I told you about my background—my family?"

"You come from Brooklyn or someplace," I said lazily.

Alan leaned over and kissed me thoroughly. "That," he

said, "is for remembering only the important things. It never mattered to you, did it—that my father was illiterate and my mother scrubbed offices at night, and my uncle . . . Well, the less said about my uncle, the better."

"I don't care what he was."

"But I cared," Alan said. "I was such a damned snob—all children are, I guess. You know, that is something people who have it take for granted—a sense of self-worth that stems from decent living conditions and family stability. I buried the slum kid under a pile of college degrees, but he was still there, with a chip on his shoulder as big as a house, looking for insults where none were intended. Nobody put my back up worse than these soft-spoken, smug aristocrats. I don't know how your grandmother spotted my weakness, but she sure as hell knew how to exploit it."

I sat up with a start. "Alan! You mean she told you I looked down on you because . . . Surely you didn't believe that?"

"The professor didn't; but Al Petranek fell for it."

"Five years," I murmured. "We lost five years that we can never get back. When I think what she did to you—"

"To me? What she did to *you* was child abuse, pure and simple. The sheer malevolence of the woman . . . Are you sure that trunk didn't contain black candles and unholy devices, and a copy of the contract she signed with Satan?"

He spoke lightly, but his face was anxious as he rose on one elbow and looked at me. Smiling, I shook my head. "I'm not suppressing that memory, Alan. I never got a good look inside the trunk. Something white and crumpled—fabric, from the feel of it; but whatever it was, it was at the very bottom of the trunk. There was plenty of room inside for me."

Alan sat up and reached for his clothes. "Let's get out of this filthy place. I'll never forgive myself for dragging you up here."

"It was the best thing you could have done. You've exorcised the last of my ghosts, Alan. I'll never be afraid to come here again."

"Well . . . Maybe it wasn't such a bad idea, at that." Alan tossed his shirt aside and reached out for me.

Some time later I left him rummaging happily among the books in the library and went back to my reconstruction. I was so dizzy with happiness I felt drunk.

At first the strips of modeling clay went in all directions. But they were easy to peel off, and after a while I got myself under control. Gradually the work cast its own spell. My fingers moved with a skill I hadn't known I possessed.

Alan's low whistle of surprise woke me from a daze of concentration. Hands resting lightly on my shoulders, he studied the cast in silence for a time. Then he said, "That's good, Julie. That's damned good. I didn't know you were such an expert."

"I'm not. This is just a matter of filling in the blank spaces, following the contours of the bone."

"Speaking of bones, yours aren't bad." His fingertips traced them—temples to cheekbones, the angles of the lower jaw; then they curved and tightened, tipping my head back. The kiss had barely begun when we both heard footsteps, and Alan swore.

"Close the door," I suggested brazenly.

"I have to go."

"Oh. Well, of course, if you're in a hurry—"

Careless of Mrs. Danner's proximity, he lifted me out of

the chair and convinced me that he was as reluctant to leave as I was to have him go.

"I'm already an hour late for a meeting," he said.

"With someone who might give you money?"

I smiled, but Alan didn't. "I wouldn't go if it weren't important. Are you sure you'll be all right?"

"Of course."

"I may not be back till late. I hope you aren't going to sleep downstairs."

"Not me. Once was enough."

"Be sure you lock up."

"I will."

Mrs. Danner had passed the door and gone into the kitchen. Alan kissed me again. "I think I'll call and tell them I broke a leg," he murmured.

"Get going. We need that money."

"What a beautiful word."

"Money?"

"We."

After an interval—a long interval—we went to the kitchen. Mrs. Danner was wiping the sink. Alan greeted her; she mumbled something and went on wiping. Alan said casually to me, "Someone has been in the library, no question about that. I couldn't tell whether anything was missing, the place is in such chaos, but I made sure no one will get in that door without setting off an alarm."

"How could—"

Alan cut me off with a shake of the head and a meaningful glance at Mrs. Danner. "Oh," I said. "Thanks."

I followed him into the yard. When we were out of earshot of Mrs. Danner he said, "There's no way those doors can be made secure. But at least the word will get back to one of the possible suspects."

"Do you think it was Joe Danner?"

"I think Danner was interested in the library. The only reason I can think of why he would carry a pair of scissors was to cut something out—a map, for instance."

"A map!"

"He may have been bit by the treasure bug," Alan explained. "Think how pleased his God would be if he were given Blackbeard's loot. Joe is smart enough to know that libraries contain old books with old maps; not smart enough to know that none of them would be of any use to him." He glanced at his watch. "Damn. I wish I didn't have to leave."

"There's nothing to worry about. Things are no different now than they have been all along."

"That's what worries me."

Romantic novelists gush about a thing called the inner glow of happiness. There may or may not be such a thing, but happiness does show on the outside. Martha noticed it. I guess that had always been her secret—not clairvoyance or a pact with the Devil, but the same skill possessed by successful fortune tellers—the ability to detect and interpret small involuntary muscular movements. Not that it took much insight to see the change in me. I couldn't seem to stop smiling.

Her comment was a sarcastic "You look very pleased with yourself."

"I'm in a good mood. Since when is that a crime?"

"Why?"

"Why not?" I riposted brilliantly.

Martha's lips twisted in the movement that always preceded a particularly withering comment. She glanced significantly at my left hand, and I laughed. "Martha, you have a one-track mind. If and when I get engaged, you will be duly informed. Now what would you like me to read? We finished *Death on the Hearthrug* yesterday."

Martha was still wide awake and staring when Shirley came. Earlier, I had heard the sound of a car leaving. It had not returned, so I gathered Ron had borrowed it again. Shirley's worn expression also suggested she had had an encounter with her eldest child, but I didn't want to raise a subject that obviously upset her, and she did not volunteer anything.

The kitchen door was locked. I also locked the door of my room before I went back to work.

Dark pressed in at the windows and the trees muttered softly as the breeze moved their branches. I had expected to be nervous, despite the locks and bars, but I wasn't; the presence of Elvis, sprawled on the rug, twitching and whining in his sleep, was as good as a tranquilizer.

It was well after midnight before I realized that my hands had lost the delicacy of touch so essential in this final stage. I had roughly blocked in the facial planes indicated by the markers and the connecting strips of clay; now came the part that was almost pure guesswork, for some of the structures of the living face leave no imprint on the bone. Had her lips been full and red, or narrow and pale? Her nose retroussé or aquiline?

When I leaned back and looked at what I had done, I had a flash of something like déjà vu. It came and went so quickly I couldn't pin it down. I had begun with the easiest part, the forehead. People don't have fat foreheads, and a young woman's brow would be smooth and unmarked. The setting of the eyes presented problems, but I had blocked them in too. Enclosed in the modeling medium, the glass reflected the lamplight as living eyes might have done.

Tentatively I smoothed away a slight bulge in the clay

over one temple. The fleeting impression was gone. I only hoped I had not yielded to the temptation to reproduce a face with which I was familiar.

I put the cast on a shelf in the closet, unlocked my door, and peeked out. Elvis rose and stretched. He appeared unperturbed. I counted on his instincts more than on my own. I let him out for his last run. There was no comforting square of light visible tonight. Alan must not have returned. I wished now that I had decided to sleep downstairs. The room was as secure as human effort could make it, and Alan could have come to me there, no matter how late he returned. Tomorrow night we would make better arrangements. My body tingled at the thought.

Elvis was pleasantly surprised when I attached his leash and led him up the stairs. He had to inspect the new room, sniffing in every corner, before he jumped onto the bed. His eyes were bright and his tongue lolled out, as if he were laughing.

"Enjoy it while you can," I told him. "You're excellent company and I'm glad to have you, but I rather wish you were someone else."

People do silly things when they are feeling sentimental. I talked to Elvis; if he hadn't been there I would have talked to myself. I studied my features in the mirror, and for the first time my face pleased me; it looked almost pretty. Instead of braiding my hair I let it fall to my shoulders, and I spent a ridiculous amount of time brushing it. I put on my best nightgown, an imitation Victorian garment of white cotton, with lots of lace and ruffles. I postured and smirked at my reflection. After I got into bed . . . Well, never mind what I thought about.

Tired as I was, I didn't sleep at once. I was too happy. I had just begun to drift off when the dog shifted his weight and sat up.

Approaching sleep had dulled my senses; at first I thought I must be dreaming, reliving the experience of the night before. It was against all reason that lightning could strike twice—and not even in the same place. How could Elvis hear sounds from the floor below, through closed doors and miles of corridor?

He had heard or sensed something. This time he didn't growl. I touched him and felt the stiffened hair on the back of his neck, over rigid muscles.

I had not locked my door. I didn't even have a key for it. I did have a light, and as my fingers found the switch of the bedside lamp I blessed Edison and all the other scientists, from the first discoverer of fire, who had freed mankind from the terrors of the dark.

I wasn't especially afraid. The sounds of this part of the house were new to the dog; perhaps he had heard an animal in the bushes under the window, or a night bird. I said softly, "What is it, Elvis?"

He turned his head and looked at me, in a gesture so human it was rather startling. Then he jumped off the bed. Stiff-legged, he crept toward the door.

Then I was afraid. I had never seen him behave like that. His movements were dragging and reluctant, as if he were forcing himself to face a danger that terrified him.

It cost me a considerable effort to turn out the light. But to open the door without doing so meant exposing myself to whatever walked in the darkened house. I heard the dog whimper low in his throat as I passed him. I wanted to whimper back.

The hall outside my door was pitch-black. Something was wrong. There should have been light to the left, where the sconce outside Martha's door was always left burning.

Then I heard the sounds the dog's keener senses had

caught. Not footsteps, but the creak of the aged boards of the floor under the pressure of feet. The dog had not moved. I heard him panting heavily, as if he had been racing for his life.

I opened the door wider and stepped out. Another creak of sound and another, closer . . . Someone was moving along the hall—toward my room. It had to be my burglar. But how had he made his way into the house and got all the way upstairs? And why wasn't the dog sounding the alarm, as he had the night before?

I didn't dare think about the answers to those questions. If I had, I would have jumped back in bed and pulled the covers over my head. Instead, I turned on my flashlight and directed it straight at the end of the corridor.

The beam caught her full-on, in a frame of brightness. I saw the long gown and the heavy stick, and the face frozen by shock into a plastic monster mask. I saw the shotgun she carried.

Elvis had crept unnoticed to my side. He let out a long wavering howl, a cry of pure terror. Martha's lips parted. She croaked, "You came back. Again. You . . ."

Her hands lost their hold on gun and cane and she toppled forward. The whole house seemed to shake with the force of her fall.

thirteen

The amazing thing was that she was still alive. My body went into automatic overdrive, performing the necessary actions with machinelike efficiency. I had to slap Shirley to waken her; my mind noted, "drugged," even as I ran back to kneel by Martha.

By the time the ambulance arrived, we had done all we could. It wasn't much; but the harsh breath still rattled in and out of Martha's open mouth and she was still alive when the medics carried her out.

They left the front door wide open. I knew I ought to go down and close it, but I didn't have the strength to move. Shirley and I sat side by side on the top step, like two survivors of a tornado. Elvis tried to crawl onto my lap. His head lay heavy across my knees. We were still sitting in exhausted silence when a car came roaring down the driveway and screeched to a halt in front of the house.

Alan's headlong advance halted briefly when he saw us. Then he ran up the stairs and dropped down beside me. "You're all right! I passed the ambulance, and I was afraid. . . ."

I crawled onto his lap, in the same manner and for the same reason Elvis had tried to crawl onto mine. "It's good to see you," I said inadequately.

My account of the night's proceedings left even Alan at a loss for words momentarily. Only momentarily, though.

"It's a wonder you didn't have a stroke yourself. To see her there like that, when you thought she was incapable of getting out of bed, much less walking—"

"I knew she was trying to strengthen her muscles, but I had no idea she had been so successful. She must be senile! Why would she sneak and deceive us? Giving Shirley her own sleeping pills so she wouldn't know—"

"It's not senility, it's pure meanness," Alan said. "I know I shouldn't speak ill of the dead, but . . ."

"She isn't dead yet." I started to rise. "I had better call Matt, and get dressed, and go to the hospital."

Alan's arms closed around me. "You aren't going anyplace except to bed." He rose in one smooth movement, lifting me like a child. Then he turned to Shirley, who was staring at us, her eyes still heavy with sleep. "Alone," he added, smiling. "She's too pooped for hanky-panky tonight."

Shirley produced a weak answering smile. "I'm pretty pooped myself; I wouldn't know what anybody else was up to. I'll telephone Matthew. It's up to him if he wants to go to the hospital, but there's nothing any of you can do for her."

I clung to Alan after he had lowered me gently onto my bed, but he stepped back, shaking his head and smiling. "Shameless woman! You look like a demure, old-fashioned girl with your hair loose on the pillow; try to act like one. Until tomorrow, anyway."

"What happens tomorrow?"

"Anything you want. Don't you understand—you are free now. This is the end. Whether she lives or dies, you'll never have to live in this house again."

Relief spread through me like a wave of sunlight. I had not had time to consider the consequences of the night's terror.

"Do you want one of those sleeping pills?" Alan asked.

"No, I don't need one. I feel . . . It's as if some dark cloud that had hung over me were gone."

"A hurricane named Martha," Alan said rudely. "Sleep well, my dearest. I'll go and tuck Shirley in too, she looks exhausted. She won't get this, though . . ."

"Poor Shirley," I murmured.

I was awakened next day by Shirley's voice raised in protest. But it was not Shirley's face I saw when I opened my eyes.

"Matt," I said. "Go away, Matt."

"I told him not to wake you," Shirley said. "Here's that coffee, Matthew, but you hadn't ought to—"

"It's after noon." Matt sat down on the edge of the bed. I groaned in protest and tried to pull the sheet over my head. He removed it and tickled my chin. Another trick from the good old days.

"I'm sorry, honey, I really am." But his broad smile belied his considerate speech. "You had a hell of a night, I know," he went on. "But there are things that need to be done. Have some coffee."

"Matthew, you just come on out of here," Shirley insisted.

"It's all right." I dug both fists into my eyes and yawned

till I thought my jaws would split. Matt plumped the pillow behind me and helped me sit up.

"Keep your hands to yourself, buster," I said half-jokingly.

Matt grinned. "I'm only human. You look good in the morning, Julie. A lot better than—"

"Please don't recite the list. Just give me that cup of coffee."

A snort of disapproval from Shirley indicated her opinion of Matt's behavior. She stomped out.

Matt sat beside me, watching me. There was something different in his expression—a new speculation, curiosity, interest. It made me uncomfortable.

"You're very cheerful this morning," I said. "Is she dead?"

Matt didn't pretend to be shocked. "No," he said gloomily. "But my God, she can't go on like this forever."

"What did the doctor say?" Shirley's coffee, like everything she made, was excellent. I felt more kindly toward Matt; not every man would have thought of bringing coffee to mitigate the pain of waking. And I surely didn't blame him for refusing to play the hypocrite about Martha. She had never wanted or earned love. It had been her choice, not ours, that she was dying with no one to mourn her.

"You know how those damned doctors hedge and quibble," Matt said. "She'll have another stroke eventually—maybe today, maybe a year from now—it will be the last—maybe it won't . . . How can they be so vague?"

"You, a politician, complain about vagueness? Really, Matt, how can they commit themselves? The odds are against her living much longer, but individuals sometimes beat the odds. And her heart is in good shape."

"Well, I've made up my mind about one thing," Matt

said. "She isn't coming back here. Now that the Judge isn't around to back her up, I can put her in a nursing home, which is where she should have been all along. I should never have asked you to take this on in the first place. I hope it's not too late for you to get another job?"

The question took me by surprise. My new freedom had not sunk in yet; I had not had time to think about the future. "I won't be going home," I said. And then, before he could react, because I had to tell someone—"Alan and I are—well, we're back together. We haven't made any plans yet, but unless he throws me out, I'll be around. There's a good chance he may get funding for the excavation, and I can help him with that."

"So that's what Shirley was hinting at," Matt said. He looked not so much disapproving as thunderstruck. "I didn't realize . . ."

"I hope you aren't going to object. Not that it would make the slightest difference if you did."

"Object," Matt repeated. His face cleared as if by magic, but there was a wistful quality in his smile. "Honey, if that's what you want, I'm delighted. You're sure?"

"Yes. Oh yes."

"Just as well. I was beginning to get some mildly incestuous feelings about you." He saw my face change and added, laughing, "I'm kidding—I think. . . . What a prude you are! Our grandmother married her first cousin."

"She made a big mistake," I said.

"Forget it. I only wish you luck."

He kissed me, with fraternal chasteness, on the brow.

"Well, to business," he said briskly. "I'm going back to the hospital in a little while. Want to come along?"

"No, I think not. I ought to call Mother, though."

"I was going to, but I thought you'd prefer to talk to her yourself."

"How about Aunt Julia?"

Matt laughed shortly. "She said to let her know if there was any change."

Mother had a summer virus. I'm sure she really believed she had. I told her there was no need to rush to her mother's bedside, since the doctors were equivocating about Martha's condition. "You will let me know if there is any change," she said. That euphemism again.

It was a wonderful day, the sort of summer day that is a feature of books about Old Virginny, and that seldom ever occurs. The only thing that kept me from going out to lie in the sun with a soft breeze caressing my body was the fact that I knew I would be eaten alive by ticks, chiggers, and mosquitoes. And the only fly in the ointment was the knowledge that I wouldn't see Alan that day. He had called earlier, while I was still asleep, to say that he had had to go to Washington, but that he would call again that evening. It looked as if the funding he wanted might be coming through. He had told Shirley not to wake me, but I wished I could have heard his voice.

Matt was scrounging around in Martha's room. I didn't know what he was looking for. He had invited me to join him, but I had refused; I couldn't pretend to be fond of Martha, but there was something unseemly about going through her most private possessions while she still clung to life.

So I went to work on the cast. At least it reminded me of Alan. But I had to admit ours was a peculiar romance if the fondest memento I could find of my beloved was a human skull.

I was smoothing clay over the cheekbones when I heard Matt calling. Just like Matt, I thought irritably—standing perfectly still at the far end of the house and yelling for what he wanted. I yelled back and went on working. He came clattering down the stairs, continuing to call out. "Where the hell are you?"

"I'm in here," I shouted.

I heard his footsteps falter and halt in the doorway. I didn't turn around. "What is it?" I asked.

"I thought . . . Shirley told me that god-awful thing got broken," Matt said.

"It was just a copy—a cast. This is another of the same. You didn't suppose the sheriff would hand over the original, did you? There are laws. You've heard about laws—passed by the legislature."

He came slowly toward the table with the fastidious delicacy of a cat edging toward a suspicious object. "I don't make a specialty of human skeletons. How can you stand to—to caress that gruesome thing?"

"*Chacun à son goût,* as the French say. Did you find anything interesting in Martha's room?"

" 'Fraid not." Matt leaned against the closet door, his eyes fixed in unwilling fascination on the half-completed face. "I thought maybe she had squirreled away some cash. You read all the time about little old ladies who tuck hundred-dollar bills in copies of Dickens and Sir Walter Scott, or in their corset drawers."

I had to admire his candor, even if I didn't admire his ethics. "Are you going to the hospital now?" I asked.

Matt pried himself off the closet door. "I can take a hint. Look here, Julie, why don't you send Shirley home and go to a motel tonight?"

It was a kindly thought that I had not expected. But I had already considered, and dismissed, the idea. "It wouldn't be wise to leave the house empty, Matt. It's no different now than it was before; it was always me and Shirley, and she's agreed to stay on until . . . until something happens."

Another euphemism. It was a hard habit to break.

Matt nodded. "Okay. Is Alan spending the night?"

"No, he is not."

"Don't be so defensive. I had hoped he would be here; I'd feel better."

"He's in Washington," I said, relenting. "It's okay, Matt, really. Let me know if anything . . . Let me know."

Shirley and I celebrated by going out to supper. Of course I didn't use that word when I invited her; I felt ashamed even thinking it. But it was like a celebration, to get out of the house, and she seemed to enjoy herself. She consented to join me in a drink; the liquor loosened her tongue and we had a good, confidential chat. She wasn't worried about finding another job. There was plenty of demand for a woman with her skills. I said I'd ask Alan if he could find a place for Ron among the football players, and Shirley's face lit up.

The sun had set and twilight was thickening in the trees when we got back. At Shirley's suggestion we had left a few lights burning to discourage unwelcome callers, but they looked lonesome and isolated in that looming dark pile. The chimneys brooded over the house like giant figures of gods or demons, remote and detached from human passions.

The telephone was ringing when I opened the front door. It continued to peal insistently while I ran to the kitchen. As I had hoped, it was Alan. "Where have you been?" he asked.

"Shirley and I went out to dinner."

"The funeral baked meats?"

"I'm afraid it was rather like that, if a bit premature. How did things go?"

There was a pause, and my heart started to sink. Then Alan said, in a strangely quiet voice, "I'm on a roll. First you, and then this . . . I'm almost afraid to believe it. I didn't dream it, did I—yesterday, in the attic?"

"If you did, we dreamed the same thing. Oh, Alan, I'm so glad. You got it?"

"The works. Funding for the rest of the season—six months, unless the weather takes a weird turn—full staff, complete publication costs . . ."

"Tell me more."

"Not over the phone. I can't wait to see you. I'm starting back in half an hour."

"Be careful."

We exchanged a few more remarks, none of which are pertinent, and I went galloping upstairs to tell Shirley.

"All the way from Washington tonight? The man must be crazy."

Her sympathetic smile made it a joke. I threw my arms around her. "Why don't you go home, Shirley? He'll be here in a few hours, and I know you miss your kids."

"No, ma'am." She shook her head decisively. "I'm not leaving you all alone here, not for five minutes. I think I will go to bed, though. It's been a tiring day. I'll sleep like the . . . I'll sure sleep sound tonight."

"Tactful woman." I hugged her again. "You go on. I think I ought to call the hospital."

The word was "no change." I asked if the senator was there, and was told he had left, but would probably look in later. Having heard the news, or the lack thereof, Shirley went to her room with one of my mystery stories, and I went downstairs.

It felt strange to wander the house without worrying about Martha's prohibitions and complaints—leaving all the doors open, letting Elvis explore as he pleased. He knew things had changed; there was confidence in the way he held his head, and his tail never stopped moving.

Alan would be hungry and tired if he drove straight through. I hoped he would have sense enough to stop for coffee occasionally—and I hoped he wouldn't, that he would come as quickly as he could. I explored the refrigerator, thinking he might like a sandwich, or soup, or something. I got out the cherished sherry and polished two of the precious crystal glasses. This night would be our celebration—the first chance we had had to linger over loving, to plan ahead and toast the future.

I was glad I had furnished the little room near the kitchen. Private and distant from the rest of the house, it was a perfect trysting place for illicit lovers . . . I wondered why that adjective had come to my mind. A touch of ESP from Shirley, perhaps? Or from Martha. She was miles away, lying in the dim borderline between life and death, but a shadow of her presence still permeated the house, and it always would, for those of us who had known her domineering presence. Perhaps that was the true kind of haunting—the memory of the dead in the minds of the living. In the same way, memory was the only certain form of immortality. Like the old couple in *The Blue Bird,* who woke from the dreamless sleep of death only when their children and grandchildren remembered them.

I stirred uneasily. Morbid thoughts, from a woman eagerly awaiting her lover. I was anxious, perhaps. It was pure superstition to think that something might happen now, just when we were on the verge of the happiness denied us for five long years. Yet I had an odd sense of urgency—of something vitally important I had forgotten to do.

Forcing myself to a brisk, purposeful walk, I went to my room and switched on the light. It didn't take long to straighten the spread and sweep the floor. I had five hours to fill—four, if Alan risked a citation and his precious neck, and drove as fast as he probably would.

I took the cast out of the closet and set to work. I was killing time, not trying to finish—though it would have been fun to have a completed piece of work to show Alan. I hoped, though, that he would have other things on his mind.

I was vaguely aware of Elvis padding into the room and collapsing onto the rug with a comfortable thud. The air felt heavy and thick; the clouds we had seen gathering as we drove back after dinner would be denser now, raising the humidity, threatening rain. Outside the window, a soft gray mist softened the outlines of the shrubbery. The crickets were practicing for a concert. Peaceful, familiar sounds—and under it all was that rising demand, peremptory and undefined.

My fingers went on moving in automatic precision as my thoughts ran down a list of duties I might have neglected. Telephone calls made, doors and windows locked, stove and appliances turned off . . . The door of my room was open. Though it was hours too early, I was listening for the sound of a car. There was no cause for concern, not with Elvis snoring on the rug. He would hear a suspicious noise long before I did; I'd have time to reach the telephone or lock myself in, whichever seemed best.

Had it been Martha who had entered this room the night before last? No, surely not. She had proved herself capable of moving around unaided; heaven only knew how often she had prowled the dark halls on nameless and unsuspected errands—but she could never have mustered the physical strength to fend off the dog and run at full speed around the house and back in an open door or window.

Mrs. Danner? Shirley's first act that morning had been to call and tell her she was no longer needed. Was she as lumpishly void of feeling as she appeared, or did her phlegmatic manner conceal rage and frustration that sometimes boiled over into violence?

Joe Danner? I had no doubt he was capable of violence, and equally capable of justifying his acts in terms of his own narrow religious creed. Had his discovery of the displaced skeletons been accidental, or was there some connection I did not fathom? What were his real feelings toward the old woman who had ruled him all his life—blind devotion, or bitter resentment?

The names repeated themselves over and over in my mind. Rose Danner and her husband, Mrs. Hornbeak, Ron, the "crazy kids" of Jarboe's theory; Rose Danner, Joe, Mrs. Hornbeak . . . Which of them? Or an unknown, driven by motives as yet unsuspected?

It seemed to me that I had only been working for a few minutes when my hands stopped moving; but my muscles ached with stiffness, as if I had been sitting in the same hunched position for hours. Tendrils of white mist plucked at the bars of the window like boneless fingers. The clock on the bedside table said twenty minutes after one. And on the table, facing me, was the completed cast, finished even to the wig, which my hands had just put in place.

I had set false eyelashes to frame the wide brown eyes and sketched eyebrows with brown paint. The parted lips were tinted pink, and a wash of paler pink covered the heavy cheekbones. The hair was thick and brown; it fell in heavy masses to where the shoulders should have been. And the features that confronted me, like an image in a mirror, were my own.

fourteen

I had lost three hours—hours in which my hands had moved independently of my mind, with a skill and precision that verged on the miraculous.

I sat back in the chair, my stiffened muscles creaking in protest, and let my hands fall into my lap. I could see the pulse beating frantically in my wrists. The only thing that kept me from fleeing the dreadful reflection of my living features was the peaceful breathing of the dog.

Gradually my own breathing slowed, and sick disappointment replaced superstitious terror. Absorbed in egotistical meditation, I had unconsciously reproduced the features I knew best—mine. The fact that the wig resembled my thick straight hair was pure coincidence; naturally Alan had selected a neutral style that could be dressed in a number of different coiffures.

I had, in short, screwed up. It wasn't a catastrophe; Alan had the mold, we could make other casts. But I hated to have him see how badly I had failed. My hand went out, fingers clawed, to tear off the damp clay.

Something stopped me, like an invisible hand closing gently but inexorably over mine. Not the sound—that came a few seconds later, as I struggled to complete the act of destruction I had contemplated. The sound was that of a soft footstep.

I was afraid to turn around. I could feel the presence, like a block of ice in the open doorway, exuding waves of cold air that brought goosebumps out on my bare arms. The dog had not barked. He had not barked the night before, when he sensed a living power of evil in the hall outside my door.

The paralysis that held me snapped, as if someone had cut ropes binding my body. I turned.

She wore the long gray flannel robe I had last seen hanging on a hook inside the wardrobe in her room. One hand held a heavy cane. I had seen that before too. A scarf or shawl, thrown over her head, shadowed her features—the bony, protruding nose, the wrinkled skin, and sagging cheeks.

The figure came rushing toward me. I managed to get out of the chair, though my knees felt like rusty hinges. I stumbled back, raising my arms to shield my face. The cane crashed down on my head.

I couldn't have been out for more than a minute. When I woke up I was huddled on the floor under the window. The hands of the clock said one twenty-five. The door was closed and the key was gone from the lock. On the floor, between me and the door, were a hundred fragments of plaster and clay and paint, mixed with the tangled hair of the wig.

The bump on the head had knocked the cobwebs out of my brain. In the initial shock I had half believed in the incredible; but I knew I had not seen Martha's ghost, sent speeding out into the night at the moment of her death.

Strong, living muscles had brought the heavy stick down on my head. And a living mind had made one fatal mistake.

The cast was the second one to be demolished. The cast, not my worthless person, had been the object of the invasion of my room. That fact could be the key to the puzzle. I felt as if the answer were almost in my hands—that I could see it hanging in the air over my head, that if I reached up I could touch it.

Finding the answer was all I could do. I couldn't get out of the room, nor should I have had any desire to do so. The mysterious figure didn't want to hurt me, it wanted me to stay locked up until it had finished its task. It had hidden its face behind a Halloween mask so I couldn't identify it. So long as I stayed where I was, I was safe. I wasn't concerned about Elvis either, though he had vanished, without making a sound. I knew why he had not barked.

I reached for the bars to pull myself to my feet. As my fingers closed over the rusted, pitted metal, a horrible feeling of claustrophobia clamped down on me. I had never suffered from any such thing, so the sensation was all the more terrifying. Part of my mind clung to the knowledge that my safety depended on remaining in the room, but another part moaned, "I can't get out—I can't get out . . ." and shook the bars with bleeding fingers.

Then all at once there was a great quiet, in my mind and in the room.

White mist lay along the ground, but high overhead the moon rode bright and perfect, dominating a blazing tapestry of stars. Blurred by the fog and by the branches of the shrubs, another light moved like a fallen moon, rolling down the slope behind the house, in the direction of the cemetery. And in my hand I held a rusted iron bar. It had not been wrenched away by the superhuman strength of desperation; it had been loosened over fifty years ago.

"All right," I said. I wasn't talking to myself. "All right."

I went to the closet and opened the door. Alan had used a hammer and drill and screwdriver when he installed the lock; being lazy, I had put them in the closet instead of carrying them back to the shed. I hoped I wouldn't need a weapon, but one never knows. I took the hammer.

Then, almost as if some other mind were moving my body, I got down on my knees and lit a match. I held it low, so that it illumined the narrow strip of wall inside the closet door. The letters would have been invisible in direct light; only the infinitesimal shadow cast by the flame made them stand out. A name and a date, and two scrawled words: "Remember me."

With the bar removed, I was able to get out the window. It was a tight squeeze. It had been tight for her too . . .

I walked through a fallen cloud that softened nearby objects as in a Japanese painting. Far above, the moon shone and the stars were alight.

The wrought iron gate of the graveyard was open. The worn gray stones showed dark in the shrouding fog. A shadowy form stooped and rose, stooped and rose again in its ghoulish task. I could hear him breathing heavily. Each shovelful of earth thudded as he tossed it onto the rising heap. How long would it take him? They had laid her six feet deep, but the earth over her was soft, unpressed by time or weather.

A vagrant gust of wind set the mist swirling and left him exposed. He had thrown off the long robe in order to work more easily. The mask was gone too—no more need for it—but if I hadn't known who he was I would not have recognized him. Dirt and perspiration streaked a face distorted by emotion into a caricature of the one I had known.

I saw something else in that parting of the fog that brought a brief touch of low comedy to the scene, like the gravedigger in *Hamlet.* No wonder Elvis hadn't warned me of the intruder. Elvis knew a pal when he saw one, and Elvis knew which side his dog biscuits were buttered on. The digger paused for a moment, panting for breath. His hand went to his pocket, and Elvis, poised and ready, caught the thrown tidbit as it dropped toward him. He crunched it and sat back, waiting for another.

The intensity of his cupboard love had kept him from noticing me. Then the wind swirled again, coming from behind me, and my faithful dog bounded toward me, barking rapturously.

I couldn't let the gravedigger complete the task he had begun. Once the object he wanted was destroyed, there was no legal proof of what I had discovered. A court of law wouldn't accept a plaster cast as evidence without the original from which it was made. I couldn't explain even to myself why it was so important that I prevent him; it was a given, like an axiom in geometry. I had not considered how I could stop him without risking another knock on the head, from a weapon much heavier than the cane. I might have had a bright idea, though, if Elvis had not betrayed me.

I knelt to embrace him. "I'm glad you're all right, you idiot," I said softly. "Hell of a watchdog you turned out to be."

"Don't run away, Julie." The voice echoed oddly in the heavy air. "I can run faster. How did you get out?"

"One of the bars was loose."

"Oh. You should have stayed where you were. I don't want to hurt you."

"Good, because I don't want you to. Why are you doing this, Matt? What possible difference can it make to anyone now?"

He lifted his lantern and set it atop one of the gravestones, adjusting it so that the light struck straight into my eyes. I shielded them with my hand.

"Why does it matter to you?" he asked reasonably. "You ought to be helping me, Julie. It's your family too—your shame, your disgrace."

"The only disgrace is hiding the truth. The crime itself—if it was a crime, and not simply a brutal, selfish piece of stupidity—wasn't yours or mine. But if we conceal a crime, we are committing an immoral act, and that is our responsibility."

"Very noble," Matt sneered. "But very impractical. If this came out, it could ruin my career."

I felt sure he was wrong. But my opinion didn't count. He believed it and he was willing to break the law to prevent disclosure. Nor could I deny that there was something in his point of view. Why drag out an old tragedy, when the perpetrator could never be punished and only the innocent might suffer?

I had no answer. I only knew what must be done.

"Tell you what," I said, with false heartiness, "let's go back to the house and talk about it."

"Fine. As soon as I finish here."

I started impulsively forward, and Matt laughed. "Trying to trick me, weren't you? No dice, dear Cousin. Once I've disposed of this—" the shovel lifted and pointed—"there's not a damned thing you can do."

From Elvis, crouched at my feet, came a muffled whimper. He was confused. The tones of our voices, perhaps the scent from our bodies, warned him that his friends weren't friendly any longer. He didn't know what to do.

I didn't know either. The hammer was no damned good to me; he could knock me flat, with the shovel or his fists, before I got close enough to use it.

I turned and ran.

He was after me like a flash. The mist was clearing on the higher ground; it offered no shelter, and the moon was too high, too bright. Elvis kept pace with me. He had completely lost his head and was baying like the hound he basically was. In the brief intervals between howls I heard Matt's feet thudding in pursuit. He was right; he could run faster than me.

I couldn't leave the path, the brush on either side was sticky with brambles and twined with wild grapevines, tight as a fence. Ahead, at the top of the rise, I saw the end of the path, where it opened on to the weedy lawn. It looked like a bright cloth woven of mist and moonlight. I don't know why it should have seemed a haven, for there was no safety and no shelter on the open ground, but it was a goal and I hurtled toward it, hearing the following footsteps come closer and closer. I broke out into the light—and fell over Elvis, who had finally got it through his thick skull that I was running away from someone who wanted to hurt me. Turning, with a mighty howl, he flung himself at my pursuer.

Flat on the ground, expecting at any second to feel the edge of the spade shatter my skull, I heard a hollow thud, and a squawl from Elvis. I raised myself on my elbows and rolled over. He loomed above me, a dark shape against the moonlit sky. He stooped, hands extended. I grabbed his leg with both arms, and pulled.

He toppled backward. I got to my feet. He sat up. The moonlight fell full on his face.

"Jesus Christ," he yelled. "What the bloody hell is going on here?"

Matt lay sprawled in the grass, his arms outflung, the shovel across his legs. Elvis doubtfully contemplated the thoughtless person who had stepped on his tail; should he resent the injury or forgive it, in view of past favors?

"My hero," I said, between tears and laughter. "How did you get here so fast?"

"I flew," Alan said.

"Angels do that," I agreed.

It wasn't the welcome I had planned. We drank the sherry, since it was at hand, and all the while Matt sat huddled on the bed in my room, with his hands over his face. Both of us talked about him as if he weren't there, which in a sense he wasn't.

"I'm sure he never meant to hurt me," I said.

"Yeah? I suppose he was brandishing that shovel for the exercise. Thank God for the dog; it was his barking that led me to the cemetery, after I had pounded on the door and then looked in your window. What I saw didn't exactly reassure me."

He claimed that he had suspected from the first that the burglar's aim was the destruction of the cast, but he couldn't understand why anyone would care.

"If you had seen the finished reconstruction you would have understood," I said grimly. "I thought at first I had goofed—copied my own face. Then I realized it wasn't mine. It was Melissa's."

The family features were distinctive; how many times had I been told that? If she had lived, if there had been those who remembered her, they'd have told me I was the spitting image of Melissa as a girl. Martha remembered. No wonder she loathed me! The Judge remembered too.

How much of the truth had he known? At the end, I felt sure he had known the whole story. Martha must have told him on the last night of his life, and the shock of it had killed him—one way or another. His dying message was for her, not for me: a promise of silence. And before his failing heart—or some other means—had freed him from the burden of guilty knowledge, he had sent me a remembrance. He never meant to betray Martha, but it had seemed right to him, as it did to me, that someone should remember Melissa.

I opened the envelope he had sent me. The message was a single photograph—the only picture of Melissa that had survived. Martha must have destroyed all the others.

I handed it to Alan. The two sisters stood side by side, one on either side of the lawn chair on which their mother was enthroned. She reminded me of Martha, not because their features were so similar, but because of their matching expressions. Martha stared unsmiling at the camera. The straight, unfitted clothes she wore did not flatter her stocky figure.

Melissa must have been about sixteen. She too wore a plain, old-fashioned dress, but the camera had captured her vibrant youth, her smile and shining eyes.

"I don't see it," Alan said. "There is a resemblance, but—"

How much of that mirror identity had been real and how much a product of—well, call it sympathetic imagination? Call it what you would, I had felt her presence that night—her desperation, her fear, her short-lived flight.

"It was strong enough to enable her to be identified," I said. "Once the family resemblance was noted, people would have started asking questions. They have long memories in this region; they pass stories down from parent to child. Shirley knew about Melissa. Run off with a traveling man, that was what Martha told everyone. No one heard of her, or from her, again. Martha lied about receiving letters and postcards from her."

"But it was an outside chance," Alan argued. He glanced contemptuously at the hunched, silent figure on the bed. "He risked so much for so little. Even if the story did come out, what harm could it do him?"

"Not enough to matter to anyone but him. Martha's influence over him was as strong as hers over me, but it took a wildly different form. He jeers at old traditions and drinks beer with blue-collar voters, but he dreamed of being lord of the manor again, an aristocrat with an honored name. You could say that Martha infected him with her own warped sense of pride; and hers weren't even the standards of her own time, they were those of her parents—Victorian prudery at its worst. She couldn't admit to anyone that her own sister had borne an illegitimate child to a low-down stranger who bedded her and deserted her.

"There wasn't enough money to send Melissa away, as was the custom for young ladies of good family who had committed a small error of that sort. I wonder, though, whether Martha would have done it even if she had had the money. I think she enjoyed keeping Melissa shut up here, a virtual prisoner. Delivering the child herself, under conditions that . . ."

I stopped, shivering. Even the wine couldn't warm me when I thought of that. Alan took my hand. "Julie," he said gently, "there's no evidence that Martha did anything worse. No signs of violence. Maybe Melissa died in childbirth and the baby with her."

"I wish I could believe that. I don't believe Martha planned to—to kill her. She hoped the baby wouldn't live. A lot of them died back then. If it did survive, there were ways of getting rid of it . . . Melissa wouldn't go along with the plan. Once she had seen her child, held it, she wouldn't give it up. Martha kept her locked in here—in this room. There were no servants, and this room was miles from the rest of the house; visitors wouldn't suspect anyone was here. Melissa managed to loosen one of the bars on the window. She was desperately afraid by then, for the child if not for herself. She got out. But she didn't get far."

"It's only a theory, Julie," Alan argued. "There is nothing to contradict the other version. It doesn't let Martha off the hook entirely, but once the girl was dead . . . Martha buried her secretly, somewhere in the woods?"

"And shot her own dog so it wouldn't go looking for Melissa," I said, shuddering. "That's why she wouldn't have another dog on the premises. Even after all these years she was afraid . . ."

Matt raised his head. "It was an accident. The baby died. She—Melissa—lost her mind. She was running wild in the woods, carrying her dead child, and Martha went after her to stop her, help her."

"She told you that?" Alan asked skeptically.

"Yes, a few days ago. She's been sick with remorse and regret all these years; she had to unburden herself before she died." Matt's face was serene under the streaks of dirt. His eyes were dry; they met Alan's with the apparent candor the practitioners of his profession learn how to simulate. He went on glibly, "Naturally I assumed Martha was wandering in her wits, that the story couldn't be true. Then I started to wonder. That's why I decided to disinter the remains."

"That's your story, is it?"

"I think it will play, don't you?" Matt smiled insolently. He rose, keeping a cautious eye on Alan. "I'll run along now. Perhaps I'll see you at the hospital tomorrow, Julie."

"Just a goddamn minute, you hypocritical bastard," Alan shouted, jumping up. "If you think you're going to walk away clean after what you did—"

"What precisely have I done? My intention was to return the bones to the sheriff's office so that he could reopen the investigation. Julie misunderstood. When she tore off into the dark, I went after her, to keep her from hurting herself."

"And it's your word against hers," Alan muttered.

"Correct."

"Breaking and entering—"

"A man can't be charged with breaking into his own house. Anyway," Matt added, "you can't prove it was me. Can you?"

Alan's fists clenched. "How I would love to smash that supercilious smirk down your throat," he said longingly.

"Let him go," I said. "He's too slippery for the likes of us. Next thing you know he'll be charging you with assault."

Matt sidled toward the door. Alan took a step toward him; Matt broke into a trot and disappeared.

Alan dropped onto the bed and pounded the mattress with his fist. "I hated letting him get away like that. I really hated it."

I sat down beside him. "I know, darling. What does it matter? We can always vote against him."

"Small consolation. He lied, didn't he? Martha told him—"

"The truth. He wouldn't have been so desperate to cover the story up if Melissa's death had been an accident.

He's known for a long time. Martha probably told him as soon as she could speak after the stroke. She felt it necessary to warn him, in case the police investigation turned up damaging evidence. She didn't know what they could deduce from the skeletal evidence, and neither did Matt—until I, of all people, told him!

"He had agreed to let you excavate because he hoped that would get people thinking in terms of old cemeteries instead of more recent missing persons. He made so many mistakes, I ought to have suspected him much earlier."

"I did," Alan said modestly.

"Maybe you were a trifle prejudiced."

"Who, me? You know I never allow personal opinion to color an academic judgment. No, honestly, I did suspect some kind of local scandal. I knew the skeletons couldn't be very old because I've seen what prolonged inhumation in this region does to bones. I even wondered whether Joe Danner's daughter . . ."

"I wondered too. But Shirley assured me Lynne Anne is alive and well."

"I know she is. I looked her up. But it could have been some other unfortunate girl in the same situation. Even in this so-called civilized society there are people who follow the old savage rules about women and fornication, and the curse of bastardy. I got that far in my reasoning, but the destruction of the cast baffled me. It was a futile gesture, since the cast could easily be replaced."

"You knew that, but Matt didn't, until I spilled the beans. When he found out, he realized he would have to destroy the skull itself. Without it to back up our reconstruction, the identification would be questionable."

Alan put his arm around me. "You're sure, Julie?"

"Very sure." I couldn't tell him all the reasons. That

eerie moment of identification was my secret, and my burden.

"Okay. But the other thing—how she died . . . Maybe you'd rather not talk about it."

"No, I have to get it out of my system. You're trying to help me, Alan, but it won't work. Martha killed her sister and she told Matt she had done it; the reason I'm sure is a little thing, a few words that no court would ever accept as evidence.

"Matt quoted part of a poem the day we buried Melissa and her child, in their rightful place at last. It took me a while to identify it, but I finally did, in a book that might have belonged to Melissa herself.

> Let us go home, and sit in the sitting-room.
> Not in our day
> Shall the cloud go over and the sun rise as before . . .
> The sun that warmed our stooping back and withered the weed uprooted—
> We shall not feel it again.
> We shall die in darkness, and be buried in the rain.

"It's a poem by Edna St. Vincent Millay, about the Sacco-Vanzetti trial. The title is 'Justice Denied in Massachusetts.'

"That's what it's all about, Alan. That's why I couldn't let him destroy her poor bones, the only evidence that she had lived and had died too soon. It's about justice denied."

Do you want to know what happened "afterward"? I wish I could tell you Matt lost his bid for reelection. Alas, he did not, and I may yet have to vote against him for governor. I doubt that Melissa's story would have damaged his chances, nor should it have done so, but in fact, the story was never made public. The district attorney's office refused to take up the case. From a practical point of view, they were quite right. The identification was questionable, there was no evidence of homicide, and every possible suspect was dead. Why waste time, when they were overburdened with contemporary crimes?

Matt continues to flourish like the green bay tree, but Joe Danner is no longer with us. A load of hay fell on him and he smothered before Mrs. Danner could dig him out. Yes, she was on the spot, helping . . . I hear she's gained forty pounds and is once again Rosie, the belle of the bars.

We finally figured out how Pauline Hornbeak located the graveyard of Maydon's Hundred. It wasn't a message from Beyond, but a combination of luck and the triumph of stupidity over scholarly subtlety. My ancestor's little book gave confused directions as to where he had found the piece of armor; in interpreting them, Alan had made too many corrections. Polly H., whose mental processes were on the same low level as Albert's, had taken him literally—and hit the jackpot. But she's never admitted it.

The case of the transported skeleton has never been officially closed, but Sheriff Jarboe admits he has no hope of solving it. "Kids grow up," he says broad-mindedly. "They won't try it again, especially with you and the prof digging all over the property."

He's satisfied he was right. I'm not. There are too many things his theory doesn't explain.

The shotgun, for example. I can easily believe Martha had kept it hidden, even from Shirley; but why was she carrying it that night? The gun was loaded. Did she plan to use it—and on whom? She hated me as she had hated the dead girl I resembled; and there were moments, toward the end, when she wasn't sure which of us she was seeing.

Had I caught a glimpse of a baby's gown, lovingly hand-sewn and embroidered, in the trunk in Maidenwood's attic? There is no tiny white garment there now. The trunk is empty. But there was something in it once—something that drew Martha up the attic stairs, month after month for unnumbered years. I wonder what she saw when she lifted the lid of the humpbacked trunk. Why didn't she destroy the clothes—or bury them with the bodies? And isn't it a little too much of a coincidence that the boys who found the skeleton—according to Jarboe's theory—should also happen upon the very garments they had worn when they died?

Too many questions . . . But there is another reason why I reject the sheriff's comfortable explanation in favor of another so bizarre and so unthinkable I don't dare express it, even to Alan.

I saw Melissa that night. No—more than that—I *was* Melissa. Her terror set my heart pounding; her fear for her child shivered through my brain. I ran with her in desperate flight, through rough pastureland and tangled woods, down into Deadman's Hollow.

That was where Martha caught up with her. That was where Martha buried her and the baby. We're certain of that now. Alan found the evidence—only a few pitiful scraps of mortality and certain stains in the boggy soil . . . Never mind the details, you wouldn't want to hear them.

I remember the night I saw Martha come into the library, her hands black with the wet, muddy loam found only in low-lying places—hollows . . . It was a spring night. The same time of year Melissa died—the same day of the year—I wonder? The very hour of the same day?

I can't forget the last words Martha spoke. I can't help believing, against all common sense and all reason, that they were not the delirious mutterings of the dying, but a literal statement of fact. You see, Martha died a few days after the events I have described. She was conscious at the end, and she asked for me. But I don't think she knew who I was. I alone heard her last words. As I bent over the bed, her eyes opened and focused with the same dark hatred that was all I had ever known from her. Her lips parted.

"Again, Melissa. Every year you come back . . . the same day, the same place . . . I burn your clothes. Not once, but every year. Every year I dig the grave . . . *Why won't you and your bastard brat stay where I put you?*"